REVERE
BEACH
BOULEVARD

REVERE BEACH BOULEVARD

BOOK ONE OF THE REVERE BEACH TRILOGY

ROLAND MERULLO

Henry Holt and Company ı New York

Henry Holt and Company, Inc.
Publishers since 1866
115 West 18th Street
New York, New York 10011

Henry Holt® is a registered trademark of
Henry Holt and Company, Inc.
Published in Canada by Fitzhenry & Whiteside Ltd.,
195 Allstate Parkway, Markham, Ontario L3R 4T8.

Library of Congress Cataloging-in-Publication Data

Merullo, Roland.
Revere Beach Boulevard / Roland Merullo.—1st ed.
p.   cm.
ISBN 0-8050-6005-7 (alk. paper)
1. Italian Americans—Fiction.   I. Title.
PS3563.E748R48   1998
813'.54—dc21   98-19908

Henry Holt books are available for special promotions and
premiums. For details contact: Director, Special Markets.

First Edition 1998

Designed by Michelle McMillian

Printed in the United States of America
All first editions are printed on acid-free paper. ∞

10   9   8   7   6   5   4   3   2   1

For Alexandra Merullo,
Eleonora Merullo, and Gerard Sikorski

"Nobody who has not been in the interior of a family can say what the difficulties of any individual of that family may be."

—Jane Austen, *Emma*

ACKNOWLEDGMENTS

First thanks to Amanda for her love and steady encouragement in the dark hours.

Special thanks to my friends Peter Grudin and Michael Miller and to my wonderful agent, Cynthia Cannell, for their time, advice, and faith.

My gratitude to all those who read the manuscript in different incarnations, especially Steven Merullo, Ken Merullo, Eileen Merullo, Vivian Leskes, Frank Ward, Ed Shanahan, Martha Patrick, Lianne Moccia, Gerard Sikorski, and Tom Alden, and to my fine editor, Tracy Brown.

For technical help on various matters, I'm grateful to Elena Ruocco Bachrach, Danny Michaelson, Ida Faiella, Jack Brienzi, Kristen Triggs, Pauline Chou, and especially to the late Anthony Merullo.

My thanks also to Rabbit Haskell, John Aucella, Russ Hammer, Craig Nova, and Tilke Elkins, who each offered a certain word and grace at a certain moment.

AUTHOR'S NOTE

I had the karmic good fortune to live for twenty years in Revere, Massachusetts, a place that deserves to be matched with a talent larger than I possess. My hope is that my affection for that place does not cloud my vision, and that no one who reads the following pages makes the mistake of confusing these characters with real people. The family described here is not my family, the friends are not my friends. The priest at St. Anthony's and the Revere police officers are priest and policeman of the imagination. With two small exceptions, the streets and buildings and the beach are written as they appear in reality. The people are just made up.

Venice, Italy, January 4, 1995
Conway, Massachusetts, September 1, 1997

REVERE
BEACH
BOULEVARD

PROLOGUE

I am an old man now, an almost-retired priest—childless, wifeless, mostly useless—passing my days in prayer, contemplation, and, during the warm months, my passion for golf. For almost fifty years, the Imbesalacqua family (Eem-bess-ah-LAH-qua; it is not such a difficult name, really), has been closer and more important to me than any of my actual blood relatives, any of my friends, any of the priests, deacons, nuns, or members of this parish. Naturally, I know the religious life inside and out. But through the Imbesalacquas, I have been able to maintain some connection with domestic life as well, some sense of the mysterious association of souls that goes by the name of family—source of so much of the world's pain and so much of its joy.

I should confess here that writing has always been a secret passion of mine. And so, given the way I feel about the Imbesalacquas, and given what happened to them over the course of the four August days described here, it seemed only natural for me to put their story onto paper.

I am tempted to claim that this is a story about addiction—gambling, in this case—or about the way families function or fail to function, or about the changing face of the blue-collar neighborhood I was born into and never left. Those are modern topics, fit for the contemporary taste.

But after searching my memory and conscience, walking the streets of our tattered beach city, writing deep into the early morning hours at this desk in this building of pious silences, I have come to the conclusion, reluctantly, that this is really a story about love.

I say reluctantly because the word "love" is thrown about very carelessly these days. It has grown feeble with overuse. To my old-fashioned sensibilities, at least, the word has come to stink of the same cheap superficiality that has poisoned the too slick, too fast, too money-and-thing-mad world in which all of us now struggle to find meaning.

Forgive me. The habit of giving sermons is a difficult one to break, an addiction of another sort.

But what has always attracted me to the Imbesalacqua family is the fact that it has been touched only lightly by the modern world. For this reason, some of the people in this story may seem to the reader somewhat out of date, perhaps even somehow not real. There is nothing I can do about that. I have written them as they are, lengthy name and all. I have set down these four days in their lives with as much accuracy as I could manage, building small bridges of the imagination only in those instances where details or pieces of dialogue could not possibly be known to me.

After struggling with various ways of presenting this family's story, I decided simply to let the people involved speak to you as most of them spoke to me—over many hours of conversation. I decided to present them in all their sentimentality, with all their blemishes and lusts and wearing the jewelry of everyday heroism with which, after all, even the modern world is sometimes decorated. This, to me, is the mottled fabric of real love. These imperfections, failures, moments of elegance, are what is real, not the sanitary sentiments of the homogenized, televised, commercially correct world.

If there is a Creator—and I, of course, have devoted my life to the presumption that there is—then He or She or It encompasses everything, even our most imperfect stirrings and strivings. If God is Love, then our lives are God's inexact reflection, a mirror of the Divine coated with dried and as yet unremoved polish. It was in the hope of cleaning away one small corner of that film that I embarked upon this project.

But I am writing here as a person, not a priest. So let me set the religious imagery aside and say simply that I loved the family Lucy and Vito Imbesalacqua made, and that it was a desire to more clearly understand my flawed feelings for them and their imperfect feelings for each other which moved me to write this book. It is, then, a love story, though perhaps not in the usual sense of the term.

I hope it will be of some small interest to those who ponder the human predicament as I ponder it: the mystery of love, the way we stretch towards it with such persistent optimism, always falling short of our imaginings and always bringing forth new visions in their emptied places.

Saint Anthony's Rectory
Revere, Massachusetts

Wednesday

1

It was a Revere night, the night the life I been holding together all these years started pulling apart. A nice Revere night near the end of August, with salt in the air and garden smells floating over to us where we sat, and the sky above Proctor Avenue lit up with a light that was like paradise breaking open and pouring down all over you.

Before the phone call came that would take my life and turn her inside out like the sleeve on a jacket, I was sitting in the yard with the woman I been husband and wife with forty-nine years, the woman who was the other half of my body. We were waiting for the moon to come up over Patsy Antonelli's roof. Big, she would be coming up. You could tell by the light between the houses that she would be coming up big on that night, the full circle of her, the full, perfect face.

"Do you have any pain, Lucy?" I asked my wife.

And she said "No," quiet, in a voice that meant Don't keep asking, Vito. So I didn't.

A little bit of a breeze knocked loose two leaves that were already gone yellow, and they came twisting down through the dark on top of our yard, and it was like somebody whispering two words you didn't understand, a threaten or a promise, you couldn't say which.

The two of them landed in the lawn, maple, and shook there a little bit, like Lucy's fingers.

The moon on that night, she was an opera in the sky. We looked up to hear it, Lucy and me, and the color of peaches was pouring down between the houses, catching in the windows of Jimmy Haydock's house upstairs. Every time you looked the song was changing: the almost red of the wet meat around a peach stone; then the almost yellow of a new pine board; then the almost white, still wet, of an old woman's eye—God's flag waving on the pole everywhere.

It was the kind of moon you only saw in Revere, a place that was squeezed off to the side, between a big city and the beach, and crowded with houses—and even then only once or two times every summer. It was a Revere night, and being alive in it I had a happiness in my body like a person doesn't feel that much anymore when he gets old. I looked at Lucy out of the side of my mind, and running right behind that happiness come something else. Maybe we wouldn't have no more nights like this, was what that something else was all about. Maybe now, me and Lucy, we were up to the number of nights God counted out for us, long long time ago. You were suppose to try not to be sad about it, but such a sadness took a hold of me then that I wanted the time to freeze solid right where she was. God, I wanted to say, this minute here is good enough for people like us. You can slow the movie down now; you can stop him right here.

But what God wants to happen is what happens, that's all. The moon, the sun, people's life pulling apart. Try stopping it.

Still, sometimes you want to. I believed in God, sure I did, but even so it didn't come out right in my mind why people had to suffer the way they suffered if there was a God up there watching out for us. Why did things so hard you couldn't think about them happen to good families? Why was there a new trouble every time you opened the paper? If I was a smarter man maybe I would know the answer, but I didn't know, and didn't pretend I knew. I just waited for what was gonna happen next, like everybody, and did the best you could in the meantime.

"Do you have much of the pain tonight?" I asked my wife again, because I couldn't stop myself.

And she said, "No, Vito," quick, so you knew it wasn't the truth.

2

After we sat there a few more minutes in the yard we heard Patsy Antonelli's screen door squeak on her hinges, then Patsy burping with his ulcer, then the sound of the little license plates on his dog's collar. A minute later the phone rang in our kitchen, you could hear it. And when she stopped there was just the crickets snoring, and Patsy telling Jupiter in a big big voice—like Jupiter was going deaf, not him—how she was the best dog in the world, how much he loved her, how they was never gonna be another dog like her, no matter how old she was now and what she couldn't do the way she used to.

And right then out our back door came the nurse's voice—"Mister Victor, for you-oo!"—the angel of the end of the world, bringing a message.

I touched Lucy on the hand and walked across our lawn into the house, Mister Victor now, on the top of all my other names. The phone we had was the old-fashion kind, black, because I don't believe in buying every new thing. She sat in the hall like a baby on her back on the white lace cloth Lucy made with her own hands, on the clear maple table I made with mine. And when I picked her up the plastic was cool like a bottle against your fingers.

"Uncle Vito," the voice said against my ear. "Alfonse."

So the stomach started going a little bit, all the past. "How you been, Capitano?" I made myself ask him, happy, just like I was talking to anybody.

"Good, Uncle. . . . How's Aunt Lucy? She in pain?"

"Try askin her," I said.

In the phone there was an empty space I did not like all of a sudden. Something in the wire, something like trouble in the end of Alfonse's voice.

"Why don't you come over for dinner Sunday and make you aunt happy?" I said, to fill her up. But a space like that, she isn't filled up so easy.

"I'm at the station."

The stomach going. The heart. Another little minute with nothing inside of her because Alfonse worked nights and never called us from the station twice in twenty years.

"Uncle, we have Peter here . . . downstairs."

"Our Peter?"

"He's okay. We picked him up a little while ago in front of Saint Anthony's."

"For what, you picked him up?"

"He's a little bit drunk, Uncle."

"A little bit drunk? How? He's not a drinker, Peter."

"Tonight he is. He was making a little noise in front of the church. Somebody called the station."

"What noise?"

"A little yelling. Calling out for Father Dom. In front of the rectory."

"What yelling? Dommy called the police instead of me?"

"The new housekeeper called, Uncle. Father Dom was out someplace, he doesn't know about it. . . . Peter's upset, calling your name, saying things."

"*My* name he's callin?"

"Yours, mine, other people's. I'll send a cruiser right up."

"No, I'll come. Lucy doesn't need now a police car in front of the house."

"I'll have them meet you a little ways down the street then, near the school."

"No, I'm comin. Five minutes, tell him."

3

I put the phone back where she went and stood a minute trying to get the breathing muscles to work the way they always worked. The nurse was wiping the sink with a dish towel instead of the sponge, listening with both ears about my family. I tried not to show nothing. I tried even to smile at her when I walked by, but the muscles in my face they went stiff on me, and the smile came out a phony.

In the yard the Madonna was lit up, like always. The moon was shining down on the bocce court. And Lucy was sitting there like the statue of a woman in a wheelchair waiting for her husband to come tell her a lie.

"Who was it Vito?"

"Alfonse."

"Is Peter in trouble?"

"No," I said, too sharp. Because she had caught me by a surprise, asking that way. The second after I said it I leaned down to her with my hands on the front of my legs, and in the moonlight the skin on her face was like an old gray shirt hanging over a forehead and cheeks and chin that was made outa marble. "He has the tickets for the Holy Name Breakfast," I said. "I'm gonna go pickem up." And inside I was telling myself it was the right thing, not to give her no more pain—which is how people do it when they lie: First they lie to themself, and then they lie to the other person.

"Can't he bring them by?"

"He's at the station. . . . I want to take a ride, get a cigar. Do you care if I go?"

Across her face then flew something I seen many years ago, when I lied to her the one other time. And for a minute it was a different Lucy there in our yard, Lucy-not-forgiving-me again. Bucket of cold water against your skin.

But we been married a long time, me and Lucy. We been through things it would be hard to talk about now, and still loved each other just the same, and so it passed right away, the bad feelin. I kissed her on the forehead where it didn't hurt too much, and left her sitting there in that light.

4

Vito made two beeps of the horn when he was going out the driveway, to say that he loved me. And when he was gone I made my mind quiet and felt myself mixing in with the music of the neighborhood: The pulley on Ellie Haydock's clothesline was whistling and stopping and whistling, because she had taken her three boys to the beach all day like a good mother and then made supper for her family and was late with the laundry; and Patsy Antonelli was banging his screen door again the way Vito didn't like, and the bang and the whistle were carrying all up and down the double row of yards between Mountain Avenue and Proctor Avenue while the crickets made their note. Every once in a while a car went passing by quiet in front of the house, and now there was a police siren. There used to be a hospital a little way up the street, and I remembered how Joanie and Peter used to get afraid, hearing the sirens the ambulances made, going there. "That's just the sound the angels make when they sing," I used to tell them, so they wouldn't worry. The police car went away toward Broadway now, leaving just the regular Proctor Avenue music, quieter, and in the middle of that soft symphony I let myself be quiet, too. And I thought: Alive, Alive, Alive.

Matilda walked out onto the back steps and came across the yard for me.

She pulled the blanket up so it covered my shoulders, and she turned the wheelchair a little bit so I could look at the Holy Mother instead of Patsy's house. She moved Vito's chair next to me and sat down like a part of the family—which I didn't mind. She was doing things for me now even my own daughter wasn't.

"Do you need to be changed, Missus?"

I didn't.

"Do you have much pain tonight?"

That night I had almost no pain, and I told her so. I told her my mother always said God took away the pain sometimes right before a person died, to give them a little rest before they did the work of climbing into the other world.

And she said, "You're not dyin on us yet, Missus."

"Not yet," I told her. "I have some little job to do still."

"You let me worry about the jobs, Missus. You done your share of jobs in your time."

No, I thought. There was still something left to do. One small job holding me like a baby holds on to your finger, and I didn't know what it could be. For a little while we sat there, side by side—a Negro in my yard, welcome as family—and let the breeze blow across our ankles and our wrists, and we watched the moonlight making shadows over the tomato plants and over the boards of the bocce court.

After a while Matilda said, "Your boy's in a little trouble tonight, Missus. I heard them on the phone, saying it."

And I nodded my head like I knew it, because in my body somehow I did, and because I was ashamed to show I had a husband who wouldn't tell me things. There was nothing wrong in the way Matilda said it. She had a son with a good heart who was in trouble too. I sent a prayer up to Saint Anthony for him and for Peter, and the two of us sat there another ten minutes not saying anything, just feeling what it felt like, having a son of your own body who couldn't swim right in the rough ocean of this world. And when her little rest was over, Matilda stood up and fixed the blanket on my bony shoulders, said she'd come back out to get me in ten minutes, asked did I want anything.

"Sure," I told her. "I want to play bocce again with my husband."

And out from her big brown body came a laugh to make the saddest person on earth happy again—bubbles of laughter that lifted up into the air above our yard and floated away down Proctor Avenue like silver balloons.

5

I drove down Proctor Avenue to Broadway, turned from Broadway onto Pleasant Street, parked there, and went up the steps of the police station with my old knees sore and somebody stirring soup in my belly. The way things were changed now, even in Revere, you could no more just walk up the steps into the police station and talk face-to-face with a real person there. You opened the front door now and found a little squeezed hall, six foot square, that smelled like scared men sweating. On your left was a window with the molding not mitered too good, and a sign on the plastic glass in English and Spanish and what must be Vietnamese or Cambodian—because there are a lot of those people living here now—telling you this was not the right place to come pay the parking tickets.

I said my name into the glass—Vittorio Imbesalacqua—but before the officer could answer, Alfonse came out of an office in the back and disappeared again. A minute later the lock snapped in the hall and, carrying a look on his face that wasn't steady, he walked out. He put his hand on my arm.

"Let's go around the block, Uncle," he said. "Let Peter sober up a little."

"He's that drunk?"

"He's just upset, that's all. Ashamed. Another little while and you can take him."

Outside, the Pontiac rested at the curb with the engine off and the headlights sending two white tunnels down Pleasant Street. Alfonse went over and shut them without making a big fuss.

We were not really nephew and uncle but something else, close as family. When Lucy and me were first married, Alfonse's father and mother used to live in the house behind our yard on Tapley Avenue, but the father was N.G., a no-good, a man who went with other women in Boston and didn't care who knew. The wife was a good wife, Carmellina, pretty as anything.

But that was the past now, Tapley Avenue, another life. Carmellina out in the garden on her hands and knees trying to make a few vegetables grow there in the shady yard she and her husband bought for themselves when they first moved to Revere from the North End. Like they were moving to paradise.

I tried not to remember it.

Side by side we went down Pleasant Street in the alive darkness. The moonlight was caught in the leaves of the old trees, and cars were parked asleep halfway up on the curb, and television voices were floating out through the screens of people's front doors. On that side of Broadway you could smell the salt from the ocean very strong, and see the fog starting to come in—smoke from God's cigar that He left in an ashtray out on the sea. A cat ran across in front of us, soft, quick, not black. And me and Alfonse we were walking through all that, through a Revere Massachusetts night, past the fronts of houses with fences guarding the small yards, the two of us talking little bits of get-ready.

"Did you tell Aunt Lucy I was asking for her?"

"I told her you were coming for dinner Sunday, so now you have to."

When Alfonse smiled it was like a lighthouse showing up the sadness in his face: nobody around who he could really call his father. His mother gone now, his wife. Before the lighthouse went out again, you could see the boy there playing on the other side of the fence, Tapley Avenue, and it was like a knife in you.

We walked, not talking about the main thing still, though in both of our minds we wanted to.

At the corner opposite the Irish church, Alfonse went in the store a minute and came out again with a box of the small cigars we liked, and we smoked while we went, two grown-up men making talk about the mayor and the Holy Name and not looking at each other in the eyes.

"The city changed on us," I said, because paper cups and scratched-off lottery tickets were laying in the gutter, and you could hear the sound of police cars in the air half the time, and I wasn't getting used to having things like that in the city of Revere.

"Uncle, you have no idea."

"All the new people moving in," I said, but he didn't make no answer. All the new people weren't in jail now; my son was.

At the next corner, Alfonse blew out a line of smoke and looked at me finally. "Uncle."

"What."

"I have something that's hard for me to tell you."

"So what? I'm not made of paper. Say."

"Peter's got himself in a jam."

I looked down the street towards East Boston and watched two people walking there, ghosts holding hands. Stoplights going yellow and red, lamps in the upstairs windows where the priests lived, on Beach Street a bus engine coughing. "It's not just drunk then," I said.

"I'm not talking about tonight. Tonight won't show up on his record or in the papers, don't worry." Alfonse blew smoke off to the side and pretended to be looking around with his policeman's eye to see if everything was all right. But everything wasn't all right. Not in this place and not in a lot of other places. And inside of us we both knew it.

"You know Eddie Crevine from Mercury Street," he said.

"Creviniello, used to be. Sure, who doesn't?"

"Crevine now. You know who he is, right?"

"Who he is and what he is, so what?"

"Peter is mixed up with him."

"With this Eddie?" I said. But once I heard the name I understood everything clear as I understood how to get in the car and drive back to Proctor Avenue. It wasn't something you lived in this city sixty years and didn't understand.

We were on Pleasant Street again. I went along slow, with the cigar burning down in my fingers, and after another few houses I rose up the courage in myself enough to be able to say, "What kind of trouble?"

"A debt."

"To this Eddie?"

Alfonse looked at me a minute, then away.

"How much? How did you know this?"

"I can't say how I know it, Uncle, because it involves a source, someone who feeds me information, and I have to keep that person secret, even from you. I have one or two things I can try, but I can't really talk to Peter anymore, you know that."

"Best friends don't talk with each other no more in this world? What, he said something to you?"

"Nobody said anything. It just happened, that's all."

But I couldn't make no sense out of this *just happened.* The worry was going inside my head like a train, new cars hitching on every minute—Peter, Lucy, Eddie Creviniello, the secrets I kept all my life and the trouble they caused me. I told Alfonse, "We'll have a talk, me and Peter," but the voice I said it with wasn't the voice my body usually made.

We went along by the last few houses that way, and then with his thumb and middle finger Alfonse shot the cigar in the gutter and asked me, finally, "One favor, Uncle."

"Say."

"Don't let him know it was me who told you."

"Sure," I said. But inside I was thinking: Even the police, they're afraid now.

6

I squeezed Vito's shoulder with one hand, left him with Lieutenant Calichman at the coffee machine, and in my office tried to focus on the Arrests and Incarcerations printout that would be sent to the

Journal in the morning and be in all the stores next week for every-one in the city to see. Near the bottom of the list was: IMBESALACQUA, PETER. Drunk and Disorderly. Saint Anthony's Church, 6:42 P.M. Arresting officers Palermo and Quinn.

I took a pencil and drew a box around his name, ran one diagonal line through the box, and scratched my initials beside it. That simple.

It was the type of small favor I'd done hundreds of times since joining the force. Everybody did it. If the offense was minor, and if you knew the offender—or his brother or wife or cousin or mother or uncle or girlfriend—then it was just the decent thing to do, that's all. On that night, though, there was some hesitation in my hand. I could feel the animal of addiction walking circles around my life again—not interested in me at all, only the people I loved.

I rocked back in the chair, glanced at the framed picture on my desk and then away, across the office and out the dark window that looked down onto Pleasant Street. Vito's car there, a woman pushing a stroller through the tree shadows and moonlight. Someone laughed quietly at the booking desk, and I glanced at the picture again, then away. Sally had said to me once—the one and only time she let me into the small room where she played out the drama of her last two years on earth—that there was addiction, and there was logic, and the two didn't ever mix. "That's why you can never help me, Mister Logical," she said.

I thought about that now, about what Vito must be saying to Peter in the downstairs cell, about all the lives I had seen the beast con-sume. Alcohol, heroin, gambling, sex, cocaine. If you did not have the urge in your blood it seemed like only a weakness—addiction—which was a kind of soul conceit, a way of fooling yourself into thinking that you, with all your hidden problems, were just naturally holier than the people whose problems were out in the open. I sat there with the ordinary night business of the station going on drowsily around me, and I tried to step over to the other side of the straight, logical tracks my life ran along, and I stayed a little while in that territory, chasing a good answer.

7

Following after a policeman whose name on the badge was not Italian, I went down the police station steps to where the jail cells were. I never been before in that place, and the scratched-up walls and sex drawings seemed to me not to belong to the city of Revere at all. More and more things it seemed to me didn't belong here, more and more of the faces you saw on Broadway, what you read in the paper, what you heard from your friends down the Soccorso Club. All these years it took me to know the city the way I knew it, and now somebody snapped the old cloth from under the dishes on my table, and everything from my wife's body to the names on policemen's shirts was all of a sudden a little bit not the same.

My son, though, my son was the same like always. Peter sat on a wood bench in the last cell, wearing a sports coat and nice shoes and holding his forehead with both hands. There was no calling out nobody's name now, no yelling, only just a forty-year-old man who looked like he was carrying a stone on his back, thousand pounds. When he heard the lock open, Peter looked up and saw me, and right away he made his salesman's smile, a beautiful smile, bashful and strong at the same time, the way Lucy's smile always was.

"Pa!" he said, "Wha-wha-what did they arrest you f-for this time?"

He stood up too fast. You could tell the drinking was still in him, and he wasn't used to it. He blinked three times; he held himself up with one hand against the wall; he came out in the corridor smiling his big smile all over me, a protection. Close up though, if you knew how to look, you could see the real Peter underneath. He hugged me, tight, the way a son was suppose to, and he said, "How's M-M-Mama?" And when he heard the answer, he nodded his head, serious;

then he put his hand on my back when we started walking and kept it there when we were going up the stairs.

It did not seem a surprise to Peter that we had no papers to fill out at the desk, no money to pay for a find, no warnings, that the sergeant there just pressed the buzzer and let us go free out the door. It was a little bit like he thought he did the police a favor, coming here. Like in another minute he was gonna try and sell the sergeant a house, and the sergeant was gonna buy it.

On the outside steps he shook my hand with a strong grip, like a thank-you, and asked for a match for his cigarette. "You shouldn't have come all the way da-down here this time of night, Pa," he said, happy on his surface but the eyes jumping like a bug all over. "Next time just let me sit there and l-l-la-lur-lur-la-la-learn my l-lesson."

He turned in a way so I could see the side of his face, and I tried to remember the hard things that happened to this boy in his life, the good blood inside him. But when I got my words out finally, there was not much of the father in them.

"What happened now?" I said.

"Na-nothing, Pa. Nothing happened."

A few more nothings like this, I was gonna tell him, and you'll be all set.

"Where's your car?"

He was washing his eyes over the windows in the police station like he expected somebody there would be looking at him. Alfonse, maybe. His best friend all his life until two hours ago. "At the Leopard Club," he said.

"I thought they picked you up in front of Saint Anthony's?"

"Who t-told you that, Pa?"

"The sergeant . . . the officer. At the desk."

Peter lifted his shoulders up and down and looked at me once in the eyes, a sad wrinkle there, you could see it, that his own father would lie to him. He let his eyes fly once to a man sitting and reading the paper in a Cadillac parked up the street, and then he shifted around on his feet, taking puffs on his cigarette like it was the only friend he had left in this world. When his friend was smoked only halfway down he dropped him over the edge of the steps, right on the police station lawn, touched me once on the arm, and walked over to the Pontiac like he was a big boss, swinging his shoulders back and forth, holding up his head.

But if you knew the person who lived inside of Peter's acting job, you could see that tonight, in the big boss, somethin was a little bit not solid.

8

I drove with both my two hands on the steering wheel and my lips pressed tight together, thinking there had to be a tool you could use to break a space for a window in the wall of a house that was closed up so many years. All the way down Beach Street I looked for it.

Peter sat on top of the seat belt instead of under it, made a pose with his elbow on the door in case anybody was watching. He went through his life now smiling at people and shaking their hands and making his talk that everybody loved to listen to, but it was all like the smoke the enemy ships used to throw out during the war: You paid attention to the smoke; it made you blind a minute; when you looked again the ship wasn't there.

"You didn't have to come all the way da-down Br-Broadway, Pa," he told me. "Another few minutes and they would have l-let me go."

I steered the big Pontiac very careful between the cars sitting parked on both curbs of the street, because every once in a while somebody there would open a door and surprise you.

"So M-Ma-Ma-Mama's doing a little b-better today?"

I made my eyes pinch on the road. Hard as I could I squeezed the wheel. People crossed sometimes not where they were suppose to. Little kids let go they mother's hand and crossed sometimes, in the dark.

"The silent treatment, Pa, huh?"

The silent treatment, I wanted to tell him. Right. Because no other treatment never works with me and you. When we crossed the Parkway and the bridge over the railroad and went past the fence and the bob wire of the horsetrack, and were within a walking distance to the Leopard Club, he said, "J-j-just let me out here, Pa. This is fa-fine."

But I pressed my foot down on the pedal and we went through the rotary, onto Revere Beach Boulevard. The moon was small as a dime now and white white.

I drove past the little bars and the pizza places that stood here and there along the beach, boxes holding light. Wood shingles worn out by the salt, kids drinking tonic through straws—that was the only things left now of the old Revere Beach the way we loved her; I couldn't help it, it made me think of my family. Boxes of light now, four separate lifes. The thin little empty park and a few trees that took over from the dance halls and the musement rides that were so famous once. The nursing home now, Kelly's Roast Beef. Now we passed the concrete apartment where Peter lived—fifteen stories, a building with nothing pretty or special in the way she been built. Now a few nice houses with yards small as the front of your car.

At the last parking space before Point of Pines I pulled straight in to the wall and closed the engine. Peter lit up another cigarette. After a minute he knocked the ashes out the side window.

I got out my door and went around to the front of the car and stood there, one foot up on the little wall for balance. Let him walk to his Leopard Club now if he wouldn't talk straight with his own father. Let him make his own road to go down in this life.

After a little while I saw a piece of the wall in front of me go dark where she was lit up. I heard the door open and shut, my son's shoes scratching sand on the hottop. I watched the cigarette fly end over end onto the sand, the ash showing red there a minute like an eye, then blinking. Out.

"I em-em-em-embarrassed you in fr-front of the whole city again, Papa, I guess."

For a minute I watched the white waves curl up they lips at me, and the lights of a police car out near the tip of Nahant Island. Blue winking.

"What were you doin at the church?" I asked him. "Goin to talk with Father Dom?"

"Who told you I was at the church, Alfonse?"

"Somebody else. The officer up front."

"Never fa-fib to a fa-fibber, Pop."

I turned my eyes then and saw next to me a middle-age stranger, the hair starting to have gray in it, the eyes falling back in baskets of wrinkles—a little bit of Peter's handsomeness given back to the world already for somebody else to have. Couldn't he see what stood in front of him, this boy, what stood there all the time in front of everybody? Couldn't he see it on his father's old-man face, in his mother's old-woman body, getting smaller and smaller now in her half of the bed? Smart as he was, good as he was in his heart, could it be he was really so blind as that?

"All right," I told him. "We won't lie then, me and you. This one time we'll say what we gotta say straight, if we never say another nothing to each other again ever."

"So it wa-was Alfonse then."

"Sure it was. Wouldn't I call his people the same way if it was him in trouble? He said you got mixed up with Eddie Creviniello. Wouldn't we try to help if it was him?"

For one part of one second Peter's eyes showed it was the truth what Alfonse told me, and I thought then about something I had made myself forget a long time. Eddie Creviniello, years ago, out in the middle of Tapley Avenue on a summer night like this. A man laying down near his feet, and Eddie swinging a piece of two-by-four down hard against the man's knees, over and over, like somebody digging a ditch with an ax. Me and my father hearing those noises from the end of the street, and seeing the two-by-four go up and come down in the streetlight, and knowing who was doing it, and knowing it was because the man had something to do disrespectful with Eddie's wife then. And not my father or me doing one thing to stop him because we were afraid next time it would be us there on the ground under Eddie. It wasn't something that easy to forget, the noise of bones breaking, of a grown man screaming in the night. But I had forgot it. Something in Peter's eyes now made me remember.

In that minute we were squeezed close together, the two of us, and my father was there a little bit too, all of us afraid of the same thing. And I wanted to reach out and take a hold of Peter in my arms, squeeze him against my chest, say the word that would make him straighten his life.

But Peter touched his shirt pocket—a pack there with no more cigarettes in it. He took the pack out, crumbled it up, and just threw it over the wall on the sand. And how could you hug somebody after that?

"Are you involve with him?" I said. "Tell me straight."

"D-did Alfonse say where he got that ra-ra-ra-rumor, Pa?"

"He couldn't tell me. Why were you outside the church when they arrested you?"

"I wasn't."

"He said you were."

"That's t-two lies he told you then, your Alfonse."

"What has he got to win, lyin to me? What, you're ashamed to say you went to Father Dom when you needed help?"

"Ask Alfonse, Pa."

"Why aren't you best friends with him no more? What, he said something to you? About what?"

No anse. The big boss was having his feelins hurt now, not talkin.

"They didn't pick you up at the church? Look at me. For once, look at me and say it straight, Peter. One time."

He turned his head and looked at me in the eyes. And I knew right away then he was saying inside himself what I said inside myself when I told my lie to Lucy. So this was my mirror to look in now. This was who he learned from.

"I was at the club with Sal and Tommy Galiberti. I got into a little scuffle with some ga-guy who was giv-giving his girlfriend a hard time. Somebody called the cops and they brought me in."

"Why were you drunk?"

"Because we drank. I had an empty st-stomach. Stop treating me like I was still in high school."

"Why did you drink? You never drink."

"I made an exception."

"Are you in trouble now? Tell me. Let me help you. Do you owe a debt to this Eddie?"

"You think I'm that st-stupid, Pa?"

Something in my mouth then was sour as a gone-by piece of bread. "I believe Alfonse now before I believe you," I said, and out in the air it sounded even sourer. It hurt Peter like a punch, too, you could see it on the skin on his face.

"Of course you do," he said, after a minute. "He's your saint. Your go-golden boy."

"Say what you mean."

"You know what I me-mean, Pa."

"No, say it."

I was making the fists with my hands now. I was standing there watching the train come straight at me down the railroad track, a forty-year train, the locomotive screamin. "Say it straight," I said, because at that minute I wanted him to.

But he said, "You don't ca-care about that. You don't care to hear anything about Alf-Alfonse and Ja-Joanie except what you want to hear. Which is fine. It used to bother me, but I don't really care anymore. I love you and I la-la-la I la-love Mama, and nothing can get in the way of that."

"You mother's gonna die soon. You're in trouble and you won't let nobody help. That's what I worry about now."

"Mama's stronger than anybody thinks."

"She's gonna die soon. What kinda dream world you livin in? In a day, in a week, in a month, she'll be gone, and then maybe you'll see it a different way, that you didn't visit, that you never said two true words to us in a row."

Another punch I hit him without wanting to. He shifted his weight back and forth. He put one foot up on the wall like a boy trying to be like his father, and pretended to wipe something off of his shined shoes.

"I'll come see her tomorrow, after wa-work."

"Sure you will."

"You'll see."

"Sure, I'll see. Your sister she comes every day. From Boston."

"Joanie's a b-better per-person than I am, that's all."

"Who said better person?"

The locomotive was coming towards me, loud. The man on the ground near Eddie's feet was screaming now, in my head, on Tapley Avenue: Guido Prenzi. You could hear him. And me and my father standing there, like the deaf people. Which better person?

"Your mother asks about you every minute, you can't drive one mile out of the way to visit her? What, two weeks now? Three? Tell me why?"

"I'm ashamed, that's why."

"For what, ashamed?" I said. "Don't you know that's your own mother, and that a mother loves her son no matter what happens, just like a father does? Didn't we tell you that all the time growing up?"

"Ha-half the time," he said. Punching back now.

He looked away, and we stood there a little while, the two of us, frozen there in the summer in a block of ice. A jet flew in low through the fog, making a noise that pushed down on our heads like weight.

"Drive me to my ca-car now, Pa, will you?" he said, when the weight passed. "I have a house to show at n-n-n-nine o'clock to-morrow. I need to go home and get some sleep."

"I'm not driving you nowhere till we talk the truth, you and me."

"Fa-fine, I'll walk."

"Walk. Go head then. But in the old days a son would tell his father the truth and the father would help if he could. In the old country, a son and his father—"

"It's not the old days now, Pa, and this isn't the old country. That's what you haven't fig-fig-figured out yet. It's not Italy here, it's not even the America you think it is anymore. It na-never was, that America."

"You so sure?" I said. "You were alive then?"

"It never existed, that place. It na-never was."

"Inside me it was."

He lifted his shoulders up and down one inch. "Tell M-Mama I la-la-love her."

"You come youself and tell her, God damn it. And if you stand here and tell me the truth I'll drive you to the car. I'll drive you to the car, I'll buy you supper, I'll pay the debt if I can. All I want is for you to talk straight to you father one time in his life before it's too late."

Peter pushed the jacket collar up around his neck and banged his shoes on the ground like it was winter. "It would be t-too much for you, Papa," he told me, not in a mean way but steady and quiet, like it was the truth. He put his hand on my shoulder a minute, saying so long; then he turned and went down the boulevard, not looking back.

9

I loved my father, naturally I did. In my own way—a deep way—I loved him and respected him, but I had understood a long time ago that his life and my life were as different as pepper and salt. Rules fit him. His tools always in their places in his workshop, a polished car with the tank never less than three-quarters full—to him, those were the things God rewarded you for at the end of everything. Joanie was the same way. And my mother, too, for the most part. For me, though, being alive meant finding the places where the rules had thin spots in them and crawling out of the trap. And so my father and I could never really talk to each other the way I would have wanted. And so, when I found myself in a little hot water, his house was not exactly the first place I thought of swimming towards. Though he kept throwing me a line anyway, year after year.

I kept my eyes up, I swung my arms, I walked along under the boulevard streetlights, tired, and saw his Pontiac go by. Flash of blue roof, taillights, not even the smallest hesitation.

Keep walking, I told myself, keep moving, stay positive. Just get back to the condo and get some sleep and it will work itself out in the morning, as always.

ʕ   ʕ   ʕ

But when I'd made it home, swallowed three aspirins, and settled in under the sheet, my mind danced and danced and would give me no peace.

The phone rang, once. I didn't move.

It rang again, twice. I waited to be sure there would be no third ring, then pinched the little plastic clip at the base of the receiver and tugged it free. I would get a voice mail system, I decided:

All the representatives of Imbesalacqua Realty are in debt at the moment. But your call is very important to us. At the tone, please touch the pound key and spell out the last name of the sales agent you wish to speak with. Your call will be answered in the order in which it was received. If you are calling from Mr. Crevine's office, please press zero. If you are calling in regards to the rent payment on our Paris Avenue real estate business, please press double zero. If you are calling on behalf of Massachusetts Electric, North Shore Water and Sewer, Atlantic Cable TV, Ace Cleaning, or the Commonwealth of Massachusetts Department of Revenue, please press zero three times and hang up. . . .

After a few minutes of this I plugged in the phone again and dialed Saint Anthony's Rectory, a number I knew by heart. Father Dom himself picked up.

"You weren't asleep, Da-Dommy, were you?"

He told me he hadn't been, that he was writing in his diary the way he always did late at night, that he was happy to hear from me.

"The diary again, ey?" I said. "Ma-man, you should try to get a book contract for that thing. All those sex-sex-sexy confessions you've heard. All those amazing conversations with Sa-Saint Peter."

He laughed and said I was the only person in Revere who talked to him as if he were a human being. Which was probably true.

"I'm ca-calling to apologize, Dommy. I'm the idiot who was drunk and pounding on the rec-rectory door a few hours ago. Your new housekeeper called the c-ca—the ca-cop—the cops on me and the cops called my dad to come bail me out, and I had to lie to my dad and tell him I'd been arrested s-someplace else."

It was quiet a minute, the cars going by on the boulevard and a girl's laugh floating up fifteen stories from the sidewalk in the sweet summer air.

"Are you in trouble?" Father Dom wanted to know.

"Nothing I pr-probably can't wiggle out of."

"Is there anything I can do?"

"Sure," I said. "You can pr-promise me that if I don't wiggle out of it, you'll rewrite the Peter Imbesalacqua story so it doesn't look like just the bi-biography of another c-con-artist ba-ba-ba-bum."

He laughed. He told me not to worry. He asked if I'd been to see my mother recently.

"Not very recently," I said. "But I have a plan to d-do so tomorrow."

Which made him happier than anything else I could have said, because he had a special place in his heart for my mother, Dommy did. One of the reasons I loved him so much.

10

I heard Vito come in, late. He took off his clothes very quiet in the darkness so he wouldn't disturb me, and I pretended to be asleep so he wouldn't worry. The pain had come back by then—from sitting out in the yard so long, probably—and I lay in it as if it were a bath of hot water, not fighting, and just moved my mind a little ways into the past. This was what I did with the weight of the pain now: not try to push it off of my body but let it do whatever it wanted to that body while I took my mind away and went back over the life I had lived, year by year. "I am not this body," I used to say to myself sometimes. "I am not this body." And most of the time it helped a little bit.

Vito's warm skin was against my arm, and I turned my mind back to the first time we met. My family was living in four rooms on the fourth floor of a brick building on Prince Street then, in the North End. My mother's sister Adelaida lived with us, Zi' Adelaida, we called her, whose husband died in the Bread and Roses strikes when they were just married, and who had no children of her own, and who would brush my hair and take me to the Haymarket with her, and sit with me at night when we could hear the horses laughing down in the street and the pots and pans knocking in the apartments that opened onto the courtyard. Zi' Adelaida had white hair like silk that she tied up in a bun on the back of her head, and a chipped front tooth that showed when she smiled, and a way of resting her hand on your arm that was like someone pouring warm milk into you.

"*Quando trovi la persona per te stessa, Lucia,*" she liked to tell me, "when you find the someone for yourself, Lucy, when you find a man you love, then you'll see what life can be."

So I used to walk around the narrow cobblestone streets of the North End with that idea in my mind, looking at the boys and wondering which one of them would be my *la persona,* my someone. But none of them seemed to be that person.

Every week or so in those days there would be somebody new in the neighborhood who'd just come over on the boat from Italy, some new family wearing the same clothes day after day, living with their relatives, walking around in the streets with their faces wide open like they were looking at gold money on the cobblestones instead of the mess the horses made. Sometimes you would see them on Saturdays at night in the summer, standing in small groups at the bocce courts, smoking, arguing in loud voices and then being best friends again the next minute, talking all the time about who could help them with a place to work or a place to live.

On one of those nights I saw this boy there with his sleeves rolled up, arms strong as the strongest grown man, and I heard somebody say he was from Revere, not the North End like everybody else, and that he was the type who always had his eye out for the girls. He waited there by the bocce courts until the men finished playing, then he stepped inside, a little bit shy, and threw the balls one by one down to the other end. When he went to get them, he saw me and my aunt.

He threw all the balls again, a game with him the only player. At the other end he looked at me, once, and at Zi' Adelaida. And when he had come down the court one more time, and when the other men were starting to move away toward their own families and their own dinners, he said, *"Jocha una volta, signorina, con me, si glielo permette sua madre":* Play one time with me, young woman, if your mother allows.

Which was not something that ever happened in the North End in those days—a boy inviting a girl onto the bocce courts, where only the men went. I stood there a minute, wanting to, but worried what people would say about it if I did, and worried about him having his eye out for the girls. And then I said, *"No, grazie,"* and took my aunt's arm, and walked with her down to the water.

And so that boy turned out to be my *la persona,* who was sleeping next to me now, and who I would live with almost fifty years, in better and worse, and make two children with: Joanie, who was always good, and Peter, who was always in trouble, from the minute he could crawl across a room until now.

Thursday

11

Two aspirins, a shower, a shave, I pulled on a pair of gray linen pants, a white shirt, lightweight charcoal sport coat, took a cab to the Leopard Club—half a mile, four dollars plus a two-dollar tip—and found the Thunderbird there, unharmed. To give thanks, to set a positive tone for the day, I treated myself to the Boxer's Breakfast and four mugs of coffee at Stevie's Place and arrived at the office in an optimistic state of mind, little bit hungover still, little bit jittery from all the coffee, but happy, positive. My usual self, for better or worse.

"Morning, boss," Elsie said from her desk, before I'd even closed the door. "Good news to start your day."

"Feed me."

She laughed her wonderful laugh, a bright tune in the monotone world. "Mr. Peter Imbesalacqua has an appointment to show a property this morning at ten forty-five. A young couple who saw the ad in the *Journal* and are very interested in moving to Revere."

"The C-Curtis place?" I said, but that was too sweet of a dream.

Elsie shook her head, smiling still, lit up, as always, with some otherworldly peace all her own. "Nine-fifty-three Reservoir. That was the picture we put in with the ad, remember?"

Good enough. It had been eight days since I'd shown a property, eight days of pacing into my half of the office and out again, treading a path of faded shellac with a mug of coffee in one hand and a racing form in the other, waiting for the phone to ring and, when it rang, watching Elsie's face as if the time and date of my last breath were being printed out there. Eight days during which the interest on my debt had piled up the way snow piles up in a certain kind of February storm—quiet but steady, gliding down through the streetlights like bird feathers, like the most gentle thing on earth. You go to bed thinking how beautiful it is—a little inconvenient but basically harmless. . . . In the morning you're buried.

It had been Elsie's idea to put the ad in the *Journal,* to gamble with money we didn't have. It was going to pay off now, I could see that. We were going to get our break.

I planted a little good-morning kiss on the side of her beautiful neck and lingered by her desk, spooning Coffee-mate into the blue mug my mother had given me for my last birthday. I'd call her today, this morning; Pa was right, Dommy was right, no excuses now. I'd settle down a bit, prepare myself mentally for these clients, then call and see how she was feeling. If this sale came through—and I had a strong feeling it would—I'd buy her a new dress, or a bouquet of fresh flowers every week for a year, pay a visit to Joanie and fix some tiny bad feelings there, buy my father a crate of cigars, take Elsie out to the fanciest Boston restaurant I could find—the Ritz, the Tower Room. One small drip of luck was all I needed now and I'd be back inside my old skin again, making jokes, giving presents, bringing a few minutes of joy into the lives of the people around me. That was why I'd been put on this earth, it had always seemed to me, to breathe that little bit of good air into lives that were miserable or boring or full of trouble, to be for other people what Elsie was for me, a spark of light in the workaday world. That was my special gift.

"Wha-what do you think?" I said. "The slump oh-over?"

A smile like the soul of the Madonna, this woman. A smile to make every stupid thing you'd ever done simply vanish from recorded history.

"Over," she said. "I told them they could see miles in three directions from the back yard. They could plant a garden, put in a pool, walk to Broadway and do their errands if they wanted."

"You p-painted a life. You're a natural."

"It's just the truth, Peter. It's a nice place to live. I wouldn't mind living up there myself."

"I'll move you up there," I said. "I'll buy the na-next house that comes on the market in that neighborhood, move you and me and Austin into it. We'll dig the hole for the swimming p-p-pool ourselves, me and him, two Saturday afternoons. We'll s-set up a telescope on the back porch and look at the Tall Ships heading out to sea. Fr-Friday nights we'll stay in, boil lobsters on the patio, watch *Ca-Ca-Cas-Casablanca*."

This new life had just appeared to me, a harmless vision . . . but I saw then, too late, the small change it brought to Elsie's eyes, the mix of sorrow and belief swimming the deep blue oceans there. I splashed some coffee into my cup and turned away, sipping, pacing, slinking into my office, knocking two more aspirins out of the plastic bottle and staring at the same blank purchase-and-sale agreements that had been sitting beside the telephone, mocking me, for months. I'd had too much coffee, that's all. Too much coffee and, without meaning to, banged the bruise of Elsie's loneliness. Puffed her up with some hope that was real enough, but still, for us, a year or two off in the distance. For thirty-five minutes I forced myself to stay in my half of the office, fiddling and diddling, watching her out of the corner of my eye, trying to work myself into a professional state of mind.

Finally, just before the clients were supposed to arrive, I ventured back into the outer room and did some more pacing there, for exercise, looking for a way to make it up to her. "What did you say was the na-name of these people?"

I'd already made an about-face and was walking at an angle away from her when she answered, and I thought she said, "They're N-G."

"N-G? Wha-what do you mean, N-G? N-no good? What's n-no goo-good about them?"

"You need to listen better, Peter."

"Wha-wha-wha-wha—what listen? What is it, a cr-credit problem? I thought you said it was good news to start the day? You call that g-good news?"

She was looking at me in a certain way she had, wise, patient. This inner-peace thing could be a little bit aggravating sometimes.

"What's going on, Elsie?"

"N-G is how you spell it. I don't know how it's pronounced."

"Sp-spell what?"

"Their last name."

"What? What ki-ki-ki-kind of name is that? N-G? Let me see this."

I put a hand on her shoulder and leaned down to read her handwriting: *Mr. and Mrs. Camran Ng.* What the Christ? "What are they, Ca-Cam-Cambodians?"

She sent me a little smirk, happy as could be.

And why shouldn't she be happy? What possible difference could it make if they were Cambodians or Italians or Martians, as long as they bought the house? They were stand-up people, the Cambodians, weren't they? They'd been through hell over there, hadn't they?

N-G. Maybe she'd just forgotten a letter. Mr. and Mrs. Camran Nog, maybe it was. What difference did it make?

Nog, Nag. Maybe the guy had a speech impediment and it was Neely or Nagy. Or Engi, maybe. Carmine Engi, a short Italian name she'd just heard wrong over the phone. What the Christ was the matter with my mind this morning? What difference did it make what their name was? I had an appointment. Actual prospective buyers for an actual house, and I was pissing and moaning now over what nationality they were?

I went and sat behind my desk. Maybe it was Nug, as in noogie, and I could make a little joke about it, give the guy a noogie on the side of his arm when he walked in the door to show I couldn't care less what nationality he was. Cambodian, Chinese, African, Hungarian, Mexican, Sicilian—it didn't mean the smallest thing to a person like me. I'd been in the army with all those people, two years of sweating and farting side by side, and never had the tiniest bit of a problem. Plus, I knew as well as anybody what it felt like to have your name made fun of. Better than anybody. If I had a dollar for every time I had to spell Imbesalacqua over the phone for some out-of-town client or bill collector ("I" as in idiot, "M" as in moron, "B" as in born illigitimate), or listen to somebody massacre it, or make a joke about how impossible it was to pronounce, I'd be able to pay Eddie off right now, cash.

I opened a fresh pack of cigarettes, put one in my mouth without lighting it—Elsie didn't like me smoking in the office—and leaned back until two of the chairlegs were up in the air, wheels spinning.

"Maybe they're Vee-Vee-Vietnamese, Else," I called into the outer office. "Which would be a lucky sign, right? I'm oh-oh-owed by the Vietnamese, you know. Was it last year or two years ago I saved the life of that guy down the beach? I told you about it, right?"

"Twenty-six times, Peter," she said.

Two years ago, it must have been. A Saturday night, late. I came out of the Ebb Tide Club and found this Vietnamese gentleman being hassled by two guido bodybuilders in the parking lot. Chased the muscleheads off with a tire iron and gave the guy a ride to his girlfriend's house in East Boston. Calmed him down, bought him coffee and a chocolate cruller at the Dunkin Donuts in Maverick Square. The proudest moment in my adult life it had been, and ever since then I'd been walking around believing there was this Savior from Saigon somewhere in the neighborhood who would do me a wonderful favor someday: hit the Megabucks and stop by the office to offer me half the ticket, something along those lines. I believed in things like that, in a kind of ultimate justice in the world. I'd do something like that myself for a person who'd saved my life, or Elsie's, or a member of my family, wouldn't I? Absolutely I would. Without question.

Maybe this was my pal now, getting out of the car in front of the office with his gorgeous wife, smoothing his white shirtfront, putting on his sunglasses very slow with both hands, like a martial-arts movie star.

Elsie and I were watching them through two different windows. "This moment," I said to her. "This moment is the beginning of things cha-changing for us."

12

It might sound like a strange thing to say, Father Bucci, but from the instant I saw Peter's face in the doorway that morning, I felt like I could see his thoughts going. I don't mean it in any magic way. Only that, just from how he first looked at me, I could see everything he was trying to keep me from seeing. The way he walked, the way he moved his shoulders and his eyes, the way he said my name. If it had been another man—if it had been my ex—I would have thought he'd been with somebody else the night before, but one of the wonderful things about Peter is I knew he would never cheat on me. And for somebody like me, somebody who'd lived through the kind of marriage I had, it's impossible to say how much a feeling like that is worth.

So I could feel his blood going. I could feel his worries as if they were whirling around in my own brain. And I spent the whole hour trying to send him calm-down messages with my body and my voice. And when I looked out the window and saw those nice-looking customers in their nice-looking car, all I could think about was a way to ask God to have them purchase the house on Reservoir Avenue.

13

Elsie greeted the clients at the door and walked them back into my office, and, though I felt guilty and phony doing it, in my nervousness I fell back on an old trick I'd learned very early in the business:

I pretended to be saying a few last words into the telephone. "All right, v-very wa-well. . . . I'm hap-hap-hap-hap-happy about it too, sir. . . . We'll see you later this afternoon. Good-bye, then."

Talking into an empty phone, now. Business was that good.

I stood up, shook their hands, and right away tried to make myself an inch or two shorter so Mr. Ng wouldn't feel bad in front of the wife. When he sat down again, I slid a bit lower in my chair and made smalltalk for a minute, gave them a chance to take in the neat office and the friendly secretary, the prints of Old Revere Beach on the walls, the nice cut of my sport coat, purchased in luckier times. They spoke English very well, the Ngs, better than my own father did, better than I did half the time. Elsie offered them coffee. They declined, shifting around a little, in a bit of a rush here. So I made my voice calm, slow—another little trick of the trade—letting the rush seep out of them, letting them see that this Imbesalacqua guy with the big nose wasn't out to cheat anyone, wasn't desperate.

Just as I'd always done in the days when I was selling houses as fast as Nicole's corner store sold lottery tickets, I ushered the Ngs out to the T-bird, drove them towards the property along the nicest route— Broadway to Park Avenue to Arnold Street—pointing out various nice amenities of the neighborhood along the way: the park with its new B-ball hoops, some trees the city had just planted, the public bocce court, the proximitry to the fire and police stations. As we drove, I tried to get a sense of their priorities: schools? privacy? kitchen? It was a Camry they'd parked in front of the office, a spotless new Camry, which meant good credit, meant sensible.

"What brings you to the great city of Revere?" I asked Mr. Ng across the front seat.

"We have cousins here. Shirley Avenue."

"Sh-sure, Sh-Shirley Ave," I said, as if Revere was Monopoly and Shirley Ave Boardwalk. "My sister and me we used to go down there and get b-bagels on Sunday mornings when we were little—a J-Ja-Ja-Jewish neighborhood then, you know?" I smiled at them. It was nice to be able to mention a sister. I knew from experience that men with sisters seemed more trustworthy, kinder, and in this case there was frosting on the cake. "She's f-famous, my sister. Maybe you've seen her on the Ch-Channel Eight news, six and eleven? Ja-Ja-Jo-Joanna Imbesalacqua? Pretty woman? Light hair? Nice big eyes?"

The Ngs did not seem to have seen her, so I moved on. "I happen to have quite a solid listing down on Shirley Avenue. In-in-in-in-income property. In case you also happen to be la-looking along those lines." I peeked at the beautiful missus in the mirror but there was nothing showing there, absolutely nothing, no in-income-property feelings one way or the other. She played poker, the missus. She and the husband, they went to Atlantic City on weekends and cleaned out the pros down there like they were playing against the Sisters of Mercy on a day trip from the convent upstate.

It didn't matter. A sale here, and I wouldn't have to worry anymore about Shirley Avenue and the Curtis house.

The odds, I guessed, were something like sixty–forty in my favor. Nine-fifty-three Reservoir, although overpriced by eight or ten thousand dollars for this market, really was a decent place to live, a three-bedroom ranch, twelve minutes from downtown Boston, in a cozy, stable neighborhood. New carpets, new appliances, a fenced-in back yard from which you could see not only the ocean, not only your cousin's house on Shirley Avenue, but a beautiful saltmarsh to the north as well. There she was now, perched on a little rise with a brand-new coat of yellow paint on her, the YOU CAN DEPEND ON IMBESALACQUA REALTY sign out front, the lawn neatly mowed by the owners' Eagle Scout nephew.

I led them up the flagstone walk and painted a life for them, a wholesome, middle-class, all-American life: kids playing whiffleball in the back yard, neighbors bringing over tiramisu at Christmas. I called their attention to the solid oak door, the security system—bolts, alarms, BEWARE OF THE DOG sign (although there hadn't been a dog there since the last time the Red Sox won the World Series)—the brand-new wall-to-wall in the entranceway. After the usual tour, I let them have their space to wander the immaculate rooms again on their own, take another glance at the cellar workshop (the bench and the toolboxes and everything reminded me of my father and sent a little tinkle of guilt over me), try the water pressure, talk about curtains, paint, furnishings. When they returned to the kitchen I was careful to drop the information that the sellers, lifelong Revere people, had already moved into a retirement community in Sarasota. I hinted there might be some bargaining room in the price tag, reminded them that interest rates weren't likely to stay this low very long, did everything I was supposed to do.

In all, Mr. and Mrs. Ng spent almost half an hour in the house— a very good sign—but there was nothing to hold on to, not a smile, not a word, not a question. They were communicating in some secret code, inspecting everything, eyeballing me when they thought I wasn't looking. They barely glanced at each other; they didn't touch or talk but seemed to be working as a team, connected by some thread I couldn't see. While we were standing around in the kitchen it occurred to me suddenly—it was the way the guy swiveled his head on his thick neck—that they might not actually be husband and wife, might not actually be interested in buying a house at all. Lately, Eddie Crevine had been rumored to be working in a kind of snakes' partnership with the Asian gangs—the Multicultural Mafia, people were calling it—and I wondered if maybe he'd sent this pair to the office on a little surveyance mission, get a sense of my finances, my attitude, try to find out why I'd missed the last two weeks' vig payments . . . ? No, impossible. It was a racist thing, making them all out to be gangsters and Kung Fu masters— same type of thing people were always doing to the Italians. . . . No, couldn't be. Buddhism. I tried to think. Loud Shoe. Gymnastics. The first people to make paper and pencils . . . No, couldn't be.

It wasn't until we were all in the car again and heading down the hill that I was able to pick up my first sense of how they really felt about the property. At the corner of Dale Street, Mr. Ng said, "That driveway. In the winter you could not go up that in our car. Too steep."

"Steep? That's na-na-na-nothing for a Ca-Camry. Front-wheel drive, r-right? You should see the driveway where I live."

"And you have problems in winter?"

"Nev-never. Not once. And Thunderbirds are not exactly known for their traction, right?"

He nodded, turned his eyes out the window, and said, after we'd traveled another block, "What about financing it through your office, if we are interested?"

"Wha-what's that?"

"Could your office help us with the finance?"

I tried to lean forward an inch and get a peek at his eyes then, because in the sixteen years I'd been selling houses in the Revere area no one had ever asked me that particular question. But he kept his face turned out the window, and I could see only the muscles at the back of his neck, thick, flat, a martial-arts neck, a killer's neck, wide as a fire hydrant. All racism and everything else aside now.

"The b-bank usually handles that," I said, as cheerfully as I could.

"We know," the missus chimed in from the back seat. "But if we could not get all the money from the bank, we were wondering if your office could help us. With finance. Is that possible?"

In the mirror her eyes were like black disks on brown steel. I smiled; I made the corner. Couldn't be. Impossible. I wasn't worth that much trouble, was I? Me and my lousy debt? "We'll ha-have to s-see," I said, and the air in the car shifted somehow and they seemed normal again, just a normal young couple worried about money. . . . With a new Camry at the curb, spotless, like a rental car. With gold jewelry everywhere, and the kind of classy clothes you saw on people who shopped on Newbury Street. No ceramic tile questions, taxes, neighbors. Just this.

I threw my biggest smile at her in the mirror. "The wa-way I do business, see, I don't let little things like fi-fi-fi-financing stand in the way of people purchasing the home they want. That's why I've been going strong now—what, fifteen, sixteen years?—while the other realtors in Revere, they're dropping out of business left and right in this m-market. You want the house, Pete Imbesalacqua will talk to some people. A little this, a little that, we'll fig-figure a way for you to g-get it."

Nothing. Not a smile, not a nod, not a look at the so-called husband. We made the corner onto Park Avenue and went in reverse order past the alphabet streets, Jarvis to Allston, steep, shady streets where I'd played blockball and touch football as a boy. All my angels were there—old girlfriends, old pals, cousins; Uncle Cammy, Uncle Bobby, Aunt Gloria, Aunt Vi, Uncle Tony, Uncle Joe, Uncle Orlando, Aunt Philomena, who had loved me like a son and made *ciambotta* for me on Friday afternoons in Lent. I sent up a little prayer to them now. *Let me not miss anything here. Let me read these people correctly, Jesus. Let them make an offer on this house.*

But by the time I parked the car and showed them back into the office, I could feel the little balloon of hope slipping out of my fingers and sailing away. Professional that I am, I forced myself to go through the motions, sat the Ngs down on my sofa, pulled up a chair, kept my voice steady, enthusiastic. It was just paranoia working here. They were real customers, the Ngs; they really wanted the Reservoir Avenue house; they just had a different way of showing their feelings.

"I mi-mi-mi-might be wrong, Camran—am I saying your name correctly?—I don't know every property this close to Boston, but I don't think you're going to find another house of this quality workmanship for this price in a neighborhood as safe as this one. I'm careful about who I show that house to, you know. It's not f-fa-far from where my p-parents live, and I'm careful about what kind of people I want moving in. But I like-liked you two the minute I saw you, I'd like to see your name over the door of nine-f-fifty-three Reservoir Avenue."

But they were at the poker table again, the Ngs. Camran looked back at me like an empty mirror, the knuckles of his fists callused in an unusual way, his whole posture sending out the message: Don't screw with me. The missus was running her eyes over the pictures on the bookshelf: my mother and father, my famous sister (who was reading out the news now in the other room, which was very strange since she didn't usually do the twelve o'clock show). Some coded message passed between Mr. and Mrs. Ng, if they were, in fact, Mr. and Mrs. I almost caught it.

I gave them a huge smile. I pushed a bit. "So what d-do you think?"

"We want time to consider," Mr. Ng said.

"Of cour-cour-cour- . . . of ca-cour . . . of course you do. A home is a key-key-key decision in the life of a young couple. You con-con-consider all you want. Go have lunch someplace and talk it over in private. I'll be here the rest of the afternoon. If you can, though, try to give me a call by four o'clock because . . . be-be-because I have some other business at the end of the d-day and I'll try to . . . well, you see, I might have another couple that I'm sh-showing it to. I'll ho-ho-ho-hold them off, though, okay, if they call? You know what dibs are, right? You have first dibs, okay?"

"Okay," the missus said. She was nodding; her husband was getting to his feet; no eye contact anywhere.

I shook their hands, I made my usual little joke about the weather. Changed so fast around here you had to keep an extra wardrobe with you at the office. At the end, I stood on my front step, waving like an eggplant leaf while they slipped into their Camry and drove away. I watched until they were out of sight, then lit a cigarette and smoked it very slowly down till it started to burn my fingers. I could hear Joanie's voice behind me in the office, her TV newscaster voice, her everything-I-say-is-the-truth voice. I had a thought then that I might walk the two blocks over to Nicole's Market and buy a few dozen lottery tickets. How else were you supposed to climb out of a hole this deep, with the fates working against you day and night?

I spat, ground the cigarette butt into the sidewalk with my heel, listened to Joanie's voice. No.

Inside, Elsie shifted her eyes away from the set and said, "I called up the Cambodian Association in Boston and found out how you pronounce it."

"Pronounce what, Else?"

"N-G," she said. "Their name. You pronounce it as if it was I-N-G. *Ing.*"

As in drown-*ing,* I thought. Sink-*ing.*

"It's the name of a Chinese clan that values faithfulness to the parents above everything else."

"G-good to know," I said.

She turned around all the way and looked at me. "A sale?"

The love, the grace—it was almost enough to save me.

"Ah." I waved an arm, shuffled into my office, and sat on the sofa with my hands between my knees. The phone calls to my condo, yesterday's conversation with Billy Ollanno about Xavier the leg-breaker, the Ngs . . . This was the way Eddie and his pals worked on you. They'd knock you off balance here, knock you off balance there, wake you up in the middle of the night with a ringing phone, send make-believe customers to see if business was better than you claimed it was. They'd set up a tent inside your mind and drink beer there, shoot off firecrackers, make it so you couldn't forget about them for a minute, for a second.

In the outer office, I heard my sister signing off for the afternoon, cheerful as a robin—"And from all of us here at Channel Eight, have a wonderful day"—and for a breath or two I held to a fantasy of going into Boston and asking her for help. It was another world Joanie lived in, another universe. I imagined myself making a journey there, an Apollo mission. Spacewalk for cash.

The scuff of a shoe, Elsie leaning against the doorjamb, strawberry-blond hair and lovely blue eyes, sunlight through rainclouds.

"Hey," she said. "Your sister just told us to have a wonderful day."

"Right. C-ca-call her up and tell her not to tell-tell-tell us what k-kind of a day to have."

Elsie smirked. "Old joke," she said, and then, when she saw how depressed I really was, "How about lunch at the boss's house?"

Sunlight through rainclouds, this woman.

14

I had performed this brightly lit, heavily powdered, twenty-one-minute-and-thirty-second ritual so many thousands of times it was as natural to me as driving a car. All that remained of the nervous terror I'd felt in my first few months on the anchor desk was a small gust of relief when the Talley light went off on top of the camera, a pleasant coasting back down to earth on the silken chute of ego. On that afternoon the moment was even more comforting than usual: one more broadcast, then seven days off.

It had been years since I'd been on this schedule—and I was on it now only because I had traded the late-night news for the noon broadcast that day, the regular female anchor having gone into a clinic for some unnamed but much speculated upon "minor procedure." During the day there was a more hectic feel to the newsroom. Still, once the broadcast was over, I knew I had three hours before we'd even begin to work on the six o'clock script, so I decided to slip out alone for a long lunch.

The makeup room wash-off, a quick change of clothes, three sips from a glass of iced coffee, and I was walking down the corridor toward the elevators, past the reporters' room, past a bank of blackboards with assignments printed on them in Adam's precise hand. Not far from the assistant producer's office I happened upon Jessica Miller, one of the college interns the station had hired for the summer. Weeknights, I'd sometimes see her, still busily copying tapes at the end of the six o'clock news. She looked at me and talked to me as if I were some kind of anchorwoman goddess incarnation; all summer I'd been trying to help her get over it.

Jessica was leaning against a doorjamb like a very small blond aircraft that had crashed there. Something about the expression on her face stopped me cold. Love troubles, I thought at first, a subject I knew well. It seemed right to offer a few seconds' consolation.

"You okay, Jess?"

Through the bottom-of-the-bottle spectacles, Jessica's gray eyes lifted to me, enormously sorrowful.

"Are you okay?"

Pinched between the thumb and index finger of her right hand was a manila envelope and a just-printed black-and-white photograph. She held them out.

"What's this?"

"D.B. says this is your six o'clock lead. I was trying to decide whether to show you before your lunch or after. I decided just to wait here, and if I saw you—"

It was a photograph of the body of a three- or four-year-old child. A male child, it seemed, though it was next to impossible to tell from the bloody face. Dark pools of bruises around the eyes, a broken maroon mouth.

"My God, Jess. An auto accident?"

She shook her head and the movement dislodged a tear, which slipped in a straight line from the outside of her eye down along her cheek and into the corner of her mouth. Not the type of display of humanity one saw very often around the newsroom.

"Abusive mother. D.B. wants to use it."

"We can't use a photo like this, D.B. knows that. Six o'clock is the dinner hour; it's too graphic. It would be too graphic even for eleven."

"Everybody was trying to tell him."

"It's tabloid. It's obscene."

"It's real, he says. He says that's what matters. A mother in Milton. She's in custody. He's gone now for the afternoon. He left word to use it. I . . . I knew you wouldn't want to, that someone like you would never—"

"What does Sebastian say?"

Jessica shrugged and made a quick, embarrassed swipe at her eyes. I hugged her; she flinched and pulled away. Before I could say anything else she was trudging off in the direction of the elevators.

I walked out of the building, across the street, through the stares and bustle of a covered mini-mall and onto the patio of Cafe Gourmet, where a cup of coffee cost two and a half dollars and the waiters were kind enough to hide me at a secluded table. I ordered the smoked salmon salad and another iced coffee and set the envelope down on the checkered cloth.

When the food came, I pushed a morsel of salmon this way and that with the tines of the fork, looked at the envelope again, but didn't open it. Around me shimmered the little well-off nation of fine cutlery and genteel conversation in which I held citizenship, but it could not soothe me at that moment. At that moment I was a teenager standing out on the patio of the house on Proctor Avenue; inside, my brother Peter lay sobbing hopelessly on the living room sofa. I could hear my mother shifting back and forth across the kitchen in a kind of twisted two-step of religious fervor, saying the rosary under her breath as if to cleanse her tongue of the other things she'd been saying not ten minutes before: "That pimply, ugly face . . . that mole like your father's . . . I can't stand to see it." And so on. Minutes of it, sometimes a whole hour of it. Streams of viciousness so unlike her that none of us had any idea how to respond—on that day, or on any of the other days.

I was sixteen. The sun scratched very slowly across the sky, and the other houses on Proctor Avenue seemed baked solid in it, un-peopled, dead. At last my father pulled into the driveway in his pickup and stepped out in his sawdusted overalls. I went across our tiny patio to accept his hug. "How's you mama today?" he started out by saying, which is what he always started out by saying in those days.

I was a spy in my own house, in those days, an apprentice re-porter. I said: "Yelling things."

"What things?"

"I don't want to say them, Papa."

"Did Peter do something?"

"He was washing his dish after he had a snack, and he dropped it and it broke, and Mama's been yelling at him"—I actually looked at my watch—"thirty-eight minutes now and she just stopped."

My father went into the house and I could hear them talking. "Lucy, what is this? Whatta you doin to him?"

"Nothing, Vito."

"Look at the boy there. That's your son there, cryin on the couch."

"What are you talking about, Vito? Of course he's my son. Who else's son could he be? I'm a faithful wife."

After another minute, Peter burst out of the house, ran past me, and went careening away down Proctor Avenue on his bicycle. Af-terwards, the three of us settled in to our polite dinnertime lie. And when Peter finally returned from his ride to the beach, Papa pretended to be angry at him, though it was really Mama he was angry at. He shouted, and Peter shouted back, and Mama straightened the already straight stacks of dishes in the cupboards and dried the already dried glasses and did not meet anyone's eye. And that was our life then, for two and a half years, and it is all planted inside us now, sprouting, bearing its evil fruit.

I ate a few bites of the salad. I touched the manila envelope with the tines of my fork. Twelve-fifty by my watch. I took the phone from my purse and dialed my brother at his office.

15

At twelve forty-five, no word yet from the Ngs and no appointments scheduled for the afternoon, Elsie and I got into the T-bird and made the ten-minute drive to my condominium for what we liked to call "the hour of peace."

She was a quiet, modest lover, Elsie. She took off her dress and underwear, laid them neatly on a chair, and climbed in under the sheet with me, all hips, breasts, and freckled shoulders: strong, quiet, kissing me the way a woman kisses when she really loves you, squeezing her arms tight around my back but keeping her eyes where I could not look at them. Complete surrender for all of about half a minute, then a kind of silent stepping back and watching, waiting for me to make room for her in the deep inside part of my life. I stroked her hair, I kissed the bottom of her ear, I sent funny little remarks across the space between what I wanted and what she wanted, but for reasons I didn't understand I could not seem to open up that room inside myself, not even for her, not yet.

Afterwards, I rolled onto my back, and in about an eighth of a second my whole miserable situation came pouring beneath the door and creeping up over the sheets and blankets. There was a crack in the Sheetrock directly above my head, which made me think of my mortgage payment, then the office rent, then Eddie, my father, my mother, my sister. A waterfall of unmet obligation, financial and otherwise. A deluge, a monsoon, a filthy flood. Where was the ark when you needed it?

Elsie wrapped one of her sleek runner's legs over one of mine and said, after a while, "The boss is far away this afternoon."

"The boss is ba-buried up to his neck in goose shit," I said.

"In what way?"

I took a breath, tapped two fingers on my belly. The bed was floating in an ocean of numbers. Shark fins everywhere, jagged reefs.

She nudged me with an elbow. "In what way, Peter?"

"In the way," I said, "in the way that I owe Edward Crevine eleven thousand four hundred dollars and I've sk-skipped out on m-my last two me-meetings with him."

A shiver ran across her body, my fear or hers I couldn't tell.

"Know what the interest is on eleven thousand f-four hundred dollars, according to Chelsea Eddie's book of interest rates and a-mor-mor-mort-mortization tables?"

She shook her head.

"Five percent . . . per week. Fa-five hundred and seventy dollars."

"God Jesus, Peter."

I could not turn my eyes to look at her. Big nose, the mole on one side of my chin, the chest hair going gray already, belly starting to sag. What a prize of a boyfriend I was, an Einstein who owed money to half the guys on the North Shore . . . bragging now about how much trouble he was in.

"Why didn't you tell me sooner?"

I turned my head towards the window so she wouldn't see.

"Your father would help if you asked him. Your cousin Buddy has the fruit business, he could do something, couldn't he?"

"Do the na-na-numbers, Else. Know what kind of business you have to have to be able to skim off six hundred dollars a week, every week? And that's only the juice, the vi-vi-vi-vigorish, the keep-Eddie-from-shooting-you money. You pay that every Tuesday, and if you live to be ninety-nine you still owe him eleven thousand four hundred bucks. It makes the cr-credit-card guys look like Cr-Christ and the Apos-pos-tles."

"What about your sister?"

"Please."

"She makes a good salary. She's always nice to me on the phone. Why not just call her and give it a try?"

"Because I've given it a try about thirty times already, is why. And the f-first twenty-five times she came across with something. And the first twenty of those times I paid her ba-back."

She was very quiet then, for another minute. Two breaths, three breaths, I worried she might be thinking of finding someone else—a guy with both halfs of his brain working, for example. "What about asking Eddie to just stop the interest for a month or two so you can pay down the principal?" she said.

"Dreamland."

I drifted along in a bleak nightmare, thinking what it must be like for Elsie to see other people buying and selling houses, day after day, while she went on living with her son in a broken-down apartment, Butchy or Skutchy or whatever her ex-husband's name was still calling her up when he was high, missing his payments, filling her bank account with nothing but cocaine lies. The memories of her old life on the one hand (bad as things had ended up, she and Skutchy had once lived in a fine old neighborhood on Malden Street, with a built-in pool in the back yard and an old Dalmatian named Whisper that had died two days after the divorce), and, on the other, the prospect of a slow slide into minimum-wage solitude—the car going, Austin going, her looks going.

"Have you tried to borrow enough from somebody else to get out from under him?"

"There's nobody left to b-borrow from. Believe me."

"Alfonse?"

I shook my head.

"Billy Ollanno?"

I made a face and shook my head—the last person I wanted to be reminded of then—and listened to the alarm clock ticking away on the night table by my ear, the whole possibility of a happy, normal existence shrinking away from me, second by miserable second.

"What about this?" Elsie said, after three or four minutes had passed. "What if I lend you two hundred dollars and you take it to the horsetrack and try to win a few thousand, at least. Start there. You've won that much or more a few of the times we went together. It's better than just sitting around waiting for somebody to come by the office and beat you up, isn't it?"

"That's what got me into the worrying-about-getting-be-be-be-beat-up arena in the first place. The horsetrack, the d-dog track, the casinos, the lottery. It's the b-biggest thing in my life, na-next to you. I only hide it because I don't want you to see that pa-part of me, that's all."

"It's not exactly a secret, Peter. I knew. People know."

I took hold of her wrist, gentle, ran my thumb back and forth across the back of her hand, felt myself sinking.

"Let me help, Peter."

"N-not this time," I said. But the kindness in her voice was a little glimmer catching and burning at the edge of the darkness. Eleven or twelve years ago I'd been in a situation almost as bad as this. There had been a sag in the real estate market, a streak of evil luck at the blackjack tables, the bank had been threatening to foreclose on a handyman's special I was living in at the time up on Washington Street. (My father was younger then, and he used to come over on the weekends and we'd work together, putting up Sheetrock, hanging doors, and so on.) I'd thought it through and took a chance: borrowed five hundred dollars from Alfonse and purchased a new suit at Filene's Basement, walked into the loan office of Revere Federated with my shoes shining like mirrors and my hair combed, and somehow talked my way out of it. Fake it till you make it. Finesse it till they can't guess it. I took pictures of the improvements my father and I had made. I played up my army record, the position my family held in the community. I found an article about market fluctorations in *Property Digest* and spent an hour in that office, selling me. Pete Imbesalacqua, picture of self-confidence. Seventy-five cents in his pocket and a gallon of gas in the car.

It worked, though. That same afternoon the bank called and let me off the hook for another month.

The next day I sold two houses.

The day after that I took a hundred and sixty-five dollars to Suffolk Downs, hit a six-thousand-dollar trifecta, and paid Alfonse back six hundred for his five.

But this was Chelsea Eddie, not the Revere Federated Bank; Elsie, not a loan officer.

"Thanks, but no," I told her, and I meant it.

She was propped up on one elbow, looking down into my face. Pretty blue eyes, freckles, peppermint Life Saver on her breath. "Why not, boss? Pride?"

"No."

"If you lose it, I'll survive. And if you win, it might buy some time. Why not?"

"Because even if I could pay you back in the ma-money sense, I probably couldn't pay you back in the other sense, that's why. Not anytime soon anyway."

"What other sense? This isn't a business transaction. What are you talking about?"

"No thanks, Else. I'd feel too much like I conned you. Even now I feel that way. For me, talking people into things is la-like breathing. I knew how to con before I knew how to read, okay? And I don't want any of that between me and you. Which is why I don't tell you about all my da-deh . . . about my da-debts, because it's a kind of trick with me, a little manipulation. . . . I appreciate the offer, though."

"God forbid anybody should try to help Peter Imbesalacqua," she said.

"I can sh-show you the list of people who've helped me. It's as long as your l-leg."

She moved her leg back and forth once across my thigh. "Tell me what other choice you have, boss."

"Go-go-go to Eddie and beg," I said. "Give him the ba-business if he wants it. Give him the car. Run to Fl-Florida someplace and start a new life under a different name."

"Dreamland. You couldn't leave Revere and you couldn't leave me, and you know it. . . . Tell me I'm wrong."

She was right, naturally. I was strapped into my little locked-up, unlucky life, rolling toward the Grand Canyon, and she had just showed me the hidden side road I might, I just might, turn onto and save myself—and I was pushing her away, as always. "You know what's funny about m-m-me?"

"I know."

"What people would never guess about me is that the one thing I wa-want in this world more than anything else is a real yard and a real house, a few k-kids of my own in that house, a paid-for car, a Disney World vacation. Just the basic pleasures, you know. The da-da-domestic scene."

"All you have to do is say the word."

"I want us to do it right if we do it."

"Pride, part two," she said. "The brick wall around Mister Think Positive. If you could feel what it felt like to be the other person."

Three years Elsie and I had been lovers (three and a half years employer and employee), and I had never yet spent a single night at her house—a dingy five-room apartment at the back of a duplex in the Beachmont section of Revere, one hundred feet from the subway line. She had a teenage son she was trying to bring up correctly, she said, and correctly meant not having Austin wake up to find strange men in his mother's bed.

"How about not-so-strange men?" I asked her once, on a lonely Saturday night, but it was no sell. Which was Elsie's way of sending me a little message. Open up to me, she was saying. Marriage or no marriage, open up to me all the way and I'll show you how a person can love you.

I could feel her body saying that to me when we were making love, and though there was no other woman I wanted in my life now, nothing else, really, that I wanted in a woman, or in a wife, I could not seem to let down some last inner guard—even here, even in these nice lunch hours. And I could feel how Elsie responded: She wasn't mechanical or cold, not at all; she just kept her own small private space safe from me, protection for protection. Fair enough.

She sat up. I ran my fingers along the bones of her back. We had been over this matrimony territory before and were used to moving in and out of it without too much lasting trouble. I would marry her when the right time came, she knew that. Adopt Austin. Have a house. Do it the way it was supposed to be done. There was no question in my mind that I would do that someday, when a certain few other issues had gotten cleared up. No question at all.

"And before I forget," she said. "Call your mother. You told me three times this week to remind you without fail to call her."

"I'll ca-call as s-soon as we get back."

"Call her now."

16

Father Dom had just driven away after giving me confession and communion, and I was sitting on the sofa staring out the front window and remembering the first time we met—before he was even a priest. In those days the woman needed a chaperone when she went anywhere with a man. And since it turned out that Vito, my fiancé, my *fidanzato*, lived not in the North End but in Revere—which was like living then at the edge of the moon—it was a long time before I ever met his family and his friends. He used to come to our house when he was finished with work on Saturday night. I can see him now, standing in the doorway on Prince Street. He had a necktie on—a little too short—and a clean shirt that stretched tight over his shoulders and came down almost to the knuckle of his thumb. White as a boiled egg, that shirt was. His brother Orlando's shirt he told me later, the brother with the long arms.

I remember him standing in the doorway, with his shoulders bursting out of the shirt and his new felt hat in one hand. I remember him sitting across the table, and me watching his hands when he ate, and his eyes when he answered my father's question—what kind of work did he do? And thinking he was answering the question as much with the way his hands looked as with the words he was saying. They were beautiful hands—strong and clean, not too big or too small, and light brown with the sun in summer like the skin of a mushroom cooked in oil—and I remember spending all the week thinking what it would feel like to have them touch my skin. I told Father Armando about it in the confession, because of the feeling it made in me, the start of a feeling. And Father Armando, who was deaf as Patsy Antonelli, yelled at me so loud—about what a sin it was, and what an evil girl I was for thinking that way, and how much trouble I was going to get into, and how much it hurt God's feelings—that I never wanted to come out from behind the curtain and show my face, and I never went to confess anything to him ever again.

The first time Vito really touched me was the same day I met Father Dom. It took almost a year to get my father's permission to go to Revere to see Vito. And when he gave it, finally, I had to take my sister Lisa with me on the trolley car. It was hot that day. August. Nineteen thirty-nine. The trolley was like an oven in our big dresses and hats and the girdles we wore then, and it carried us over the bridges in East Boston and Chelsea, past the saltmarshes with the sea reaching in with her beautiful blue arm, past the new wooden houses that were going up in Beachmont, and as far as Revere Beach—where we had been many times with our father and mother but never before alone, and to see a boy.

I remember Vito meeting us where the trolley stopped and introducing Lisa and me to his best friend, Domenic Bucci, who was getting ready to be a priest.

We just walked on the boulevard that day, in the heat. Lisa and Dommy in front, me and Vito a little ways behind. We loved the old Revere Beach: The Nautical Dance Hall and the Cyclone and the Virginia Reel, the little restaurants with front windows without any glass in them, and onions with sausages cooking on the grill so you could smell them from two blocks away. More people, even, than on the streets in Boston. Men swimming in the ocean on the other side of the boulevard. And Vito taking off his hat and wiping his forehead with his handkerchief, turning away from me a little bit when he did it—to be polite—and then folding the handkerchief four times and smoothing it with his fingers as if it was alive.

That was all. We walked and talked a little bit. We sat and listened to the band play in the gazebo. Vito bought all of us lime rickeys, and when it got late we walked back in a big crowd of people to the trolley station so we could get back to the North End before dark. And while we were standing there, waiting in the crowd, Lisa still talking with Dommy Bucci, the friend, Vito breathed in a breath like he was getting ready to swim across the ocean and back to the Old Country, and he took ahold of my hand. That was all. Only about one minute he held it, running his thumb back and forth over my knuckles and looking at me straight. Just that. But I thought my blood was going to explode right out through my skin. Straight back into Vito's eyes I looked, and every time his thumb moved over my hand it was like my whole body, from the inside out, was having a pitcher of warm water poured over it, and the water was sending a little warm shiver through me, bottom to top. And that was like some other Lucy Cascio coming to life then, some secret part of me no one knew. . . . An eye for the men.

On the trolley on the way home, Lisa said, "He's too handsome to go be a priest, that Dommy."

But I hadn't noticed.

17

Though my mind was full of trouble, my body was humming still with the warm peace I always felt after making love with Elsie, so things were, as my father liked to say, better than the worst they could be.

With Elsie in the shower and the sound of fire engines on the boulevard, I rolled onto my side and punched the speed-dial button for my parents' number. One of the nurses answered and took a long time handing over the phone. My mother greeted me in her normal way, solid, happy. Another saint.

And my mouth did the thing it did sometimes, the thing it had been doing since I was fourteen or so, and which I had stopped being embarrassed about a long time ago: "Muh-Muh-M-Ma-Muh"—thirty seconds' worth, before I could squeeze the word out—"Mum? How you feeling?"

"I'm all right, Peter. I'm good."

I pressed the receiver tight to my ear and searched her voice for signs. Once, many years before, there had been a stretch of bad time between my mother and me, a period when it was like having a different person in the house. From time to time now I thought about those days—she'd had her reasons for being upset, I guess—but I never let it get between us anymore and neither did she. There was a way in which we could tune in to each other, a kind of telepathy we had always had, and so I tried to listen *through* her voice on the phone line. At that moment, at least, she sounded fine. Upbeat as always. Glad to hear from the failure half of the two children she had raised.

"Father Dom was here a minute ago to bring me communion," she said, "and Joanie just called, looking for you. It's nice to see my priest and hear from both my children one right after the other."

"Fa-Father Dom say anything about me?"

"He was asking how you were, honey, that's all. He was saying you should stop by the rectory and have one of your talks like you used to. He misses your old talks, he was saying, that's all."

"I tri-tried to see him the other night. I went by the rectory. . . . Did Joanie sa-say anything?"

"She tried to call you today at your office and then at your apartment. You didn't get the message? Where are you?"

"I came back to my place for lunch. I m-must have just mi-missed her."

"You should have come had lunch with us."

"I should have. I'm thinking of you all the time, Ma. I'm coming by with flowers later on. Are you g-going to be up or are you gonna be asleep again like every other time I vi-visit?"

"You should visit at five in the morning, Peter. I'm always awake then. If I'm feeling good, I sit out in the parlor and say the rosary."

"I just might, Mum. Some morning you'll be out there saying your Hail M-Marys, and a dashing young real estate guy will slip his key in the front door and surprise you with a ba-bunch of flowers, you'll see."

"I'll be here," she said. "Your father's out in the garden. Should I call him in?"

"No. I'll see him tonight."

"You're coming for supper?"

"I don't want to pr-promise supper, Mum, but I'll be there a little after. If not tonight, then er-er-early tomorrow before work, but you'll see me within a day. Okay? Anything you wa-want? Chocolate eclairs or anything?"

"No, sweetheart. You don't have to bring anything. Just come by and visit us. It will make your father happy."

"I will, Mama. Ab-absolutely. I have to get back to the money-making game now, okay? Love you, all right?"

"We'll see you tonight, Peter."

"Tonight or early to-mor-mor-mor-morrow. Bye, Ma. Love you."

When I hung up the phone, Elsie was standing near the balcony sliders in her underwear, a band of sparkling droplets along the back of her shoulders. She was looking in her purse for money, or her ATM card, or a check, and I got up and surfed past her and into the bathroom on a wave of good feeling. I was going to be all right now, I knew that. The big, crazy tide of my luck was changing. I could smell it.

I showered and dressed and, in the end, after twice more turning Elsie down, sincerely turning her down, I finally gave in and let her help me. By the time we returned to the office—by way of her bank and Mario's Pizza—I had a plan, at least, which was more than I could say for all of my previous forty years. A plan and four fifty-buck bills in my pocket. I'd bumped into Billy Ollanno at Mario's, asked him for tips on a couple horses. And I'd returned to an interesting phone-machine message from my sister, who thought it might be nice to have a quiet dinner together in the city that night, if I could get away.

So instead of making more humiliating cold calls on the Curtis house, begging; instead of pacing the office and constantly getting in Elsie's way, waiting for an offer from the so-called Ngs or for newlyweds with good credit to walk through the door; instead of wallowing, I did something: picked up the phone and set up the dinner date with Joanie (via her secretary), took the last two hundred dollars from the rent money in my safe, added it to Elsie's loan, gave her a nice kiss for luck, and made it to Suffolk Downs by the fourth race. Billy O's tips scribbled on a matchbook cover, four hundred dollars in my pocket, Elsie's love on my mind: a new attitude.

18

To be completely honest, Father Bucci, I worried it had been the wrong thing, giving Peter money to gamble with. My girlfriend Rosalie, my sister, all the magazines, all the talk shows—everybody said it was the wrong way to go. I listened to Peter's car pull away from the curb, and for a little while I sat in the old-fashioned wooden swivel chair and let a wave of sadness wash over me.

It took about one thought for that wave to carry me back to the apartment in Winthrop, my mother sitting there on the plastic-covered divan with the TV going day and night and the cat in her lap, and my stepfather out on the tiny balcony staring at the airport runways and smoking himself to death. It was the make-no-sense life, that was the connection. Good people, smart people, living lives that made no sense, stubborn, wrecking themselves, catching everybody around them in their sad, sticky unhappiness. It had been the story of my life for as long as I could remember ... until the day I walked into Peter's office looking for a job. Then another story started.

On my desk there was a recent picture of Austin, lounging at the beach with his girlfriend, Darcy. I stared at it a minute and whispered a little prayer for him, and it pulled me right out of the mood. Really, it's so simple, what people want. Somebody to lift them up, respect them, forgive them, see past their faults to the core of them and somehow show some love for that core. The complications only come when that's missing. I may not be the smartest person on earth, but I understood that, at least. And a long time ago I had made up my mind that that would be my contribution to this world: As much as I could do it, I would give Austin and the people close to me the feeling of being loved. That's what was on my mind when I offered Peter the loan. It was the right thing, then.

There was a sound at the door. I turned, hoping for a walk-in, and saw a man standing there with a neck like somebody's thigh and thick black eyebrows that needed to be trimmed in the middle.

I set my coffee on the windowsill and stood up. I smiled and went towards him—exactly the way Peter wanted me to greet his clients— but at first the man did not seem the least bit interested in talking to me. He was running his eyes over the walls of the room, more like a wiring inspector than a client.

"Good afternoon," I said. The sound of my voice seemed to hook his attention and reel his eyes towards me. He was holding his hands out away from his body like a sheriff in the Wild West. I almost laughed. "May we help you this afternoon?"

"Petah heah?"

"No, he's stepped out. He's showing a house. May I take your name and number and have him call you back?"

"Stepped out?"

"Yes, he's—"

"Stepped out wheah?"

"He was with a client—somewhere in Revere—and he was going to Boston afterwards, I believe. I'm not sure."

The man was staring at me now as if nothing else in the world existed, and he no longer seemed like the kind of person you could laugh at. For some reason I found myself holding my hands together in front of me, down below the buckle of my belt. It was a little girl's posture, a way I could not remember standing in years and years. I thought of Peter's safe, wondered if there was any money left in it.

"Bah-troom?" he said, pointing with his chin.

"No, that's a closet. The bathroom is in the back office. You're welcome to use it."

But he had already started towards the back office, and I didn't know what else to do, so I followed him. When his eyes were off me and I had a second to think, it occurred to me that this might be Chelsea Eddie or one of his men, come to talk to Peter about the debt. I glanced at the telephone and pictured myself calling the police—and saying what?

I followed the man into Peter's office, watched him push open the bathroom door. Trying to keep a distance between my body and his, I reached around the jamb to turn on the light, and he was suddenly holding the top of my arm with his fingers, snug, like a blood-pressure cuff, not hurting. I started to pull away, and the fingers tightened. His face was three inches from my face and I was sure he was going to rape me then, right there in our tiny immaculate bathroom, with people walking by on Paris Avenue, oblivious, and the telephone ringing, and Austin on his way home from eleventh grade.

He used only the leverage of one hand on my arm, and he half lifted, half pushed me backwards until I sat with a bump on top of Peter's desk, knocking over his Celtics mug, spilling pencils and felt pens everywhere.

"Wheah's Petah?"

"I told you, he—"

I felt something hit the side of my face, and for an instant I thought he was holding a piece of wood or metal, his hand was so hard. Blood in my mouth, hot pain up and down the side of my face, little blazes of light behind my eyes. I had been hit before—three times with Butchy before I decided I'd had enough—but there was something different about this. There was no feeling in it, as if he was just slapping dust out of an old rug. His fingers on my arm were like five little padlocks, and his eyes were dead eyes, light blue, flat, empty. "Lie again," he said. "Go head." He lifted his hand and took hold of my throat. "Go head, lie now."

I held my eyes on him for as long as I could, thinking of Peter, of the ways people could betray other people, so easily, and that I didn't want to do that now no matter what it cost me. My field of vision clouded at the edges, my chest shuddered up and down. I clawed at his arm, a piece of iron, and then I started to think of Austin. To live for Austin. I tried to look at the window, to signal, to call. Just as I was blacking out, the man let go and I took in huge gulps of air, three breaths, four breaths, five, thinking only of that now, my air, my breath, me. He put one finger under my chin and lifted my face.

"So wheah did you say now he was?"

I shook my head and gasped.

"So should we gonna do this heah again?" he said, touching my throat, just touching it, and I said "Suffolk . . . Downs" then, automatically, without holding back even a part of one second.

"You shuah?"

I nodded, still gasping, and with the hand still circling my arm he pushed, once, and I rolled away from him like a rag doll and fell hard on my palms and knees on the floor between Peter's chair and the desk. One drop of blood dribbled from my mouth down onto the wood. I just waited there, coughing, shaking, thinking of a way I might run and throw myself through the plate-glass window, or scream, or find something to hit him with. There was a steady trickle of liquid on the desk, which I thought at first must be Peter's coffee being dumped out on his papers. But it came dripping over the edge and down the outside of my left arm, sharp-smelling, and I jerked away from it fast and banged the back of my skull against the metal edge of Peter's chair so hard I almost knocked myself out.

Stars. The smell. The world spinning. I heard the man's zipper. Footsteps. The door slamming so hard that every pane of glass in the office rattled.

19

Saddle weights, track condition, post position, early burner, late-comer: The language of racing felt like my true native tongue. And the track itself—Suffolk Downs, with salty breezes shifting in off the ocean, and the sweet smell of cigar smoke, and crowds of bettors in sport coats and short dresses and baseball caps lining up at the win-dows—felt like my truest home, a place where the rules were as familiar to me as my own face in the mirror.

I bought a program for a dollar, gave the college kid selling them a dollar tip, then opened to the fourth race and read the coded entries as I walked down towards my lucky spot at the rail. I had a system, naturally, like everybody: raw speed at the top of the list, then the jockey, then the trainer, after that pure intuition. Down the page I went with the tip of a black felt pen, making check marks, question marks, circles, exclamation points. If I saw a red flag—tendency to fade in the stretch, a history of trouble in the turns, a jockey you couldn't count on—I made a neat box around the horse's name and drew a diagonal line through it right away so as not to be tempted in a moment of weakness. I underlined four-furlong times, assigned a certain number of good points and bad, tallied them up in the margin, mixed in a measure of hunch—my father's license plate number, my sister's date of birth. Then, when it had all been checked and rechecked three or four times, I wrote out the order of finish at the top of the page: 8-3-1.

To be honest, this was not really my own system but something that had been handed down to me by my mother's brother, Peter Cascio, the man I was named for. When I turned fifteen, Uncle Peter took me here as a birthday present and gave me twenty-five dollars to bet with—a phenomenal sum for a kid in those days. "This heah's a little world of itself, Petey," he told me that afternoon. "You watch the way they lead the hoss out. Is he walkin good? Ah they trine ta hide somethin? You watch his poop—don't laugh—you sniff the air, you check the Place and Show pools late to see the action of the large money, you walk back and forth along the rail and check out what kinda shape the track's in—dusty, muddy, soft—right? Then you do the numbahs. See this? Watch how I do this."

A hundred times I stood next to him here and watched him decorate the page of a racing form; a thousand times I rode around the city of Revere with him in his silver Cadillac, listening to his stories. It was the very worst period of my life, a terrible time—my mother still going a little crazy on us, my sister off in the Ivy League winning scholarships while I fumbled and joked my way through high school, the draft waiting for me on the other side of graduation, Alfonse and my two favorite cousins and my friend Leo Markin over there in Vietnam, my parents doing battle, girls calling, Father Dom talking to me about the importance of peace of mind.

Peace of mind. The one person in my life, the one person in the whole city of Revere in those days who seemed to have even the smallest little pimple of peace of mind going for him was Uncle Peter. He laughed, he smoked a fancy pipe, he flirted with women and they flirted back. He ate what he wanted to eat, and drank what he liked to drink, and drove the wrong way down one-way streets, and dropped dead of a heart attack on the golf course one September afternoon, fifty-nine years old.

A million times since that September I'd had conversations with him. Now, standing in my lucky spot—the fence near the final turn—a cigar in one hand and the program in the other, I called upon the amazing grace of Peter Cascio one more time, tried to feel that grace and that luck in my own blood and transfer it into the horses' bodies: 8-3-1.

Ordinarily I considered Place and Show betting to be a sign of moral weakness, but that day I made an exception. It was not the time to take chances: not with Elsie's money, not with Eddie's. I went up to a teller who didn't know me, bet ten to Place on the eight, ten to Show on the three, and made myself walk away.

The bell sounded. The horses broke and pounded along the near straightaway, settling in along the rail as they made for the first turn. They took the turn in just the order I expected, took the second turn also according to plan: the six and the two wearing themselves out setting the pace. In the far stretch, both of them faded, as I knew they would, and the smarter jockeys held their mounts along the rail in tight formation, the eight creeping up into the lead now, slowly stretching it out.

For a few seconds between the third and fourth turns my view was blocked by the angle and the rail, and I swung my eyes up and towards the beach for luck. When I looked again the horses were driving right at me, leaning through the turn in front of me, the heat of it in my blood now, in my hands, the beauty of it, the speed.

Out into the stretch they went, silks flying, pieces of turf kicking up and back, running just exactly the way I knew they would run: 8-3-1. They crossed the finish line and the numbers went up. The trifecta paid $1,342.80 for a six-dollar bet, and if there had been a grave dug for me right there I would have laid right down in it and told them to get out the shovels: 8-3-1. One hundred dollars on that trifecta and I would have been cashing in my winnings, filling out the IRS forms, driving straight to Eddie's house and paying him off, cash, with a little something left over for gifts for my mother, Elsie, my dad.

8-3-1. Instead of trusting my instincts, I had bet like an amateur, like a coward. Place and Show. And so here I was, shuffling up to the window like a guy in a leisure suit and cashing in for the massive sum of seventy-four dollars and forty cents. Sandwich and coffee money. Toilet paper money. Up in heaven, Peter Cascio was laughing at me.

That was it, then, a lesson from God. I rounded my winnings off to an even hundred and put it on the seven to win in the fifth.

The seven finished third.

Now God was laughing.

⑥ ⑥ ⑥

But I'm the type of person who learns from his mistakes. I've had a lot of practice at it. So from that point on I returned to my usual system—one trifecta, two other horses to win—separate wagers.

The system bailed me out. Race by race I made my pocket fat, losing sixty and winning a hundred and five, losing eighty and taking in two hundred. In the eighth, going with a little flicker of intuition, I bet twenty dollars across the board on a little-known ten-to-one shot named Sally's Dream, watched her win going away, and walked up to the window with no expression on my face—as I'd been taught—and collected three hundred and twenty-two dollars, even. More like it.

By the next to the last race I'd built the original four hundred worth of capital up to just over nine hundred. Which, if you subtracted Elsie's loan and the rent money I'd borrowed from my safe, was just about enough to pay the vigoroffski on one of my missed weeks.

I consulted the matchbook notes before the last two races: Billy Ollanno had given me Maudlin in the eleventh and Dancer's Gambit in the twelfth. But I bet Maudlin to win and wheeled three trifectas around her and she finished eight lengths back. And so, as the horses were being led out for the twelfth and final race, the voices were loud in my ears from both shoulders. Go to Eddie with the four hundred beans, they said. Walk out now, Little Pete. Walk out.

But it would have been crazy, walking. Immature. With the exception of the previous race—Billy's fault—my luck was running sweet as ice cream. And I'd slipped away from Eddie two Tuesdays in a row: there wasn't a chance in twenty thousand the man was going to be happy with four or five when he was owed twelve. It would be insane, leaving now. You had to have discipline in situations like this; you had to keep a perspective.

So I stayed with the system, worked the figures, wrote my numbers at the top of the page: 2-5-8. Plus a backup trio, since it was the last race: 6-4-3. And went to the windows.

The problem was, though, that with each notch I moved up in the long line, I kept seeing other combinations that might work, kept looking for ways to cover all the bases that needed covering. By the time I finally stood face-to-face with the teller, I was reading off lists of numbers like columns in the phone book: eleven different trifectas, one hundred ninety-eight dollars all told.

The two was my wheel horse. If they finished 2-5-8, I'd win six or seven hundred, minus the one-ninety-eight I'd bet. Two with the 6 and 4, or 6 and 8, and the payoff would be a few hundred at best. Two with the 3 and 7—my longest odds—and I might leave with four or even five large, depending on how the odds changed in the last minute or so of betting, when the guys with inside information put their money into the system.

While the jockeys slipped their mounts into the starting gate I stood in my lucky spot and shifted up and down on the balls of my feet, twisted the cigar between my lips the way my dad always did when he played bocce, muttered a small prayer. Fidgeting. Hoping.

It is a beautiful thing, horseracing, really. The smell of the track and infield, hay, horseflesh; the sound of the hooves, of people's voices rising up in a wild cheer and falling off again, like the end of some National Anthem of Getting Rich; the sight of the nearly perfect animals—God's favorite creatures—and the brave little men and women who sit up in the stirrups, flying, barely touching the earth. If you think about it, horseracing is one of the few truly natural entertainments left in this sterilized, closed-in, machine-soul America, a kind of reward God thought up to compensate us for the pain of living. Next to the time I spent with Elsie, it was *the* sweetness in my life.

Just as I was thinking this, though, naturally, some redheaded guy steps down the slope and decides to stand next to me. Talkative type. "I like dat dare numbah one," he says, not looking at me. "I love dat dare one."

"Screw the one," I almost said. "Let the one choke. Let the one come in on the next race, pal."

"Look at the butt end on her, willya? Ever see a hiney like dat?"

"Gorgeous," I said.

The bell sounded. The gates slammed open and the one broke first in an elegant way, stretching out a quick length lead with her beautiful butt end. The one. Billy's horse, the redhead's horse, the only horse I'd crossed off my program. The only sonofabitching horse that had to finish out of the money completely in order for me to survive this day. I came that close to turning and walking right out without even waiting for the end of the race.

Mister Good Diction beside me, naturally, starts breaking eardrums: *"YOU ONE! GO YOU ONE YOU! YOU BEAUTY YOU!"* He swings his head at me once, like we're brothers getting out of jail on the same day, happy for each other, us against the world. "Whattid I say about that numbah one. You gut it, right?"

"Sure," I said. "Two hundred on the na-nose."

"GO YOU ONE YOU! GO! GO! GO!"

Almost enough to make you abandon your lucky spot.

At the first turn, Billy's one went to a length and a half lead on the pack, and the guy beside me was peeing his pants, popping up on his toes and down again and huffing and puffing so much I was tempted to start looking around for the ambulance guys with the heart attack machine. I took the cigar out from between my teeth and let a little smoke drift his way, hoping that would put him over the edge. But he kept breathing. I moved my eyes in a slow, flat, hopeless oval, all the beauty of the sport gone for me now, trampled, buried.

The one held her lead through the turn but did not extend it. She held her lead through the second turn and did not extend it, the next four horses working to stay close. *"One, eight, four, two, three,"* the announcer called, but I listened as if from a thousand miles away, turning my head in half-inch ratchets, fingering my mole, rivers of sweat sliding down the insides of both arms. I was gone now. Gone. Screwed. Dead. History. I should have been content with the four hundred. I should have walked out. I should have played the 8-3-1 the way I'd wanted to in the fourth race.

And then I heard, *"DON'T DIE ON US NOW, YOU SWEETHEART YOU! DON'T YOU DAYUH DIE NOW!"*

At the end of the far straightaway, as the pack stretched out and thinned behind her, Dancer's Gambit was beginning to show just the smallest wobble in her stride. I noticed it. Mister Silence of the Library beside me saw it. Her head was jerking up and down a little bit more than it should have, the jockey asking her for something extra now, a little too early.

"ANOTHER TWENTY SECONDS NOW, SWEETHEART! OH DON'T DIE!

"She's fadin," he said. "Son of a bastard, look."

"N-naw, she's fine," I told him, reversing the psychology on the fates. "Watch her ba-bounce back now. Watch."

"You think? *GO YOU BABY NOW GO!"*

I whispered a little silent prayer to Saint Jude, patron of impossible cases: Let Dancer's Gambit choke on her own spit and die, Saint Jude, just this once. I'm begging.

Twenty more yards and the lead began to slip. Half a length. Quarter length. I whispered another little prayer to Saint Jude.

"OH JESUS PLEASE!" the redhead said, trumping.

"One, eight, two, three, five. It's Dancer's Gambit into the far turn."

I moved half an inch closer to the rail.

All through the turn the one stubbornly held to that lead, neck-and-neck with the eight, jockeys rubbing knees, crops working, hooves pounding. Coming into the final turn she finally actually faded—not far enough—to second, and I could feel some small little thread of hope lifting me, the rush of it in my arms and legs. How many people could do this, I said to myself at that moment. How many people could put their entire life on the back of a horse? I deserved something for this now. I deserved something good here.

"DON'T YOU DAYUH FADE, YOU ONE, YOU PIG, DON'T YOU DAYUH!"

"Eight, one, two. As the thoroughbreds enter the home stretch it is Mmmmolly My Queen and Dancer's Gambit. Sheeeebah. Witch's Brew. Caroliiiina Rrrrrobert."

I fixed my eyes on the one horse's head like two daggers. Let her slip now, Saint Jude. Let her slip, let her fall back, just this once! Once!

The eight was pulling steadily ahead, with the two and then the three creeping up on the struggling Dancer's Gambit. Let her stumble a little bit now, Jesus. Eighty yards.

The voice of the crowd swelled up and up and seemed to move right through me, toenails to throat, drowning out my pal, who was in mourning for his one, and pulling from my lips a sound that was half tortured scream, half prayer. The horses seemed to shift into slow motion, the space between the leaders and the wire stretching out instead of shrinking, muscles rippling, jockeys' whips floating up and back and knifing dreamily down. The eight glided past, black as oil, her skinny little legs thrown out front and back. The eight and then the two, and, after the two, Billy Ollanno's ridiculous one, still hanging on, with the five, from nowhere, pounding along beside her as if in harness.

They passed beneath the wire at an impossible angle for me to judge, and the crowd noise faded and died.

"She took second, at least," said the jumping man. "I covered my ass wit some Place bets. You?"

I raised the cigar to my mouth and took one small sip of smoke, held it in against the thumping of my heart. Cool now, to the very end. Leave here with two hundred or leave here with eleven hundred—the difference between those two numbers was the difference between living and dying for me, no exaggeration. Life and death. The race was over. In three seconds the numbers would come up in lights, and my future would be printed out there, one way or the other.

No begging now.

One time, Jesus.

"She placed, you could see it. Showed, at least. At the very worst, she showed."

"M-maybe," I said.

A very long minute. An unbelievably long minute, and then the first two numbers flashed up on the tote board:

8

2

And beneath them, in red lights, the word PHOTO.

The guy next to me sucked some wind. I waited, quiet. I could feel my heart kicking and leaping, lion in a cage. Behind me the crowd had gone mostly silent, a few seats slapping up, one or two drunks yelling, the shuffling and muttering of losers leaving.

"What'd you really have?" the guy asked.

I pretended my eardrums had been blown out. I could feel the wind brush across the sweaty skin of my forehead and neck. I could feel the damp sleeves of my shirt against my arms. Another endless minute of heartbeats and manicured infield, and then two numbers rose up in the middle of that lawn like visions in the sweetest of all possible dreams:

5

1

OFFICIAL

"Fourt?" the guy beside me said. "Fourt? No friggin way. Not possible. I wanna see dat photo myself."

I did not move. I showed nothing. Another second and the pay-offs sprang into place. I made a quick calculation, checked again to see that the one was, in fact, sitting there at the bottom of the four-number list, that I wasn't hallucinating, that I was, in fact, holding a 2-5-8 Trifecta box ticket, any order a winner. In the end of ends, even bad-luck Billy Ollanno had not quite been able to ki-bosh me.

Even after the guy stumbled off and most of the crowd filed away behind me, I stayed where I was, taking in long, slow breaths of sea air, throwing up a little prayer to Uncle Peter, shifting the stub of cigar back and forth in my fingers, round and round, then, finally, snapping it over the rail and onto the torn-up track.

Saint Elsie.

I collected my winnings and walked out into a parking lot littered with losing tickets, eleven hundred seventy-four dollars folded in new bills in my pocket, the beast of regret walking an inch behind me: Two more races and I'd have won enough to pay off the debt in full. It caught up with me then and worked me over, that regret, pummeling me in the places it knew I was soft, making me bleed inside with thoughts of what might have been, what could have been—until, like a drug that had been invented to stop the hemorrhaging, a small fantasy came to me: I saw myself at Wonderland Dog Track that night. I formed a mental image of myself in the clubhouse there, Elsie beside me, a wad of fresh money in my jacket pocket. I saw myself driving from Wonderland to the Leopard Club, summoning Billy O to the end of the bar, handing him twelve beans, cash . . . with instructions for him to pass on what I owed to Chelsea Eddie and keep the balance for himself. The evening card at Wonderland. Seven P.M.

No, I heard Joanie telling me. No. No. No!

Yes, why not?

No!

The hot parking-lot sun reflected back at me from off a small ocean of cars. Men and women, winners and losers, walked between rows of fenders, dropping programs in the gravel, tearing up tickets, jingling change. Shading my eyes with one hand, I finally located my white T-bird among the hundreds of twinkling windshields, and who should be half sitting, half leaning on the hood with his massive arms crossed on his chest? Xavier Manzo.

Xavier waved in a casual, horrible way, the hand floating up two inches and dropping again. I waved back like I was happy to see him and shuffled towards the T-bird through the lines of cars, yard by yard, because there was no other thing to do.

Ꝏ Ꝏ Ꝏ

Up close, Xavier was a particularly unattractive fellow: coal-colored hair that stuck straight out from his scalp like a low thick forest of quills, and a single eyebrow, a black untrimmed shrub, that drooped a quarter of an inch as it crossed the bridge of his nose. His lips were thick and uneven, and he did not speak too good. Up close, though, what you noticed most was his pale blue eyes, Baby Jesus eyes in a World Wrestling Federation body. When I came to a stop a yard or so in front of him, my legs were vibrating from the soles of my feet to my hip joints. I managed a smile.

"Za-Zave the R-Ra-Rave," I said. "You came to f-find me about buying a piece of prop-property, am I correct? A na-na-na-na-nice two-bedroom condo overlooking Nahant B-Beach?"

Not a molecule moved in Xavier's manly face. The baby blue eyes could have belonged to a marble statue, washed once with ink in Michelangelo's workshop. In the middle of my fear (this happened to me occasionally), I had a perverse urge to slap him on the shoulder and laugh. I mastered it.

"Billy gives you the message las night?" he said.

"Sure he did. I tr-tried calling Eddie at his club—tw-twice—but it was busy both times. I wah-wah-wah-want wanted to set up an appointment for Saturday n-night if I c-could."

"Eddie wants tonight."

"Tonight? Tonight I can't poss-poss-possibly do, Zave. What about tomorrow?"

"Tomorrow Eddie's had meetins. He wants tonight."

"Meetins, huh? Tonight I just can't do, ba-buddy. I'm late as it is. On my way to B-Boston to meet a client who's th-thinking of buying the C-Curtis house. Tell Eddie that, he'll know what it m-m-m-means."

Xavier just stared at me, his face as wide and empty as the back side of a warehouse building. After a minute he blinked; my shoulder twitched.

"I have to ka-keep this appointment, Za-Zave," I told him. "R-really, I have to. This cli-cli-cli-client is primed to make an offer. If I keep him waiting now the whole show goes right out the window. And you know how long Eddie's been trying to unload the C-Curtis house, r-right?"

A single ripple of doubt crossed the pale blue eyes. One of my legs stopped shaking. I leaned my weight on it, shook my watch free of the jacket cuff, stared at the hands without seeing them.

"Eddie wants for tonight. Don't screw wit me."

"What? Who's screwing with you, Zave? How am I suh-suh-supposed to have a meeting on two hours na-notice?"

"If you didn't pull out ya phone for once at night, you didn't have maybe a hundred hours notice."

I was stubbornly shaking my head, other plans for the evening. I was imagining myself at the dog track. If not the dog track, then something else, a very quick trip to Atlantic City, a lucky lottery ticket, or—it had just come to me—the possibility of Joanie herself making an offer on the Curtis house as a gesture of sisterly love.

I pulled the folded crisp bills from my pants' pocket and began peeling back twenties and fifties. "Here, here's fa-five hundred bucks for Eddie, then."

"You know we don't handled Eddie's money when the debt was late."

"All right, so here. Take this for yourself, then." I pushed two fifties into a hand thick as a catcher's mitt. "T-tell him what I said about the Shir-Shir-Shirley Avenue house—that'll make him happy two ways: I'll give him my commission on it, and his friend—what's his name—will finally have unloaded the pee—the pee—the pee-piece of garbage."

"Curtis."

"Curtis, right."

"You just said it yaself a minute ago."

"I can n-never remember those American names, Zave, you know that. And if you don't let me get into Boston by seven o'clock, the whole deal is off and we'll all be-be-be-be screwed."

"You bullshit the same way otha people breathe, Petah. One day not too soon, you're gonna bullshitted the wrong Eddie."

"I'm not that stupid, Zave, r-really. You know your business, you just don't know my business, that's all it is. In m-my ba-business, if you're dealing with a client who has the ma-money to pay for an apartment house, cash, and if you pr-prom-promise you'll meet him in Boston at sa-seven, then you show up at seven, not seven-thirty, not na-nine, not the next night. This client is a big investor on the East Coast. He could ba-buy and sell you and me both without blinking."

I waited, trying to hold my eyes still, to stifle the mad twitching of my left leg. I had seen Xavier Manzo hit someone once, at about this distance. It was a winter night two or three years ago, and we were both at the bar at the cursed Leopard Club (I was through with the place; I hated it), relaxing after our own fashion: me nursing a beer and adding up debts in my mind, Xavier fondling a glass of rum. I could feel just the smallest irritation radiating from his body—irritation at the tattooed guy beside him, who was drunk and yelling ridiculous little love messages to the stripper on stage. The guy beside him ranted; Xavier stared at the woman's nipples, didn't say a word.

Toward the end of the routine his tattooed neighbor started waving his arms in a pitiful way, whistling, calling out, anything to get the woman to look over. When she left the stage finally, without so much as smirking at him, the guy had the bad fortune to spin on his stool in frustration, arms still waving, and knock over his glass of beer in such a way that one little fleck of foam flew out and landed in the hair of Xavier's forearm. Xavier looked down at it like it was alive, a foamy white insect, and I saw his hand move—eighteen inches, no farther—and a bright rose of blood and broken teeth bloom where his neighbor's mouth had been. The fellow slid to the floor, making little whimpering noises. Santa, the bouncer, looked the other way. Xavier poured the last of the rum across his knuckles, disinfecting, shook his cut paw a couple of times over the bar, and walked out.

I stood in the middle of that memory now, shaking, waiting. Xavier folded up the two fifties, very small, molded them into the shape of a small plum, and pushed the plum with one finger down into the handkerchief pocket of my linen jacket. With the same hand he made a gesture: Go.

I flinched. I turned, hair crawling on the back of my neck. Pushed my key very carefully into the door lock—and then went into a kind of trance, and I did not see anything else or hear anything else until I reached the tunnel tollbooth, where I tossed two quarters into the bucket and let out a big breath. Alive.

21

"What about Xavier?" I asked him. I'd spoken quietly, but the words knocked against the square marble columns and echoed up to the fifty-foot ceiling. Billy looked like an animal with one leg caught in a trap, ready to chew it off.

We were sitting in the left front corner of Saint Anthony's, near the votive candles, just the two of us. The cop and the stoolie. Given the kind of people we were trying to avoid, it had to be as safe a place to meet as anywhere on the face of the earth.

When Elsie called me—whispering into the phone, crying, half hysterical—I made sure she was okay, calmed her down as best I could, then dialed Father Dom to see if I could use the church, something I'd done once or twice in the past. I left my house, called Billy Ollanno from a payphone at his house, and told him to meet me at Saint Anthony's—to use the back door and to park his car somewhere no one passing by could see it.

Billy had been on my mind even before Elsie's call. Three weeks ago, I stopped a car making an illegal left onto Dedham Street. Billy Ollanno, it turned out, was driving, although it wasn't his vehicle. He looked off balance there, the way he was perched behind the wheel, so I made him get out. When he got out I saw what he had been sitting on—a nice little packet of poison—and I did something then I had not done in many years: Instead of going by the book—confiscating the substance, arresting him—I let him go. Billy had a two-page sheet of minor and not so minor offenses, and another drug conviction—even though the amount was small—would have been enough to send him away again. I knew that, and I used it. Not to torment Billy—I'm not that kind of cop—but because I despise the people Billy works for, despise what they've done to so many individuals, so many families. For all the time since Sally's death—ten years—I had been looking for a way to strike back at them: the right way, the perfect way.

And it seemed to me at that moment, sitting in the church where Sally and I had been married, that I might finally have found it.

I could smell the sour sweat from Billy's body. I did not look at him. In front of us, Father Dom was getting ready for the next morning's mass, straightening out the altar cloth, cleaning a speck of dust from his chalice, ignoring us. He had locked the three front doors himself and was just keeping an eye out now for a minute, making sure we had the church to ourselves. Thursday afternoon, late. My question about Xavier floating up there near the ceiling with the angels.

"Whattaya want to know about him, man?" Billy said, and I turned, finally, to look. He was high. The muscles of his face were doing a little overstimulated dance, and his eyes were jumping towards the stations of the cross on the wall beside us as if they showed scenes from his own past and his own future. Billy being stripped and beaten. Billy falling the second time.

The night before, I'd had a terrible dream about Sally, and it was haunting me then, in the place from which she had been buried, in the place where I had come—before her death and after it—to pray and to beg and to light candles that burned down, like the last of her will and her strength, to nothing. She came to me in the dream, sitting in a car, her face healthy and full of life, the way it had been when we were first married, and she said, "The ocean of your pity between us," and drove away again.

"What's going on in Xavier's mind now?" I said to Billy, but I was looking at the cross and I was thinking of Sally, and Peter. The ocean of pity, the frustration, the impossibility of ever helping people who did not believe they needed help or deserved it.

Billy swung his face forward. He studied Father Dom a minute—

though Dommy couldn't hear us—then raised his eyes to the mural above the altar. "What mind?" he said.

Which was a perfectly typical answer for Billy Ollanno. Which was why he had so many friends.

"What difference does Xavier's mind make, man?"

"It's a puzzle piece. You were at Concord together, you know him. What is he up to now, going to Peter's office in the middle of the day. What's that all about?"

"Nothing," Billy said, one half decibel above a whisper. "How'd you hear about that so fast?"

"How did you?"

Billy started to shake, to gnaw at his leg bone. He took a handkerchief out of his back pocket, held it in front of him and stared at it like he'd forgotten what it was for, then pushed it back into his pants. "He takes orders, that's all. Xavier."

"It's not personal, then? He wouldn't do it just to get back at Peter for something?"

"Nevah. That's not the way he is."

"What happened to him at Concord? What was he like there?"

"You know."

"If I knew, would I ask? Were you friends with him?"

"Friends?" Billy let out a high warble of a laugh that flew up and around the church like a trapped bird trying for open air. "Friends, huh? Man . . . I was . . . man. Friends, huh?"

"What then?"

"What, huh?" His eyes scrambled across my face, over the twitching candles, up towards Father Dom. "I ended up more like his wa-wife than a friend, that's what," he said, in a pathetic whisper. "More like a effin wife. . . . And it would probly still be that way, even now, if Eddie wasn't around to feed him a girl from the club once in a while. He's like a dog, you know? He listens to orders like a dog, he eats the way a dog eats, and . . . and he does the other thing like a dog does, whoever's there, that's all. He takes, that's all. If he's bigger than you, if nobody has him on the leash, he takes."

"Why did you come back to the club, then? What happened?"

"Same thing that happened for you to get me to come here. I got caught doing something I shouldn'ta been, some little nothin, taking something they said didn't belong to me, that's all. I can't leave the state, you know that. I'm not exactly a person everybody's dying to give a job to. And I got caught doing some little nothin when I first got out. Eddie coulda killed me for it, but instead he took me for a ride on the Lynnway and made me pull my pants down, and he grabbed my . . . my eggs, you know, my balls . . . in one hand and he said if the next light turned red before we got there he'd cut them off, right there; he had a knife on the seat. Yellow, the light was. We went under it yellow. He let me pull up my pants and he made me a deal—I'd do this and that and I could keep my—you know, my . . . equipment. And he uses it to work me now, same as you with this other thing. Pay me half what they're suppose to pay me. Make me do little favors nobody else wants to. Run a little stuff here, Billy, carry a little stuff there, nobody will never catch you, we'll take care of it if they catch you. Sure. Take care of it how? What am I suppose to do now that you caught me, go tell Eddie? He works me like you work me, that's all. That's my life, man. That's what it is. One or two little mistakes and you're a slave to some effin guy forever."

"What about Peter?"

Billy swiveled his head and studied the empty pews behind us, glanced at me, sank down an inch lower in his place. "You know, dontcha?"

"Sure I know. What I want to find out is what stage it's at. Eddie's sending Xavier over to Peter's office. What stage is it at?"

"It's just business, just money," Billy said, but for a small-time crook and bullshit artist he was a pitiful liar. And there was something about him—there had always been something about Billy—that drained away all my natural sympathy for people. He had not supplied the drugs Sally used, I knew that. She had ruined her own life, not Billy, not Eddie, not me. But I had known Billy growing up, and I had seen him drift, very gradually, out of the life the rest of us lived and into the life he lived now. And I hated him for that, as if he personally represented what I saw happening to the good people in this city, the good families. As if he were the Devil or the Devil's advance man, a mascot for the new America.

And he hated me the same way. To him, I represented the system that had caught him, imprisoned him for being who he was, taken away his last drop of self-respect. He would just as soon have seen me dead.

Sitting there then, I had a flash that my little escapade in rule-bending would end one of two ways: Either I would be standing on a bloody street somewhere, looking down at Billy's body, or he would be standing there, looking down at mine.

"Is it just the debt?"

He shrugged and pouted and tried to cover up, but I could see that I'd hit one edge of something.

"Is it?"

"I dunno; you know, who can say with that guy? Who sees inside Chelsea Eddie, you know? You hear things. They say his wife is playin around, for one, which makes him nuts, natchrally, who wouldn't, righ?" He looked at me then, to see if this was a surprise. It wasn't, and I didn't pretend that it was. "His wife is playin around, one. Some Vietmese guys came to the club to talk to him, all smooth, two. Tough guys, you know. His friends are all in jail, three. Somebody took his pitcha down the beach two weeks ago and put it on the paper, righ? Four. How happy could you be?"

I knew there was something else. I felt a little sadistic twitch then, looked up at Father Dom, swallowed it. "Listen," I said, in a slightly kinder voice, "Peter's in a jam here. He considers you a friend. Help him out."

A flash of feeling went across Billy's face, and I almost forgave him for the person he'd turned into. Father Dom finished his preparations and disappeared through a door behind the altar, and the church was just haunting me then, old feelings rising up in a way they hadn't risen up in ten years.

By the end there had, in fact, been an ocean between us. Sally swimming stubbornly out away from me, away from her family and friends, from everything she had been. Nobody had an explanation for it. It had nothing to do with us—we were happy together, faithful and happy. It wasn't because she couldn't have children—even though, afterwards, people said that's what it was. It was addiction, pure and simple, and addiction doesn't need any other reason to kill you. Addiction puts its claws in a person, and it pulls them down, that's all: small troubles and small lies, growing over the years just the way a child grows. A small, untreated sickness turning into a chronic infection, turning fatal. I could feel the same thing happening to Peter now, the next closest person to me on this earth, my truest friend, my brother. It was like watching half your family die of cancer, very slow.

"In a world like this, a friend counts for something," I said, but I was saying it to myself then, not to Billy.

"I know that, man. Dontcha think I know? Leo Markin was my friend and he goes and moves to a desert island, righ? And my one other friend in the city, you think I forget who that is? All the kids we went to school with, who comes down and spends a hour with Billy at the bar? Billy, who gives them free drinks every other time, who introduces them to girls, who does them little favors when they need something? What, I forget the name of that person?"

"Help him out, then."

"Sure, I'll help. I'm already helpin. I come here today and I meet with you on—what?—ten minutes notice. And if somebody finds out about it, they'll take me up on the Mystic Bridge late some night and let me jump off . . . if I'm lucky."

Someone rattled the front door handle, waited, rattled again, then walked away. Billy perked up his ears like a terrier and went into a small fit of chemical twitching.

"Wow, I hate this place, man." He turned towards me, his whole body jumping, poison running the blood. It made me remember things I would rather have not remembered. I turned my eyes forward and let him sweat a little bit more.

I should have taken her and moved to Alaska. Found a job there, started another life. But I had been tricked by the memory of the family she'd come from, the memory of the woman she had once been. As if that was some kind of protection.

I swore to myself I would not make that same mistake again, with Peter. No assumptions now, no excuses for me, no blind hoping for the best. "You're staying here until you tell me what you can tell me," I told Billy.

"Yeah, fine," he said, shaking like he had been frozen in a block of ice for the last two days. "Rafaelo Losco was my godfather, don't forget, though, man. Lived behind Petey's parents his whole effin life, told me things."

"Really."

"That's right, man."

"Told you what things?"

"I know who you are, is what."

I turned and looked into his twitching, terrified face, waited a few seconds, and when I saw he wasn't bluffing I said, "I know who I am too, Billy. That's not the way out for you now."

"It ain't, huh?"

"Trust me, it ain't."

Billy held out another minute or so, then the tough-guy act melted into a puddle at his feet. "All right," he said, twisting one ear in each hand, as if he was tuning himself into the truth channel. "All right, then, all right. . . . It's the sister, man, what I hear. Petey they could let go of. Run him twenty years and keep him paying a little bit this week and a little bit next week and not worry too much about it. But the sister's trouble for Eddie, that's all. And he don't know what else to do but put the pressure on Petey to try to get her off his back. That's what you hear, you know. The press. The TV lady."

"You're not saying that just to get away?"

"What get away? Get away where? The club? You call that gettin away?"

"You're sure?"

"Who can be sure with Chelsea Eddie? You think he comes down and has a drink with Billy O and tells me all his secrets? I hear this and I hear that, that's all. You wanna know what I know, there it is—a lot of thises and thats, man."

"He protects you, though."

"Sure, he protects me. He protects me, you protect me. That's my life now, man, what am I suppose to do?"

"Go."

"Now? Where?"

"Out through the altar door where the priest just went. He'll sneak you out the back."

"Oh, man, there?"

"And call me when you know something else."

"What about the other thing, then? The . . . you know . . . dope."

"I'll forget that other thing like it never happened."

"You will?"

"Call me one more time, tell me one more thing to help our friend, and it never happened."

"Man," Billy said. He looked at me like he might kiss my hand or shoot me, he wasn't sure which. Then he hunched his shoulders, stood, and skittered up the side aisle, keeping his eyes down as he passed the saints. I watched him step through the marble altar-rail gate, make a quick sign of the cross over his chest—a childhood habit—and then circle like the shadow of the Devil, along the brown marble wall that curved behind the altar. There was the sound of a door closing, a series of soft echoes, and I was left alone there in the locked church in a stew of a hundred doubts, thinking about Joanie.

22

I parked in a guarded lot on Newbury Street and tipped the attendant five dollars in advance as a way of sharing my good fortune and protecting the T-bird at the same time. And since I had an extra few minutes, I decided to walk around the block with my jacket over my shoulder, let the little chat with Xavier fade into the background a bit so I could greet my sister in a more or less calm state of mind, more or less as an equal.

I'd had a nice afternoon at the track—not a huge afternoon but a nice one; I had eleven hundred seventy-four dollars in my pocket, won in small doses, which meant the IRS hadn't gotten involved; Joanie had invited me to dinner; my mother had sounded happy on the phone; Xavier had let me off the hook.

Everything pointed to a shift in fortunes. I fixed that idea in my mind, and after a stroll through the busy Back Bay, arrived at the base of the Prudential Tower at exactly ten minutes past seven—just right.

The express elevator carried me to the fifty-second floor. I found my beautiful sister there, sitting at a window table with her chin in one hand, staring north towards the city she'd abandoned. Joanie was wearing a businesswoman's dress, something she might have read the news in on a rainy afternoon. Expensive as a small car, sexy as a shopping bag. "Hey, J-Jo." I pecked her on the cheek, slid into the chair opposite, offered a smile.

She smiled back. But somehow, in the light of that smile, my big lucky afternoon at the horsetrack seemed like so much Mickey Mouse.

"S-sorry I'm a little late. I showed a house at six, and Els-Els-Elsie had left already for the day, so I had to stay around and make out the purchase-and-sale myself."

"Congratulations, Peter."

"A referral. Three-three-three-three and a qua-quarter percent of a hundred twenty grand. Enough for a couple new suits. No big deal."

She was watching me, seeing right through me. I turned my eyes out the plate-glass window. Off in the distance, beyond the tight bunch of skyscrapers, I could just make out the crescent-moon curl of Revere Beach Boulevard in the fading light. I'd turned into a liar now in middle age, a phony salesman, a guy who couldn't pay his debts. The conversation I'd had with my father the night before was floating around in the air near my ears like bad music.

"Business is strong?"

"Na-not bad. Revere seems to be bouncing b-back, finally."

"Not what I hear."

I gave her a one-syllable laugh, brotherly enough, but the whole act had gone rancid now. People at the other tables were shooting little envious glances at my famous sister, and she was sitting there in her jewels and styled hair, at peace in her body, healthy, wealthy, famous, sure of herself, two beautiful, confident eyes looking down upon the lower worlds. "You're getting ba-ba-bad information, J-Jo. You never should have m-moved out."

"You never should have stayed," she said, and the waiter came and saved me from another lecture.

Joanie ordered the vegetarian omelet; she was always going on one special health diet or another. I chose veal Milanese and insisted—against her halfhearted protests—on an expensive bottle of Italian red. A little wine would loosen us up, let me be more honest with her maybe, let both of us drop our defenses.

It seemed to work. As we ate and drank, the last of the light drew back off the stone and steel skin of the city and settled in around us in a warm, comfortable way. I gave her the news from Revere: cousins I'd seen around; people we knew from high school who were getting married again or divorced again; who'd gotten rich or gotten sick, been arrested, hit the lottery, moved away. As I talked I watched her watching me, and it occurred to me that God had messed up and given her the eyes Xavier Manzo was supposed to get—dark chocolate, almost black, piercing whatever she pointed them at like crucifixion spikes. Joanie had inherited our mother's good looks, and even now, in her early forties, her face was holding on to its classic lines. Nice lips, blond-brown head of hair, nice cheekbones, nice shoulders beneath the librarian's dress, a beauty mark to the left of her lips, Cindy Crawford style. I wondered then, for a minute, what kind of perfect imaginary man she'd been waiting for all these years, what had kept her from marrying and starting a family. The huge ambition, maybe. Or all the moving around she'd done in the early part of her career. Or maybe the gene for commitment had just slipped out of our blood when we were in the womb: not a child between us, not a husband or wife, not a single grandkid for the old folks to fuss over.

❦   ❦   ❦

We both ordered the apple strudel for dessert and took our second glass of wine in small, thoughtful sips. By the time the waiter stopped by to warm up our coffees, it had gotten dark, and strings of lights had appeared below us like diamonds sewn onto the city's black dress. My sister and I had been brought up to believe that family was the most sacred human institution, and maybe that was true because I felt a deep comfort with Joanie on that night—Joanna, she wanted us to call her; I would try to remember that. I could feel the link to this girl. I could sense colorful little pennants of good memory waving at the edges of our conversation: Joanie teaching me to swim in the cold water at Revere Beach; Joanie proudly introducing me to her roommate when I made my one visit to Cornell; on my thirtieth birthday, Joanie throwing a surprise party at Casa Ministieri in the North End and presenting me with the entire collected works of Dostoevsky, a rare edition, which I kept on a shelf at the office but hadn't had a chance to look into yet. . . . My sister, my blood—she must have sensed I was in trouble.

"I was th-thinking of you this week," I said. I shook two sugar packets together, stirred, tapped with the heavy spoon. "An interesting property came on the market. M-my exclusive."

"Moving back to Revere is somehow not in my plans, Peter."

"I wasn't thinking of it as a p-place you'd like to live, Jo, come on. It's just that a p-person could m-make a for-fortune owning this building and renting out the apar-par-par, the apartments; I've been in the business long enough to see that. So I thought of you, f-figured you'd have the capital, figured you'd be looking for a little tax break. . . . A considerate br-brother, that's all."

She smirked.

"You used to make that f-face when you were in junior high."

"It's the face I make when people say they have a special deal that's going to make me rich overnight."

Richer, I thought. I leaned forward and topped off her wineglass, then sat back and took a sip of my own, trying to keep the smile there, to keep loving her, to hold on to the good memories and let go of the bad. Father Dom had taught me this trick once, long ago, where you breathed in and took all the troubles of the other person's life onto you, then you breathed out just good feeling, just kindness. I was trying it now. Breathing in all the sad parts of Joanie's life (though really, how much sadness could there be in a life like hers?) and breathing out love. Breathing in all our old arguments, breathing out Family. I tried to put only kindness into my voice. "Think about it, J-Jo. I've been in business for myself, what—six, seven ya-yee-yeh-years now? Have I ever come to you with a property?"

She shook her head. Defensive. City suspicious.

"We might not want to adma-ma-mit it, you know, but we're at a place in our lives now where it's not such a b-bad idea to look down the road a little ways. It might be nice to incur a steady income without w-wa-working. Maybe you already have the investments and everything. I mean, I have a la-la-la-little something set aside too, you know, an IRA and some T-bills and whatnot . . . st-stocks. But this is cash, every month. Another day or two and somebody will hear about it and gobble it up, but now it's there, on my desk, nobody Elsie's . . . else's."

"Thanks, I'm not tempted."

"No problem."

"I just bought a new apartment at Grayson Towers."

"On the water. Na-na-na-nice. No problem, then."

I tried to stay positive. I remembered she'd complained to me once that I never asked about her, that the conversation always revolved around me: my *drama*, she called it, my *melodrama*. As if she didn't have one too. "How's your la-love life? How's the job?"

"Both fine."

"Boss still up to the same whattayacallit? Unwanted grab-assing, as we sa-say in Revere?"

She shook her head, her eyes slipped away and then quickly back, and in that second her face changed the way the ocean can change on a summer afternoon when the sun goes behind a cloud. She seemed all of a sudden like somebody else, a sad, lonely woman trapped in a world of phony glamour. Fame without fortune. People staring at her wherever she went, coming up to her on the street, pesting for autographs. Idiots calling the station and asking her out. Unlisted phone numbers, dark glasses, not a day's peace. For a moment then I had an urge to reach out and put a hand on her bare arm, to reconnect her again to the simpler world she'd run away from, to let her know she had a family, a brother, a real hometown, friends who would stand by her if things ever started to turn sour here on the Boston side of the river.

But Joanie had never really liked being touched, and I wasn't sure how much of it would be a type of con on my part, another lie.

I asked her what she was working on, and she brightened some.

"A series of investigative pieces."

"Something different for you, no? Is that why you were on the na-noon news instead of six?"

I poured another glass of wine, leaned back, tried to appear interested. It wasn't easy. So much going on in my mind at that moment, so many plans, numbers, meetings, phone calls: a hurricane of worry.

"We've had a small bump down in the ratings," she said, "and the powers-that-be came up with the idea for this series, and I more or less volunteered to anchor it. I'm taking a week off to get ready. They're trying out this newsmagazine idea—"

"Diane Sawyer," I said.

She gave me a smile. "It's the trend now, industry wide. Only ours will be a little bit different, a sharper edge than the typical local network stuff, riskier subjects. And it's something I care about personally, so—"

"Ma-Ma-Ma-Ma-Mama and Papa will miss seeing you at six o'clock," I said, in as cheerful and upbeat a way as I could manage. "It's like d-dessert for them, watching you. Their piece of pie after supper." I rested my fingertips on the edge of the table, watched the blinking wingtip lights of a jet lifting off from Logan, and felt the building starting to slide out from under me. I concentrated, tightened the muscles around my stomach. I ran through my calculations: what I owed Eddie, Elsie, what I had in my pocket, what this meal would cost, what kind of story I was going to have to make up for my landlord on Monday. What I was going to do for food now.

Gas. Spending money. Elsie's salary. Against that mountain of in-debtedness, the money I'd won at Suffolk seemed all of a sudden about as significant as three shitty pennies in the gutter, a seven-hundred-dollar blip on the screen, a joke. By next Tuesday I would owe Eddie Crevine a total interest payment of seventeen hundred and ten dollars. I already owed my friend Augie Recupero five hundred since last Christmas—when I went to Atlantic City hoping to win enough to buy Elsie a diamond, and things hadn't exactly gone my way—so that option was out. Elsie was out, my father and mother, Alfonse, my shrinking roster of friends. I'd mortgaged the condo way beyond what the loan officer called the bank's "comfort zone," taken out what collateral I could on the four-year-old Thun-derbird, pawned a favorite ring and a set of cuff links an old girl-friend had given me.

I went down the list of people I might turn to for a loan, but it was a crappy, useless list, empty of promise as a smelly beach shell. My mind dropped to the bottom of it and fell off into the void. The Ngs, maybe. Maybe the Ngs had called and left a message on my machine. Six and a half percent of a hundred and twenty-seven . . . say a hun-dred fifteen if they negotiated. Seventy-five hundred, minus—

"Have you been to see Mama?"

"What?"

"Mama. Have you seen her?"

"Sure, a ca-couple weeks ago."

"Talked to her recently?"

"This afternoon on the phone. I'm going to see her later tonight, or t-t-tomorrow."

"I spoke with Dr. Pierni. He says she has a month or less. He says less would be a blessing."

"A ma-ma-ma-ma-month or less, what are you talking about? I had a ca-conversation with her on the phone at lunchtime. She said she was fa-fine."

The smirk again. Joanie looking at me like I was ten years old.

I turned my eyes out the window and tried to imagine being on this earth without my mother. She'd said she was fine. She sounded fine, a little tired. I was going to visit her tonight, with flowers . . . to celebrate the Ngs buying their house. If Joanie and my father would just let me up for a minute, I was going to set everything right.

"So this series you're doing," I said. "Wha-what's it on?"

"Organized crime."

I wasn't sure I'd heard right, I couldn't have been hearing right. . . . A month or less . . . Organized crime.

"And my brother drifts away," Joanie said. "It must be terrible to have to listen to someone else talk about themselves for more than a minute or so at a time, hey, Peter? It must seem so irrelevant."

"I'm sorry, J-Jo. Christ. I'm just exhausted, that's all. I'm, I'm— Go-go-go on, I'm listening."

She reached a braceleted arm out for the check, and I was nearly angry enough—at her; at the way things seemed to always twist wrong for me—to let her get it. "It's mine," I said.

"*I* invited *you*."

"I know. It's m-mine anyway. You got it last time. Christ, hold on, will you? Are you that pissed off at me? I told you, I'm beat, but I was la-la-listening. Go on."

"I've lost the thread."

"Come on, Jo."

"Let's split it."

"My God, will you? I said it's my ta-turn, it's my ta-turn. What is it with you tonight?"

To my complete surprise I saw that her eyes had filled with tears, that a rich young couple at the next table was watching her, staring, that my famous sister and I had a little scene going here at the Top of the Hub. I shot the yuppies a nasty look and they went back to their zinfandel and low-fat baklava, their clean little lives.

"What's going on, J-Jo?"

She shook her head, pinched the water out of the bottoms of her eyes with her thumb and forefinger, and wiped them on her napkin.

I reached across the table and took her hand. "To hell with these people," I said, loud enough for them to hear. "What's the m-matter?"

She shook her head and stared out at the city.

"Jo? Come on."

She shook her head again.

"You despise m-me, don't you," I said. From nowhere.

She ran two fingers down her forehead, blinked, met my eyes, then went back to the dark long-distance view. "I despise the life you lead," she said, so quietly I could barely hear.

I took my hand away. "What do you na-know about the life I lead?"

"You lie for a living, I can see it. You've been lying to me all night, I can feel it."

"What? Says who, lying? Wha-what lying? Wha-what was a lie? . . . And you don't lie for a living?"

"I try not to, no. I try to listen when people talk about a subject other than me. I visit Mama and Papa as often as I can, and I don't try to pretend it's a made-up story when I hear that my own mother is dying. I don't see you for dinner once every three months and use the opportunity to make a sales pitch."

"What sa-sales pa-pa-pitch? It's the ca-ca-ca-cur-cur-cur—It's the Cur-Cur-Curtis house, that's all. I wasn't going to take any commission on it, I swear I wasn't."

"No? Why bother then?"

"Why ba-bother?" I looked at the couple beside us—total concentration on their last sip of zinfandel now, the wallet coming out, the big credit card—and leaned across the table so there was only a few feet of space between Joanie and me. "Why bother?" I said. "You want to know why bother?"

"Of course."

"Ask your sources who give you your information on the Mob. Maybe they'll tell you why bother."

"Meaning what?"

"You go fig-figure it out," I said. "You've ga-got your reporter's face on now, look at the way you're leaning forward, all pa-perky all of a sudden. That's why you invited me to dinner, wasn't it? Pick up a little street information for your newsmagazine? That's it, isn't it. La-look at you."

"I'm sorry I said I despise your life, Peter. I—"

"You haven't the s-smallest l-little clue about my life. You sit there in your makeup and your fancy clothes and you report the na-news about the whole rest of the world, but really you don't have the ta-tiniest clue about how other people live, what it's like to suf-suf-suffer, really suffer, to really be in a situation you can't buy your way out of."

"That's partly true. I'm sorry. I—"

"Then just don't st-start in on my life when you don't really know what that life is."

"Fine, I—"

"And ga-go find somebody else for your information from now on. And work your hotshot TV job for another few years until you're too old, and then ga-go find some rich guy from Well-Wellesley or someplace you can marry just to—"

"I'm gay, Peter," she said, very quietly.

"Say what?"

She looked at the next table, waited for them to stand and start for the exit. "I'm gay. I'm a lesbian."

I had been reaching into my breast pocket for the money, half crazy. I stopped short, stared across the table at her, and said, when I saw it was the truth, "Hah."

And a second later: "That answers those nine million questions."

And two seconds after that: "Do Ma-Mama and Papa know?"

She shook her head.

"And you call *me* a liar."

"Don't go on the attack."

But I wasn't thinking of attacking. And, for the moment, I wasn't thinking of Xavier or Eddie or my debts. In the files of my memory a certain puzzle piece was snapping into place again and again, completing one scene after the next—odd moments and confusing little looks and comments, all sticking onto one word now: gay. My gorgeous sister was gay. Queer. She liked to do with women what I liked to do with them.

"Do they know at work?"

"Planning to blackmail me?"

"There's that suspicious streak again, sa-see? I wasn't going to blackmail you, but you're doing a show on the M-Ma-Mob, right?

And it doesn't enter your mind that maybe *they're* going to try and blackmail you?"

"They wouldn't dare. There are too many gays in the business."

"Too many nice gay Italian Catholic girls on the na-nightly na-news? Who all the old women in the North End adore? Who get invited to be guest speaker at every Italian-American b-benefit and church dinner from Hanover Street to East Providence? Who are inves-ves-vestigating the Mob?"

Something passed across Joanie's face then—eyes, cheeks, lips. Vulnerability, maybe, although vulnerability wasn't a word you really would ever use in connection with my sister. It took her less than an eight-count to recover. She glanced over my shoulder at the view of the Back Bay and the river, and when she turned to me again it was like looking at a pretty face on a TV screen.

"What was the house deal you were telling me about?"

"The house deal? Fa-forget that now. This what you just told me is a huh-huh-huh-, a huh-huh-, a hun-, a hundred times more important than some c-crappy ha-house deal."

"No, I want to hear about it."

"Forget that now."

"You say I don't know anything about your life, and you're right. I want to know."

"Believe me, you don't."

"Peter, come on. I'm trying to make a change here. Try back."

There was another shift now, two drops of sisterly closeness in her voice, love even. I felt a shot of hope go through me. Maybe the dream life was harder on the inside than it looked from the outside, being gay and everything. Maybe it wasn't the picnic it seemed to be, all glamorous dates and big paychecks. Joanie nodded then, like she was reading my mind. All I had to do was move my lips apart about an eighth of an inch and the whole Curtis house spiel came bubbling out.

I knew it by heart. In my panic to sell the place, I'd made the pitch to at least thirty prospective buyers, run down a list of less and less likely landlords and investors from Chelsea to Manchester-by-the-Sea. Twelve apartments in a spacious triple-decker off Shirley Avenue, two blocks from the ocean. Each unit had two bedrooms, a kitchen, den, and full bath, and the building had enjoyed a hundred percent occupancy rate for the last three years running. It was not the most beautiful piece of property in the city, but that was exactly the point: Some cosmetic work—a coat of paint, new set of front steps, that kind of thing—and it could be sold for twenty percent profit overnight. Or the rents could be nudged up ten or twenty bucks a month and you could put that against the mortgage princi-pal. Three or four years from now a building like that, two blocks from the beach, would be worth half a million, minimum.

I went on a little bit longer than probably I should have, telling her about the new sewage treatment plant that was going to clean up the water down the beach; about the possibility of selling the house in a few years and investing the proceeds in a safer market in town, Beacon Hill, Back Bay; about the job the new mayor of Re-vere was doing, the nice families who still lived there, the city yard's new street-cleaning machine. I let myself get a little bit wound up in a tale of easy money, that's all. I started to spin a life, do what I did best.

When I finally stopped to take a breath I noticed she was sitting back in her chair, watching me like I was a fish in an aquarium. I swam on. "It's a seller-da-da-da-desperate situation, Joanie. The guy's asking three hundred and fi-fifty thousand, which is twenty-five below assessment. And I happen to know you could get him to knock it down to three thirty-five in about two seconds."

"Who is the illustrious owner?"

"La-Louis Ca-Ca-Ca-Curtis," I told her, but I could see in her eyes and hear in her voice that the house meant nothing to her. She had no more interest in saving her brother, in getting involved in Re-vere again, than I had in reading the fucking TV news with makeup on. I watched the waiter return with the change like I was watching a citizen from another civilization. Prim, smug, young cheeks shaved clean as a porcelain vase, the kid was a smirking ambassador from Oz. Screw him.

"Why is Mr. Curtis in so much of a hurry?"

"Screw him, too. The ga-guy's wa-one of the wa-worst slumlords in Greater Boston, a house burner, a shit. I hate him. I wish I'd never gotten involved with the ba-bastard, all right?"

"There is so much anger in you," she said quietly.

"There is like hell."

"Who are you angry at, Mama?"

I locked my eyes on her, shaking, lips twitching. "Leave Mum-Mum-Ma-Mama and Papa out of it. I'm not angry. I'm screwed, d-dead, that's all."

The check was paid—I threw an extra finnif onto my twenty percent because, really, the waiter had left us alone, and because I wanted to show him I could move in his world, and because it didn't matter now anyway—five extra dollars wasn't going to ruin me any more than I was already ruined. My plan had sailed like the *Titanic* into Joanie's icy edges. I could feel myself filling with water, going down. The conversation was dead, the plan was dead, I was dead, but I could not bring myself to make a move for the door. My sister was gay and had to hide it, my mother was sick, my father hated me, in another week Elsie was going to be out of a job, and people like Eddie Crevine were riding around in limousines with a beautiful young wife, earning money hand over fist from other people's misery. Where was the place for any kind of God in a life like that, could somebody please tell me?

All of a sudden then I remembered why I'd walked all the way to Saint Anthony's from the Leopard Club and my conversation with Billy Ollanno, the day before: I had wanted to find Father Dom, ask him that question, and see what kind of answer I got. Where is the place God stands in an upside-down mess like this, Dommy? Where is the smallest shred of God-evidence in the middle of this frying pan?

Over the years we'd had probably fifty private talks there in the living room of the rectory, the old housekeeper bringing me Boston cream pie and coffee, the fire in the fireplace going, Father Dom joking with me, pushing me, challenging me, once in a while slipping me ten bucks to put on a horse at Suffolk because he secretly loved to gamble, Dommy, and it wouldn't look right for people to see him at the track. I left Billy Ollanno and the Leopard Club and walked all the way to Saint Anthony's because the drinking had somehow brought those talks back to me. I wanted there to be an answer—not an answer for a kid, for a nineteen-year-old, but for me, now, an answer for a full adult.

"Why don't you buy it yourself if it's such a wonderful opportunity?" Joanie was asking, and I came within a whisker of telling her. Ribbons of traffic moving north and south over the Mystic Bridge. Freighters in the harbor. The little half-wedding-band of yellow lights along Revere Beach Boulevard. I opened my mouth, closed it tight.

"Tell me," she said.

"Tell you be-because you care, or tell you because you're a reporter doing a series on the M-Mob and you want some information?"

"Come on, Peter. I'm your sister."

The truth caught in my throat. Any chance of being equal was gone now. I was a fool, an addict, a liar, *less*. It was clear as the layout of the city streets below.

"Peter."

"I'm in d-debt," I said, making a quick survey of the room to see if anyone had heard. "I'm in debt very da-da-deep, J-Joanie."

"From gambling?"

"No, from my ch-charitable contributions. Of course from gambling. What else?"

"I thought you were going to quit. I thought we made a pact. You were going to quit, and I was going to slow down."

"I did quit for a little while."

"You did? What—"

"Six or seven weeks. . . . And then I t-told myself I could t-take it or leave it. . . . So I took it. Don't make that fa-face. Please."

"I'm sorry. I'm just . . . I thought we were through with this."

"We aren't."

She went right back to the verge of tears again and I could not bear to look at her. It was almost impossible to take the next breath, but somehow, when Joanie said, "Tell me what happened, for God's sake," all I had to do was open my mouth, and my lungs and heart and intestines were out there on the table within about three seconds.

"I had a huge streak of la-la-luck when I first went back to it is what happened. At the be-be-beginning of the year I had a streak of la-luck like gamblers dream about their whole lives—at wa-work, at the track, lottery tickets, ke-ke-ke-keno. Everything I ta-touched turned to money. I decided I could take twenty thousand dollars to Atlantic City and earn enough there in two days never to have to work again. I could ma-mar, ma-mar-mar-marry Elsie, finally, and set her up in a real house. She has a son, Austin; I was thinking I could more or less adopt the k-kid, you know, send him to a good college some-someplace. I was thinking I could maybe make things a little easier for Ma and Pa."

"Peter, what *happened*?"

"I . . . I drove down, I settled in at the Claridge—they treated me like Sinatra: la-limo, room with a view of the oh-oh-ocean, free dinners—and I went through the twenty thousand in one night. They offered me a line of credit; I took that too, won back about half, then ba-bl-bl-blew everything."

"My God, Peter. Twenty thousand dollars! I can't—"

"That's n-nothing. I had *forty* thousand dollars worth of chips on the craps table a few years ago in Va-Vegas, and by the time I was done that night I had to borrow the money to get a cab home from the airport."

"You're bragging now."

"Bragging? Who would br-brag about a thing like that? Are you kidding? Let me tell the story, you'll see what there isn't to br-brag about. . . . After that, I came home and started working seven days a week, but from the day I got back, the real estate market went sa-south on me and kept going. I had the credit line—a hundred a month; the m-mortgage on the condo, seven-seventy-five; the office rent, four-twenty-five; two years left on the car note at two hundred a month. Pl-plus Elsie's salary, gas, insurance, advertising, clothes, pocket money, little da-da-da-, little deh-, little debts I had here and there that I wanted to get free of.

"I worked my rear end off and I hardly ga-gambled at all, truthfully, and between February and April I made exactly one sale. One sale. Sixty-five hundred dollars in four months. I went to every bank in the city, I went to friends, acquaintances. I piled up debts so high I couldn't think straight, couldn't eat, couldn't sleep through the night. Half a dozen times I pi-picked up the phone to call you, but all I ever got was your ma-ma-ma-machine and I couldn't say a word into it, I was so embarrassed.

"Finally I was so damn desperate I went to Ma-Ma-Ma and Pa, took them up on a two-thousand-dollar la-loan—"

"You did *what*?"

"I was da-dead wrong. I adma-admit that."

"Peter, do you have the smallest clue what their finances are like, what it costs to have the aides there around the clock? You lose in one night everything they've been able to save in fifty years of working!"

"Ma-Mama offered, Jo, I didn't ask. I ca-can't f-forgive myself for it, believe me. Why do you think I haven't been back there? You think I can fa-fa-fa-face them now? Stop looking at me like you're gonna shoot me, will you? I said I was sorry. . . . I'll p-pay them back—"

"*This* is what I despise," she said, and I could see she meant it, but there was nothing to do except keep talking.

"So on my birthday some of my buddies threw a little p-party for me at Joe Bones' pub. I had a couple beers, I stayed there talking late with Ba-Ba-Billy Ollanno, spilled my whole story, naturally. Billy, that sn-snake, he cozies up to me at the end of the night and says, 'Why don't you go see Chel-Chel-Chelsea Eddie again, ma-man? He la-loaned you money before one time and you paid him back, didn't you, Pa-Petey? He thinks you're a class guy.'

"So I made the call and went to see Eddie at his shop in Melrose. He was na-nice about it. His ja-ja-juice is five percent, same as always. Five dollars per hundred per week. Which at the time seemed almost like ch-charity. . . . Ja-Joanie, please, look at me a little bit different, will you?"

"It's not five percent, Peter. It's two hundred and sixty percent, compounded."

"I can do arithmetic, thanks. . . . But I was sure I could p-pay him back, you know. I stayed optimistic."

"That's your problem, staying optimistic."

"Let me finish, will you please? . . . Two more weeks went by without a single sale. Not one winning night at the tr-track, not one la-lousy commission other than a few rentals I collect on. Chump change. I go to Ed-Ed-Eddie again, ask him for another seventy-five hundred. He said no at first—if you don't pay them they don't keep making la-loans, naturally—but I talked to him for a while the way I do, and he ended up giving me what he had in his pockets—just under fa-four th-thousand.

"By the time the next Tuesday rolls around, I'm having to come up with five hundred and seventy dollars a week *interest,* and Ed-Ed-Eddie is starting to change a little bit on me. 'I'm not a ch-charity,' he's saying now. 'I understand personal problems and business problems as good as the next guy, but I'm not a charity. Don't forget that,' he says.

"I keep getting ma-more and more nervous about it, Jo, but there's nothing I can do, not even anybody I can tell. You've heard the stories about Eddie, haven't you? There were rumors going around about other guys who hadn't pa-paid up, and the ki-ki-kinds of things that had been done to them, gruesome things, in-in-inhuman kinds of things. You know his first wife disappeared, right? Just disappeared one day, gone, buried someplace. And all those stories are going around and around in my head, cutting me, making me crazy.

"Then, f-finally, I get what looks like a little break. It turns out Eddie has another guy who owes him money, this La-Louis Curtis, also a gambler. Curtis has a house off Shirley Avenue that he's thinking of getting rid of to try and clear his account. Eddie t-takes me for a ride, says he'll see to it the house is listed with me, and when it sells the ca-ca-commission will go to pay off my debt. That's the b-best he can do, he says, and he's only doing it because he's known our family such a long time, because his brother grew up with Pa-Papa or something. It felt like a gift from heaven.

"So from ma-morning until night I make the calls, Joanie. For the first ten days after that conversation I hit up every landlord I've ever heard of. I even approached my own loan officer, and the girl who cuts my hair—Angie Panechieso. My old girlfriends, their husbands. Anybody I can think of who has so much as a hundred dollars left on their cr-credit card. Da-dope dealers, city ca-councilors, st-st-state senators, the ga-guy who owns Cindy's Subs down the beach. Nothing. Zero. *Lo gatz.* One la-lousy call from all the ads we placed. One call.

"August twentieth I ma-ma-mi-miss my first p-payment. August twenty-seventh, another one. By this time, Eddie is hav-having people call me, at home, at work. I eat about one meal a day now—my pals Steve and Kenny Mer still let me run a ta-tab at their place. I can't even afford to get my shirts done. I owe everybody and his brother, but nothing is happening on the market. Nothing. The city is dead.

"Now I have a meeting with Eddie on S-Saturday night, and all I have to off-offer him is nine hundred dollars. Against about seventeen hundred. I didn't call you because I didn't want you to see me like this, that's all, and because you've come through for me in the past, and I didn't want to prove to you once again that I'm only a screw-up. . . . On my way in here I thought of the C-Curtis house as a way you could help me out of a tight spot and maybe get something for yourself for once, but I can sa-see n-now . . . now. . ."

I could not go on. I put my face in my hands. The hatred in my sister's eyes when I'd mentioned the loan from our parents; the stories about what Eddie had done to people; the thought, just the thought alone, of Curtis and his piece-of-garbage house which nobody in his right mind would ever make an offer on. . . . My shirt was sticking to my armpits.

When I looked up again, my famous sister was staring back at me the way you stare at a kid who confesses to stealing a pack of gum at the corner store. I almost hated her for that look, and at the same time I was ready to forgive her instantly in exchange for one kind word, one suggestion, the most minuscule bit of assistance.

But I was dreaming again. She sighed; she bent her lips back between her teeth like she was in physical pain; she said, "We've been here before, haven't we."

Just like she was talking to a kid.

"No, we haven't, Ja-Joanie. Not here. This is life and death now."

"It's been life and death before."

"No. I maybe *said* it was before. This time it *is*. There's a gigan-gan-gantic difference between those two things, believe me."

"Believe you? After tonight's performance? *Business is excellent, Joanie. I just made a small sale, enough for a couple of new suits. I have a few T-bills, an IRA and whatnot. Revere is the new hot place to live.* Count the lies there, Peter—in what, an hour and a half? Count the lies."

I drew my neck down into my collar, let go of the table, and slid to the back of the seat. She was right; naturally, she was right.

"I know the hell you've been through in your life; I remember it, even if you don't. I've wanted to talk to Mama and Papa about it for years now. But I can't stand to see you lying like this—to me, to us, to yourself. I simply can't *bear* to have you taking money from them at their age and using it to gamble. You're so wrapped up in yourself you can't even see how wrong it is. A little while ago I told you something I've never told anyone from Revere, something that colors every minute of every day for me. And you forgot it in the time it takes to blink."

"I did not forget it. How-how could I forget something like that? I thought you wa-wanted off the subject, that's all, I thought it made you uncomfortable. You got me started on this other thing and I got c-carried away. I do that sometimes, you know I do. I w-wish I'd never mentioned it now."

"Go to the FBI if this is true," she said. "Start by talking with Alfonse and getting his advice, if that's more comfortable for you. The Witness Protection Program. You'd be doing a lot of people a tremendous favor. You and Elsie could have the life you say you want."

"You really are living in a dr-dream world, you know that? You don't understand who this guy Ed-Ed-Eddie is. You da-don't have any idea how he looks at things."

"I have some idea."

"No, you don't."

"I grew up in Revere too, you know. I have an idea who he is, what he does. I'm in the process of finding out more—he's part of the first segment of the special we're doing."

"You're doing the sp-special on *him*?"

"Partly, yes. I was going to tell you but I couldn't get a word in."

"You *m-mention* him? By *name*? On *TV*? Oh, my fucking word, you'll be in the cemetery be-be-before I will."

"You should watch the show next week. Your Eddie is not as big a secret as he'd like to be. He's been in the paper lately, he's—"

"Na-next wa-week! I might not be alive next week! Sure, smirk, who gives a shit, right?"

"There's nothing I can do about it, Peter."

"Of *course* there is. Are you k-kidding me? There's five or six things you can do. For starters—"

"In the long run, there's nothing anybody can do. We love you. We've tried to talk to you for years now, but the message doesn't get through. This is something *you* have to take care of yourself. You, yourself. Not me. Not Mama and Papa. You, you, you."

My arms and legs were twitching, Joanie was crying. She placed her napkin on the table in a delicate way—all fingertips—and looked out the window so the people at the other tables couldn't see. Whenever there was a break in our conversation it seemed as though the other diners stopped staring and went back to their meals. But it couldn't be. I'd been leaning towards her the whole time, speaking in a whisper. I wasn't even sure *she'd* heard all the details. She couldn't have. If she'd heard me right, she wouldn't be sitting there like that, making that face. She wouldn't be saying there was nothing she could do.

"I'm sorry," she said, but it didn't sound like sorry to me. "I know how hard it is to change, believe me. Years and years ago I tried to get you into a program. Papa and I tried at least three separate times. Father Bucci tried. Alfonse tried to talk to you half a dozen times. You wouldn't listen, and you're still not listening, and you turn your own stubbornness around to make it seem as if people don't care about you. Many, many, many nights I lie awake thinking about you, about everything that happened and everything it's led to, worrying, looking for an answer, a solution. Do you realize that? Do you?"

I shook my head.

"I tried to get you to see a counselor. I paid up the best group therapy program in Boston in advance a couple of years ago, remember that? Eleven hundred dollars just to reserve a space. People wait years to get into it. I scheduled you, you promised you'd go, and then you never went."

"You don't understand, Ja-Joanie."

"I understand perfectly. I've—"

"No, you d-don't. I na-nee-nee-need to pay *Ch-Chelsea Eddie.* N-now. D-day after tomorrow. Or I'm a dead man. And you're talking *pr-pr-programs.* Don't you get it? Don't you see that the last thing in the world I need now is this god-god-goddamn queer bullshit about *pr-programs* and *gr-group therapy* and *counseling*? Can't you see even that?"

She shrank back from me like I had thrown a punch.

My body was twitching and jumping but I forced myself to sit there, sweating, watching her, waiting for the blood to show, the connection, the family. It didn't. She sat staring back at me, smarter, better, cold, aloof, and finally I could think of no other move but to get out, get away from her eyes on me, her words crashing down on me like artillery rounds.

I pushed back my chair, mumbled a bitter good-bye, and strode out between the tables. At the far edge of the lobby, the elevator stood open, almost full. There was a nun in the front row, naturally. The nun saw me coming and held the doors open, and when I stepped in and made an about-face, hoping against hope to see my rich sister running after me, I caught just a glimpse of her, sitting at the table, staring across the room at nothing, hurt-looking as a person could be. *Goddamn queer bullshit,* I thought I'd said to her. But the doors had closed, and the nun was smiling at me like the solution to all my troubles could be found in regular prayer, and the elevator would not stop until the first floor now, and I was too pissed off in any case to go back there and tell my sister I had not meant the word that way.

23

When the elevator doors closed and Peter disappeared, I had to clasp my hands together beneath the table in order to keep from signaling the waiter to bring a double vodka tonic or another bottle of wine. It could not be true, everything he'd told me. Such a perfect link between my work and his pain, my success and his failure; it could not possibly be.

After a time I set my napkin on the table, stood, and walked out through the usual stares and whispers. Down and down, I tried just to breathe it all out into the elevator air. Just breathe, just walk through the lobby very calmly now, breathe it out, let it go.

In front of the Prudential building I hailed a cab, sank back into the shadowy anonymity of the rear seat, and watched the glittering Back Bay night drift past. How was it that these people could cruise about in such sleek, polished lives—retirees walking dogs, couples happily strolling, men jogging, women wearing pearls and gold and sitting in restaurant windows—while my brother's life was like a rust-bitten jalopy with loud music blaring out the windows and the engine stalling at every light? Why was it that some people spiraled up and up, stacking one success upon another, while others—Peter and a whole tribe of Peters—could not so much as keep seventy cents in a checking account?

On Atlantic Avenue I paid the driver and, slightly woozy from the wine, made straight for the lobby, tucking the purse under one arm and gripping my keys tightly in the opposite hand, feeling as if, during the course of our dinner, Peter had somehow attached an invisible tube to my life and would now drain every good thing from me, body and soul. I have always been a bit paranoid about my personal safety—more so since moving back to Boston and taking the anchor job—and for a moment then I was absolutely certain someone was following me, stalking me, watching from the shadows.

Such was the price you paid for having the life you had always wanted, in a world of people chained to misery.

24

Leslie had called me at work and said she would be spending the night. When I opened the apartment door I saw that she had let herself in and was sitting at one end of the couch in a pool of yellow lamplight, her hair freshly colored and cut, her legs crossed at the knee. I kissed her, took a bottle of Evian, a lemon, and a glass from the kitchen, and sat down not far from her in the half-dark. She showed me the paperback she was reading, *Mrs. Dalloway;* said, with her usual sardonic wit, "Erotic thriller"; then set it aside and switched off the lamp.

We sat in the darkness with a bit of space between us, a bit of muted traffic noise floating up and through the open window, a bit of month-old malaise I could not quite identify.

I closed my eyes, sank down into the cushions, and imagined that all the troubles Peter had poured onto the table that night were grains of sand that had spilled onto my kitchen floor. I swept the sand carefully into a plastic bucket, carried the bucket to the window, and tried to empty it out there, fourteen stories above the city. . . . But a gust of wind blew half the sand back into the apartment. It floated into the bedroom and living room, coating my skin, sifting down into the fibers of the carpet, covering every surface with blond, irritating grit.

"Sleeping?"

"Doing a visualization exercise."

"Is it working?"

"No."

I tried taking long, even breaths, drawing the knotted feelings up and out of my stomach in a neat line of air, cleansing my system of toxins with each exhalation.

I tried picturing myself and Leslie strolling through knee-high grass, a mountain pasture somewhere in Switzerland.

I tried forming a mandala in the center of my thoughts and dissolving every worry into it.

"How was your dinner?"

"Awful."

"How awful?"

"He says he owes a loanshark eleven thousand dollars. He says the loanshark is about to kill him."

"Pleasant, uneventful brother-and-sister get-together, hey?"

"No."

"You're in that related-to-an-addict funk again."

"I know it."

I finished the glass of water, kicked off my shoes, and lay back on the headrest with my feet in Leslie's lap. Leslie was a kindhearted person—beneath what could sometimes seem like a cool exterior— and I felt more at ease with her, in some ways, than with anyone I'd ever dated. But she had not suffered very much, and the people around her had not suffered, and so the idea that a human life could actually be ruined beyond repair seemed always to remain a slightly perplexing abstraction to her. Her work was rational work— cost–benefit analyses, venture capital—and I think she expected the rest of creation to be equally rational and predictable, a neat, sane world that could be summed up in a few business school equations. We had been having a conversation about Buddhism once—two of our friends had taken a trip to Tibet—and Leslie had actually said, "It makes more sense than most of the other ones, but it's a little outdated, don't you think? I mean, *life is suffering* is hardly the motto for the modern condition."

A police car wailed and faded below, someone else's suffering, someone else's news story now. "The sound the angels make when they sing," my mother had called it when we were small, but the shriek of sirens always made me think of pain and trouble: murders, overdoses, kids being hit by cars. Leslie was humming a few bars from *La Bohème*—"Musetta's Waltz," it sounded like. I thought, again, of Peter. "I came out to him," I said, and she switched from her humming to a murmur of surprise.

"For God's sake, why?"

"I don't know why."

"You don't know why?"

I raised my head slightly and tried to read her tone, her unreadable and lovely Nordic face. "It just happened. . . . I think . . . I think it was because he was something like the way he used to be when he was a child. For the first few weeks of kindergarten he used to come home with this wonderful bewildered expression on his face, as though he couldn't believe he wasn't the only little boy in the world."

"It's called being spoiled."

"He couldn't seem to fathom the idea that there were strict rules, that you really did have to stay in your seat at certain times. He was always being punished in one way or another—no star on his forehead, warning notes on the back of his report card. I remember my father had to ask me once what 'flamboyant' meant . . . as in 'Peter seeks attention with flamboyant behavior.' He'd come home on the verge of tears, but he was too much of a little man to cry in front of anyone, even then, and so he'd get all wound up when he saw me come up the walk, and he'd race around and around in circles in the back yard, his little legs churning up the dirt, his little arms jerking back and forth. We thought it was hilarious. We used to call him our little scooter."

"You were too easy on him," Leslie said confidently. She began a gentle massage—toes, bottoms of the feet, ankles, calves. "Your parents were too easy."

I had an image of my brother standing at the edge of the kitchen with his arms wrapped over his ears and tears trickling down his cheeks. Sixteen years old and standing there, frozen in pain beneath a barrage of maternal viciousness. *Too easy* had not the smallest thing to do with it.

"I'm listening. Keep going."

"He was so sweet then. He had such a tender little self for the first two or three grades, until adolescence, really—you should see the pictures."

"I have."

"And there was a bit of that vulnerability in there tonight, somehow, behind all the . . . all the bullshit. And I think I had this urge to be myself with him again the way we used to be, only in an adult version, to let him in on the big secret that other people have complications in their lives too."

Leslie's hands were gently kneading the muscles above my knees, a slow, luxurious advance that would have been most welcome on any other night. I shifted my hips and pushed my legs together an inch, but she missed the hint and kept working. "So he heard you were gay and it enlightened him. He's going to change his ways."

"He said it explained a lot of things. For a minute he seemed to really care. At the end he made one wisecrack."

"Hmph."

"He was upset. He takes after my father in that way. He winds himself up, says something he wishes he hadn't said, then feels rotten about it for weeks. . . . My father didn't call, did he?"

Leslie shook her head. "Someone called, but they hung up before saying who it was."

"On the machine?"

"No. I picked up. I thought it might be you. Sorry."

She took hold of the balls of my feet and shook each leg separately so that the thigh muscles swung out and back a little ways, like loops of stretched wet cloth.

"I don't want to make love tonight, Les."

"That's fine."

"Now you're angry."

"I am not."

"You're angry that I traded dinner with you for dinner with Peter on a couple hours' notice, that I came home so late, that you drove all the way over here and waited up and now I'm not in the mood."

"Keep telling me I'm angry and I will be."

"You're angry that I spend so much time at my mother's."

"Stop it, Jo."

"You're angry that I don't want us to live together, to try to have a child."

"In about two seconds I am going to take a quart of your no-fat soy milk from the refrigerator and pour it all over you, okay? I just have a less sentimental view of life than you do, that's all. If he were my brother, I'd simply never speak to him again until he stopped throwing his money away on ridiculous fantasies. Period. End of agony. At a certain point you need to just write people off if they're causing more trouble than they're worth."

"I can stop giving him money. I can stop calling and trying to convince him to change his life. But I don't think I could ever *write him off* as if he were some kind of bad investment."

Leslie shrugged her shoulders in the darkness. "Nothing will ever change, then."

"When I've been that close to somebody, I can never really cut them off entirely. It almost doesn't matter what they do, I still have some hope for them, some soft space."

"Cut the cord, sweet. You'll be doing yourself and everyone close to you a favor. Instead of what you're doing now, which is just trying to keep from feeling guilty."

"Easy for you to say. This is the woman whose only brother is a neurosurgeon, whose sister-in-law publishes mystery novels while raising two perfect children, whose parents sponsor twenty people in the AIDS walk every year—"

"Sure. But I'd do it, really I would. That's the difference between you and me."

She lifted my feet from her lap, gave them a last squeeze, and padded off down the carpeted hallway. No good-night kiss, no last affectionate word. *That's the difference between you and me.* I listened to the click of the light switches in bathroom and bedroom, the whisper of a coverlet being thrown back, the bedsprings' faint protest.

I sat up and sucked the lemon in the bottom of the glass, a habit from childhood, and for almost an hour I sat alone on the sofa, listening to the ebbing sounds of the city evening—a favorite symphony moving *piano, piano* toward its middle-of-the-night hush. Tough love, all the advice-givers said. Tough love. It made sense, of course. Made sense, and at the same time went absolutely and directly against the grain of what Italian-American women most prided themselves on: our warmth, our notion of family and sacrifice, our First Commandment of generosity. . . . Tough Love. How much toughness? was the question. And how much love?

I thought I heard a very soft knocking on the hallway door. Another apartment, I told myself. But then I heard it again, four regular taps, as if someone were hitting just the end of one strong finger against the metal. For some reason, I was quite sure it was Peter, come to apologize, knocking very lightly in case I was asleep. So much for conscientious doormen.

I went over and looked out the peephole. An empty piece of corridor. I unbolted and opened the heavy white door and stuck my head out just far enough to see to either end of the hall. All quiet. I stood there like that a minute or so, waiting for my brother to peek around the corner, grinning; then I ducked back inside and bolted us in for the night.

The numbers on the VCR read 11:43. I wandered over to the windows. Beyond the light-checkered towers of the financial district I could see the stripe of Tremont Street running southwest through the heart of the ghetto, saffron bulbs glowing. I thought of my mother: sleeping now, I hoped; medicated beyond pain, I hoped. I thought of Peter, racing frantically around the city, fibbing, grinning, stammering, trying to scrape together enough money to save himself from another man's wrath. Over the past decade or so, to my shame, I'd occasionally caught myself wishing he was dead, that the dance was over. More often, I'd had fantasies of leaving everything behind, leaving Boston again, taking a job in another market, Atlanta or Honolulu or Seattle, so that Peter and his troubles would be only a voice on my answering machine.

But I did not want to live anywhere else, and I did not, of course, want him to die. What I wanted was some true link to my earlier life, my Revere life, one person from that other world who knew me as the person I truly am and loved me anyway. It was pure loneliness I felt then, a loneliness so profound it seemed to have taken root in the tissue of my womb. What I wanted was a brother.

On impulse, I went to the telephone, dialed the Revere Police Station, and asked for Captain Romano.

"Alfonse, it's Joanna."

"Joanie, cousin!" he said. "Everything all right?"

"More or less. Do you have a minute now? I know you're just about to finish your shift."

"I have an hour now, for you, two hours if you need it."

"Are we being recorded?"

"Not on this line, cousin."

"I had dinner with my brother tonight, a little while ago. . . . He has a certain kind of debt. Do you know anything about it?"

There was an empty moment, whisper of some wordless discomfort in the line. "I know about it, Joanie."

"You do?"

"A little bit."

"Well he wanted me to help him with it, and I said I wouldn't. . . . But now I'm sitting here thinking it over and I'm not sure. I feel foolish calling you. I know it's been a long time and I only seem to call when I need something, but—"

"You can call me anytime, I told you that. I almost called you myself tonight, believe it or not. Your name came up in a conversation this afternoon, and I almost called you."

"You did?"

"Sure I did. I think about you and your family all the time. I drive by your house every night on my way home from work, kind of check on your mother and father in secret, you know?"

The image knocked me silent a moment: a man who was not even really related to us going out of his way at midnight, after working an eight-hour shift, to see that my parents were safe. I pictured him standing in some small, grimy office, surrounded by sleepy men in uniform and desks covered with stacks of official forms, a misplaced character, a knight out of some nobler century. I pictured his wife, Sally, shuffling along Broadway with one hand on the store windows for balance, clothes just hanging from her shoulders, the ravaged pretty face and vacant eyes. I thought of the *Journal* clipping my mother had sent me when she died, two days before Christmas, ten or eleven years ago, Wonderland subway station.

Not long afterwards, I'd come home from St. Louis (where I was working as a reporter for KLNM) and gone to offer my condolences at the family home on Ambrose Street. Alfonse hugged and kissed me at the door, served me a glass of anisette and a plate of orange slices in olive oil like a nineteenth-century Neapolitan landowner, then broke down at the old-fashioned Formica-topped table. I had never seen grief like that in a grown man. He must have wept for fifteen minutes without being able to speak or look at me, and, strangely, among the awful mixture of emotions I'd felt, there had been some envy. Here, I thought, here is a person who loves at a level I cannot even imagine.

And here, I thought now, on the other end of this phone line, is a person who knows how to love in the face of addiction, through the pain of it, the stupidity of it.

"I'm wondering if you can offer me any ideas, Alfonse. I need a new way of looking at it. I need a new way of looking at it or I'm never going to get to sleep again for the rest of this century."

"You know how I feel about Peter, right, Joanie? I don't have to tell you that, do I?"

"No."

"You know I'd do anything for that guy, don't you? Anything. I'd hand over my life for his life in a second."

"I know, Alfonse. It's not you I'm wondering about, it's me. I have enough money to pay off his entire debt, tomorrow, without even noticing, but I've done that before, probably ten other times, and it never seems to change anything. He doesn't stop gambling. He doesn't really even try to stop."

"He's never going to stop, Joanie."

"Never? Not a hope, not a chance?"

"Not until it hurts him so bad that it's not worth it to him anymore, which hasn't happened yet. Close, a few times, but it hasn't happened."

"This time is different, isn't it?"

"It's different, it's worse. In other ways it's exactly the same. . . . I let your father know about it. I thought that was the right thing to do."

"I don't want my father spending his money on this," I almost shouted into the phone, and Alfonse went silent again, as if the fire in me had scorched him. I held tightly to the receiver; I breathed, waited.

"What I was trying to say, cousin, is that, much as I love Peter, there's nothing I can do for him at this point, other than pay the loan—which I can't really afford. And there's not very much you can do either."

"You don't think I should pay it, then?"

"I don't think you should get involved in this at all, if you can help it. The only answer here, if you ask me, is to walk this thing right to the edge of the cliff with him and hope he gets scared enough to see his life a little clearer."

"I don't think I have the courage to walk it to the edge of the cliff this time."

"Sure you do. And so does your dad and so do I, okay? We'll walk him right to the edge, and when he really believes they're going to push him over, when it's really real to him, then maybe, *maybe*, we can try something, all right? But if we save him too soon he'll never even know the cliff was there."

"I know that. I'm just terrified we'll walk him to the edge and he'll jump off before we can stop him. Out of some crazy pride or something."

"If he does that, then it was him who did it, not you and not me, okay? How's your mom doing?"

"The same. Not well."

"I'm praying for her."

"So am I." But it wasn't true, and I felt somehow soiled, saying it. False and rich and soiled, a liar, a traitor. "I'm doing a special project at work," I told Alfonse, as if trying to regain a handhold on the truth.

"I know."

"You know?"

"Of course. Everybody here knows. One person you work with at the TV station tells somebody, that somebody tells somebody else—a Boston cop, maybe. The Boston cop has a friend on the force in Revere. It's a whole gossip network in this business."

"I'd like to talk to you about it at some point in the next week or so. Maybe you could come into town for lunch and we could—"

"Anytime," he said, and there was another strange pause, some shift in the climate of the conversation that I felt clearly but could not fathom. "You should be very careful with that project, Joanie. You should be careful not to make it seem like it's something personal . . . not just with Peter, I mean, but with the way you approach it. Do you know what I'm getting at?"

"They'd never touch me. The press and the police, they'd never touch either one of us."

"They have different ways of touching people. Just watch yourself, all right? We'll have lunch together soon, and we'll talk about it, okay? I'll give you whatever information I can, which is probably not that much, to tell you the truth. Or you can come over here and I'll make supper. We'll have a date, two cousins."

It was a sore subject for us, this date business. It was a sore subject and something we'd never discussed in our adult years, but Alfonse seemed comfortable joking about it now, seemed to feel close to me in spite of everything. Utterly different as our lives had turned out to be, it seemed to me at that moment that we'd remained linked in some subtle way. It made me think of my parents and their *paesanos* from the Old Country—passing bowls of fresh cherries across the back fence, visiting each other after mass on Sundays, connected, still, by the rules and traditions of their old village, by the rules and the soil of Revere.

"Just watch yourself, okay, cuz?" he said again. "Give your mom my love."

There was something in Alfonse's voice then, an Old World tenderness, that threw a bridge across the vast space between his life and mine. Which was exactly what I'd been hoping for when I lifted up the phone.

25

It was not a night for going straight home. After I said good night to Joanie and hung up the phone, I spent a minute with Captain Ciccolo, who ran the midnight-to-eight shift, then left the station and drove towards the beach.

The air was warm and still, a perfect late-summer night, with a few stars shining above the roofs of the houses on Beach Street, and the moon halfway up in the sky, one day past full. Bell Circle had its traffic problems as always: double lanes stacked up at the north–south lights. A knot of teenage kids were standing out in front of the Dunkin Donuts on A-1, flirting, horsing around. Shirley Avenue was all shadows and litter and sealed-up storefronts, people sitting out late on wooden front steps. But most of the city was asleep, you could feel it, and, for all their troubles, most of the people here were decent and honest people, just trying to be happy and good at the same time. I knew that—in spite of everything I heard and saw at the station— and at certain moments it gave me a little comfort, a little faith.

I drove to the beach and cruised back and forth along the boulevard, not paying any attention to what might be happening there in the alleys and bars and along the dark narrow stretches of park. Strictly off duty. I thought, for a while, of pulling over in front of Peter's building, going up, knocking on his door. But I knew he'd need another day or two to stop being angry at me for calling Vito. Another day or two, and maybe we could talk.

So I just cruised back and forth awhile, thinking about what Billy Ollanno had told me, what the mix of truth and lie might be there, winding down from the feeling Joanie's voice had raised. There was some old persistent connection between Joanie and me, out of line now, out of the question, but I felt it still, and it needed some time to settle.

After I'd driven the length of the beach twice, I circled around by the dog track and pulled into the lot near Wonderland station, another little pilgrimage I sometimes made late at night. Twenty or twenty-five people, men mostly, stood on the platform, alone or in groups of two and three, waiting for the last train back into Boston. They'd been at the track, probably, won a few dollars or lost a few, stopped in at the Cavalcade for a nightcap before getting on the subway and riding home. I turned off my engine and watched them, heard the train pull into the station on the opposite side. I listened to the squealing wheels.

In all the years I'd lived in Revere, I'd only ever heard of one person falling off that platform and beneath those wheels. She had been high, no doubt—by that time she was high every morning and every afternoon, and sometimes I would drive around half the night looking for her. It was Christmastime. The platform was crowded with people going into town to shop, and maybe there had been something just too sad about the holiday for her, or maybe she was disoriented or dizzy and had taken a step in the wrong direction at the wrong moment, or maybe somebody pushed her. The criminal investigation led to nothing. No one came forward with any leads or pieces of evidence, no eyewitness reports that were reliable enough to make it a definite suicide and not something else. And no one, not Father Dom, not my friends, not Vito or Lucy or Joanie or Peter, had ever shown me a good answer for that last step of hers—whatever or whoever had been behind it—for the complete ruin of the life of a good woman, for my complete inability to help.

In the time that had passed since then—ten years and eight months—I had just learned to live with the idea of Sally's absence, that was all. That was all I knew how to do. Just live with a thing without talking to anyone about it, without complaining to God, without analyzing it or trying to figure out the why. It was a trick I'd learned from the way my mother had brought me up all those years, alone, in disgrace, poor, somehow at peace with it without liking it very much. What she and I shared was this kind of very deep and quiet sadness—not only because of the things that had happened to us but because we lived in a world in which things like that *could* happen. Even now, people tried to tell me this and that, console me, absolve me, advise me, but I was beyond all that, really. I was a planet moving along in empty space. And people were throwing little stones of sympathy up towards me, sending single women my way, nudging me towards solutions—counseling, the Church—that I did not really want.

I sent a little quiet word up to Sally then, and to my mother, and to my own idea of the Spirit I believed had some say over the way human beings lived their lives. That was my way.

After a while I started the car, drove up to Proctor Avenue, and past Vito and Lucy's house—dark now, except for the nurse's light— the people inside just living, just waiting, in some kind of fragile good faith, for what was coming next.

26

Out in the back of the house I was sitting, where it was almost dark. There was a little bit of noise from the nurse's radio, and a little bit of light from the kitchen and from one car going by slow in the street. But it was pretty quiet there. And I was sitting out with my sweater on, waiting for Peter to come visit, like he said he was gonna do.

It was late now, so probably he wasn't coming. Which was the way he did it, Peter, telling you he was gonna do something, and promising he was gonna do it, and convincing you he was really gonna do it this time . . . and then not doing it.

Still, his heart was a good heart, and once in a while he surprised you.

So I sat outside past midnight in the back of the house, holding a little piece of maple in my hand that I was supposed to be sanding for the jewelry box I was making for Joanie's birthday. Every time a car went by out front I would think maybe it was Peter, come to see his mother and talk a little bit with me. But it wasn't.

After a while I went inside to the bedroom and sat on the chair there and took off my clothes without making no noise. Lucy was awake—I could tell by the sound she made breathing—but she didn't say nothing to me, which meant she had the pain now and didn't want to talk or to listen. I took off my clothes and got in the bed with her, not pressing down too hard, and I made it half the way through a prayer to Saint Jude before falling over the edge of this world and into my old man's sleep.

27

They didn't like me to get up and walk by myself, in the day, even, and especially not at night. Vito, Joanie, the nurse, Dr. Pierni, everybody told me the same thing: What if I fell? What would happen then?

Then, I told them, then I would lay out in the hall on the carpet and wait until somebody found me. What, the pain would be worse? I'd lose my beauty sleep? I'd die there maybe instead of dying in bed?

Every once in a while it was good to show people you still had a full person inside you, no matter what the body that held the person looked like.

But that night I did not have the energy to sit up. After Vito went to sleep, and after the pain went away, I tried twice to sit up and couldn't do it. I couldn't sleep, either, so I took hold of Vito's arm with my hand and lay there, thinking, with my eyes closed.

I remember everything about the first night we were in a bed together, husband and wife. My Aunt Adelaida had told me the secrets I had to know, and my girlfriends had told me, and my sister Rosa, but my body did not know anything then, only my mind. Which is like people who think they know everything about being sick and dying, but really don't.

I remember getting undressed in the second-floor bedroom in the dark, and the sheets feeling like other cool skins against my skin, top and bottom. When Vito's shoes made their noise on the wood in the hallway, when the glass door handle turned and the door opened and closed, it was as if those sounds were inside my body, moving. Vito said, very quiet, "Lucy, you awake still?" Like I could have gone into that bedroom on that night because I wanted to fall asleep. I turned down the sheets and the blanket with one hand on his side and tried to watch him taking off his clothes in the dark.

The man's smell, the feel of your hands and arms on the big muscles of his back, the feel of his big body resting on you. The kissing—which we knew already. The feeling of the warm blood in us—which we knew.

And then the feeling we didn't know—I didn't know it, anyway—the pain first, Vito saying, in Italian, *"Dimmi se ti fa male,"* Tell me if it hurts. And me not telling him. Then the feeling of all the warm world inside you, in your fingers and your feet and your mouth and your place there, and your body taking over and moving in a way you knew something about without even knowing you knew. The pain being buried underneath one sweet second piled on top of the next, and the next, the feeling of being one person made of two bodies—what could be better than that?

And then, another few minutes, finding out the thing that could be better, the surprise of it, like you were dying falling into it.

And afterwards feeling your husband next to you, and that you both were a part of the world of men and women now.

When Vito fell asleep then, half leaning on me still, I put my hand down along my belly very quiet and touched that place once, though I knew it was probably a sin to do that. Warm like a stove after cooking, and with a little blood there and a little something else.

And the next morning there was rain against the windows—good luck for the day after the wedding—and the smell of gas from the stove, I remember. Before I got up to make Vito his breakfast, I took hold of his arm just the way I was holding it now, forty-nine years later, and I put his hand on me so that he knew my body wanted not to wait until the night to be sure it could have that happiness again. I was worried then what he'd think, a woman, a wife, doing that. But Vito and me we were made the same way when it came to our bodies, and he didn't mind it one bit.

And that was how we were for four years until our life changed: a good Catholic woman and a good Catholic man carrying around this night secret in their bodies that nobody on the outside could see. Sleeping in an ordinary bed like this bed, a bed with a better world inside it, a world my body could not feel anymore but my mind still remembered.

Friday

28

Friday morning I woke up at six o'clock, not exactly a typical hour for me. It was the sound of rain on the windows that woke me, and for a minute when I opened my eyes I wanted just to sink back down in the sheets and come up a few hours later into a better world.

I shook it off and got out of bed, got myself dressed, my failures following me from bedroom to bathroom and back again like a muddy tail. I almost called my mother and offered an explanation for not having shown up the night before, but that would only seem like another con to her now, another trick. I knew that. The only thing that would make up for it now was for me to just go and see her. Give her the priceless gift of my actual presence.

I drove down the boulevard to Stevie's Place, eleven hundred dollars in my pocket, treated myself to a sausage-and-pepper omelette there, and used the loose bills to pay down my tab by about half. Afterwards, I should have gone to see my mother and then headed straight to the office, paid Elsie back her two hundred, and locked the rest in my safe so it would be there when it came time to meet with Eddie on Saturday night. But I did not do that. Instead, I stood out under Stevie's dripping awning, staring across the boulevard at the ocean, listening to the car tires on the wet street, and thinking a lot of not-so-good stuff about the past.

Eleven hundred dollars in an envelope in my sport-coat pocket.

I went and sat behind the wheel of my car. Eleven hundred minus Elsie's two (I would give her two twenty-five or two fifty as a return on her investment) meant I'd have about eight hundred to take with me to the meeting tomorrow night. I owed Eddie just over seventeen, and I could picture myself sitting in the back of his limo, passing him the envelope, Eddie taking out the money and spreading the bills in his fat fingers. "What's this bullshit?" he'd say, when he saw it was only half what he was expecting. "What's this bullshit supposed to mean?"

I could picture it.

I turned the key and sat there with the wipers going and the rain tapping like fingernails on the roof. There was always a chance the Ngs had been real customers. That they'd looked at another property or two with somebody else and realized what a bargain the Reservoir Avenue house was, called my office late last night, were waiting there now for me to open shop. . . . Always that chance. Even so, I wouldn't see that money for weeks, and by then I'd owe Eddie another fifteen hundred, the electric company, the landlord, Elsie, my parents, on and on. . . .

What I had to do was to make money at a pace faster than the pace at which my debts were accumulating. And there was only one way to do that.

I filled the tank at Joey Lewey's on Revere Street because I liked to send some business his way when I could, liked to tip the young Cambodian kid pumping gas there who reminded me of myself when I was first starting out in the working world, all eager and friendly and determined to find his success. From there, I should have driven straight down Broadway and gone to the office. But it was early still, raining, and the light in front of the fire station was green, and since I was headed that way in any case I just kept going straight through it, south; then, at the Chelsea line, west. Then up the ramp and onto the bridge and south on the bridge through Boston with a certain mood clinging to my skin like a wet, sweaty sheet.

There had been a lot of talk in the previous year about the new Indian casino that had opened up in Connecticut, less than two hours drive from Boston. Ads on the TV late at night. Billboards on the Southeast Expressway. Stories in the *Herald* about people who'd driven down there and found the atmosphere to be more congenial than Atlantic City, the dealers slightly less sharp, the parking safer. I'd always had a kind of special place in my heart for the Indians, long before they caught the attention of the politically correct types and turned into Native Americans. Father Dom felt the same way. We talked about it dozens of times—the underdogs, the guys out there on their own, fighting the Big Man and his guns, living free. So now they had taken back a little of what was really their own land to begin with and were making millions off the stupidity of white people. Good for them, then. Good for them.

I told myself I'd go down there and just scout out the situation for an hour or so, run through one hot streak at the craps table or at blackjack, leave some nice tips for the dealers, and be back in Revere in time to take Elsie out for a Friday-night dinner, three or four thousand dollars in my pocket, maybe more.

I'd just drive down there now on this drizzly, depressing morning (no one would stop by the office on a day like this anyway), call Elsie from a rest area, and tell her not to worry. I'd solve this thing myself, in one day.

My route took me right past the new building where Joanie had her apartment, and I sent a little apology her way, a little prayer. Once the congestion of the Southeast Expressway was behind me, I stayed in the slow lane and cruised through the flatter, richer, South Shore suburbs in the rain, the radio on, the wipers knocking, my mind blowing up a hundred thousand bright balloons of possibility. . . . I made it as far as Walpole before turning around.

I don't know what it was—maybe someone was praying for me, maybe I'd finally learned what I had to learn about how stupid I was being—but in Walpole, not far from the prison (possibly it was the signs for the prison), I took an exit, looped around under the interstate, drove up the ramp onto the northbound side, and kept my foot on the accelerator all the way back through Boston.

In Revere again, although I knew I had done the correct thing, I was hit by a solid black cloud of depression. The mood would not let go of me and so I just drove and drove, circling up towards Breakheart Reservation and down again, out towards Nahant Beach and then back, thinking the whole time about the money in my pocket, how I might use it to free myself once and for all, the things I might do for people with my small casino fortune, the love I might show in this world.

I thought of going by my mother's, of calling Joanie at work, going to the office, going straight to Eddie's house to pay him what I had, going to see Father Dom. . . . But I did none of those things, just drove the shiny wet streets of the homeland until the needle on the gas gauge was down below E and the urge to gamble had almost—almost—been driven out of me.

29

On Friday morning I awoke to a very light rain pattering against the glass of the bedroom windows and to a vague sense of my brother's presence. I knew I had dreamt of him—though I could not remember exactly what he had been doing or saying—and his voice seemed to be lingering in the apartment now, a muted cry emanating from the walls and wet windows and the plants standing hopefully on the sills. Leslie had left early for the office without waking me, without a good-bye kiss, without leaving a note on the kitchen table as she usually did. And the wine I'd drunk with Peter ran in my blood still, leaden penance for a lead-colored morning.

First day of my vacation, and there seemed nothing better to do than shower and dress and head to the office.

Downstairs in the parking garage I discovered that both rear tires of my car had been slashed and flattened. Peter again, I assumed. In a fit of pique, of desperation, he must have come knocking at the apartment door and then been too embarrassed to show his face. He must have come down here, looked for the SBT-ANCH plates (a birthday surprise from Leslie), and gotten carried away. I was furious, naturally.

But after I'd called the AAA number and was watching their mechanic change the tires as easily and quickly as I changed blouses, after I'd calmed down a little bit, it began to seem suspect, that assumption. My reporter's instinct began cutting a nice even swath through all that righteous anger. Over all our long history of argument and reconciliation, Peter had never done anything remotely violent to me or to my property. Knock on the door and then hide . . . maybe; he had a childish side. But slash his sister's tires because she wouldn't buy a broken-down apartment house and help him pay a debt? It just didn't mesh with the Peter I had known all my life.

Which, for all of four or five minutes, was comforting.

I made it to the office only about twenty minutes later than I had planned and ended up spending almost four hours there, talking mainly with the executive producer about the taping of the first segment (which was to be a kind of general introduction to the Organized Crime series, a sampler of the new Asian and Russian gangs, inner-city drug trafficking, and La Cosa Nostra). During a brief meeting with the two senior researchers I slipped in a string of questions about Eddie Crevine—for Peter's sake and, now, for my own.

Crevine, they both said, was a maestro of invisibility—the perfect focus for our kickoff segment. He ran his operations via quick meetings in the open air or in the back seat of his unbuggable limousine. He surrounded himself with a very small coterie of utterly trustworthy thugs who would serve a hundred and twenty years rather than rat on him, and he funneled his earnings into legitimate businesses so swiftly and deftly that the IRS's best sleuths had not yet been able to find an excuse to indict him. His exact position vis à vis his mobster colleagues was, at the moment, still somewhat vague. No one seemed to be sure where, precisely, he stood in the hierarchy of the crippled New England Mafia or how much the Asians and Jamaicans had cut into his earnings and his power on the street, only that he had a reputation for ruthlessness and unpredictability, that he was a man of immense and easily wounded pride, and that he divided his time between what was ostensibly a plumbing supply shop in Melrose and the old family home in Revere, less than a mile from my parents' house on Proctor Avenue.

"So," Michael Simonds, WSBT's chief researcher said to me, in the middle of the session, "a Revere *paesano,* eh? Did you family know his-a family back in the old-a neighborhood, uh?"

I forced a smile—used to this—and, in very precise detail, imagined slashing the tires on his Lexus on some very cold February night.

At lunchtime I left the station lot and did my best to set the project behind me . . . which turned out to be impossible. In the space of twelve hours it had gone from being a source of pride and excitement to this sticky, mocking enemy. Nasty jokes, late-night harassment, quadrupled worry about Peter. Be careful not to make it personal, Alfonse said. Was this what he meant?

Driving north over the Mystic River Bridge, I felt as though the new tires of my car were pulling the stitches on the damp coverlet I'd sewn over my two separate selves, exposing a sordid schizophrenia—the professional Joanna Imbesalacqua, pretty and famous and presumed heterosexual, carefree as the Back Bay on a summer night; and my actual hidden self, messy, nervous, tickled constantly with uncertainty and fear, a mother dying and a lover drifting, and a brother who'd sold his soul.

For some reason I associated that messy, truer half of me with Revere, which was why Michael's little quip cut so deep. In some way—no matter how much I made or how much I changed or who I chose to sleep with or how I pronounced my *r*'s—I would always be a Revere girl: loyal to a fault, inherently provincial, the keeper of friends' small secrets. And about fifty percent of me was completely at peace with that.

I could see the city now from the crest of the bridge—low, crowded hills in the near distance, telephone wires, triple-deckers, tidy ranch houses like the one I'd been raised in. A stew of humanity that included the glittering remnants of immigrant dreams and the squalid realities of postindustrial blue-collar America, people as mild-mannered and generous as my mother and father and as vicious as Chelsea Eddie Crevine.

Once I actually reached the city, once I left the highway, circled down the exit ramp, and began making my way through the tired streets, the fake little gem of my Boston life seemed to drop out of sight. The rain stopped as I turned onto Proctor Avenue. I drove up the familiar street, past the familiar housefronts standing tight together, and felt myself moving deep into a darkness that swallowed everything else. I could not think about Peter then, or about Leslie, or about Eddie Crevine. I could not think about anything but the impending loss of my mother's presence in my life.

In her simple, modest way, my mother had cemented the family together, even in those years when that cement was composed of an ugly near insanity. Those years aside, her kitchen was the place you gratefully returned to after the triumphs and disappointments of the working world and the dating world—the one solid unchanging place on the planet. You set yourself down there over coffee and homemade lemon pie, and all the great societal dramas were reduced to trivialities. Somehow, without education, without liberation, without ever having traveled the world (she and Papa had made one trip to Italy, on their fortieth wedding anniversary, and one trip to upstate New York for my Cornell graduation), my mother had staked a claim to the center of the emotional universe. Amidst a life of toil and anonymity, and some secret buried anger, she had somehow learned the art of giving and forgiving. Now all that was being squeezed out of her, drop by painful drop, and there was nothing anybody could do but watch.

There was nothing anybody could do, but I wished I could devote myself more fully to her, sit with her day in and day out as Papa was doing, so that she had some close, constant, female company as her body wasted away. The damp faces of the neighborhood houses seemed to be whispering to me as I passed, urging me, and I wished I were selfless enough to take a leave of absence from my Boston life, move back into my old room here, and cook and care for Mama instead of paying other women to cook and care for her. That would be my own rock to stand upon. When she was gone, I would have that at least, the memory of that sacrifice.

A month or less, Dr. Pierni had said. But who knew how long it would really be? And who knew when Papa would begin his own decline (little chance of Peter taking time off to be with *him*). If I left Boston to care for my mother, I would almost certainly destroy the relationship Leslie and I had worked so hard to build. I would run the risk of being marooned in this city, smothered. I would lose my grip on a career it had taken me twenty grueling years to build, and turn into an old-fashioned Italian-American spinster daughter, padding around the kitchen in apron and slippers and curled, colored hair, poring in secret over the Personal ads in the *Phoenix*, lying to old family friends, walking the streets wrapped in a blanket of lone-liness, an alien, an outcast, a queer.

Surrounded, suddenly, by such a vivid image of myself growing old that way, childless, motherless, friendless, inauthentic, I pulled at last into my parents' driveway and had to sit there for a minute, grip-ping the wheel in both hands, telling myself again and again that I was doing everything I could reasonably be expected to do—for Mama, for Peter—that being a loyal daughter and a loyal sister did not require self-annihilation.

About half of me was convinced.

30

Inside, the house was so quiet I could hear the parlor clock ticking. Helen, the bleached-blond daytime aide for the privilege of whose presence we paid nine hundred twenty dollars a week, slouched on the living room sofa immersed in *People* magazine. She glanced up, angled a finger toward the back bedroom, but did not bother to rise.

In the bedroom the yellow muslin curtains were drawn against the day, and my father sat beside the bed, holding one of my mother's frail, bruised hands. When I touched his back he stood up slowly, kissed me on the forehead, motioned for me to take his place.

My mother was buried in one of her drug-induced approximations of sleep. For a time I sat holding her fingers and watching her breast swell and fade beneath the thin blue nightgown. Her face was gaunt and puffy, her gray hair sticky with sweat and pulled messily back from her forehead, the eyelids lined with delicate blood-vessel tracings in which a very faint pulse ebbed and pushed. I touched three fingertips lightly to the top of her shoulder and tugged the blanket up to her collarbone, but with my father there in the room I felt too self-conscious to speak.

He stood there for a minute or two with a hand on my back, saying nothing. Then he leaned down and whispered, "She'sa sleepin solid now. I'm goin out in the garden a little while," and left us.

How strangely peaceful I felt, alone with her. How perfectly that city and that house and that room closed out the complexities of the greater world. And how wonderful it was not to have to contemplate and announce those complexities for one whole week, not to feel yourself diluted by the sheer mass and number of them at the same time you were pretending to the whole of eastern New England that no other reality existed or mattered. My mother's great gift—to us, to me—had been the sense that she had found some smaller, truer, more private Top Story. It was exactly that perspective that was being lost to us now, withering away in this bed.

For a quarter of an hour I sat there, in the warm stuffy room that smelled of liniment and perspiration, and just watched her breathe. What had she done, I wondered, when *her* brother—another Peter, another gambler—came to her for help? Given him money? Made excuses? Said a novena for him at the church? Why, even with her love and her wisdom—so much greater than mine—had none of it ever changed him?

After half an hour she stirred, moaned, shifted her legs in tiny movements beneath the blankets.

"Mama, it's me. Joanna."

"Joanie." She turned her head but seemed not to have the strength to open her eyes. A droplet of spittle stuck to the corner of her mouth. I wiped it away with a damp facecloth, then wet a finger in the water glass and ran it over her parched lips and the tip of her tongue.

"He went away from the people and spent forty days in the desert," she said hoarsely.

"Mama, it's me."

"Joanie went away from the people."

"Jesus did that, Mama."

"He went away from all the people."

"I love you, Mama."

"Really?" she said, and I had to pinch the skin of my forearm to keep from bursting into tears.

"His love is the light . . . on earth. The light is the light. . . . What's that noise?"

I swallowed, coughed, could not get a word out.

"Joanie?"

"Nothing, Mama. . . . It was raining. . . . That was just the wind blowing the branches of the plum tree against the house."

"It was raining?"

"All morning."

"Where's Peter? Did he clean the gutter?"

"Peter's away on a trip. He loves you. He calls me every day to see how you are. . . . Mama?"

Beneath the half-closed lids my mother's eyes switched left and right as if following text on a TelePrompTer. A spasm rippled through her, toes to the top of her head. She moaned. Her eyes drifted upwards, her head tilted another few degrees sideways on the pillow. I was certain then that she was slipping away, and though that was what I told my friends I wanted for her—a quick death, quick and morphine-cushioned—still, at the sight of it I leaned over the bed, squeezing the bruised hand hard. "Mama, Mama, it's me. Mama!"

For an instant she seemed to stop breathing entirely, to go absolutely still beneath the sheets. Then her eyes moved downwards again, and she let out a muted shriek that seemed to rise from the depths of her and reach the surface as one high note, held for half a second. I stroked her bony thigh through the coverlet, brushed away a tear. It seemed clear that I had just summoned her back, and I was proud at first and then miserable. Back to what? To agony and dementia and this restless chemical sleep? A second-by-second torment? A living hell?

I held her hand and kept my eyes on her twitching face. The idea of a soul was something I had long ago stopped believing in. But at that moment, with her body and her personality reduced almost to nothing, something like the pure essence of my mother seemed to glimmer there in the center of the sickbed. Still fighting. A sack of bones, blood, and one small speck of feminine will, indisputable.

I heard a creaking of shoe leather and turned around. Helen was there, had been there, was moving toward the bed. "Time to give her some medicine now and change her," she said, as though speaking to an older child of a younger. She tried to push forward between the chair and the bed, and the rough touch of her knee against mine flipped some switch. I took hold of her wrist in a vise grip. "You just wait a goddamned minute to change her. You wait a goddamned minute, and you wash and brush her hair every morning, or I'll see to it you never set foot anywhere near this house again, do you hear me?"

"Your mama don't like people washing her hair these days. Gives her pain," she said. She freed her wrist and turned away.

She pulled aside the blanket and rolled my mother's stick body partway onto its side. *I called her back,* I wanted to shout. *Not you. She came back for me, not you.* But I could not so much as whisper the words aloud, could not bear to be in that small curtained room with my own shame.

Helen continued working, as if unwrapping something fragile and valuable but no longer human. I stood, stumbled out the door, and went down the blurry hallway to the bathroom, where a chorus of ugly accusations waited for me in ambush. I locked myself in. I sat on the edge of the tub with my face buried in my hands, feeling like a made-up useless doll. No tears, no thoughts, only bitter breaths and a sourceless piercing pain that seemed to go on and on, pressing and pressing down on me like love's failure. It was a child's agony, immune to the salve of logic, and it belonged solely to that house.

31

After ten or fifteen minutes, I splashed cold water on my face and brushed out my hair with my own brush (still in the medicine cabinet after all these years, as if my parents expected I would get tired of my other life eventually and come back to my true home). Without so much as glancing in the mirror, I unlocked the door and walked through the kitchen, out into the back yard.

There was my father on his hands and knees between rows of staked tomato plants tall as my shoulders. He was wearing a pair of farmer's overalls, a gift from our late neighbor Rafaelo, and they looked out of place on him—too American, somehow, too much like a costume for a sitcom grandfather. A reed basket stood just behind him in the dirt, two-thirds full of his prize tomatoes, so ripe and plump they seemed about to burst open and spew pulp and seeds everywhere. When he turned toward it with another handful of harvest, he saw me, grunted, and clambered to his feet.

He studied my face a moment, told me to sit, said he would bring outside a "nice ice coffee" for me. But I toweled off the lawn chairs and made *him* sit, went into the kitchen, and put together two tunafish sandwiches, dripping tears down into the bowl, swiping at my eyes with the back of my hand, pouring cold coffee into the same unbreakable blue-tinted glasses Peter and I had used at this table thirty-five years ago.

We sat in the yard with our backs to Proctor Avenue, the clouds beginning to break apart above us. He was very slightly hunched now, my father, bald on top beneath his favorite straw hat, his shoulders thinner than they had once been but still powerful. His ears,

large to begin with, had grown larger of late. His eyes looked per-
petually wet, as though the old vigor—fifty years of manual labor
with a total of three sick days—was slowly oozing out of him there.
"The last few days she goes in different moods with the medicines,"
he told me. "Sometimes she sleeps good, a real sleep. Other times she
makes herself get up outa the bed, and walks into the parlor by herself, and I find her there in the morning, all crooked in the soft chair,
solid asleep. She's better at night, Joanie. You should stay and have
supper. After supper she'll be up."

"I have tickets for the Red Sox, Pa."

"The baseball," he said, but he looked down at his hands, then
back up as if the idea of a daughter choosing a game over her
mother's sickbed was more than he could fathom. "Two nights ago
the other nurse and me we got her up and pushed her out here in the
wheelchair, and we had a good time, you mama and me."

"She was talking nonsense just now."

He peered hard at me, sandwich plate tilting precariously in his
lap. "That'sa no the nonsense, Joanie."

"What: I say I love you, Mama, and she says Christ was in the
desert for forty days—that makes sense?"

"Sure it does. If you had religion ina you life, it would make sense
to you too. She's takin on other people's sufferin now, you mother.
She's carryin the load of it in this world, so people like me and you
don't have to."

I made a face and turned away. I would not be drawn into an argument, not today. He was a kind man, too kind at times, a wonderful father, really, but there were certain subjects you just did not
discuss with him. You could not say the word "abortion" in his presence. You could not talk politics or question the edicts of the One
True Church. He kept a picture of the Pope on the wall of his basement workshop. A picture of the Pope and, in a slightly lower position, a portrait of John Volpe, the plain Italian workingman who'd
risen, against all kinds of odds, to be governor of Massachusetts, then
gone to Washington and Rome and made his people proud.

Over the years I'd periodically fantasized about telling him I was
gay. I suspected my mother had known it for a long time now, so

perhaps he wouldn't be surprised. He'd suggest I go speak to Father Dom, say he knew one or two good Revere boys who'd never married, or whose wives had died, who were lonely, who'd be happy to go out on a date with such a beautiful girl like me.

One of my former lovers had come out to her father—a man like this, an old-school Hungarian bricklayer—and when she'd told him she was gay, he'd puzzled over the word a minute, then answered, "Good, Sharon, that's what your mother and me we always wanted in life for you." When she told him gay meant homosexual, he'd been embarrassed at first, then angry, then, after an hour or so, apologetic. She'd been on a weekend visit, and her father had come up to her on Sunday night as she was leaving and said, "But honey, what do you *do* with another girl?"

Or so the story went.

My father reached out, rested his wide coarse hand on the top of my forearm for a few seconds, then took it away. To the west, rays of sunlight were breaking through the ragged rainclouds, lasers piercing torn denim. The phone was ringing in Antonelli's house—notes from a childhood aria—ringing and ringing over the new fence that separated our yards. When it finally stopped, my father said, "So how is you life now? I see you almost every day, I don't even ask."

I said I'd volunteered to take on some extra work, a special project, and that I wouldn't be on the news now for seven days. When he asked what the project was, I told him, bluntly, without apology.

"La Cosa Nostra?" he said very quietly, as if he could not quite believe it might be spoken about, in public, even now.

"Not only them, Papa. It's a whole series. All the organized crime groups, all the gangs."

But for my father there could never be any other type of organized crime. I could see only one side of his face—the strong jaw and large ear, the most Roman of Roman noses. For a long time he sat very still, balancing the plate and glass on his lap and staring out over the back fence. At last he said, "Remember one thing, Joanie. Those people are people in God's eyes, like me and you."

"They're animals."

"No. It's a mistake to think that. I'm not telling you now how to do your job—I don't know nothin about that. But some a those fellas, I grew up with them. They went the wrong way, and the things they do are terrible things. But in a lot a ways they're the same as you and me."

"Don't be naive, Pa."

"It's not for you to call me naive," he said. Bucket of water on my big-city conceits.

There was the growl of a garbage truck on Proctor Avenue, the singsong poetry of girls jumping rope on the sidewalk, then police sirens from the direction of the beach. I replayed my phone conversation with Alfonse, changed my mind three times before speaking. "Those fellas you grew up with might be about to shoot your son in the head."

We sat for a full minute in silence, and then, still not looking at me, he said, "Peter owes a debt."

"A very substantial debt. Many thousands."

"Twenty thousand?"

"No, Papa. *Many.* He—"

"I saw him the other night."

"Here?"

He shook his head. Sunlight was swimming in our little box of a yard now, the laden limbs of my father's fruit trees giving way and shifting back again in the breeze. "Down the beach. I went for a cigar . . . a little walk, that's all. You mama makes me go out sometimes so my heart stays strong. . . . I saw him there and he wouldn't talk to me about it. I don't know the right way to talk to him no more. I never knew it."

Another silence fell over us; the breeze momentarily died. I asked my father what he thought they would do to Peter now.

"Now," he said, as surely as if he'd been asked to spell his last name, "now they try to get Peter to talk to you, ask you not to do your new TV show."

"If I stopped at this point, somebody else would just take over."

"Then they try to get something from him, some favor. Something he has."

"He has nothing."

"Then they hurt him. Unless we pay, they hurt him."

"Neither you nor I is going to pay a cent this time, Papa. Not this time. Not to a person like that."

"This time is the most important time," he said. "He could kill a man, this Eddie, like you and me kill the mosquito."

"No, Papa. No. No. No. It always comes down to this. We care more about Peter than he cares about himself."

"This time they could kill him, Joanie."

"We're not paying Peter's debts anymore, period! End of discussion, Papa!"

He frowned and turned his head away a few degrees. "You don't need to talk like that," he said. "You mother she used to talk to me like that when she got mad. Remember? But you don't need to. Not with me."

"Sorry. I'm . . . but don't you see how it works, Papa? I've paid his debts twenty times over the last ten years, did you know that?"

"That's what the family is for."

I made myself count three breaths, three quick heavings of history.

"Did it do any good? Did he stop gambling for one month, one week? Did he learn about money the way an adult has to learn? Did he try to change his life the way adults change their lives?"

"You should love him, that's all."

"Love him! I *have* loved him! I *do* love him. But does loving him mean—"

"Don't make a show for the neighbors."

"Does loving him mean we keep him a child for his entire life? Does it mean we keep sending him the message that it's okay to throw money away hand over fist?"

"What does it make you so mad for if I help him?"

"Why? It's obvious why."

"It's not to me obvious. Why, because you think we're giving him the money you give us?"

"It's got nothing to do with money. It's . . . you're ruining him, you and Mama, by not letting him take care of himself. I think sometimes I love him more than you do. . . . I think about what will happen to him when—"

He held up his hand, unwilling to consider that particular *when*. "I'm goin tomorrow to have a little talk with this Eddie who he owes money to," he said. "I knew him a little bit growin up. I knew his brother, Aldo, who they killed in Korea. I'll talk with him."

While your daughter is on the TV screen doing her best to put him in jail, I thought, but I had clamped my lips together by then, and vowed not to speak another syllable. Family protecting you against the merciless outside world—it went back to the isolated valleys of the Contadina, tight little villages of peasants bound together by a dialect not spoken on the other side of the hills, kept alive only by their unbreakable bond to each other as the *padrone* squeezed the sweat and blood out of them, as the land was conquered and occupied again and again. The first commandment was: Sacrifice everything for your family, for your *paesani*. It was bred into the bone, that law. It had traveled across the ocean in our chromosomes. No matter how much damage it caused, no matter how many lives it ruined, no matter how outdated it became, letting go of it was like losing an organ.

I stared down at the half-eaten sandwich on my plate. "Whichever way I look there's sadness now."

"Look up."

"Oh, please."

"You know something better?"

I shook my head.

"This is not the last life, Joanie," he said. "That's all you gotta remember."

But there was no comfort in that for me. I could take no solace in a Church that raised its own members to glory and condemned the rest of creation to eternal fire, that excluded me simply on the basis of who I loved. For the past fourteen years, in various cities, I'd read the news aloud to millions of people every evening, and in that time it had become utterly apparent to me that there was nothing special or sacred about human beings. We were all just so much gristle and electricity, hormones and ego. When we died, our bodies rotted, like pieces of wood, like dogs, pigeons, uneaten food. That was the merciful end of it. I wanted it to be otherwise—I thought of the little sparkle of spirit I had seen in my mother's body a few minutes before—but that was only the dream world again, a Friday-night Back Bay fantasy, another opiate.

I gathered up our plates and went into the house. My mother was snoring in the bed with her head turned away, eyes shifting beneath the lids, working, searching. I brushed my fingers lightly over the crossed bruised wrists, kissed her lightly on the shoulder. I whispered my love, promised to see her again in a day, conveyed another imaginary message from Peter. On the way out I came upon Helen, nicely installed in the softest living room chair. We did not exchange so much as a glance.

After trying to press upon me everything from an old cardigan sweater to a pound of macaroon cookies one of the neighbors had brought by, my father held the door open for me and followed me outside to my car, a lonely old man now, about to be abandoned by everyone. Before I turned the key he leaned down toward me with his hands on top of the door and asked again how my life was.

"I told you, Papa. All is well."

He nodded, skeptical, looking straight into me. "You life other than work, I mean."

"I bought a new apartment, on the waterfront, fourteenth floor. I'll have you over for dinner some night when Mama . . . when Mama's feeling okay."

"I could meet you friends. That would be nice for me."

I said it would be nice for me as well. I accepted his kiss and backed very carefully out into the blurry street.

On the way back toward the highway I decided to drive by my brother's office, not thinking of anything in particular, just drawn to him, just wanting to hold the family together in my mother's last days. But a plastic CLOSED sign hung on the door, and the blinds were down—at two-thirty on a Friday afternoon. I ended up driving halfway back to the bridge, then pulling into a parking lot in Chelsea, putting my face in my hands, and weeping there, a Contadina peasant woman in her sea green BMW.

32

But somehow, just driving back in the direction of Boston—the streets of Chelsea, the parkway, the long gentle rise of the bridge—brought me a certain muted comfort. In a way I could not define, Boston was connected in my mind to the rational wide-minded world, and when the tollbooth appeared in the middle of the bridge, it was like a customs checkpoint rising up between two nations. I tossed my quarters at the bucket and steered gratefully south toward the city.

I was tempted to drive back to the apartment (the newness had not worn off yet; I still felt a certain thrill, opening the door) and spend the afternoon alone, working on the script, reading and resting before the game. But something drew me back to SBT. When I parked in my reserved space and slipped into the building through the side door, it was like slipping back into a glitzy but comfortable dress. There were messages littering my desk, piles of folders and videotapes stacked neatly on the dusted blotter. There were parts of my life I could not allude to here; still, it was a sanctuary, this place. The windows offered views down into Chinatown and out over Dorchester and Mattapan; there were Frankenthaler and Motherwell posters on the walls. Hidden in an envelope in the top desk drawer was a snapshot of Leslie in a white cable-knit sweater, sitting in a pile of scarlet leaves outside our favorite bed-and-breakfast in Vermont. Of all the roles I played, this was the one I liked best.

Margie tapped on the jamb and stood in the doorway with a hand on one plump hip. "I thought this was your vacation week. What do we have to do to keep you away from this place?"

"Fire me."

"For what possible reason?"

"My secret addiction."

"I put on a fresh pot the minute I saw your car."

Margie's phone rang once in the outer office. She put the tip of a painted thumbnail between her teeth, bit down on it gently, and drifted. Her husband was a Boston detective, handsome as a movie star, who worked in the city's worst neighborhoods; she had two young children in day care in West Roxbury, a mother in a nursing home with late-stage Alzheimer's, a heart the size of Massachusetts; a tendency—understandable enough, given all that—to think about her domestic problems when she was supposed to be thinking about work. I sometimes thought that was the essential difference between us: Margaret Jefferson, executive assistant, had trouble setting her home life aside; Joanna Imbesalacqua, executive, did not.

"Margie?"

"Sorry. . . . There's a producers' meeting at four-thirty but no one's expecting you. D.B. sent down a couple of what he calls 'our mafioso tapes'—he gets all nervous when you go on vacation, you know—and George left a message saying he'll pick you up in front of your place at five forty-five. He has the tickets."

Her telephone sounded again, one ring. She turned down the corners of her lips.

"Can you call Rebecca and Zachary and ask them to see what else they can dig up on Eddie Crevine? We're very thin on the visuals in the first segment."

"Will do, captain. D.B. wanted to say something to you about that, I think."

"Any breaking news?"

"A five-alarm in Dorchester, which they're pretty sure was set." She gestured toward the windows. "You can see the smoke from here. See it? Way off to the right? . . . Angela Lee is there with the second unit. They think there might be some children still inside."

"Was Julius all right without me last night?"

"Oh, you know." She glanced over her shoulder. "He stumbled and bumbled a little bit, the way he does. He said 'the six o'clock *nude'* once, instead of the six o'clock *news.* People are kidding him about it still. . . . You didn't watch?"

"I was out on the town."

"D.B. put Cynthia on with him again, but she's as nervous as he is without you around."

"He needs someone younger, maybe."

"Don't get going on that younger thing now." The phone started up again in the outer office. Margie didn't even move until the third ring. "Been getting hang-ups all day," she said, over her shoulder, buttocks flexing beneath her too-tight dress as she walked. "Lots of nutcases out there."

In the soft chair in one corner of the office, I set myself up with a mug of coffee and a stack of tapes, blinds drawn, door closed, and spent an hour and a half studying clips of *consigliere* leading their clients out of court. How they strutted, these men. How unbelievably proud they were, how adolescent. From somewhere a scrap of verse floated into my mind: "The killer\ hides his Buddha\ beneath a thousand skins\ of anger." But I could not see the Buddha in them, or the Jesus, or the buried, misunderstood saint. They were walking evil, nothing more.

In fifty minutes of small spliced segments, there were only a few fleeting glimpses of the notorious Edward Crevine. Which was a problem. We'd have to go with stills in the first segment; stills, hearsay, speculation. I remembered Alfonse's offer to help, made a note to call him later in the evening—we had six days still. Very briefly I toyed with the idea of trying to convince my brother to give an interview, voice altered and face in shadow, a way of helping me put pressure on the man he owed, perhaps help send that man to prison. But I had always been careful to keep my personal life at a safe distance from my work, and I wanted to help Peter, if I could, not use him, not endanger him.

So far, though he'd been in his filthy business for several decades, Crevine had been too smart or too lucky to have been captured at close range by the electronic eye. The key that might unlock his life for us would have to come from a second tape, filled with scenes from the career of Crevine's late mentor, Angelico Pestudo—flamboyant, odious, in an out of Walpole prison like a bird returning to and leaving its seasonal nesting grounds. I spent a long time with that tape. For the most part, all it did was reinforce my perceptions of him: conceited and mean-looking, a nasty goombah in two-thousand-dollar suits. One clip was different, though: Some enterprising reporter holding a videocamera had caught Pestudo with his guard down, frolicking with his granddaughter in a park in the North End. They were playing a game in which the girl would get a running start of six or eight steps and throw herself against Pestudo's chest, and he would swing her around in a circle and say what sounded from a distance like, "My leetle pumpkinetta-betta! My leetle pumpkinetta-betta!"

I copied the sequence numbers onto my legal pad and played the scene over again. For a few seconds Pestudo seemed like any other ordinary sweet grandfather—unarmored, slightly foolish, his pure white hair swept neatly back, the old hands catching his granddaughter under her arms and lifting her up and out in a jubilant circle.

But then—almost as if she'd been bred to do so—the little girl pointed at the camera and said something to her grandfather. Pestudo set her down and charged across the dirt like a bull, murder in his eyes and a string of the foulest curses issuing from his mouth. Halfway across the playground he stopped and grabbed a stone from the dust at his feet, came forward a few more jerky steps, and flung it at the camera with an awkward motion. The screen showed a flash of blue sky and went blank.

I rewound the tape and stared again at the kindly Italian *nono* spewing vitriol. It seemed likely to me that the first segment of our series would set off a similarly vicious blaze in Eddie Crevine. And perhaps because of that, because of my ambition and so-called professionalism, my own brother would end up lying in a puddle of blood—just the way Angelico Pestudo had ended up, in the gutter outside his West End Social Club.

I clicked off the VCR, walked over to the phone at my desk, and dialed Peter's apartment. Fifteen rings, no machine. I checked the clock—three-forty—dialed his office, and after the third ring heard his secretary's happy Revere-accented voice on the line, all optimism and lopped-off *r*'s. Just as the message ended, just as I was searching myself for a voice with half Elsie's kindness in it, the door opened. I glanced up, spoke, in my irritation, only a false, businesslike "Goodbye, then," and slipped the receiver back into its cradle.

33

D.B. always entered my office without waiting for an invitation, as if to make sure I understood who was the boss here and who the mere celebrity. "That's the way," he said, when he saw the stack of tapes. He was wearing a dark blue pin-striped suit and a checkered silk tie that didn't quite match. He walked over, stood so close I could smell the starch on his shirt collar, and said, "The smartest, sexiest, hardest-working news anchor in New England." A typical opening for him.

I collected the tapes and carried them around behind my desk. D.B. took a seat opposite, crossed his legs, tucked in the edge of his tie. "Do you know what they mean in sports when they say someone's a franchise player?" he said.

"They mean that if the player isn't happy and decides to leave, the franchise goes down the tubes."

"Exactly. They also mean the player is a star, and the star gives the fans more than anyone else gives them, works harder, looks better on the field, has better numbers, gets paid more."

I studied him a moment, a craggy-faced, unattractive adulterer with padded shoulders, watched him break eye contact with a self-righteous smile—the man who liked to show pictures of brutalized children on the evening news.

"This morning, I was starting to worry a tad. How, I thought to myself, can she have a special project coming up in six days and decide to take the week off?"

"I took a week off from the *anchor desk*, D.B. I told you I'd be coming in to meet with Rebecca and Zachary. I have my outline for the first segment, we have clips. Andy and I have the script ninety-five percent done."

He went on smiling and looking around the office as if not hearing me, a favorite trick of his. "I was thinking we could have a nice quiet dinner on the waterfront and talk this thing through."

"Tonight?"

"Of course tonight. When else? Time is short, Joanna. I suppose you're going to tell me you have a date."

"I'm using the station's Red Sox tickets with George and some friends."

He raised and slowly lowered his brows, another trick. Making fun of George, maybe ("Georgie, our weatherperson," he usually called him), or releasing a little puff of jealousy, or just trying to knock me off balance by hinting that he knew my deepest secrets (and George's). Which, I was fairly sure, he did not.

"You're not serious with him, are you? Our Georgie?"

"You're not supposed to ask questions like that of franchise players."

"Well, I'm asking."

"And I'm not answering. It's good for the station to have people see us together in public. A love interest on the six o'clock news, a boost for the ratings, right?"

The frown and lowered lids, the loafer tassels going, the sudden switch to his executive voice. Depriving me of his friendship now. How would I ever survive?

"Let's talk about a couple of things, then, shall we? Off the record." He tugged his trousers a bit farther down on his heavy thighs, glanced at the door—which he'd left partially open—but did not bother to get up and close it. "You're not feeling a-tall ill at ease on this project, are you, Joanna?"

"Not in the slightest."

"Not feeling a-tall compromised?"

"Meaning what?"

"Meaning . . . your private life is not interfering in any way with your work, is it?"

"Meaning what, D.B.? We can't have much of a heart-to-heart if you're going to speak in code."

For five or six seconds he fumbled with his tie, fidgeted in his seat, plucked at the hair growing from his ears, would not quite look at me. I was sure, then, that he was going to ask about Leslie. But when he finally met my eyes he said, "I mean, your being from Revere and all, as are some of the, oh . . . subjects shall we say?—of your report. No hometown loyalties getting in the way? No subtle embarrassments? No dilution of the journalistic purity?"

"Have you ever seen any hometown loyalties get in the way?"

"Never," he said, and he laughed in the direction of the open door as if I'd just told him a slightly off-color joke.

"And the 'subjects,' as you call them, are Vietnamese and African-American and Cambodian and Jewish and Irish and Jamaican and Russian—"

"Of course, of course, don't get touchy. But the Mafia is the real hook, don't you think? And, from what Andy has been telling me about the script, you're going to break this Crevine fellow out of his nice comfortable box of anonymity, make him out to be one of the candidates for Godfather of Godfathers, isn't that so? We're about to start running spot ads for the special, so if that's *not* so, you had better let someone know very soon."

I stood, strode over and closed the door, returned to my seat, leaned back, clasped my hands over my waist, and eyed him calmly, the way he was eyeing me. "I feel like you're holding something back, D.B."

"She's a sharp one," he said, to some invisible observer.

The sharp one glanced at the digital clock on her desk.

"All right, what I'm holding back is this: The station has been receiving anonymous telephone calls, hang-ups mostly, but the occasional vague threat. Which means we're doing something right. And which also means the word is out already about the specifics of what we're planning. You haven't told anyone?"

I could hear Margie bumping around in the outer office. "Not a soul."

"Well, I'm starting to have the feeling this is going to turn into something larger than we'd planned. We've decided—as of this morning—to go a bit higher-profile with the project, heavy promotion during the nightly news and sprinkled here and there on our prime-time slots. A little something in the Sunday *Globe,* et cetera. Given all that, you can't blame me, can you, for wanting to have a chat with my franchise player to see if the fact that she's working part-time on this high-profile series means anything special?"

"I was always intending to work on it part-time. I'm a full-time anchor, remember?"

"Of course you were—of course you are."

"What are we talking about, then? I'm approaching it the way I'd approach any other project that—"

"Really?"

"Of course, really. What are you after? Why are you probing like this?"

"What about your brother?"

"What *about* my brother?" I had a sudden glimpse of a scene from last night's dream: Peter holding a six-pack of beer and, standing on a sidewalk somewhere, grinning, oblivious. "I didn't even know you realized I had a brother."

"We received a call this morning—straight into my line—which mentioned a brother."

"In what context?" I swallowed, did not move my eyes.

"I couldn't be sure."

"D.B., stop playing games. You have your concerns and I'm trying to address them. Let's get it out in the open, no bullshit."

His head jerked back a quarter inch, and then the smile came out, an oily, slithering smile that spread across the bottom of his face like a wound.

"I had a call this morning that vaguely threatened your brother's life if you were to go forward with the project, and I wanted to raise that with you. That, believe it or not, is what the board pays me for, asking questions like that. What does your brother do, if you don't mind me asking?"

"He sells real estate."

"In Revere?"

"Yes, my family lives there. Everyone but me."

"Why would he be mentioned, then, in a phone call like this?"

"Beyond the fact that he's my brother, I haven't the faintest idea."

"Really?"

"Of course, really. We've had threats to the station before—by the dozens when we did the police corruption series—why are you suddenly losing your nerve?"

"I came to see if you were losing *your* nerve. Have you been threatened at all?"

"No."

"Anything out of the ordinary happen?"

"Not that I can think of, no. A flat tire this morning—two flat tires, actually."

"Slashed?"

"Yes."

"Okay, that's exactly what I'm talking about. Do you want off the project?"

I pressed my lips together, swung my head away from him. The blinds were still drawn, and I stared at the even bands of sunlight between them for as long as I dared. Peter was making the calls himself, I was almost sure of it. But it was not Peter I was focused on now. My skin seemed pulled tight around me suddenly, and within it some awful, primitive beat was pounding, the same ferocious pulse that had propelled me, bump by bump, through journalism school, through a long series of reportorial jobs in places like Boise, Idaho, and Chico, California, lifting me gradually higher and higher until I found myself flying through an executive stratosphere peopled by various hideous mutations of the creature who sat now in my office, pushing me. D.B. had no idea how typical he was, how many men—and women—like himself I had eaten for lunch on my long climb. He had, in short, not the slightest idea who he was fucking with.

"My contract requires me," I said, "in addition to the regular anchor responsibilities, to do a reasonable number of promotional, community, and charitable appearances and at least once a year, if called upon, to oversee a special project of duration not longer than six weeks. I was called upon. I helped come up with the concept paper for this series. I'm working on it an appropriate number of hours. I've taken part of my vacation time to focus on this first segment and to get the whole thing up and running. Lois Stearns is the special assistant on it, so if you're worried about our preparation schedule, you might talk to her, but at this point it seems to me everything is moving along quite well." I turned my eyes back to him. "If you want me off the project, D.B., or off the anchor desk for that matter, say so and I'll start looking for another position tomorrow. If not, let me get a little more work done here before I have to leave for the game."

He watched me like an interrogator, one second, two seconds, and then sent such a counterfeit smile in my direction that I wanted to pick something up off the desk and throw it at him.

"That's my girl," he actually said. "That's passing the test all right." He reached into the side pocket of his suit jacket, withdrew a business card, and snapped it down on my blotter like a trump. "Edward Crevine's home number is written on the back," he said smugly. "Still have a few sources of my own, you know. Thought it might be of use to you at some point. Call him up, harass him a little bit, the way he's been harassing us. Use your name if you want to, or not. Hell, use *my* name if you want to."

The card itself meant little to me. I already had Crevine's home telephone—both home telephones—but I held it by its edge and tried to follow a logical line of thought through a whirlwind of absurd suspicions. "Yes, fine, thank you," I said, but the conversation seemed extraordinarily strange to me suddenly, our station manager turned investigative reporter. Exceedingly strange. I pushed the card into my daybook and made my face flat and blank and unreadable, an anchor-desk trick.

"Pop open those blinds a minute, can you, Joanna?"

I obeyed, a solid, rigid crust over bubbling lava. D.B. stood, leaned on my desk, and pretended to be studying the skies. "Looks showery to me," he said. "What about this—if the Sox are rained out, we'll continue this conversation over a fancy dinner in the North End. Deal?"

I took and released a breath, ran through five replies, then finally looked him in the face and said, "Our Georgie is calling for a clear night."

34

Two-thirty P.M., it was, by the time I decided to make an appearance at the office and see if we'd had any luck with the Ngs. I pulled the T-bird into the alleyway behind my building (no sense letting Xavier and everyone else in the world know I was sitting there, waiting to be harassed) and went in through the back door.

Elsie wasn't at her desk—which was a surprise—the bathroom empty, the venetian blinds down, the SORRY WE'RE CLOSED sign propped up in the front window. The message light on my phone was blinking, which meant she must have called in sick, must have been calling me at the office and at home all morning while I was out burning gas and wrestling with the Angel of San Casino. I paced back and forth twice between the rooms before pressing the button.

This is Mr. Ing, the voice said, very false now, obviously false. *We're calling to tell you no, that house is not interesting to us. Thank you for taking your time to show us.*

Message number two: *Peter, it's me. . . . I came in for a while and you weren't there, and I called you last night and this morning at home and you weren't there either. . . . So at lunch I locked up and left. I'm worried. I'm feeling terrible that I told that man you were at Suffolk Downs. Did he find you? Are you all right? When you get in please call me, okay? I'll keep trying you at the condo. But please call me as soon as you hear this, okay?*

I went into her half of the office and stared at the top of her desk. The note pad and pen, yesterday's *Herald,* Austin's picture. A yellow Post-it that said *Cambodian Social Alliance. 286-8081. Right pro-nunciation is* Ing. *Tell P.*

I listened to her message two more times. Worried or not, it was strange of Elsie to leave the office uncovered. I'd call her right now and make sure she was okay, let her know it wasn't a problem that she'd told the Hulk where I was: he would have found me sooner or later, anyway. After that, I'd pick up a bunch of flowers at Mulligan's and bring them by my parents', see my mother, try to make some sort of peace with them.

In a minute I would. I'd just walk around the office a minute and iron out my thoughts; then I'd turn the day around. There was money in my pocket, wasn't there? I was still breathing, Elsie was still breathing, my parents and Joanie were all right.

But after three laps across the office a certain bad breeze started blowing through my mind. It began to seem obvious that it was harmful to my mental health to be indoors, that the mature thing to do would be to step out into the alley and have a smoke before calling Elsie, so she would hear from me when I was in a positive frame of mind, upbeat, calm.

Dreary weather still, but the rain had stopped. In the alley I shook a cigarette out of the pack and walked up and down next to the T-bird awhile, taking a drag now and then but not really inhaling. I lit a second one, crushed it out before it was halfway smoked, started towards the door and the telephone. But then there was the tobacco taste to deal with. And I was out of Life Savers. And it was only half a block to Nicole's Market. She had Life Savers, bottles of lemonade . . . half a block. Obviously the logical thing was to take a walk over there before getting on the phone.

The little tinkling bell on the door, shelves of tomato sauce and white bread, five-dollar-a-tube toothpaste, the gorgeous Nicole herself perched on a stool behind the counter with a nice smile for me and her eyes on a miniature television. I could hear the organ music: something not so good happening in soap-opera land.

Beside the cash register stood the blue lottery machine, whispering. And behind it, curling out from their plastic dispensers, were a dozen different types of instant tickets, loops and loops of them, five hundred chips of hope.

"How-how've those instant tickets been doing lately, Cole?" I heard myself saying.

She looked up and smiled. "Nothing, really."

"No b-big winners the last few weeks?"

"A ten-dollar guy yesterday. Fifty-dollar lady last week."

"What's the ma-maximum pa-payout on those new two-dollar games?" High Roller.

"Twenty."

"Twenty thou? No kidding. You get some kind of b-bonus, don't you, if somebody hits for that much?"

"Two hundred dollars and a beautiful sign for my front window."

"Two hundred bills, ey?" I fingered the change in my pocket, looked over my shoulder. If somebody comes into the store now, I said to myself, I'll take it as a signal from God and just walk out— no tickets.

But no one came into the store. More organ music now, Nicole's pretty smile. "Give me a b-bunch, then," I told her. "I'll dress up the front of your estab-est . . . I'll d-dress up your est-est-establishment here with a nice sign, care of the Ma-Massachusetts Lottery Commission. We'll have our picture in the *Journal* together, you and me."

She showed me a smirk. "What size bunch, Mr. Trump?"

"Mr. Trump, ey? The five-dollar tickets doing anything?"

"Same nothing."

"Give me a ha-hundred, then, I guess, if you have em."

"Hundred dollars' worth or a hundred tickets?"

"Um . . . ha-hun-hun-hun-hundred tickets. Why not, right? What's the wa-worst that can happen?"

"The worst that can happen, Peter, is that you lose five hundred dollars in about five seconds, that's the worst that can happen."

"Sh-sure it is. But seize the day, correct?"

"In my case, it's more like the day seizes me," she said, but she drew out the long ribbon of tickets, folded them in even thick stacks on the counter, and was kind enough to put them in a paper bag for me so I wouldn't have to step out onto the sidewalk looking like a guy with a gambling problem.

I left ten fifties on top of the machine, new and crisp and fanned out as neat as a hand of cards.

Back in the office I called Elsie immediately. The line was busy, so I made myself comfortable behind the desk, broke three Life Savers from the roll, and arranged the tickets in five piles on my blotter.

I touched redial—busy again.

Elsie must have cleaned off my desk during the few hours she'd been in, because the gray metal next to the blotter was shining like it had just been carnauba-waxed. The pencils and pens in my Celtics cup had been dusted, the old ones thrown out, some type of nice deodorant sprayed around. A saint, for sure. I decided I'd scratch the first ten tickets, then call and let her know there was nothing to worry about. If I happened to win the twenty grand—I knew what the odds were, I was no fool; even so, somebody had to win it, didn't they?—I'd pay off Eddie within the hour, close shop for a couple weeks, and use the rest to take Elsie on a Royal Caribbean.

But before I could pick up the letter opener and start to work on the first ticket, a burst of fast knocking sounded on the glass of the front door. The blinds were drawn tight, and my visitor couldn't see the desk from there, so I sat still and breathed and waited for him to go away. More knocking. Some people had trouble with long words like C-L-O-S-E-D.

I moved two inches to my left so I could see the shadow the person made on my blinds—somebody small, not Xavier, not Elsie, who had her key and wouldn't be knocking in any case. The knock again: rat-a-tat style, timid, nervous, a little kid's knock. It took me less than two blinks to figure it out.

"Go around ba-back!" I yelled, and a minute later Billy Ollanno was sitting there in the office, angel of the underworld, bringing me a message.

I hadn't thought to hide the lottery tickets—they were still there in neat piles on the desk—and Billy's eyes flickered towards them and away as if somebody else's tiny brain had been planted there behind his puppet face.

"I come here on my own, Petey," he said, leading off with a lie. He

had his hat in his hands, a wrinkled red cap that looked like it belonged on a second-grader. "I didn't see Xavier in the club last night,
Petey, but, but I heard from the other guys that he come ovah here
and scared your girl a little bit yesterday, and then he found you
down Suffolk."

"Scared who? What are you t-talking about?"

Billy seemed to be high—no huge surprise there. He was rocking
back and forth in the chair, and his eyes were jumping from the window blinds to the lottery tickets and back again, like there was a
mouse racing around the room and God had given him the job of
keeping track of it. He held the hat between his knees and kept ro-
tating it, fingering it, tapping it against his trousers.

"Your girl. The secretary. Ellie."

"Elsie, not Ellie. Who t-told you that?"

"I heard it. I dunno, Petey. Somebody."

"Who?"

"Ain't it true?"

"Who's the sa-somebody? Sa-somebody who?"

"Richie, the other bartender. He heard it from some guy. She's all
right, though, righ? . . . I come up here on my own because I tole you
if you was ever in real trouble I'd let you know, you know? And it's
not like that. . . . I mean, I didn't hear nothing, like they say, from the
hosses mout. But somethin Al—something Richie said, I mean, made
me think—well, he . . . well . . . what it is is, you shouldn't leave Revere now if you was thinkin of leaving."

"Why would I leave Re-Re-Revere?"

"Why? I dunno why. I mean, you pissed off Eddie Three Hands,
dincha?"

I studied Billy for a few seconds, tried to fit the puzzle pieces together. After a minute, I pulled the money from my inside jacket
pocket. I set the envelope down on the blotter in front of me, like
the lottery tickets were invisible, pulled the money out one inch and
riffed the edges of the bills so Billy could see there were twenties
and fifties, a lot of twenties and fifties, but couldn't get the exact
count.

"I have what I owe him r-right here," I said. "Xavier c-called me at the c-condo last night, la-late. I t-tol-tol-told him I had the money. It's all set."

"It is?"

"Sh-sure it is. What, you think I'd run out on a debt, is that what you're saying?"

"No, no, no, Petah. No way, man. Madonn, I'm just glad for you, pal. I mean—Jeeziz, man. I'm effin happy. Look at me. Look at my face, willya?"

The face was a cocaine puppet's face, smile painted on, Billy's own goofy brand of meanness slithering around there behind the smile. To emphasize how happy he was, he jumped out of his chair and came over to me, and for one instant then I thought he might be carrying a pistol, and he would take it out, and that would be the way my life would end—Pete Imbesalacqua shot dead by the most pathetic little *skutchamenza* ever to walk the streets of Revere.

But Billy only approached the side of the desk, with his hat in his fingers, and seemed to want to hug me. I stuck out my hand—a defensive tactic—and he shook it wildly. "Man, I thought you might be gettin ready to slip out on him or somethin, you know? Go to the cops or somethin. Man, what a mistake I made. Thank God, man. Thank God. So you're gonna meet wit him then, righ?"

I was smiling now, too, putting some life into the handshake. "My oldest friend thinks I'm a stoolie," I said. "N-nice."

"Nah, nah, nevah. Course I don't. I just was worried about you, that's all, Petey. You gut a little temper, I know that. You know it, righ? I thought: They scared his girl, Petey's gonna take revenge now. That's the way he is. He's gonna try and put Big Zave away for a few years for intimidatin or assaultin or somethin. Or stiff Eddie for his money now, you know? I shoulda known better, man. I apologize, all righ?"

I thought maybe I should hug Billy after all. Hug him, take the silver letter opener Elsie had given me, and drive it through his heart from the back. Drop the body off in front of Eddie's house with a note on it: *For Elsie.*

De Niro would have.

But I only threw his smile back at him and said, "I just talked to her five minutes ago. A little bit sh-shaken up. But they didn't t-touch her, correct?"

"That's what I heard, man. But you can never know, you know? I mean, I heard it from somebody who heard it from somebody, you know? She talked to the cops, I guess, which was probably a mistake. But so she's okay, that's the main thing, righ?"

"How do you know she t-talked to the cops?"

"How do I know? I dunno. . . . You know, people. . . . She's all righ, though, huh? She ain't gonna prest no charges, righ, or nothin?"

"Never. She's not that way. I don't even think she wa-went to the cops. That's b-bullshit, Billy. That's a st-st-st-story."

"It could be, man. You know how people are."

"She'd never do anything like go to the c-cops."

"Eddie's pissed over what Zave did, and Zave's sorry he did it, man. If I know him at all, he's feelin really shitty that he ever even rose his voice to a girl. He loves em, that guy. He adores em. You should see the way he treats the girls at the club. He's gentle for a big guy, really." Billy's whole body seemed to get twisted up in this package of lies he'd been sent to deliver. He stood there with his shoulders crooked and his knees half bent, and such a pathetic expression on his twitching face that I suddenly understood the reason I'd stayed friends with him all these years: Charity.

"I gave her the day off. She doesn't know anything about my d-debt, understand?"

"Sure."

"Understand?"

"Course I do, man."

"Tell Za-Zay-Xavier I'll be at the meeting like I'm supposed to be. Tell him you saw the m-money yourself. Tell him I even had enough left over for a few lottery tickets."

"Sure, Petey. I'm happy for you, man. It'll make my day to go tell him."

Billy backed away a couple feet, then straightened up and met my eyes, almost like a real person.

"What's your buddy Alfonse up to?" he said, twisting his mouth all weird when he said the name.

"What?"

"Alfonse. You know, Romano. The cop."

"I da-don't see him."

"You don't?"

"Never. I'm through with the g-guy. He doesn't know about the debt either."

"Good," Billy said. There was something new shining in his face now, a little eel slithering there under the skin, below the pathetic goofiness, below his own special brand of evil. If I had to name it I would have said it was triumph crawling around there, but triumph and Billy Ollanno were not words that fit that well together.

"Eddie's guy on the force says he's been actin weird lately, you know? Hanging with FBI guys, Mister Strict on the street, actin weird."

"I'm da-done with him."

"You are? Good. He's changed on us, Petey, righ?"

"Ab-absolutely."

"Some people say he's been tryin to fool around with Eddie's wife. Alicia. You heard that, righ?"

"What?"

"Alfonse. You know. In bed."

"What are you talking about? You can get some-somebody killed making up a story like that."

Billy laughed three notes of his hysterical laugh and looked away. "Women, right?"

"Women, bullshit. Don't you da-dare m-make up a story like that, don't you d-dare even whisper it outside this office, hear me?"

"Sure, man. I didn't mean nothin by it." He was backing slowly towards the door, swinging his eyes around the room again, a few billion twitching cells of moral confusion. "What happened wit the house. You know, Curtz? Anything?"

"C-Curtis."

"Righ. What happened?"

"How do you know about that?"

Billy shrugged, let one hand flutter up near his ear. "Ah," he said. "People, you know?"

"Listen, Billy," I said. "Listen to me n-now. You just go ba-back and tell Eddie, or Xavier, or R-Richie, or whoever it is you run to with your news reports, that Pete Imbesalacqua doesn't r-run and he doesn't squeal. All right? I have the money and I'll be there tomorrow night when I said I would, and if there's any more fa-fa-fucking around with my girlfriend or my family or Alfonse or anybody else, then my sister's gonna get involved, okay? Na-not-not-not because I'll ask her to but just because that's the way she is. Family, you understand? The press, understand me? She'll come down on Eddie with everything she has. She'll show up at his house with a ca-camera crew, she'll interview the girls at the club and let them tell their stories with their fa-fa-faces hidden and their v-voices changed. So just tell whoever it is that I p-pay my debts and I keep my mouth shut and that oughta be the end of it, okay?"

"Your sister, huh? The lady-on-the-news sister? She's goin after Eddie then, huh?"

"That's right."

Billy was nodding, backing out now, but his eyes were scraping the edge of the envelope, making a desperate try to get a count of the bills. I stepped forward, and we danced a little no-touch waltz there for a minute, three yards apart, Billy looking, me squeezing the envelope in my hands to make it seem about twice as thick as it was.

"It looks like you got, what, Petey, about five grand in that there letter?"

I stared into his face as if staring at my whole childhood memory album, gone rancid.

"I mean, everything's gonna be good then, righ? So maybe even come by the club tonight and we'll have a couple drinks and celebrate, all righ? On the house. Why dontcha come by around eleven. . . . And you and Eddie—tomorrow night is still good, righ?"

"The Lounge. Eight-thirty sh-sharp."

"Good, then. Beautiful. I'm happy, man, okay? This makes my day, buddy."

He slipped out the door and skittered away down the alley. I watched until he was out of sight, then closed and bolted the door and leaned against it, squeezing the knob hard in both hands. Not twenty seconds after Billy left, the phone rang. I waited for the machine to click on and heard a woman's voice, very faint, like she was holding the phone away from her. "Good-bye, then," I thought she said. The line went dead.

It had almost sounded like Joanie.

35

It was an hour or more before I could bring myself to call Elsie. Even the lottery tickets couldn't pull on my attention during that hour. I sat in my office with the lights out and the traffic going by beyond the blinds and just stared at the wall. I could tolerate having these kinds of people in my own life; I was used to it. Bringing them into Elsie's life, though, was something I hadn't counted on. A new low for me.

At quarter of five I punched redial again and waited for her sweet hello.

"You all right?"

"Peter? Where are you? Did you get my message?"

"I got it, I came in l-late, I'm sorry. What happened?"

"Nothing, I . . . did he find you, that man?"

"He fa-found me. Don't worry about it. He would have fa-found me anyway. What did he do to you?"

"Nothing."

"Don't lie to me, Elsie. What did he d-do? D-did he t-touch you?"

"No. He scared me, that's all. He has a terrible face, terrible eyes. I shouldn't have told him where you were. I'm sorry."

"Did you call the police?"

Three heartbeats of silence. "I . . . after he left I called Alfonse at his house. I was afraid for you. . . . Was that wrong?"

"No, it's . . . d-don't worry about it. This is the wa-way these people do business, okay? You can't read too much into it. They're just trying to make sure I don't skip out on the ma-ma-ma-ma-m-meeting tomorrow night, and their way of doing that is to ra-run around scaring people a little bit, doing what they did to you, m-making phone calls, paying a visit, ta-talking t-tough. That's all it is, though, talk, believe me. You probably shouldn't have called Alfonse, but that's all right now. I'm going to the meeting tomorrow, I made out f-fine at the track."

"You did?"

"Sure I did. Thanks to you. And I'm going to pay you back, and meet with Eddie and make a pa-payment there too. And then something will break for us, you'll see. That's the way my luck runs. Something will come along and save us, right?"

"Will you please come and stay here tonight, then?"

"I can't do that, Else. There's still one or two er-errands I have to take care of."

"But they'll be calling you at your place, you won't be able to sleep. Come over and I'll make up the couch."

"Thanks, but I'll be fine. I put out the word just now, so they won't come by and b-bother you anymore; they won't even bother me. It's all set."

"What about tomorrow? Can we do our regular Saturday breakfast at least? Austin was asking."

"Sure we can. Of course. Stevie's place, twelve o'clock."

"Do you want me to come in now?"

"There's no business, Else. Nothing going on."

"What about the Ngs?"

"No l-luck."

"Can't you come over, Peter?"

"I can't now, Else. Just d-don't worry, all right?"

She said she wouldn't, but I could hear otherwise in her voice, in the way she told me be careful, in the way she told me good-bye. I laid the telephone back in its place, wondering if I should go and spend the night there after all, since she had offered the invitation. No, it would be too miserable—me tossing and turning on the couch, Elsie in her room, Austin in his—we'd just end up giving each other nervous intervenus through the walls. I would make it up to them at the breakfast, that's all.

I carried the little stack of tickets over to the coffee table, sat on the sofa, and began very methodically scratching them with the edge of a key.

The first eight I scratched were just cardboard, more weight for the recycle company. The ninth was a two-hundred-fifty-dollar winner. I sat back a minute and stared at it, then carried it over to Elsie's desk and slipped one edge under the corner of her blotter so she'd find it there on Monday morning and be pleased. Even if the unthinkable happened and I didn't make it through the week-end, she'd at least find the ticket there and understand what I felt for her.

Ten more useless tickets, then a fifty-buck winner, then twenty-nine losers in a row. No chocolate. A contribution to the State. A foolishness. A death wish it had been, doing this. I scratched the next to the last ticket, putting all my focus into the edge of the key. Fifty dollars again. I was in the red a hundred and fifty, still, with one ticket left. I scratched. Zero. Nothing. *Niente.* No good.

I stared at the dead ticket for thirty seconds, rechecked the numbers, scratched away a bit more of the colored coating, thought, for some reason, of my father—who had lived seventy-three years without ever being this stupid.

There was no other option then. Nothing to do but buy another fifty tickets, keep trying until my luck turned. I went out the door, around onto the street side, and walked back to Nicole's with a big smile on my face ... for the benefit of anybody who might be watching.

36

Seventy-three years I been alive on this earth, and I seen a lot of hard things to see, in that time, and heard a lot of hard things to hear. In the Old Country, in Squillani, our village, I watched the men dig into a building that was knocked down by the earthquake and take out the body of a little girl—Philomena Benedetto—with her mother standing there screaming her name. And in the service I seen a man not too far from me get knocked off the ship by an explosion, by a Japanese bomb, and burn up in the water, still alive. I seen the faces of women who were pregnant when they shouldn't be, and listened to the sound of what that meant in they voices. But nothing never cut me so deep as the sound Lucy made now when the worst pain came on her.

She was in the bathroom with the nurse that day, I remember, and she was screaming, "Saint Theresa, help me with the pain, Saint Theresa!" in a voice that was like a razor going up your backbone, peeling the skin.

So I went outside on my steps and watched the light going out of the sky from the direction of the beach. Mary DiRuzza walked by on the other side of the street, made the sign of the cross in front of her Madonna, and then waved to me, when she was getting in her car, and called out how was Lucy. And I called back, "Okay, Mary," but without any heart in it, and it made me think for some reason of a time when Mary and Joe they used to come over and sit in the back yard with us after supper, eating chestnuts that were so hot you almost couldn't hold them, and throwing the shells in a bowl, and how they'd bring over presents at Christmas for Joanie and Peter—who loved them like a mother and father.

Thinking about that made a picture in my mind of when the children were small and I would carry them to their beds at the end of the day so Lucy could have a little rest. Carry them in, with them in their pajama, one on each arm, and pull the sheet and the blanket up over they bodies that were so clean-smellin. Sometimes I would sit with them between their two beds and tell them a story from the Old Country—a funny story or a happy one—and they would try to help the way I talked. Joanie was in the second grade then, already the smartest in the class, and she got a kick out of teaching me. "*Sweet dreams* is what you should tell us, Papa. That's the right way." So I would say *Sweet dreams,* instead of "Have-a nice-a the sleep," which is the way I used to talk then. And Peter would say, "*That's* right, Papa!" even though he didn't know what he was talking about . . . because he wanted to be like his sister.

Sometimes I would tell them the story how I used to go out with my father and shoot rabbits in the hills near Benevento, and my father he would let me carry the rabbits by their big ears home for supper. Or how I used to have to walk down to the piazza with the bucket knocking against my knees, and pull the water there from the well, and carry her all the way back up the hill for my grandmother to cook with. . . . Or the one they liked best, about how I come over on the boat, by myself, fourteen years old, squeezed in with all those other people in the bottom part of the boat, who were sick all the time in the buckets, and who smelled by the end the way people should never have to smell. And how when we came to land finally— at the harbor, Boston—I saw my Uncle Sabatino standing there on the dock, with his white hair pushed straight back, holding a banana in his hand for me, which I hadn't never seen. I would try to tell them what it felt like to look down from the boat after all those days on the ocean and to know this was *America.* To look down into the crowd of people there and see Uncle Sabatino, who was like a God for us in the Old Country, and the banana.

Standing out on the steps now, in this America, with the cars going by quiet and a little wind knocking the leaves of the trees, it made me feel better to think about the way our family used to be in those years—the way we went to the beach on Sunday, the four of us after mass, Lucy and me holding our shoes in our fingers and the water like the ice against you ankles, and Joanie and

Peter trying to teach themself to swim because we couldn't teach them. . . . And my brothers and sister and their children coming over on the holidays, and all of us like one person in the kitchen eating the food Lucy cooked. . . . And how Lucy and me we used to come out at the end of the day and sit in the yard if it was warm, thinking that Peter and Joanie were asleep in they beds now, and the house was clean, and there was a little money in the bank, and we were going to mass on Sundays, doing everything the way you were supposed to.

It made me feel a little better then, remembering the family we had at one time. But Lucy was still suffering, and I knew it, and so instead of trying to keep remembering the good things, I said a little secret prayer, probably a sin, asking God to take her.

One minute after I said that prayer, I saw a car moving up Proctor Avenue from the direction of Broadway, too fast. She come up past the school, past Antonelli's house, and slowed down to make the turn in our driveway and stop. White. My son's car. Almost a miracle.

Peter got out with a worried skin on his face, but in his arm he had a pile of flowers you could fill up a small house with and a little paper bag in his hand. Going down to meet him I almost tripped on the edge of the patio, I was so glad. He shifted the flowers into his other arm and held out his hand to shake, and we shook, the two of us. That was all you had to do, father and son. Not that it made you forget all the troubles you had before. But it made you put those troubles in your pocket a little while, which was the way a family worked when she was working.

"How's M-Mama?" he said, and he looked a little better than he looked the other night, in the jail. Nervous around the eyes, like always, but a little bit better.

No more lyin now, I said to myself. "You mama's in the bathroom now, bleedin from inside," I told him, and everything that was solid in his face broke apart.

"*Santa Teresina, ayutame!*" we could hear now from inside the house, so I went back up and closed the door tight, and me and Peter stayed outside. It made me think then of when Lucy was having the babies. Me and her brother Peter we would stand outside in the hall-way in the hospital and we couldn't look at each other, because half of you wanted to take that pain on yourself, if you could, and the other half was afraid you'd ever have to.

Peter put the big flowers and the bag down careful on top of the picnic table, and we walked a little ways away from the house.

"She was not too bad today," I told him. "Then a little while ago she said she had the bleedin again, and the nurse took her in the bath-room, and all of a sudden the pain come over her."

His face was gone all white now. "We sh-should call Dr. Pierni, Pa," he said.

"Dr. Pierni knows."

"We sh-sh-should do something."

"There's not that much you can do. She doesn't want to go in the hospital, you mother. The nurse will give her something now, and she won't feel the pain in a little while, and then maybe we can go in and talk to her a minute before the medicine puts her asleep. She wants to see you, she was askin."

But everything in Peter's face was broken—you could see it even just in the streetlight, even with the yard going dark.

"How's you girl?" I said.

"Fa-fa-fa-fine, Pa. Elsie's fa-fine."

"Best girl you ever had," I said. "By a long shot."

"I know it, Pa."

"How-a you?" I asked him, after another minute, and he seemed as if the question knocked him out of a sleep. He looked around at Proctor Avenue and the cars and the other houses like he was just now seeing them the first time.

"I'm all right, Pa. Th-things'll be all right with me."

"You eatin okay? You look thin. Why don't you come tomorrow night when I make supper for Joanie. Eat with us."

"I'm doin good now, Pa, ex-exercising, you know."

"What kind of exercisin?" I said.

"Running," he said, and he made his smile, and you couldn't be sure what he meant.

I was on the edge of saying, What about the debt?, which is what

I usually would say. But that time, for once, I must of learned something about how to talk to my son, because I didn't say it.

For another little while we just stood there in the yard, shoulder by shoulder, and I was trying, one after the other, to think of things to say. I thought for a minute about asking if he wanted to go to the father-and-son breakfast at the Holy Name, but I knew he would say, Sure Pa, sure I'll go, and then when the day came he'd make an excuse. I didn't want to talk about Joanie visiting, because that would make him feel bad that he hadn't visit. I couldn't talk about Alfonse, or the debt, or Eddie, or the real estate business, because all those things would make him feel only more weak and broken up than he was already, and I didn't want that now.

What I wanted was to build him back up again the way I built the garage back for Joe Accettullo, who had the termites. One piece after the next, taking away the rotten parts and the eaten-away parts and putting new wood in there and nailing it up so even a hurricane could come and not knock him down again. I tried to think of the way to do that. But Peter started smoking a cigarette, and I was worried that, in another minute, he was gonna tell me he had a meeting to go to, and get in his car and drive away again, and so when it came up in my mind all of a sudden I just said, "What about a game of bocce, me and you?"

A surprise on the face, a little wiggle in the chin like he wanted to smile but he wouldn't let himself. Peter looked at me in the eyes one minute, then away again. "It's too dark."

"We had someone come and put the outside light in. I can open it."

" 'T-turn it on,' Pa, you say in English, not 'open.' "

"I can turn it on, then, if you want to play."

"All right, sh-sure."

When I went in the house, Peter stayed outside in the yard, but there was no more yellin now from the bathroom. The door was still closed, they were still in there, but there was no more yellin, and I said a prayer that there would be no more pain for Lucy, and I thanked God that He ever invented bocce, and I opened the outside light.

In the yard, Peter took off his jacket and hung it up on a picket of Rafaelo's fence, with a handkerchief spread out between the collar and the wood so it didn't get dirty, and he was standing at one end of the court where the shadows were, holding the little ball that we call the *pallino* in his hand. He threw the *pallino* up in the light, and we watched it come down against the stone dust that I raked out very even, come down and bounce once, and then roll a few more feet toward the board on the left side of the court.

My turn to go first then. I picked up one of the lined balls and turned it around and around in my hand, letting the dust get on my fingers so they would hold better, letting my arm feel the weight. One leg forward. The hand down now and turned back, so the ball would have the going-backwards spin on her when she flew, the English.

I bent my knees and leaned forward and threw. Little too hard. She came down and rolled against the side board, bounced off, and went another little ways down, almost to the end of the court. A bad shot for me, six or eight feet away from the *pallino*.

"I left the door open," I said.

Peter didn't answer. When he played a sport he was always what you call a "shaper," which means he made a big show. Dancing around when he played the basketball in high school, making big noises when he fell, doing more than he had to do with his arms, showing off for the girls. And it was the same even now, with the bocce, even though there were no girls watchin. He threw away his cigarette on the lawn; and instead of holding one ball, he held two, one in each hand; and instead of just standing and throwing, he moved his feet around like he was digging them in the stone dust that had been so smooth, and he shifted his position, and wiggled his el-bones, and knocked the two balls against each other, and pinched up his face, concentratin. And when he threw, he let out a little noise and ran forward a couple steps, and the ball went way high in the air, so that she came straight down and didn't roll nowhere, and wasn't nowhere near the *pallino* when she stopped.

So his ball was farther away than mine, which meant he had to throw again. He dug the feet in again, and shaped, and swung the arms, and threw, high, and this time his ball ended up closer.

But I was an expert at the *botch,* even at the club they said so. I made my next ball go out and up in a high hook and come straight down so she landed hard, right on top of my son's ball, and kicked him out of the way—down in the corner of the court—and left herself sitting, still as a stone, right next to the *pallino.* So I had two points now, the two closest balls, and Peter would have to knock me out.

"N-nice, Pa," he said. "You were always a pr-pr-pro at that."

Peter tried to do a *botch* himself, and he missed. His ball flew up and out, missed by a half inch, and rolled all the way to the back. One more ball for him then. Most people at the club they would try to play it safe in this kind of a situation, rolling a ball in pretty close to keep the other fella from coming in for eight points—because the way we made our rules, you got the double score if you had all you four balls closer. He shouldn't take any chances then; he should play it careful. But Peter didn't play that way, which was the way he didn't live, which was the problem.

Roll in there close, I wanted to tell him, because it was something I knew about, bocce. Don't let me get the eight. But for some reason that night God was helping me, and I didn't say nothing, and Peter tried to *botch* again, and missed again, and left the door wide open. So I came in for the eight.

Eight–zero already, and we were going only until twenty-one.

But Peter was a good player at one time, and we went back and forth, up and down the court, and he little by little caught up. We didn't say nothing else. It was a quiet night, and cool, because it had rained during the day. And although every once in a while a car went by on Proctor Avenue, or you could hear Patsy Antonelli talking to Jupiter next door, or a person talking on the phone in Jimmy Haydock's house, you had the feeling somebody had thrown a blanket over the neighborhood and it was the time for sleep. The bocce balls knocked against each other with the sound of two bowling balls knocking; or they bumped against the wood sides of the court like the sound of a drum; or one of us would say the score in a small voice—fifteen–eleven, eighteen–fourteen, twenty–eighteen— but those noises were wrapped up in the blanket of the quiet of the night. And it was the same way with the troubles between us. For the time we played—maybe thirty minutes, maybe twenty-five— those troubles came knocking out in the air; you could feel them. The arguments we had all our life with each other. The ways we were different. But for the time we were playing, those troubles were wrapped up in a feeling I had all my life wanted to have in that yard and that house: the feeling of a family just going through time together, just being together in peace.

In the end we were twenty-twenty, and I should have just put the balls down and shook my son's hand and left it a tie . . . but that wasn't what you did in this world. You had to win, and in bocce you had to win by two. So I threw the *pallino* out, short, and Peter shaped and shaped and shook his elbones and pinched his face, and threw his first ball, a pretty good one. We made our shots then, good against good, one knocking the other out of the way a little bit, trying for a little closer, trying to win. When Peter had thrown all his four balls, and I had thrown three, he had the two points he needed to win—two of his balls squeezing one on either side of the *pallino,* with my own balls more far down the court. What I should have done then, if I had took one more second to think about, would be throw my last ball a little bit wrong and let the son win for once, over the father. It was an easy thing to do, and sometimes even at the club I did it to let somebody else win for a change (Dommy Bucci, for instance, who couldn't play worth beans). But what I did instead was try a dangerous shot, but the only thing you could do to win: I rolled my ball in solid and bumped the *pallino* straight on, straight forward, so Peter's two balls popped away a little bit on either side, and the *pallino* got chased by my ball a little way farther down the court and stopped there. Two points for the father, end of the game.

Peter made a little cheer for me, squeezed his hand on my shoulder, told me, "You're the champ, P-Pa. You always wa-were the b-bocce champ."

And I said, "You played good too. I was lucky." But I could see the quiet feeling we had between us run off in the night like Zizza's cat when you opened the outside light.

"I'm going in and see M-Mama before she fall-fall-falls asleep" was the only thing the son could say now, even though there were five hundred other things we shoulda been saying. Peter took his jacket off the fence where it was hanging—a nice jacket, expensive— and spent a little time dusting it off and straightening it out before he put it on, and I could see now that the jacket made him feel a little bit better inside when he was wearing it. And when I understood that small thing, I could all of a sudden see past the act my son always put on for me, and I could feel towards him then, for those few minutes, a little bit like a father was supposed to.

I said, "Good. That's what she wants more than anything, to see you." But it didn't matter now because, without really wanting it, I knocked my son down a long time ago and never let him stand up all the way.

When Peter picked the flowers off the picnic table and carried them inside, I sat down in the chair I had sat in with Lucy, a couple nights before, and felt like I was sitting in a cold lake of my sins. There was no moon yet, just an empty black sky with a few little stars stuck in it, and all of space there for you to think about.

I thought to myself you were suppose to try to be a good person in this life, and I had tried to do that and had worked it out maybe not so bad. You were suppose to try to be good at things: your job, bein a husband, bein a father, little things like playing bocce and keeping the yard nice. I tried hard as I could to do those things. But now I got an idea that all my life I was concentrating so much on bein good myself that I didn't make enough room around me for other people to try to do what they had to. With Peter especially I didn't make enough. And the idea of that was like the feelin I had listening to Lucy suffer. Only really, for me, a little bit worse.

37

My mother was sitting up straight in the recliner, facing the television, and at first I thought she was pretending not to recognize me, as a joke. I came in with the flowers and laid them across her lap, a huge bouquet of gladioli, the kind she loved most, but she only looked down at them like they were sheets of rolled-up newspaper, then up at me like I was the paperboy, then back at the Red Sox running around on the TV screen, no volume. The nurse was nearby, on our divan, fiddling with some bottles and pretending not to eavesdrop on us.

"Ma-Mum, it's m-me."

"You're late," she said.

I tried to laugh, but the voice my mother said it in belonged to a time I could not laugh about, and so my laugh came out as a squeak, and the nurse looked at me like I was a transvestite.

"L-late? What do you me-mean, Mum? I'm right on ta-time, and I brought you the biggest bunch of flowers you ever saw" (and a York peppermint patty, which I had left outside in the paper bag along with something for my father), "and you did-did-did—you didn't even la-look at them."

"Late," she said, eyes straight forward. The nurse stood up and went into the kitchen, to put on a pot of tea, but kept her ears on us from over the countertop. "Joanie comes on time."

I tried the laugh again, another squeak. "J-Joan-Joanie's not here, Ma. I'm here. P-Peter."

She stared at the TV. Hot dogs cooking on a grill in someone's perfect back yard, the father in his perfect apron and the kids smiling at him and holding up perfect open buns, and the beautiful dog, and the beautiful wife coming out with a tray and a pitcher of lemonade—they'd put my dream life on the television between innings.

"It's the medicine," the nurse volunteered over the counter. "The pain medicine affects her this way when she first takes it. It will pass in a few minutes, and then she'll sleep. Don't let it upset you."

"Mum, it's me. Peter. How you d-doing today?"

"You never could and you still can't," my mother said. "And I've told you a hundred times about it, and it doesn't make any difference. All you do . . . is . . . go with your girlfriends in bikinis. Don't think I don't know about it."

"I only have one g-girl now, Ma. Els-Els-Elsie Pa-Patterson. I brought her here a few times, don't you remember? She has fr-freckles, she's pretty? She has a sa-sa-sa-sa-sa-son of her own who's the nicest kid you could ever imagine. I'll bring her next time. She's b-been asking for you."

I heard the screen door slap and my father's feet on the linoleum, but I did not look up. The house was beginning to close in on me in a certain way it had closed in on me when I was a boy. The walls were pressing against me like the eyes of the nurse, the eyes of the city, and the air was going very dry—and I had a spark of a memory then of getting up from the dinner table one afternoon after my mother had been going on and on in this same voice, and walking straight out the door, crying, even though I was too old to cry—which made it worse—and riding my bike down to the beach and out onto the end of Holt's pier and thinking that if I tied my bike to my leg and jumped in it would solve everything. . . . All sorts of memories were whirling in my brain now, as if the medicine my mother had taken was affecting us both. Billy Ollanno's visit, Elsie being tapped on the shoulder by Xavier the legbreaker, me buying every lottery ticket Nicole had in the store and ending up almost exactly where I started, almost to the dollar. Nine hundred dollars for Eddie now instead of the seventeen I owed. Who were you supposed to pray to about that?

The teapot started whistling.

"All the girls," my mother said again, like I had been Wilt Chamberlain in my younger days. "Don't think I don't know about it."

"You need to take your nap now, Lucy," the nurse said, over the counter, as if my mother was a little kid. I shot her a look, but she was in charge here, sure of herself, getting ready to go off her shift.

I reached down and took my mother's arm, the skin all wrinkled and spotted and cool. She pulled herself up to standing without any hesitation, grunting once but coming straight up. She shuffled her feet a little bit and started off down the hall, her fingers cutting into my forearm like claws. My father was following us, then the nurse, a whole slow parade of misery.

When we reached the back bedroom, my mother shuffled her feet again, made a kind of pirouette, and dropped herself down on the bed so fast I lost my hold on her. The nurse was watching, my fa-ther—I had drifted away for an instant and almost let her fall flat. She was pulling her nightie up over her knees now, showing everything. I bent over and tried to turn her back towards the pillow, hoping the nurse would maybe figure out that now was the time to lend a hand.

We ended up with me leaning over my mother like I was a wrestler about to pin her to the mat, and my mother yanking her nightgown up way too high, and my father standing a little to one side, trying to get hold of her hands and stop her, and me knocking my hip against the table so that three or four small bottles of medicine rolled off and bumped down onto the carpet. My mother's head went back at a bad angle onto the pillow. My father pulled the sheet up over her legs. She kicked it away.

"We'll s-set the flowers up in here for you, Ma," I told her.

"Your arms . . . skinny."

"Lucy," my father said then, sharp. "Peter came to see you." And his voice seemed to reach in through the medicine and wake my mother into her true self. For all of half a minute she looked straight at me, seemed happy to see me, seemed to be struggling with her throat and lips to make a few words come out.

This is you, I said to myself, this is the real you.

"Peter," she said, in a pleased voice. "Peter, I'm so—" and then it was exactly like her face had been pushed back underwater with the eyes and mouth still open.

The nurse went through the motions of arranging the sheet and blanket. She straightened up the medicines on the table, then left us.

My father and I sat by the side of the bed, watching my mother fade deeper and deeper into sleep, not looking at each other. I made myself reach out and take my mother's cool hand, though it seemed to me I might only be doing it for my father's sake, for show.

The train of my mind was taking me in a certain direction then. I couldn't help myself, I walked a trail of remarks back and back. *All the girls . . . skinny arms . . . pimply face . . . ugly man's body. . . . Don't love you . . . never wanted you.* Over and over like a record playing, some days. And other days nothing but love shining like a bright light every time you stepped into this house. How could a person be two people?

I had asked Father Dom about it once—what could I do to change it, to fix it, to make my mother stop when she got started down that road.

"You can't do anything, Peter," he said. "All you can do is, in your own life, try to live without protection."

It made no sense to me.

"Your mother's protecting herself when she does that," he said.

"From what? From me? What ca-could I do?"

"From being hurt. Inside."

"But who hurt her?"

"Nobody in particular," he said. And then: "I'll talk to you about it more when you get older, I promise I will, but for now just remember that some people have something like a bruise inside them. A wound. They can't let that wound ever be touched again, it's that sore, so they find different ways to cover it over, and those ways hurt other people sometimes—and the cycle starts all over again with somebody else's bruise. All you can do is try in your own life to break the cycle. Not let yourself have too much of that protection, if you can. Let yourself be nailed up on the cross."

At the time it made zero sense to me. Sure, Dommy, I thought, what are you, nuts? Let myself be nailed up on the cross? You've been into the altar wine a little too much again.

Now, though, sitting there staring at my mother—her body too weak to do any protecting of anything—I remembered what Dommy said and it almost seemed right to me. There was some real wisdom buried in all his religious rigmarole, but when I tried to take a solid hold, it just flew away from me. A smart Catholic bat in the house, impossible to catch.

After fifteen minutes, when it was obvious my mother wasn't going to come to again for quite a while, we leaned over the bed one at a time, kissed her forehead, and told her we loved her.

In the yard again, it was like my father and I had been carrying a sheet of plate glass between us all our life and one of us had just now taken a wrong step and smashed it to pieces against the doorknob. Such a feeling of failure in the cool air. Nothing to say, and everything we weren't saying lying in bright bloody splinters around our feet. You had to take a step eventually, but neither of us wanted to.

"That's how she is now, sometimes," my father said finally. "She's sufferin. It don't mean nothin against you."

The words hung there in the air and unrolled for me another memory. My mother in the house saying things about my nose and my hair and Alfonse and my girlfriends. And my father standing out here with me like this, possibly even in this very same spot at the edge of the little patio we had built together, the two of us just standing here side by side, not touching, and him saying, "It's my fault, what's goin on in this house now. It's me, not you mother. . . . Someday I'll tell you. Someday we'll have a talk."

But the someday never came; the talk had never happened. Not with him and me, anyway. What happened instead was that all of us had signed a kind of unwritten contract, in secret. Push forward, push forward, we would all of us just push forward and pretend to be building our nice pretty lives on a foundation of fibs. . . . Not that there hadn't been good times in this house. I could remember a hundred good times, a thousand. But in some way I could not understand, those good times had been half poisoned by this lie we made, this way we had of not talking about things that should have been talked about.

Papa followed me to my car, but we were both beaten down somehow. We'd had our few minutes of peace playing bocce, which was something. But now a lot of lousy history seemed to be floating up around us again in the night, loud as a teenager's music. We shook hands all right—there was some kind of iron, unbreakable love there between my father and me, in spite of everything we couldn't say to each other. "You came anyways, that's what's important," he said. And I looked at him a second and didn't even try to get a word out.

I rolled the T-bird out of the driveway, then pulled halfway back in. My father took a step towards me, with this look on his face like I was going to say the thing to him we both knew we should have been saying, or like I was at least going to tell him I loved him, which I hadn't done. "There's a p-p-paper b-bag on the picnic table, Pa," I said, into that look. "Sa-something inside for you. I forgot. Cigars."

"For what?" he said, which was what he always said when we gave him a gift. Christmas, birthday, Father's Day, always the same line: *For what you did this, spendin you money?*

"Vito," my mother would tell him, putting her hand on his arm and giving a little push, "it's a present. From the children."

"For what?"

I leaned my head out the window, already with the car in reverse. "A smoke on me," I told him. Which was the best I could do at that moment.

On the way back to the condo, my mind was spinning like I'd just stepped off the Wild Mouse at the old Revere Beach, the Revere Beach I knew as a kid. I thought about going to see Elsie, after all, or about driving down to Saint Anthony's and having a chat with Father Dom, get my head straight again. I should have, too, because what I ended up doing instead was driving into the Leopard Club lot, finding Xavier Manzo's black 280Z there near the side door, and letting the air out of his two back tires—a joke, sort of, a kid's trick, kind of thing I hadn't done in twenty-five years.

Saturday

38

I must have walked again in the middle of the night without knowing it, because when I woke up I was sitting in Vito's chair in the living room, with the blanket over my legs and the rosary in my hands. Through the picture window I watched the night change into morning, houses showing themselves more and more there on the other side of the street—slanted roofs, open windows, cars in the driveways—and the birds waking up one by one and sending their different pieces of news out into the air. *Hail Mary*, I said. . . . *Fruit of Thy womb . . . Hour of our death, Amen.*

By the time I finished my prayers, sunlight was coming in strong through the window and cars were starting to go down Proctor Avenue, one after the next. I let my eyes move toward the front door, hoping to see Peter there, smiling, making his jokes. But he didn't come last night the way he promised he was going to, and he wasn't there now, so I prayed for him another few minutes—my heart to his heart to God's; then I turned my mind to Joanie.

Later, after some fuss with the medicine and some worse fuss in the bathroom, the nurse put me in the wheelchair and rolled me up to the kitchen table. Vito sat down and wished me good morning in Italian, something he had done every morning since the day after the night we were married. He took a sip of his coffee, a little milk and no sugar, like always. It was half past nine by the clock, late for him and his *buon giorno.*

"Did Joanie come yesterday?" I asked him, because I had seen the flowers.

He nodded his head and wiped the coffee from his lips with his thumb and one finger. "She was quiet. She didn't want to make you wake up."

"I dreamt about her all night, Vito. Over and over. She was jumping rope, she was crying. She was racing down the street in her car."

The nurse set up a long line of pills on the tablecloth—in a straight row, the way I liked them.

"She's doing a special project now for the TV, two months," Vito said.

"What kind of project?"

"She didn't say."

"Was I sleeping when she was here, or was I talking crazy?"

"Sleeping."

"Don't fib to me, Vito, anymore."

"Talking crazy."

"It's the medicine you take for the pain, Missus Besalacqua," the other Negro nurse said, in that kind voice she had, almost like she was singing when she spoke. I tried to look up and see her, but my neck muscles wouldn't work anymore, and I ended up lifting my eyes and seeing only as far as her chest. She worked weekends, this nurse, if I remembered it right, and she wasn't lazy. She made the Cream of Wheat soupy, though. Carmen. "I seen lots of people like that on this medicine. They say all kind of foolish things. You're not too bad as far as it goes. Some of them start swearing like the Devil himself."

"Which medicine does it?"

Carmen put her finger on the tablecloth beside a blue pill no bigger than the button that holds down the collar of a man's shirt.

"I don't want any more of them, then," I told her.

"You wouldn't stand the pain, Missus. Even if you don't take this one here, you'll see. A little while now and the pain will be too much for you because you gone the whole night without taking it."

I lifted up my arm and, with the nail of one shaky finger, knocked the pill out of line, almost off the edge of the table.

"Peter was here last night," Vito said, over the top of his coffee cup, because he would say anything these days to keep the peace.

"And was I crazy in front of him too?"

"You were just sleeping. Deep. You set the world's record yesterday with the sleep."

"I'm having feelings about him now, Vito, that he's in trouble. I had a dream about him the other night; you just reminded me. That I was saying terrible things to him and he was afraid of me. It was as real a dream as this minute."

"You never did that," Vito told me.

"I never did?"

"Never. I'd tell you if you did."

"Would you?"

"Sure I would. You never did it."

"Did he say anything when he came?"

"He said he's workin, like always. He brought you the flowers; you didn't see them?"

I knew Joanie brought the flowers, but I went along with it so Vito wouldn't feel bad. "That's all, working? No trouble?"

He was shaking his head and looking a little bit to the side. "Just workin, like always."

"So how come he never visits when I'm awake? Is he afraid of me?"

Vito reached over and stirred my Cream of Wheat to keep it from making a film on top. "He calls," he said, but he said it like a boy making things up the way he wanted them to be.

"And why does he call but he doesn't come by to visit the way Joanie does? Tell me."

"He came last night. I told you."

"But why does he wait two weeks between coming?"

The eyes again, the sad look. I tried to move my arm and give him a little push in the shoulder to show I was only playing a game, but my arm wasn't working now the way it had worked for seventy-one years. It had gone into retirement, that arm. When I sent it the signal to move, it only twitched, so that I knocked the pills out of line with the edge of my hand. Vito looked at them, then across the table at me, like he wanted to say something else but was ashamed to.

39

After a little while, Vito finished his coffee and said he was going out in the yard. Carmen wrapped a shawl around my shoulders and rolled my chair onto the patio. From there, I could watch my husband work in the garden the way I used to work, and feel the sun on the skin of my hands and arms—all bruised now, like I'd beaten someone up with them.

Vito worked very different in his old age from when he was young. What used to take him a few minutes then took him now half an hour.

Not long after he went down on his knees in the garden, the pain came up through the medicine and took hold of me and made me forget about everything. Vito, the children, my house—everything else disappeared. It started at the level of my belt and went up my backbone and down along my legs like someone had struck a burning-red tuning fork in my womb and the sound was echoing all through the bones. Wave after wave of fire going through the bones, through the flesh and across the skin, burning. I closed my eyes and tried not to make any sound Vito would hear. On and on and on it went, squeezing a rough hand around the softest inside parts of me, burning.

And then, at last, I could feel the ripples passing down into my fingers and toes, the heat of it growing less, fading away. And when it was gone, my mind went soft and blank for a minute and then clear and sharp as the sky. I could see Vito walking out of the garden toward me, the buttons at the neck of his long-sleeve underwear shining like three rhinestones in the sun. There was sweat on the bald top of his head, and he had one pepper in the basket, a green miracle, which he set on the table like a gift.

"I'm gonna go wash up and then walk down to confession, Lucy," he said. "Will you be okay? Do you have the pain?"

"I'm feeling all right now, Vito."

"You been out here a long time."

"I'm all right."

"Father Dom is coming up for lunch tomorrow after mass, don't forget."

I asked him what I should cook, and it came out the way I meant it to, and his face broke open in a smile at first, and then my little joke seemed only like another stone in the heavy sack he was carrying. The smile fell away. He wiped a sleeve across his eyebrows.

"And Alfonse too," he said, after a minute, like he was afraid to say it. "They're bringing food from Maggio's. I told them you might sit with us a little while or you might not, dependin how you feel. Okay?"

I told him fine. And when he leaned down and kissed me and was walking away, I said, "Don't be sad about anything, Vito." And it made him stop still, half turned away from me. He started to say something—I could see his Adam's apple move, and his lips go apart—but nothing came out. After a minute he kept going toward the house.

40

For me, walking anywhere in Revere was the same as walking through my own life. There wasn't one street where a friend of mine didn't use to live, or a brother or sister or a cousin, or that didn't have something I had built from scratch or fixed up. On the way to the church I went past some of the jobs I did many years ago: a nice set of steps with a fancy railing at the corner of Cummings Street, the cedar shingles on Gino Aucella's two-story gambrel near the end of Proctor Avenue, a whole house I made on the corner of Broadway. They were pretty much the same way I left them. Windows, gables, soffits, trim, new wings I built with wifes who were pregnant looking over my shoulder—everywhere I went in Revere I saw things that made me think about those days, riding around in my truck with my tools and my wood and my boxes of nails, a young man, strong, with his business and his family going along pretty good. I built things; on the surface, that was my life. That and Lucy, my brothers and sister, the children. On the surface.

But at night, after dinner and after telling stories a little bit with Joanie and Peter when they were still young enough to want to hear the stories I had to tell, at night I would try to spend at least one hour reading books. It was slow for me, reading the English, but after all day of hammering and cutting and moving around like a machine, I liked that slowness. I read the history books, stories, the lives of people who had been famous—whatever Father Dom told me I should read.

Sometimes, if it was a special book, like Nicolo's *Gift of Michelangelo,* I would take it in the truck with me to work and read a few pages at lunch to break up the banging of two thousand nails in a plywood subfloor, or painting the ceilings with a stiff neck, or putting the asphalt shingles on a roof, row after row in the hot sun with your knees achin. I'd turn the pages slow in the cab of my truck, alone, with a sandwich and my thermos bottle on the seat next to me, and the motor going if it was winter, and it would put my mind in a different place from where it was when I worked. If there were other contractors on the job, electricians and plumbers and plasterers, they would kid me about the pornography I was hiding in the glove box, ask me could they have a peek. And when they saw what it really was, they would laugh in a way as if a carpenter reading a book was a kind of craziness, a hornet that could swim, a priest playboy. People like that, they wanted every thing kept in a neat little box so they didn't have to strain their minds too much. To hell with them anyway.

꧁   ꧁   ꧁

Instead of taking the shortcut through the projects, I went down Broadway to Revere Street—not so many hills that way. One or two of the stores on Broadway were boarded up, but there were a lot of little restaurants where you could get a cup of coffee and some breakfast, and the banks had put new fronts on, so the city looked pretty good to me that day in the sun. Young girls stood on the corners in pants that were too tight, smoking, playing the music loud out of their boyfriends' cars. They barely looked at me and I barely looked at them, which was the way it's suppose to be. When I was young, though, I used to look at them a lot, the girls, and sometimes I would do the things that men did. That was just the way I was made. After I met Lucy I made one mistake there, too. One big mistake in forty-nine years being married. I almost forgave myself for it. Lucy forgave me, I knew that. Maybe God eventually could forgive me. I would turn my mind away from that time now, from the pain of the way Lucy was to me and the way I was to her. I would think about other things now, not that.

I made it far as the highway and rested there, waiting for the green light. From that corner you could see the tiles on the roof of Saint Anthony's—color of dry blood—and just when I was looking at them, the bell struck eleven o'clock in the tower. The sound was sharp at first; then the sharpness faded and there was an echo that reached in and vibrated up and down in your bones like God sending you a message: *Not too long now for you, Vito Imbesalacqua. Get ready now. Get everything straightened out.*

I crossed the street, swiveling my stiff neck at the bunched-up cars. I'm trying, I wanted to say. I'm trying hard as I can. It's not so easy.

41

I looked up and saw Saint Anthony's standing in front of me—big as the churches in Italy—rough brown stones laid perfect one on top of the other, and the tile roof, and the stained-glass window in the shape of the wheel of a bicycle. The only part that wasn't perfect about her anymore was the front doors, plastic doors now—so all the old people could open them, although at one time they had been real, solid oak carved with roses and a cross.

Inside, she was cool and almost dark, and the hundred rows of pews were shining soft with sunlight that came in through the stained glass. There were flowers in a nice vase on the altar. Built into the front walls there were blocks of brown Italian marble, polished like glass and cut with the names of families who had given money to help build the church. My parents' names were there. My brothers and sister—Carmine, Orlando, Tony, Bobby, Philomena—gone now. Gone over to a better place.

At Father Dom's confession box the light was on, no one waiting. I knelt down in the closest pew and made my Act of Contrition, said a prayer for Lucy, for Peter and Joanie, for Alfonse and Alfonse's wife like I always did, for Larry Masse, who just passed on. I asked God to show me if the big thing I was thinking of doing that day was the right thing, and to help me with it if it was, and not let me make a fool out of myself if it wasn't.

I pushed aside the heavy red velvet and knelt in the darkness of the confession box and waited for Father Dom to be done on the other side.

In a minute, Dommy slid the panel back. So much as it had changed over the years—his nose growing, his neck sagging—the outline of the face still held in it the same Dommy Bucci from Tapley Avenue, thirteen years old, the first friend I made when I came over on the boat. Some part of his voice was still the voice at the back door after supper on a summer night, calling you out to play in a time when the streets were made of dirt, and the lamps on the poles were the old-fashion kind with little upside-down dinner plates over them, and the men wore felt hats wherever they went.

To what other priest in this world was it better for me to make my confession?

"Bless me, Father," I told him, "because I sinned. These are my sins: It—"

But Dommy said, "How is she, Victor Bones?" right away, before I could really get going.

"She's okay, Father. In pain, but okay. . . . It has been—"

"Is she up today?"

"She's up. She was sittin outside in the sun when I left her. She told me to go take a walk for my heart. She told me she was all right. . . . It has been—"

"Is she eating anything?"

"She's eatin okay, Father. At breakfast she was eatin good. . . . It has been one week since—"

"What does Dr. Pierni say?"

"He says same as last time. Let me make my confession, Dommy, so I don't die all of a sudden and go straight down to hell."

"So make it. Who's stopping you?"

"It has been one week since my last confession. . . . I lied to my wife, telling her she never said bad things to Peter all those times when she was a little bit crazy, and telling her she's not talking nonsense now on the pain medicine when she is, and that her son isn't in trouble, even though *trouble* is like another middle name for him since he was a baby. . . . I lied to my son that it wasn't Alfonse Romano who told me he was locked up, when it was; then I told him the truth five minutes later even though I promised Alfonse I wouldn't. And I lied to my daughter that I was just going out to get a cigar when I saw Peter, but I wasn't."

"Vito."

"What, Father?"

"Get to the sins."

I closed my eyes and peeked around the dark places inside me, the places you can go through a whole life and not let yourself look at face-to-face. Walking down to the church on Saturday mornings, it always seemed like I was dragging a big sack of sins through the streets of Revere so everybody could see. But once I got here, inside, and kneeled down that close to my oldest friend, the most important sins seemed to run away and hide like beetles in the cellar when you open the light. I didn't think about them again until I was back out on the street, walking away, and then it was too late.

"Vito."

"What, Dommy."

"Get to the sins. It's Saturday, people are waiting. I have a tee time at Bellevue at one-thirty and I don't want to fall behind."

"Nobody's waiting, Father."

"Get to them anyway."

There was a crucifix next to my shoulder in the dark. I looked at Him. I took a big breath to get started. "I have a conceited, Dommy. I have a conceited that tells me I'm a good man."

"You *are* a good man. You're one of the best men I know."

"I have a conceited that tells me I'm a special in God's eye, me and a few other people."

"You *are* special in God's eye. But so is everyone. Some people see it and save themselves, some people don't see it and make themselves suffer, or they lead lives that are only a waste of time. Understand?"

"No, Father."

"Think of Peter and Judas, like I gave the sermon last Sunday. Both of them betrayed Jesus, right? But Peter trusted Jesus would forgive him, and Judas didn't think he could be forgiven, even though he could have been. Peter went back to Jesus. Judas went away and hanged himself. There's your difference, okay?"

"Okay."

"Understand?"

"I think so. I'm trying to."

"Go on."

I took another breath. I tried not to be afraid. "I pray for my own wife's death."

"That will come when God wants, Vito."

"I want Him to know Lucy don't have to stay around because of my sake."

"If you know it, then He knows it. Go on."

But I couldn't go on. Outside, in the pews, there were noises now, shoes knocking, people coughing and sneezing and blowing their noses like people always do in church, whether they have to or not. Some of the worst sins were coming back to me, and all of a sudden it seemed like maybe Dommy Bucci wasn't the best priest to pick for your confession after all. But there was nothing you could do about that now.

"Last night I was playing bocce with my son, late, and I figured something out. And my sin is that it took me all these years to figure it out, all these years bein not such a good father in that way."

"You're a good father, Vito. Stop it."

"Not so good, Dommy. I don't want you to say so just because you're my friend. Peter is in trouble now with bad people. He has a debt, he's been in trouble all his whole life. Lucy says I lose my faith when I talk to him and she's probably right because I didn't protect him the way I should when he was a boy. He came by the house last night, and we played a little bocce, and when we were done playing I saw all of a sudden how maybe it was me who been wrong all these years, not him."

"What are you talking about, Vito, a sin you committed forty years ago?"

"I'm talking about loving my own flesh and blood."

Dommy was quiet for a minute then on the other side of the screen, and my whole body was empty inside and cold, like it was me who was dying, not Lucy. After a while he said, "Some people are harder to love than other people, Victor Bones. If a person doesn't love himself, it's hard even for God to love them."

"But why wouldn't a person love himself?"

"There could be all kinds of reasons."

"But it would have to do with the parents, wouldn't it?"

"Not always."

I was having a little trouble breathing then, thinking about what

Lucy and me might have done different, and how our mistakes had gone down into the lives of the two children we had been responsible for and caused trouble there. I wanted to stop myself from saying what was coming next, but I had gotten that far, finally, and I worried if I stopped too long I would lose the momentin. The real sins about the kind of father I had been, they would sink back, deep, and I'd never find the courage to pull them up again. I made myself go forward. "Joanie is a good daughter, Dommy. Smart. But Joanie . . . Joanie . . ." Lucy had said something to me once about our daughter and I didn't believe her. But what she said made me pay attention, and now I thought . . . I was almost sure . . . I had wanted to say it to Dommy for a long time now.

"Go on."

"Joanie, I think . . ."

"Go on, Vito."

"She's not gonna get married, Joanie. . . . She's a pretty girl and never brings a boyfriend by the house. I think she's a woman who . . . a woman who—who loves other girls."

On his side of the screen, Father Dom was so quiet I thought he been knocked over by the huge size of the sin—either Joanie's sin for being that way or my sin for saying she was that way when she wasn't. I waited. Footsteps echoing in the big church, people coughing. Either he was struck dumb or he'd gone asleep. Which happened once before, Father Dom sagging down there in the chair in the confession box with the little light on, snoring. That time, I had to make a noise against the screen with my fingernail in order to wake him up.

But after a while I heard a rushing of cloth behind the screen, a sigh, the deep voice. "Vito."

"What?"

"Did you read the books I gave you all these years?"

"Sure I did. All of them I read."

"In those books, did you ever read that there were always men who went with men and women who went with women? Did you read what Nicolo says about Michelangelo, for example?"

"Sure I did. I didn't believe it one minute what he said. I knew he was making it up out of jealousness. I—"

"Who do you think created those men and women?"

"There's only one possible One who created them."

"Okay . . . so try to look at it like God looks. Those people, the men who love men and the women who love women, God made them that way. Maybe they are sinners, sure, but there's a lot of men who love women who are sinners, no? And a lot of women who love men. The other ones, like Joanie is and Michelangelo maybe was, they're beautiful just exactly the same in God's eye, you see?"

"When you say it, I see it, Dommy, but not on my own."

"What they have to do in life is to see that they're perfect. Once you see that, you don't really sin anymore, understand? You almost can't sin then, because you don't need anything else other than what you have already, and because you could never hurt another person once you really believe that. You see?"

"I'm trying to, Father."

"Look, there are people like Joanie in the Kingdom of Heaven. There's priests and nuns like that—or at least who have those feelings. . . . Some of those priests are people you might know. Understand me?"

"No, Dommy."

There was a long space, like Father Dom was trying to figure out the right way to make me think about it. Years ago, he told me once or twice that I became like a little boy when I went in the confession, and part of that maybe was true. I had never been the smartest person in the world, and I always believed it was better to let people give you advice, and tell you to read books, and tell you what they thought those books meant. It never hurt to let people do that, a priest especially. In the end you made up your own mind anyway.

"There's some people you might have known all your life who are that way. Understand?"

"Not exactly, Father."

"Who might have been friends with you a long time ago and then become priests."

I didn't saying nothing then. I wasn't thinking straight.

"Vito."

"What, Father?"

"There are priests you might know, who might have borrowed your new baseball glove once and lost it at the park behind the Paul Revere School, who are like that, the way Joanie is, except on the man's side, even though they didn't ever do anything about it. *Capisci?*"

I kneeled in the dark without moving even my little finger. There was the crucifix next to me. There were all the people waiting outside. "But you," I said, when I could talk finally. "But the Pope said that—"

"The Holy Father is a good man."

Someone kneeled down in the opposite side and Dommy made his voice low as natural as if you touched a button for the TV.

"But to most people about most things he has to speak as a father to children. Sometimes a father has to speak to his children in a certain way until they're old enough to understand. And sometimes they're never old enough, and you have to tell what seems to be a fib in the human sense, okay? In the human sense only. Okay?"

"Okay," I said, but inside I was thinking, You have more conceited even than me.

I was gettin ready to say a word to defend the Pope, to say he spoke for God, and however he said it must be the right way, but Father Dom—like he was all of a sudden embarrassed by what he just told me and wanted to get away from it—began racing through his prayers so fast not even the angels could follow him, the words mixing and bumping together in a fast little opera he was singing there in his throat. "For your penance," I heard finally, in English, "one Our Father and one Hail Mary for wasting God's time. *Capisci?*"

"*Capito.* . . . It was a fib you just told me now, to make me feel better about Joanie, right, Dommy?"

"That doesn't matter, Vito. We're old, you and me. What matters is what I said about how to love people. That's the specialty of old people, loving. The specialty of young people is the other thing, okay?"

"Okay, Dommy. Sure. It's just that the family I ended up making isn't the family I thought I would make, that's all."

"Don't worry about that now, Vito. Just hold on to the inside love, that's all. You follow?"

"Sure, Father." And I did follow him then. I followed him pretty good.

"Who is Peter in trouble with?"

When I said the name I heard him make a little noise like he bumped himself in the shins.

"I'll pray for both of them."

"I'm going to talk to him now. Eddie."

"Where?"

"At his house."

"Are you sure you want to do that?"

"No."

"I'll pray for you, then, and for Lucy. I'll be praying the whole time I'm playing golf. Every time after I hit the ball I'll say an Our Father for you and a Hail Mary for her, all right? Go in peace."

"Okay, Dommy," I said. "Tomorrow we'll see you?"

But the screen had snapped closed and I could already hear a woman starting to confess her sins from the other side. I closed my ears on it.

I left the confession and walked to the altar rail with my hands held together, my eyes low, my shoes making tapping noises that flew up the marble columns and knocked back and forth against the high ceiling there. I was married in this church, my children were baptized here, my brothers and sister buried from here. Like everywhere I went now, it was filled with the loud noises of memories for me, the hymns of an old man's mind. For a minute, though, in the middle of all those sounds, my mind was at peace.

I made my penance and tried to hold my attention still in the middle of me with a kind of prayer my mother taught me sixty-five years ago. When a thought came into your mind—about Lucy or Joanie or Peter or Father Dom—you just said a small piece of the prayer to the Blessed Mother and watched the thought float away. Mary would know a thing or two about the way the parents suffered, I told myself. She would know.

I said a prayer for my confessor, like always, made the sign of the cross, nodded to the three brown marble blocks with IMBESALACQUA cut into them, and stood up.

I lit a candle for Lucy, then one each for Peter and Joanie. I stood in front of the row of small fires, asking God to give my son and my daughter peace in whatever way He decided was right. I thought of Father Dom again, prayed again, kept my thoughts pure.

My prayers were finished; the candle fires were wrestling with themselves. To hold it tight in my mind for the job that was ahead of me now, I peeked up at the mural that had been painted on the ceiling above the altar. It made me think of a special painting I saw in Italy, something I had forgotten about lately, and which made me happy to remember. Bellini was the name of the painter.

We took one trip in our lifes, me and Lucy. On our forty-year wedding anniversary, Joanie and Peter gave us a trip to Italy—Rome, Venice, Florence—a beautiful vacation with a company from the North End. Ten days. By then I had already read the book on Michelangelo the first time, and I stood in the Sistine Chapel with my head bent back and my mouth open, staring up at something so perfect you couldn't talk about it. Then, later, we walked into Saint Peter's Church and stood in front of the Pietà, the only sculpture Michelangelo ever signed his name on. Twenty-five years old and he could take a piece of marble and cut it in such a way so you look at it and feel a little bit of love for yourself in there. After that, Michelangelo stopped signing his name on anything, because he knew who he was already and didn't need to tell nobody else. And if Nicolo's book was right, and if Father Dom was right, then Michelangelo had been a man who loved men. A man who loved men and he was close enough to God to make something like the Pietà, like the Sistine Chapel. That showed you something, didn't it?

I slipped a folded-up dollar bill in the metal box, took the thin wooden stick in my hand, and moved the fire from Joanie's candle to one that was empty. Step by step you said yes to more things and no to less things; that was the way to do it. If you practiced enough, in the end, when you had to say yes to the hardest thing, you could do it without so much trouble because you been trying it with smaller things your whole life. That was the lesson Mary had to teach, wasn't it? Wasn't that what the Pietà made you think when you looked at it, saying yes to what you wanted to say no to more than anything? Sure it was.

I walked back down the side aisle and came upon my Alfonse there, kneeling in a pew behind a row of six ladies with blue hair. Alfonse made a signal to me, and we met in the back, next to the bowl with the holy water in it, and had a little conference there, whisperin.

"You talked to Peter?" he asked me.

"I tried. Joanie told me he has a debt, maybe twenty thousand, I think she said. I'm gonna go see Eddie now and ask him to forgive part of it."

"No, no, Uncle. He'll never see you. He'll never admit Peter owes him money. That's too risky for him now. And you'll never find him—he moves around in different houses. Please don't do that."

"I'll go to his house on Mercury Street, where his parents lived. That's where he would be on a Saturday. I knew his brother Aldo, who the communists killed in Korea; he'll talk to me."

"You'll do Peter more harm than good at this point, Uncle. It's not just an ordinary debt now, it's a principle. Eddie feels insulted."

"So the more people who hear about it the better, then. The less chance he's gonna do anything to hurt Peter."

"Just the opposite, Uncle. It will look like Peter is going around the city telling everyone about Eddie and his business. Wait a few days, give me time to try something first. I talked to my friend in the FBI today; we have a plan; give me a little time."

"But maybe it can't wait, Capitano."

"I think it can still wait a little bit. Let me try and make sure before I see you tomorrow, okay? If it can't wait I'll call you tonight and tell you."

Alfonse was leaning towards the confession, a man in a rush, and I wondered if he played the golf on Saturdays, too. He knew good as I did that it was the traditional thing for the father to go and talk face-to-face about the debt. That was the way they always did in the old days, and sometimes the debt was forgiven for a favor you would do later, and sometimes it was cut down. What was he telling me not to go for, then? What was in his mind?

But Alfonse was one of those people it wasn't so easy to tell what was in his mind. He was smiling one of his sad smiles, hiding himself in the face, so I swallowed what I wanted to say to him.

"Go say you confession, Capitano," I told him, because I knew what I was gonna do by then anyway, for my son, and nothing nobody said was gonna stop me. "We'll see you tomorrow."

42

When I woke up on that Saturday, the first thought I had was, Run. Just lock up the condo, get in the car, and drive out of the city of Revere forever. Gone.

But after I'd been standing in the shower a few minutes I started picturing Elsie and Austin sitting at Stevie's Place, waiting. I started imagining what it would feel like for her to be stood up in front of her son—after everything else she'd been through the last few days. There was still a whole chorus of voices telling me to abandon ship, but I kept my mind focused on Elsie and Austin and ended up getting myself dried and dressed and stepping out into the hallway no more than four or five minutes late.

It was no picnic, walking out into the open air, knowing what I knew about Eddie and Xavier and what they knew about me, thinking about being with Eddie face-to-face that night. Still, there I was, out on the sidewalk for everyone to eyeball. And I was out there with a little bit of style, it seemed to me, walking along the boulevard like any other successful businessman about to treat his family to a late breakfast on a gorgeous Saturday morning. I held a memory of the old Revere Beach in my mind's eye, the Dodgems, the Wild Mouse, the Cyclone, the smell of fried dough and pepper steak, the families who used to come down here by the tens of thousands on a warm Saturday morning like this and spread out their blankets and chairs. It was my little kingdom, this three-mile stretch of sand, one of the jewels I held inside me—the beach, my family, the city of Revere. That was what kept me smiling now, walking tall.

Finesse it till they can't guess it.

The instant I pushed through the door into Stevie's Place I knew I'd made the right decision, not running. There was such a look of happiness on Elsie's face. And the boy, though he tried not to show it, was relieved for his mom, you could see that.

I kissed her, gave Austin's hand a firm shake, and sat down with my spine straight and my shoulders back so as to be a good example to him in his growing years. "Eight m-minutes late by the clock," I said to them. "Next week it'll be seven minutes. The week after that, six. By Christmastime I'll be here t-twenty m-m-m-minutes early."

They laughed. Cindy the waitress brought me a coffee without asking, but there was something a little bit peculiar in the air, something I could not quite get ahold of. I looked around at Stevie's boxing trophies, the marble-topped bar where he served his famous pizzas, the big windows facing out onto Revere Beach Boulevard. Something was a little bit off.

For the first few minutes Elsie watched me practically without blinking, holding her water glass tight with both hands like I was about to burst into flames and she would have to be the one to extinguish me. Austin seemed upset about something too, which wasn't the usual chemistry between us. He kept looking down at his juice and up again with his big sad eyes, fiddling with his earring, hooking a lock of hair behind his ear exactly the way his mother did, though you would never tell him that, naturally. "You," I said, pointing with my coffee mug. "A pee-pee-pee-piece of advice from an older man: Don't get in the hab-habit of keeping your girlfriends waiting, understand?"

"Right, Pete."

"Listen to me when I ga-give-give advice," I said, carrying on with the smart-uncle voice because I didn't want silence, didn't want questions about last night or about Xavier, not now. "The fe-female of the species is something I know about, okay? L-look who I ended up with. Pretty good, don't you think?"

Now Elsie was smirking, Austin smiling behind his orange juice. They were probably only worried about my meeting with Eddie, I decided. I would keep things light, then, keep their spirits up.

With a little this and a little that, I managed to move the conversation along pretty strong until the food arrived. I told them about the time we'd been on maneuvers in the Gulf of Mexico with the navy and had flown out a mile in the choppers, then been dropped down into the water from thirty feet up. Fatigues, boots on, the whole scenario. "The idea was to tr-train you not to pa-panic in the ocean swells, see, to test out your swimming muscles, your n-n-nerve. But hell, I figured I'd been testing out my swimming muscles and my n-nerve my whole life right here in Revere, so I let the other guys start kicking and stroking and I just flo-flo-floated a while, getting my bearings, trying to find a better way. After a minute or so, I took off my boots and tied them to my belt, snug, and did a n-nice easy breaststroke all the way in to shore. Most of the other guys got there ahead of me, naturally, but when the sarge started to ch-chew me out I told him, Hey, look at these guys and look at me. Who's in better shape right this minute to fight the Va-Viet Cong? Who's wheezin and who's laughin here? Who was making all kinds of noise when they got in near the beach, and who was quiet? After that, whenever anybody fig-figured out a smarter way of doing something, they called it the Imbesalacqua M-method, after me. Still call it that in my oh-old outfit, from what I hear."

"It was cool in the army?" Austin asked me.

"What cool? Twenty years later it's c-cool. While you're there, it's like somebody gets together the worst food in the world and the worst clothes in the world, and gives them to you every day for two years as a g-goof gi-gift, and makes you live with a thousand other sweaty guys in a hot little m-metal hangar in the middle of nowhere. Plus, Ve-Vietnam was going on then, and two of my cousins and Al-Al-Al-Alfonse and my ba-buddy Leo Markin were over there, so I was worried about them constantly."

"Why didn't you end up going?"

"Why? Because they assigned me into some jee-jeep-repairing school, and I fumbled and screwed up there a little b-bit, and by the time I graduated they were t-taking guys home, not sending them. My usual last-minute luck . . . Listen, forget the army. Go to work, start a biz-biz-business, smart kid like you. You can come in with me if the m-market ever turns around."

When the food came, I tried to draw the boy out of his shell a little bit, tossing him the usual questions adults ask people that age to cover the fact that their own dreams haven't worked out too fantastic. School, sports, music, the usual stuff—but I was watching Elsie out of the corner of my mind the whole time, trying to gauge how bad Xavier had scared her. It wasn't that unusual for her to be the quiet one and me the talker, especially at our Saturday morning breakfasts. Sometimes when I got Austin going on rock groups or the purpose of staying in school, or the Bruins or Celtics or Red Sox, she would just sit back and work through her oatmeal and fruit salad in a contented way, chipping in a word now and then. After all, she and Austin had the whole rest of the week to talk with each other, and it seemed to soothe her to let us knock things back and forth, the two guys. Between her father and her Skutchy husband, she hadn't had a huge amount of wonderful luck with the male side of the coin, so it didn't take very much to please her in that department. Lucky for me.

I watched her that morning, though, and I felt something different floating near the table. Elsie had showered and done up her hair, and she looked especially beautiful to me then, not just in the physical sense. It was a little bit more real to me at that minute just what I would be giving up if I ran, what kind of friend I had here in this woman. I knew she was angry at me for being the kind of idiot I was, for bringing the Xavier Manzos of this world into her circle of acquaintances. But angry or not, disappointed or not, afraid or not, she was still there. And so was I. Some sweet domestic hummingbird was flying around near the table that morning, in spite of everything, and for once I wasn't even thinking of waving it away.

I could not seem to stop talking, though, to slow down.

"What, you think Va-Vaughn for MVP? You're n-nuts, my friend. Vaughn's a flash in the pan, you'll see. Valentin's my MVP this year. You know how hard it is to play shortstop and hit home runs?"

"You're just saying that cause he's white."

"What? Else, you hear that? T-teh-tell the young m-man here how many black and Spanish friends I had in the service. Tell him about the Vietnamese guy I s-saved."

"He did," she told him, and I listened close to her voice and could tell nothing. "Just don't get him started on the subject."

"Without Vaughn and Canseco they wouldn't have been any-where near first place last year," the boy told me. "You can't win now without power hitters. You can't draw crowds, and without crowds you can't get the money to pay for the pitching you need."

"M-maybe," I admitted, letting the kid score a point or two in front of his mother. "C-could be. I'm a little prejudice towards shortstops, I guess, probably, because I played some shortstop my-self when I was your age. Nothing special, you know, but I did make the All-Star team in La-Little League, and they had a banquet after-wards, and I got to shake T-Tony Conigliaro's hand and every-thing—a great player, Tony was, you wouldn't remember him. . . . I have a fr-friend who thinks he can score us three tickets for the play-offs, by the way, if you're int-int-interested."

Cool or not, sixteen or not, there was a spark in Austin's eyes. It was the truth, too, about the tickets. There would be three tickets waiting for us in October. If the Red Sox made it to October. If I did.

We went all the way through the meal like that, me stringing to-gether one story after the next, Elsie watching, Austin struggling to hide whatever it was he was hiding behind those serious eyes of his. It was a miracle the way this kid could pour food into that skinny body. Besides the stack of pancakes, he vacuumed up half his mother's homefries, a grilled English, washed everything down with three coffees, two orange juices, three or four glasses of ice water. After a while he had to pee—no wonder. He excused himself and went off towards the bathroom, and Elsie and I were alone at the table then with the last crumbs of our breakfast between us, and it wasn't easy.

"I'm s-sorry I didn't come by la-last night," I said. "I was too nervous, that's all. I went to see my pa-pa-parents and after that it was so late. . . ."

Elsie's face was changed now, and I understood she'd been wearing a mask for her boy, pretending not to be half as angry as she was. Which was fine.

"You know how I am, right, Else? I'm s-sorry, really. And I'm sorry about what happened to you at the office. Sorry's not the word. I'm . . . a-sh-shamed beyond anything I've ever done."

"Are you going to meet with Eddie tonight?"

"Ab-absolutely."

"I don't know if you should, Peter."

"I should, of course I should. What else is there?"

"But you don't even know what you're going to say, or if you have enough money—"

"Sa-say-say-saying things has never been my problem, Else. I'll know what to s-say when the time comes, believe me."

"I feel like you're pushing me away. Or showing off or something. . . . I don't know. I don't mind so much usually, but this time it scares me."

"What did he d-d-d-do to you?"

"Nothing. He grabbed me, that's all."

"Grabbed you? How did he gr-grab you?"

"He grabbed my arm, that's all. And I was afraid, so I told him where you went. I've never met someone with such a . . . such a dead look in his eyes. I'm worried, Peter. I'm scared to death. I don't think you should meet with them."

"How, exactly, did he gr-grab you, that—"

"Just to turn me around. He let me go right away, he didn't hurt me."

"Elsie, l-look at me. How, exactly, did he gr-gr-grab you? Sh-show me."

She reached across the table, squeezed my shoulder for a second, then let go. About as much like Xavier as Jesus was like Hitler.

"That's all?"

She nodded. She frowned. "Austin's not here. So cut out the macho stuff, will you? What are you going to do?"

"I'm just going to meet with Xavier, that's all. Ta-touch him on the shoulder like you just touched me."

"Peter, stop."

"All right. Look . . . I've never been in a situation la-like this before in my life, okay, even me. I'm wetting my pan-pan-pants, okay, I admit it. I haven't the faintest idea what I'm going to do or s-say or what Eddie's going to do. But I'm not going to run—on them or on you. That m-much I know. Other than that . . . something will come to me, you'll see. Just stay p-positive with me now, all right?"

I saw Austin step out of the men's room, checking his fly with one hand. Elsie's mouth was shaking; she was on the verge of breaking down. I reached across the table and put my fingers on her wrist, gave her a smile. "He won't b-bother you again, that's all. I guarantee it. W-we'll be all right now, okay?" She tried to speak but couldn't manage anything else before we became a threesome again.

"So where are you guy-guy-guys off to today? M-mall rats again?" I swung my arm in the general direction of the Meadowglen Mall and knocked over a water glass, nothing in it.

"I'm taking him to the Fine Arts Museum," Elsie said, after a few seconds of swallowing tears and trying to get her breath back.

"What? You're jok—" I started to say, but she gave me such a blade of a look that I caught myself, glanced at Austin, reached across the table, and tapped him lightly on the arm. "F-f-for a minute there I didn't believe it. The kid here and culture—it didn't seem to work. But m-maybe I was wrong about you all these years. Maybe there's something else going on in there besides Gr-Green Day and Nine Inch REM and so on."

"Not Green Day anymore," Elsie reminded me.

The boy himself was squirming a little bit. "Want to come with us?" he said at last, serious as could be.

"A Bellini exhibit," Elsie said. "He was Italian."

"Bellini, huh? I knew a Bell-Bell-Bellini in Ga-Garfield School. Sebastian Bellini. We used to call him the Wrench. Kid was a c-car freak." I looked from Elsie to Austin, hoping for a smile, but there was nothing but ache on their faces, and it was all I could do not to get up and sprint for the door. I couldn't remember the last time I'd knocked over a glass at the table—I prided myself on things like that, on the way I moved, on being calm under pressure. . . . My mind kept racing off on little two-lane roads of meaningless chatter, and I kept having to catch it and bring it back, concentrate, think about my words before I said them—it wasn't like me at all. "W-well . . . I'll tell you the truth then, all right?" I said. "My father and m-m-mother were art lovers; you'd never know it to look at them, but they were. . . . And they took Joanie and me into town I don't know how many times to go to the museums. Joanie loved it, but me . . . it j-just never grabbed me. And I'll tell you the truth, Austin, all right? I re-re-re-regret it. I do. It just never t-took."

"Give it another try," Elsie said.

"Not today. I can't today."

"Why not?"

I thought at first she was just paying me back a little bit, pressing me, which was fair enough—unlike her, but fair enough given what she'd been through. But when I looked a little closer it seemed all of a sudden maybe I was wrong. Maybe she wasn't trying to pay me back at all but just sincerely wanted me to be with them. And when I saw that, and understood it, the muscles around my mouth started twitching on me, and my throat went a little choky—King of the Macho Men.

"N-not today, Else."

"Why?" the kid said. He'd picked up the ball now, Mister Museum all of a sudden.

I wavered, recovered, snapped the pen out of my shirt pocket, and flattened a clean paper napkin on the table in front of me. "All right, watch," I said. "Watch v-very close." In my wobbly, old-man's penmanship I printed: *I.O.U. Austin and Elsie Patterson, one visit to a museum within this calendar year.* Dated it, signed my name with some fancy curlicues, like I was signing a house contract.

"G-good enough?"

Austin took the napkin, stared at it a minute with his eyes wide like a funny guy in the movies, and folded it neatly into his left shirt pocket. "You'll regret this, Pete," he said, in a manly way all of a sudden. Manly, sure, but something in the smile and tone of voice came straight from his mother's vocabulary of the heart, a gesture so beautiful and natural that I could not keep myself from comparing this boy in front of me to myself at that same age. I would never, ever, have had the brains to go into the bathroom and get myself straightened out, then come back and try to smooth things over for my mother the way Austin was doing now. Just the opposite, in fact. At sixteen, I would have been blind to anything but my own pain and urges—I was still mostly that way. And so God was paying me back now for all those years of selfishness, making me squirm a little bit before my luck changed, mixing me in with bad people. It was obvious as could be.

Elsie didn't mention the money I owed her, and I didn't mention the lottery ticket stuck in the corner of her desk blotter. We sat there a while longer just winding things down, and then, at quarter after one, she started making moves to leave. As a kind of penance for being a week late with her salary, I reached out and picked up the tab, though it was usually her treat on Saturday mornings.

Elsie's turn for the bathroom. Austin and I stood out on the sidewalk in our sunglasses and stared across the boulevard at the sea. Cars hummed past in front of us in the warm air, and on the opposite side of the street, against a background of the most perfectly blue sky, Reverites were jogging, strutting, walking dogs. I wanted to tell Austin about the way the beach had looked when I was sixteen, what it felt like to come down here with your circle of friends on a Saturday night and just cruise the crowded strip . . . but all through breakfast I felt like I had been juggling about six heavy bowling pins in the air, and now the effort of the performance had caught up with me and I was all of a sudden exhausted. I couldn't seem to compose a sentence in my mind, couldn't think of a single joke, a single wise word. At last, I fell back on an old safety valve. "So how-how's your girl? What's-her-name."

"Darcy."

"How is she?"

"Fine."

"St-still together?"

Austin nodded, tucked his hair back.

"You c-care for her?"

There was a pause of all of two seconds before he said, "Sure," in his grown-up voice, the voice I liked best.

Another silence fell over us. What was Elsie doing in there, writing a poem? I felt my mind start to wander down towards the dark lower regions of the evening, a small panic swelling up, faces, scenes, the nasty promise of a ride in Eddie's limo. Out of the blue, Austin said, "You care for my mom?"

"What?"

"I said, Do you care for my mom?"

"Why are you asking me that now? Because of what hap-hap . . . because of what hap-happened at the office the other d-day?"

I glanced sideways, and although it was impossible to be sure, I thought the kid might be having some tears there behind the sunglasses, "a flood situation in the eyes," my old man used to call it. I looked out at the street so as not to make him embarrassed.

"You're gonna hate me n-now forever because of that, right?"

A little twitch of one arm, a deep breath. He was making fists with his hands, fighting himself.

"No," the kid said at last. "You're all right."

I turned and put a hand on his arm. "Listen, okay?" I coughed, cleared my throat, used the word. "On the scale of pe-people who l-love your mother on this earth, you're in f-first pl-place and the guy standing next to you is a close second, okay? Half a length ba-back, all right?"

After some swallowing and squeezing down of his eyebrows, Austin nodded. After another few seconds he said, "You ever tell her that?"

"No."

"Why not?"

"Because I'm an idiot is why not. Be-be-because the m-macho disease caught me when I was about your age and I still haven't quite re-re-recovered yet, that's why not."

He let out a choked laugh, then found the courage to take off his glasses and wipe a hand across his eyes, no pretense.

"And la-listen to one more thing," I told him, taking him by the elbow now. "I'm not a jer-jer-jer-jerk-off like your father, all right? I'm gonna set it right what hap-happened to your mom, as best I can. Hear me? I've already s-set up some revenge action and so on that I can't talk about now, and tonight I'm going to a m-m-meeting and I might end up putting away some bad people for a long time, m-making sure nothing like this ever happens to us again. Okay?"

What a stupid thing it was to say to a boy. Nobody, nobody at that age especially, wants to hear bad about his old man, no matter what kind of loser the guy is. It was an accidental hurt, but a hurt just the same, and now Austin had two things never to forgive me for.

Before I could think of a way to repair the damage, Elsie came out the door, and we were the sunglasses trio. I touched Austin once more on the arm in farewell, in apology, and put my hand on Elsie's shoulder. She had been crying, I could see that. I was making everybody cry now, messing up all the lives within twenty miles of me. "I'll c-call you as soon as the meeting is fa-fa-finished," I said, in as confident a voice as I could manage.

"Come over, Peter. Please. We'll make brownies or something. A pizza. Austin will stay in and we can talk."

"I'm not sure how late it will go. L-let me call you first, okay? I'll call, and then if you still want me to, I'll grab some pizzas at Bon-Bon-Bonadino's and come over."

She nodded, sad, tired of it now, and I put a little bit extra into the hug, holding her chest tight against me and planting a kiss on her ear. But when I let go of her I knew it wasn't even close to enough, that hug. She and Austin turned and walked down the sidewalk, and if I hadn't been so down I might have run and caught up with them then and gone into Boston just for the ride.

When I saw Elsie's car pull into the street and right away make a U-turn, I thought maybe it was because they didn't want to drive past me again. I was too pitiful to contemplate, standing there, alone, broke, a bullshit artist with bub-bub-bub-bubbles in his mouth.

They'd seen right through the breakfast act, both of them, and now I was left with that, and the rest of the day to get through, waiting for some guardian angel to come and make me an offer I couldn't refuse.

43

After my confession I walked out of the church and sat in the parking lot in the plain blue car and stared at my hands on the steering wheel. I had come to Saint Anthony's more to get Dommy's advice than to confess my sins. That was what Peter and I had done since we were teenagers—go to Father Dom and hear, straight, what other people would tell us only in a vague way, a too-polite way . . . or not tell us at all. This is where I had come when I was first choosing between the laws of the Church and the laws of my body, and when I was getting ready to leave for Vietnam, and when I first realized Sally was addicted to cocaine, and after she died—twenty or thirty times in the month after she died. This was the place I came when I found out, from my mother on her deathbed, that Vito Imbesalacqua was my father and not just a family friend. And this was where I had come now, trying to figure a way to save my father's other son.

I didn't remember whether it was in the Old Testament or the New, but there was a saying in the Bible that went something like: Just when you thought you had your soul swept out nice and clean, that was the time the Devil was most likely to sneak back into it. And so I had wanted to find out if that was what was happening here, if my big idea about saving Peter was coming from the goodness in me or from something else. Did I want him alive and cured? Or did I secretly want him to stay the way he was—always struggling, always screwing up—so I could have someone to compare myself to and feel better than? So I could be Vito's good son?

"Your motivation is the key," Dommy said. "If the motivation is sincere, then the deed, even if it's imperfect, has God's blessing."

Which was fine, motivation. Except what I wanted to ask was: How are you supposed to know, in the deepest, murkiest part of yourself, what your motivation really is for doing a particular deed? How are you supposed to get that kind of perspective?

But I hadn't asked. In the end, faith or no, good priests or no, Bible or no, you figured out certain things only in the quietest part of yourself, hidden from everybody . . . and you lived there with the consequences, either way.

I started the car and drove through the tangled traffic of Revere Street, past the funeral home, where I could see myself still, a thirty-one-year-old widower sitting all night by the casket of my twenty-nine-year-old wife, putting the question—why?—again and again and again, to a cold emptiness. I had struggled then—I was still struggling—to hold on to the idea that, beyond that emptiness there was someone or something watching out for us: Mary or Jesus or one of the saints or one of the people who had passed on. I believed in that. In spite of everything that had happened to me in my own life, all the suffering I'd seen in other lives—in spite of all that—I believed.

Even so, believing didn't always mean things would work out the way you wanted them to, not on this level. The trick, Father Dom had told me a long time ago, was not so much to keep yourself pure but to keep yourself small. To hold what you wanted like a small jewel in a small box in your shirt pocket. To see, in the huge rest of the world, what God wanted and yield to that.

That was the trick, I thought, driving towards Nicole's. And sometimes you could manage it alone, and sometimes you couldn't.

44

I stopped in at Nicole's for a take-out coffee and the Saturday *Herald*, drove by Peter's office to make sure he wasn't there, then circled back towards the beach, working it through in my mind. As I passed Saint Anthony's again and came closer to the boulevard, I decided—instead of going up to Peter's apartment as I'd planned—just to park the unmarked car out front and kill two or three hours there, waiting. A little childish, maybe, a little superstitious, but it would be putting some of the responsibility in God's hands, that way. I'd sit there for two hours with my coffee and my paper, and if there was no sign of Peter maybe that would be God's way of telling me the motivation was suspect, that I shouldn't be sticking my nose in this time.

So I pulled onto the boulevard, parked a few spaces down from the front of Peter's building, took exactly two sips of my coffee, and who should come walking out of Stevie's Place and down the sidewalk just then?

For the first few seconds I just watched him, and the watching brought up such a flood of feelings I was sure I wouldn't be able to do what I'd set my mind on doing, right motivation or not, sign from heaven or not.

If you didn't know Peter, you would have thought he was just another middle-aged guy out on some errand on a summer weekend, coming back from a walk or a very late breakfast. He had this small, stylish swing to his arms when he moved. In the army he'd learned to hold his shoulders back and his chin up, and if you didn't know him you might have thought he was someone with a fair amount of money in the bank, or a wife and kids who made him happy, or some secret knowledge about the way the world worked.

If you knew him, though, you could see something was off. A tightness in the neck, a nervousness around the eyes that didn't quite match the rest of the picture. Peter's little secret about how the world worked was starting to unravel. And he was trying, body and soul, to keep anybody from noticing.

I flashed my headlights on and off twice. He squinted, stared, kept coming, and when he realized who it was there behind the windshield reflection, you could see the confusion pushing up against his fake-confident surface. Half of him wanted to smile, relieved; you could see it. And the other half wanted to make a dash down the nearest alley. But I just waved him over like there wasn't the smallest particle of bad feeling between us, and reluctantly, proudly now, half-bitter, my friend and half brother angled over towards the car.

"Sit here with me a minute," I said, when he showed his face in the passenger-side window.

"Can't."

"Come on, Pete. I just want to talk a minute. Let's take a ride down to the circle and back. We're friends still, no matter how ticked off you are."

"I'm la-lay-late for the office," he said, but underneath the words there was the same fear you saw in the face of a nineteen-year-old with the flashlight in his eyes and alcohol on his breath. Peter was better at hiding it, a lot stronger on the inside than most people gave him credit for, but you could see what was going on plain enough.

"Don't give me a story about being busy," I said. "I went by your office four times yesterday. There was a CLOSED sign in the window all afternoon."

He stared a minute, made a move to turn away.

"Look, whatever I did, I'm sorry for it. Just take a ride with me. Five minutes."

He turned back, moved his face an inch closer, and tried to make it mean, but meanness didn't work on Peter's face. He tried to screw his eyes down tight and twist his mouth into a kind of snarl, but there was so much going on behind the mask that even the master of disguise couldn't disguise it. Little twitches here and there, a glance at the back seat—like somebody was about to jump up off the floor there and grab him by the throat.

"Calling my f-father to the station like I'm an eleven-year-old? Hav-hav-having your g-guys pull me over every time I roll two miles an hour through a stop sign in the middle of the night with no other car within twenty miles? *Whatever you did?*"

"I didn't tell anybody to pull you over, ever. Look, just sit here with me awhile. I just ran into your dad at Saint Anthony's and I want to talk to you about something. Two minutes."

He made as if to turn away again, but there was a small hesitation, an opening almost anybody else would have missed. And in that instant an idea flew into the swept-out room of my mind, an angel or a devil, I didn't know which.

"Pete," I said, like I'd been telling lies my whole life, "we're both in the same kind of trouble here."

"Same k-kind of trouble, huh?" He let his eyes run along the boulevard and the line of cars parked there before they drilled into me again. "What, you're in d-debt up to your ass with Chel-Chel-Chel-Chelsea Eddie too?"

"I'm sleeping with his wife," I said.

"Sure you are. I'm Ma-Mike Tyson."

"I mean it."

Over the years, Peter had mastered all the tricks a person could do with his face. He could twist his mouth this way and make you smile, do a little twitch with his eyebrows to make it seem like you'd just said the stupidest thing imaginable, turn on the salesman's charm like it was a second sun. Meanness aside, he could do anything with the muscles near his eyes and mouth, and he was trying to turn the mask blank now, to show nothing. But there was a flicker. A flicker of surprise at the fact that he wasn't the champion sinner and all the rest of his friends champion saints.

He didn't reach for the door handle, but after a few seconds he squatted down and rested his arms on top of the door, his chin an inch above the back of his hands. He hadn't shaved that morning—absolutely unheard of for him—and it made him seem sloppy and tough, years older. He waited a blink or two, suspicious, then: "With the beautiful Alicia? You? M-mister Clean?"

"Why would I make it up?"

"Why would you do it in the first place? What do you have, a d-death wish?"

"Maybe. I hadn't thought of that. Let's take a ride down the circle and back. Ten minutes, that's all I'm asking."

We drove to the rotary at the south end of the beach, angle-parked against the curb there, and killed the engine. Behind us was the apartment building where Sally's mother had lived until a year ago—outlasting her daughter by almost a decade—and behind that the parking lot of the Leopard Club, one of Chelsea Eddie's dens, the little hellhole of smoke and bare flesh where Billy Ollanno twittered and twitched and sold his watered-down drinks. Peter's eyes slipped towards it a minute, then away, same as me.

Eddie and his associates were just a part of our life, that's all, as much a part of the landscape of our childhood as basketball and church and this beach. We'd grown up on stories about the Mob, a whole mythology of ruthlessness passed down to us by our fathers and our uncles, by friends who'd heard things, seen things, who knew people, who were maybe a little bit involved themselves. They were a kind of Gospels in reverse, those stories, and they claimed a place in the deepest part of you, just like the real Gospels did after you'd heard them every week for your whole childhood. The parables, the lessons, the fear and death—all the truths and half-truths that surrounded what people called the Mob, the Mafia, La Cosa Nostra, the underworld—all of it slept there in your memory for years and years, rising up again only when you rubbed the wrong way against the actual reality of it. And then the mythical figures turned into a herd of devils, horror-movie monsters, only real now, hungry, half a block behind you and gaining.

"I saw your dad at confession."

Peter smirked, left hand cupping right fist, and stared straight ahead through the windshield. But on the other side of that hardness I could see the true face of my friend, and in that face, some tide was swelling up, forty years of these streets and these people and this gray sandy strip. Forty years of living by the rites of Roman Catholicism, and the imported blood rites of southern Italy, and the rites of blue-collar America. Loyalty times loyalty times loyalty. Angry as he was at me then, he could not break that code. I knew that, and I used it.

"Listen, I'm sorry about the other night. I shouldn't have called your father. But when I heard you'd been picked up, I figured that was my chance to try and talk to you about the debt. I've been hearing things for weeks now, and you've been avoiding me. So I went out to the desk and tried to say a word, and you wouldn't let me get anywhere close."

Nothing. One quiver in the muscles of his neck.

I reached out and put a hand on his shoulder for a second. He turned.

"Look," I said, "I know Eddie . . . in ways you can't imagine. You're thinking now that maybe he's just going to let you walk out on the debt because Joanie does what she does, or because your father knew him years ago, or because you're a good guy and everybody likes you, or because it isn't that big a deal to him, a few thousand bucks. But it's a wrong way of thinking, Pete, believe me. In the first place, every little transaction is life or death for Eddie Crevine now. The bosses are all in jail, and the underbosses like Eddie are all trying to position themselves for a move. For a long time the Asians have been breathing down his neck, to the point where he's having them do some of his deals and cutting them in on the action. But that's not enough for them lately. The territory that used to be Eddie's, no questions asked, is shifting, up for grabs, and just when he's trying to move *up*, not slip back. If he lets you slide on something like this, he's going to look soft. How long you think the Vietnamese are going to let a soft touch keep running the North Shore? How long you think Eddie's pals will let a soft touch swim with them?"

But Peter had turned again and was showing me only his profile, his father's nose and his mother's eyes, green eyes filled with a hundred lifetimes worth of hurt, imagined and real.

"And in the second place, the information I have is that it's not you Eddie cares about so much, it's Joanie."

He blew a short breath of air out between his lips.

"Think about it. You might make Eddie look a little bit weak, locally. But Joanie's about to make him a household name all over New England—you know about her project, right? Staying out of the limelight is the only thing that's kept Eddie alive all these years while all his former bosses, every capo and don from here to Philadelphia, is either under indictment, in prison, or dead. That's Eddie's secret strength; you know it. That's what he learned from the mistakes of Angie Pestudo. It's too dangerous for him to go after Joanie directly, but he can get to her by hurting you, and he'll do it in a second, believe me. I know him now like I know my own name."

For the count of five, Peter only kept staring straight ahead, out over the hurricane wall and the coarse brown sand the state had brought in to keep Revere Beach from being washed out to sea. He stared and stared, his neck and shoulders tight as a towing cable drawing three thousand pounds of twisted metal up from the bottom of a pond, the veins on his forehead showing, his lips working, until when he finally managed to get the words out it was more like spitting than speaking.

"Y-you know Eddie? You stu-stu-stupid ass, you know Eddie and you're sleeping with his wa-wife? Every barfly in the city knows she's cheating on him, thanks to Billy Ollanno and the l-likes of him—who came to my office yesterday, by-by-by the way, asking what was going on with Alfonse Romano, why you went b-bad on us, why you changed, threatening to let Eddie know what his wife was doing, and with who. Xavier and Michael are pr-probably spending half their time following her around wherever she goes, so who do you think you are, Hou-Hou-Houdini? That you can screw Eddie's wife—his *wife*, for Chrissake—and get away with it? Wa-what do you think, it's an act of charity or something, p-putting her in a spot like that? If she gets caught—*when* she gets caught—they'll cut her b-belly open and dangle her from the top of City Hall by her intestines. And you're screwing around with *her*? Of all the women in the city? And you s-say you na-know Eddie?"

"We're careful."

"Oh, give me a f-fucking break. *Careful.* How careful can you be with a guy like him? He has eyes and ears in every bar and corner market. Goons in cars, watching. Ga-guys who owe him so much and are so desperate they'd love to have some little scrap of information to pass on in exchange for not having a piece of wire wrapped around their neck. Careful, ma-my ass. What do you do, Mister Careful, fly to Ma-Mars and make love with her, then fly back?"

I finished my coffee, shook the last two drops out the side window, checked the mirrors and the other cars parked along the beach wall, the handful of people sitting there in the sun.

"She goes to Angie Panechieso's place to get her hair cut," I said, turning it into truth in my mind so I could say it the way I wanted to. "Saturday nights after supper when almost nobody else is in there and Eddie has his regular pool game in his cellar with his Mob buddies. His meetings, and so on. She sits in the chair, and Angie works on her hair a little while. Then, if it's all clear, Alicia gets up and goes down the hallway like she's going to the tanning booth, but instead of actually going into the booth she walks right by, takes Angie's keys and a blond wig, and goes out the back door. She uses Angie's car. She drives ten minutes or so to this little motel in Swampscott, and I'm there with a rented car, always white, parked in front of the room. When she finally gets there, she has about fifty minutes to spend with me. Fifty minutes, once a week. First thing she does is call Angie to make sure everything's clear. One time it wasn't. She had to drive right back and go in the rear entrance and walk up the little hallway like she'd just come out of the tanning booth because there was a woman in the shop, snooping around, with a boyfriend waiting outside in the car."

"Nice. So you have Angie's la-life on the la-line, too."

"She introduced us. It was her idea. They've been friends since junior high, you know that."

"And you think this is such a gee-gee-genius plan that nobody will ever catch on to it? N-nobody will ever make a mistake? Eddie Three Hands, the most suspicious sonofabitch in the universe, will never even s-suspect that his beautiful wife, who's thirty years younger than he is, might be fa-fooling around? Christ, I think I've even seen her there once or twice myself when I went to get my hair cut. Everybody we know goes up to Angie's to get a c-cut or a t-tan or whatever. Even old Stevie goes up there, for G-God's sake. Even Fa-Father Dom. What's the matter with you?"

"I'm in love. I was in love once before, and she got taken away from me. This is the second time, all right?"

He snorted.

I had to look away then, out through the windshield at the sun sparkling on the waves, two skinny Cambodian kids chasing a crippled seagull along the shore while their mother or grandmother or aunt squatted on her heels near the edge of the water, gazing east. It was a story I had heard once, word for word, from a Chelsea cop who was playing around with the wife of his own supervisor. That was all—a little rearranging of the facts to suit my purpose, to help a friend. But it was a lie just the same, and I wasn't used to lying, and all of a sudden my motivations seemed suspect again. I tried just to break it down to the basics: Peter was in trouble, Peter was family, Peter wouldn't listen to any kind of normal argument. The only thing that would ever change him would be something like this. I could try this, or I could stand to one side and let the ship of Peter and Joanie and Vito's fate just take its miserable course, piloted by Eddie Crevine. Which would mean being passive again while the people closest to me were destroyed. . . . Which was a mistake I did not believe I could let myself make twice in one lifetime.

"I have a favor to ask," I said, pushing the words out of my mouth and into the warm air. "I don't want you to do it, necessarily, I just want you to think about it."

"I know the fa-favor and you know the answer."

"I want you to think about testifying against him. I'll do everything I can to make sure nothing happens to you or your family. You have my word on that. You can marry Elsie and take her and her boy out of this place. Go out to the West Coast and start a new life, have a house, a child together, get into a different line of work. Eddie's sixty-six. We put him away for fifteen years on a loan-sharking charge, on the RICO statutes, and that's the end of him."

"We?"

"I'm asking you to consider it, that's all."

"What a d-deal, Alfonse. You g-get to be the hero of the Revere Police Department, you get pr-promoted to assistant chief, you get to sleep with your Alicia without looking over your sh-shoulder. And I get to tes-tes-testify against Eddie and Xavier in court and then have my face changed and go live in fa-fucking North Dakota someplace and never see my family again as long as I live. Thanks, you're a tr-true friend."

"What are your options? Ending up in pieces in the trunk of your car? Turning out like Billy Ollanno, working for Eddie for the rest of your life because you owe him?"

"I'm not m-made like him and I'll never be like him, and you know it."

"Fine, I'm sorry. But still, I'm asking you: What are your options? You always think money's going to just fall in your lap from someplace, and this time it isn't, and you can't face it. You've got a problem the size of North America—with or without Eddie Crevine. Tell me, what are your other choices?"

"I'll figure something out," Peter said, miserably. "It's you you should wa-worry about. You know how c-close they are to finding out who the lucky idiot is who's been m-making Mrs. Eddie? You could be d-dead before you get to work tonight."

"Right. That's part of why I'm asking you."

"M-maybe you should have asked me *before* you g-got involved. I would have given you a good piece of advice: St-stay-stay away."

"I could say the same to you."

"Right. Twin idiots," Peter said, out the window. "The m-moron br-brothers."

I turned my eyes to see how the word had been meant, but Peter's hands were squeezing together, the fingers white, his jaw was locked up, and it seemed wrong at that moment to raise such an enormous subject between us when I had managed to hold it down in the shadows since the night my mother died. Tell Peter, Father Dom had urged me—Dommy, who had known about it for four decades and told no one. Tell Peter, tell Joanie. But I had gone six years without telling them, and it seemed absolutely wrong to start talking about it now.

So, like a magician working some new trick he's still unsure about, I reached into my shirt pocket, took out the object I'd been carrying around all day, and put it on the seat between us. Peter turned his eyes down over his shoulder and then out the window again. "No, thanks," he said. "And ta-take me back now, will you? I have a business to run, whether you believe that or not. I've killed half the day as it is."

"Look again."

"I said no thanks. I've sa-seen cigars before. I'm not in the m-mood for one now. And don't make me walk all the way back to my car to pa-proo-proo-prove you're a better person than I am."

I lifted it off the seat and tapped it against his elbow. "It's not cigars. Hold it in your hand a second."

He took it. I watched his eyes as he felt the weight of it.

"There are two real cigars in there, if you flip the top open, but the rest of it's a plastic case around some of the best Swiss machinery in the world. Neat, isn't it? It's only the weight that gives it away. They even put a little acoustic padding around the inside of the cardboard everywhere but near the microphone—so if you just touch it without actually holding it, you think it's an ordinary box of stogies."

He started to lift it closer to his face, but I put a hand on his arm and held it down below window level. "You don't even have to turn it on. Just set this switch here and it turns itself on the instant anybody within about ten feet of you starts talking. You just wear a sport coat and keep it in the inside breast pocket so it's up high enough. It's so quiet you can't hear anything, even if you put your ear right down there next to the carton. I got it from an FBI buddy, brand-new."

Peter held it on top of his leg, stared at it, turned it once this way and that, flipped the button on and off, started to hand it back.

"No," I said, but there was a huge balloon of doubt swelling up inside me. "Hold on to it. I know it's a big risk. I almost didn't give it to you because of that. But you're going to meet with Eddie tonight, right? If—"

"Who told you that?"

"Alicia."

"B-bullshit."

"How do I know it then? From Billy Ollanno, last time I stopped in to catch a few drinks at the Leopard? Last time we went to church together? . . . Look, if they pat you down beforehand they'll be looking for a wire, not a box of cigars. So what you do is you put something else next to it in the pocket just in case, some real estate papers or something in an envelope, but against the back side, not the microphone. It's a big risk, Pete, but if you go to court against them we have to be sure they'll do time, and having something like this is a thousand times stronger than just your own testimony. Alicia can't testify, she's his legal wife. Everyone else in Eastern Mass is afraid to. . . . Whatever you do is a risk now. That's where you are."

He was holding it down on the seat without looking at it, and I could see from his posture how torn he was. He knew I was doing it out of love for him, and he knew how deep a hole he'd gotten himself into—if it had come to something like this. But there was the pride, still, to deal with. When a person's been beaten down that low, when your addiction is exposed to the world that way, when you're that afraid, the pride just rises up and takes over everything else.

"You'd d-do this?" he said, after a minute. "You'd ask me to d-do this before you'd ask if I could use some mon-money to help pay him off?"

"Loaning you money doesn't do any good anymore. You haven't figured that out yet; that's the whole problem right there."

"And you know for a fact this time isn't different, right?"

"Is it?"

He looked away in disgust. His face was shaking now, and he didn't want me to see it. Two full minutes passed before he could say anything else. "Like they say, I guess, t-times like these are when you find out who-who-who your friends are."

"That's right."

"Saint Alfonse," he said, in a flat, wounded voice, a voice that had had all the optimism knocked out of it and most of the love.

It hurt to hear that, and it hurt that he couldn't break the pride down enough to talk to me straight about it—to say yes or no, but straight. It hurt me and reminded me of Sally, but I knew it was just the fear talking, the addiction. Not the soul. Not Peter.

"T-take me back now, I'm late," he said.

"Fine."

"I don't w-want this little g-g-gizmo here, either."

"Fine. It's your debt, not mine. I can't make you take it."

"And you can't make me a la-loan either, I bet," he said, after a minute. One last desperate try.

"I can't right now, no. And if I could . . . I don't think I would this time."

"Even though you know I'm ma-ma-meeting with him tonight, and he's going to wa-want everything I haven't given him for the last three weeks, and I don't have e-e-even half of it."

"That's right."

"There's a ca-cousin for you."

We rode back along Revere Beach Boulevard in a bitter silence. It seemed to me somehow that the ghosts of all the old amusements were standing up to watch us pass, two brothers caught in their separate destinies, separate miseries, but connected still. Young men and women in shorts and T-shirts were jogging the sidewalk with Walkmans over their ears, kids sprinting up the sand, waves breaking, seagulls calling, but it simply was not the place it had once been. There was no life here now, just poses, snapshots, suntan oil and show-off bodies and greasy paper plates in the gutter. A shallower, greedier America. There was no real Revere here anymore.

I stared at the teenagers standing in small knots of tanned skin around somebody's new car, flirting, posing, just starting in on their second sixteen or eighteen years of life, the section where innocent little habits grew fat and monstrous, and the decisions that had once seemed so unimportant turned out to have real consequences after all. The section where, instead of opening up wide into more and more options the way it seemed to have been doing all these years, your life started narrowing down, just a few degrees at first and then faster, sharper. If you slipped at that point and did one or two things wrong—happened to marry the wrong person, develop the wrong kind of habits, turn out to have the wrong kind of luck— then, when your third sixteen or eighteen years came along, your life could all of a sudden narrow down to something so small and nasty you wouldn't believe it. You'd refuse to accept it. You'd fight it and fight it, and after a while you'd see that even fighting it didn't change anything, and you'd have to come up with another tactic: being better, or being worse, or living one kind of a lie or another. Or making yourself completely naked and humble in front of your own fate and living it out honestly, minute by minute. Which almost nobody could do. Almost nobody, myself included.

I was thinking like that then. I was looking back over the life Peter and I had had together, and the life Vito and Lucy and my mother had, and I was struggling to hold on to a little handle of faith, to believe that things might somehow change for the better again for people like us; that God—whoever or whatever God was—would shine a little luck down on the broken-up lives in this place.

"What are you going to do then?" I said, when we'd driven past the bandstand and the bathhouse and the lonely, ragged strip of grass that passed for a park.

Peter just stared out the side window without moving.

"This is better than a loan, what I'm offering you. This is a way out, forever. A new life . . . with Elsie. A new place."

Nothing.

"Do it for Joanie then, if you won't do it for yourself. Joanie and your parents and me."

A little twitch of the lip when I mentioned Joanie. Nothing to hold on to.

"What connects me and you—nothing can break something like that, Peter. I'm doing this out of love, that's all. You can believe it or not. It makes no difference."

Not a word.

In front of his building, as if to reinforce my new reputation as a bad guy, I made an illegal U-turn and pulled the blue car to the curb. After we'd sat there a minute without speaking, Peter said, in a voice that came straight out of the place in him that was all bruises and self-pity, "Th-things turned out nice for you."

What things? I wanted to say then, out of my own bruised places. What, my wife dying while she was still alive? My mother going the way she went, like an Atlantic Ocean of pain evaporating drop by drop? Which things? Growing up with no father in the house, and then finding out he'd lived within walking distance of me my whole life, and then having to call him "uncle" every other word to keep from saying what I really wanted to say ... for six years? ... What things?

It was absurd, it was the logic of a person who'd come out of a coma and found himself buried to the chin in wet concrete. From where that person was, any other life looked like heaven.

But I swallowed all that and said, "Why, because I'm in love with a woman who's married to a devil?"

Peter's eyes jumped across the seat at me and held contact for a few seconds, gauging me, looking for the lie. It seemed to go on and on, and then, finally, he said, "M-m-m-me and you, we turned out different, that's all." But he grabbed the recorder and slipped it into his sport-coat pocket. Without so much as a grunt of good-bye, he got out of the car and closed the door, hard, and started walking down the sidewalk, the same way he'd been going when I first saw him.

45

Afterwards, I did not know if I was the Devil myself to have done what I did. Deciding to put another person's life in jeopardy, when there was no danger in it for me. Lying and manipulating in order to get that person to do something he should have been left alone to decide for himself.

But Peter *was* alone with it now, I told myself. He could show up for his meeting with Eddie or not show up, try to tape the conversation or not, find a way to come up with the money he needed or not come up with it—and just hope for another amazing twist of luck. If you spend any time around them, you understand right away that gamblers aren't really in it for the money. I knew people who'd won hundreds of thousands of dollars in one night of gambling, enough to live on for the rest of their lives, and then turned right around and played until they gave it all back again. It was losing they were addicted to, not winning. The whole, awful, buried driving purpose of their lives was to push fate until it matched the voice inside them that told them what losers they were—unlucky, unholy, evil, hopeless.

I knew how that voice had been planted inside Peter, and I also knew—better than he did himself—how wrong it was, how inaccurate. He had his chance now, probably his last chance, to stop listening. His father and mother, Father Dom, Joanie, Elsie, me—we were all trying, in our own way, to get him to do that. That was why I'd given him the tape player: in the hope that Eddie's voice recorded there might erase the echo Peter danced to. In the end, though, no matter who'd planted the voice, no matter why, he had to decide for himself whether or not to keep listening. Same as everybody.

I drove the streets surrounded by images of him: coming through my front door on the day Sally died, not even stopping to knock, just barging in and weeping all over me, like it had been *his* wife, not mine. And in the winter of my mother's sickness, a miserable winter when I would work the four-to-midnight shift and sit up with her most of the morning hours, Peter would knock on the front door late—midnight or one o'clock—with a basket of fruit he'd picked up someplace or a pizza my mother couldn't eat. Or he'd take the night aide aside and slip her ten or twenty extra bucks so she'd be especially careful moving my mom, washing her.

Had somebody tried to tell me a friendship that strong could just snap off like the end of a brittle bone, I would have bet everything I owned against it. Peter would have bet twice what he owned. It had always seemed to me that real friendship was like a piece of new steel: The more you heated it up and banged on it, the stronger it became. In time, there might be a little rust on the surface, a few nicks and scratches. But steel was steel; friends were friends.

I wondered then if I had made a mistake, not telling him we had the same father. "Secrets eat people alive," Dommy had said to me more than once: people, marriages, families, souls. Tell him, tell Joanie. Maybe, I thought on certain days, Dommy himself, or Vito, or someone else had told him, the way someone seemed to have told Billy Ollanno. It would be just like Peter never to let on.

Wrestling with it still, I drove, as if by some blood instinct, towards Proctor Avenue. Slowly up the rise I went, past the statues of front-yard saints and virgins: monuments to the special people, people who had no evil inner demons or who had somehow learned to tame them. I turned into the driveway, got out of the car, walked up to the door, and rang the bell of a house where I never knew, I never really knew, whether or not I was welcome.

46

When I rang the bell of the brown-shingle house on Mercury Street, the person who answered was a beautiful redhead woman just about Joanie's age, last thing I expected.

I was tryin, all during the walk from Saint Anthony's, to keep my mind in the clean place where Father Dom left it. I tried not to think about what Alfonse told me, not to let the fear take me over, not to imagine Eddie Creviniello's legbreakers throwing me down the front steps and smashing my knees with lead pipes because a son of mine owed them money and wouldn't pay. But I imagined them, and I was afraid, and a face like this woman's face was the last thing I expected when I pressed my finger against the plastic doorbell button. Eddie's daughter-in-law, she must be. But she did not look like she belonged in this kind of a house—too happy inside, too much like a young mother in her summer dress. And her face was not a face that belonged to any of the Revere families I knew.

"My name is Vittorio Imbesalacqua," I said, when I recovered from the surprise of her. I was standing on the top step with the straw hat in my hands, and I could feel the sun shining on the bald top of my head. I saw her look at me up there, quick, and even though I didn't care no more what people thought about my looks, a little piece of embarrassment went over me. She was a pretty woman, watching me now like she wanted me to be her special friend, but it couldn't be. "I'm here to talk to Eddie Creviniello about my boy," I said.

"Eddie's not home at the moment," the woman told me in a voice that was sweet like a bell ringin. "Can I leave him a message? I'm Alicia, his wife."

Wife. The word almost knocked me down backwards. How could this be Eddie Creviniello's wife? Eddie was sixty-six or sixty-eight, and this young woman . . . how could it be?

"No messages," I told her after a second. And now that I wasn't gonna be seeing Eddie, all the tight muscles in my stomach went loose on me. For a minute then I thought I would have to ask to go to their bathroom. Out of embarrassment, out of not knowing what else to do, I made a little bow in her direction, because she was a woman, still, and I was a man.

I made sure my feet were planted solid on the thin front step to get ready for shifting my weight and turning around and starting back down, but the way she was holding the screen door out with her arm made a turn around on that side too hard. So I waited, not wanting to put my back on her, or to fall and make a fool out of myself, and in that minute my mind made a change. "No," I told her, like another man inside me had decided all of a sudden to start talking. "No, I think from how you said it that he *is* here."

"He's not, though," she said, only a little bit less nice.

"I don't want to make you lie, miss," I said. "A long time ago I knew Eddie's brother, Aldo, who the communists killed in Korea. I would never bother him at his own house if it wasn't somethin important. I won't be long, because my wife she's home dyin."

The woman only looked at me a minute, started to tell me no again, but I held up one of my hands and I told her, "I won't cause him no trouble, miss. It's Imbesalacqua, with the 'I' first. Vittorio. But they call me 'Victor Bones,' some people. Or 'Vito.'"

When she let the screen door close, I had to step down one step backwards, but I did it without putting my back on her. Then she shut the wooden inside door—solid on her hinges, like they used to build them in the old days—and I waited in the sun, keeping my eyes straight forward so no one inside would think I was spying. When the door opened again he was Eddie Creviniello himself there, the hair cut in a whiffle, all gray, his chest naked, and a little bit of shaving soap stuck on the bottom of his ear, which I saw but didn't say nothing about.

At first, Eddie was angry in his face, but then he covered over the angriness with a phony surprise and said my name like in another minute he was gonna try and run for the mayor. He invited me inside, shook my hand too soft, and made me sit in a white leather chair in the TV room while he went to put on a shirt and while the pretty wife went back and forth in the kitchen, making me ice coffee with milk and then carrying the glass and the napkin into the TV room, and asking about sugar, and smiling like she wanted to be your friend if Eddie didn't find out, and then running away.

When Eddie came back he had on a shirt the color of a new pair of pliers. There was a fancy glass on a napkin next to his chair, and the shaving soap was washed away, and the wife had gone out the back door into the yard without saying nothing else. At first my mind was thinking: Guido Prenzi on the street. The two-by-four. Eddie riding past my father and me afterwards, and me and my father pretending to be looking the other way, two deaf guys, two guys who were blind.

But in his shirt and trousers now, Eddie seemed just like any ordinary fella, getting old and trying not to let people see. His face was fatter than it used to be years ago, round like the cushions on the stools at Buddy Goodyear's coffee shop, and he had learned a new way of walking, the arms sticking out a little ways from his body like he was holding a few magazines up there under the shoulders.

"I was taking a nap, Victor," he said. "I didn't know it was you. How are you? How's the family?"

"Lucy's dyin," I said, because I didn't want to lie so soon after confession, and because it was the main thing on my mind. But right away I was sorry. It showed on Eddie's face that he didn't care Lucy was dyin, although he said what you were supposed to say: that he was sad to hear it, that he hoped it was a mistake, that there was always a chance things would turn around.

"Not always," I said.

Eddie took a drink from his coffee. He was one of those Italians who were built wide, with big thighs pushing out against his trousers, and the two bones of his wrist as far apart as a package of cigars, and soft fat fingers with no rings.

"I remember you coming here to have dinner with us before Aldo went off in the service," he said.

"I had dinner in this house lotsa times before that. Dinner and lunch, too. You mama's *cavatelli*. I remember you walking around this room with diapers on you."

Eddie made a noise that was like a laugh; then his eyes looked at my glass of coffee to see how long it was gonna take me to finish.

"I remember you when your last name still was Creviniello. It had a better music that way."

"For us," Eddie said, making his laugh. But now a little stain of meanness had showed up in his face, and like magic it pulled up the fear again in my legs and in my belly. His voice turned a little bit hard. "Most people can't pronounce something that long, so we changed it."

"We never changed it," I said. "Imbesalacqua. To hell with them if they can't say it."

A bad quiet fell over us then, because I had a disrespect for Italians who changed their names, and I couldn't pretend nothing otherwise. All of a sudden I remembered my father talking about that same thing on the back porch on Tapley Avenue. It was after I came home from the war, and we were all sitting on the porch together, listening to a record from Tony Bennett, the singer, who was really Benedetto. "Maybe he had to," Lucy said. And my father said, "How come-a DiMaggio no have to? How come-a Frankie Sinat?"

I remembered it, clear as the minute.

From out in the yard came the sound like somebody jumping in a swimming pool. I turned my eyes to that direction, and when I turned them back, Eddie was tapping his foot.

"I came about Peter," I said, and the minute I got the name out of my mouth, the fear crawled back up in my chest and started jumping around there like I swallowed a little fish who wasn't dead yet. For one second, looking at Eddie's eyes, I had the idea I was too late already, that something already happened. "My boy."

There was no change in Eddie's cushion face except the eyes held still on me now, tight. And the foot wasn't tapping no more. We sat that way a minute; then Eddie said, "He was in the service too, wasn't he?"

"He was. I was." I took a drink from the coffee because my tongue was sticking to the top of my mouth and the words were coming out like dry balls of paper, one at the time. I could feel my body shaking now the way Lucy's shook, and I did not know anymore if it was the fear or something else. "I came about his debt to you."

"What debt, Victor?"

"He owes you a debt that with the interest I think is twenty thousand dollars. I came to have a talk about it. In the old days that's the way they used to do."

For a minute Eddie only stared at me, not blinking, and in that minute, I understood in my mind that here was a man who could kill people and not care about it. Once in a while down the club somebody would say something about this guy they called Chelsea Eddie, a story about a body with no head the police found in a car once when one of his bookies tried to cheat him, or why nobody ever figured out where his first wife went, or what he did to the girls that were whores because of him at his club, or what he said to one of the teachers of his son, who told him the son was no good in school, because he wasn't. But to hear those stories and to be in the same room with Eddie was different as the word "tomato" and eating one. To be in the same room with him like this made you feel there was another life underneath the life you saw every day, a devil's life. Eddie stared and stared at me, then let go a small little laugh, something so phony I felt embarrass for him and had to look away.

He took a mouthful of his coffee and washed it around inside his teeth. "I'm not in the bank business, Vic. I have a plumbing shop in Melrose. I've been a plumber all my life. You got bad information, that's all."

Now I stared at *him,* not blinking. I squeezed my hands tight in my lap so it looked like I was just folding them together, and I stared, and when Eddie held the smile on his face that was like a fat grapefruit, I said, "Plumbers don't have soft hands like you," and I saw him look down into his hands like they just that minute been stuck on the end of his arms.

I was wearing the long-sleeve white shirt I always put on for confession, and I started undoing the buttons. I undid them all down the front and pulled the shirttails up out of my pants. Moving awkward in the big leather chair, careful not to knock over the glass of ice coffee on the table next to me, I pulled the two sides of the shirt off my shoulders. "See," I said, and my throat pinched in on the end of the word so she almost didn't come out. "No tape recorder machines, Eddie. I didn't come here from the police. I came to talk to you about my son. With respect I came, and I get only lies from the minute I push the bell until now."

He looked at me a minute. "Put your shirt on, Victor," he said.

I pulled the halfs of my shirt together but I didn't try to close the buttons. I stared across at this man who talked to you like he was ten years older, not ten years younger. Who lent people five dollars and made them pay back twenty. Who changed his name and still brought disgrace on the Italians. Who was treated with respect wherever he went because there was nothing he wouldn't do. And who had a wife like the one who opened the door for me, beautiful, sweet women whose job it was to lie to anybody who rang the front bell. How could you try to be a good man in this world when people like this could hurt you and your family and smile afterwards?

"All right." Eddie wasn't smiling now but pinching the little sack that hung down under his chin. With one hand he pushed down on the arm of his chair and shifted his behind from the right side of it to the left. And with the other hand he took hold of the little sack of skin like it was the place where he held his supply of true words and he had to squeeze it three times to convince them to come out. "I didn't want to say anything about it because I didn't want to make an embarrassment for your son in front of his father, and because I didn't want to cause you any more pain, with your wife sick the way she is."

Men who let you get upset and then talked to you in a calm voice, to make a fool out of you.

"It's just a business debt, off the books, that's all. Peter needed some money because real estate was slow in the city, and we have a mutual friend who knew my plumbing business was doing pretty good at the time—I don't do the plumbing anymore, Victor, which is why my hands aren't as tough as they used to be. I'm the boss; I don't do that work anymore; I'm in the office all the time now: paperwork, meetings. . . . I made Peter a friendly loan, that's all. Without any interest. Zero. And he hasn't been too good about keeping up with the payments."

I just stared at him now, because the one thing I never in my life been able to stand was people lying into my face.

"But it's not twenty thousand, not even close to that."

"How much exactly? I'm going Monday to the bank. By the lunchtime you have everything he owes you."

"I'd have to look in my books to say exactly."

"I thought you just said it wasn't in the books."

Eddie made the muscles jump on one arm. "Don't make me out to be a liar, Victor, okay? I was doing your boy a favor, not trying to hurt him. . . . I meant not on my plumbing business books. Which it isn't. Why should it be? I keep it written down, though, naturally."

"Look, then, Eddie. I'm waitin here."

He shifted his rear end back to the other side of the chair and made a face that was like a smile and a curse at the same time. "Let's say eleven thousand and we'll call it over," he said. "It's a little bit more than that, but for old times' sake let's say eleven thousand, cash, and wash our hands about it. . . . Peter wouldn't want you to do this, though."

"You don't tell Peter, then. When you meet with him, you just say there's no more debt, that's all, not who paid. You have the money by the lunchtime Monday. I give you my word on. Eleven thousand, cash money."

"But you're retired, Victor. Where are you going to get that kind of money?"

"I have some savings accounts, don't worry. And my daughter Joanie helps us with the investment. I'll get it and you have it by then. I give you my word on."

Eddie was making some new kind of faces now, pretending it would make him feel bad to get the money.

This is a person, I kept telling myself. God loves this person just like anybody. But I could not stand to look at Eddie no more, to hear his voice, to be in the same house with him, because the carpet and the walls and the pictures on the walls were all covered over with lies then, and this had been a solid family who lived here at one time, a good family.

"This is nice, you paying for your son," he said. "I appreciate this. But let me tell you one thing, Victor, just me to you. Your kids are making my life hell lately, and I don't know what I ever did to you or your family to deserve it. Your girl is poking around places she shouldn't be poking, one, saying things about me she shouldn't be saying. And, two, this boy of yours, if you don't do something about him he's going to be trouble for you all down the line. I'm telling you this as a friend. He's a con man, your Peter. He says he's going to do one thing; then he goes and does something else."

As a grown man, I hit somebody only one time with all my strength. When I was a boy there were some fights, and I won a few of them and lost a few and run away from a few others. But as a man only one time did I really hit somebody, a little thing that started it, a workman in the lumberyard saying the word "guinea" when I was in there buying some lumber once with Peter, who was six or seven then. The man didn't even say it to me, didn't even say it in a way to be mean. But it seemed wrong to use a word like that in front of a boy, and so I told the man I didn't come there with my money to hear those kinda words. And the man went a little crazy right next to the piles of two-by-eights. He came and pushed me in the shoulder, in front of my son, and he said the word three, four times, crazy—*guinea, guinea, guinea*—waving his arms, throwing spit from his mouth. And so I hit him in the middle of the chest, one time, all my strength, and knocked him over flat like a blanket on a bed. And that was the end of words like that from that guy.

Now I had a minute when I wanted to get up and hit. If I had been standing near Eddie I might have, but I was an old man now; it was wrong; it would go to nothing but more trouble. Still, I could feel it in my arm, I wanted to.

"You have children, Eddie?" I said.

"Sure I do. Two boys. They—"

"And they all the time do what you want?"

"No, of course they don't, Victor. I didn't mean any insult to you or your family."

"Then don't talk about my family that way if you don't want no insult, okay? You gonna get you money, don't worry about. But money is money, and talk like that is-a somethin else. I could talk that way to you, maybe. Maybe other people could too, but I don't."

It was like Eddie was smiling at me then without smiling, like he was trying to say, just with his eyes, I could kill you. So I tried to say back, just with my eyes, Big deal, you could kill me. What, that's something a man can brag about, killing another man? But it was a stupid game, and I was too old for it, and I didn't care no more who could kill who, who was stronger than who. After a minute I couldn't stand to be in the same room with this kind of a devil, that's all. I left the ice coffee almost full, I took a hold of my hat and tried to stand up, but the chair was too soft, it took me three times to push myself forward and out of her.

It took me three times, and on the last time a pain went up my back like a knife cutting, but I was standing on my feet. And instead of asking me to stay a little while and finish the coffee, which is the right way to do when somebody comes to your house, instead of that, Eddie was making a big fuss about walking with me to the door, saying about how nice Joanie looked on the TV, and how come a beautiful girl like her wasn't married yet, and how come she never came by to say hi to old friends like him . . . and about the way the city used to be years ago, all the families like one family, eating at each other's houses, watchin out for each other's brothers and sisters and cousins, the good old ways of doing things, face-to-face like this. All of it just to cover up what he said before. The big Mob guy.

I couldn't listen. All the peace of the confession was gone from me now. That Peter came here in the first place, my own son! That the kind of father I was, it was easier for him to borrow this dirty money than come to me and talk straight.

When we were going out on the top step, Eddie said, in his snake voice, "But whoever this person is who's telling you things, you should have a talk with them, Victor. I know it couldn't have been Peter, but whoever it was says I'm charging interest, that it's up to twenty thousand—that would be illegal. Some person is giving you wrong information, spreading bad things about me, I'm telling you."

At least, I thought, at least in the old days the Mob guys didn't try to pretend they weren't. Whatever else they did, in the old days they didn't lie to you like this in your face. I felt a small chance now to do something, a small opening in the fog that was all around me. There were people in my life who were important too, and they seemed to come help me at that minute. When Eddie and me we got to the bottom of the front steps, I turned to him and I said, "It wasn't one person, it was two who told me about the debt."

Eddie lifted his eyebrows in a fake surprise. He leaned the top of his body back a few inches like the words had pushed him.

"And they were smarter people than you, people who didn't change they names, neither."

"Who?" Eddie said, in a nice way, like he was a friend asking. *My daughter on the TV and Alfonse Romano the captain of police,* I was right on the edge of telling him, but just at that minute I remembered something the fellas at the club said about this Eddie. Eddie Three Hands, they called him sometimes. And that meant he would seem to be doing one thing but really be doing something else. With the extra hand. He was trying to get the names from me now, that was all, get the names and then figure out some way to hurt Joanie, hurt Alfonse. It was clear now. I looked at him straight. "Doesn't matter who," I said. "*I* got the numbers wrong, not them. You'll be old as me someday, and you'll have to forget things and watch people you know die slow, and you'll have to face God one day too, that's all."

I could see—even though Eddie tried to keep his face from showing it—that this speech knocked against him pretty hard.

Not afraid now, not afraid for once, Vittorio Imbesalacqua turned his back on Eddie Creviniello without even shakin hands, and I stepped the three steps to the end of the walk and turned left there, downhill, with my spine straight and my chin up.

The screen door slapped closed behind me—the big Mob guy didn't even wait for me to get out of sight—but over Eddie's fence I could see the red hair of his wife, the liemaker, her pretty eyes there above the wood pickets. She was watching me now, watching the old man go, and my shirt, the both sides of her were all flappin open.

47

"How you feeling today, Aunt Lucy?" he was asking me, a man who had never really done anything wrong all these years besides looking too much like his father when the light hit him a certain way.

I was in the bedroom, lying down because it had tired me out too much, sitting in the yard all morning, and the pain had come back very strong. "Not too bad," I said. "Nice that you visit, Alfonse."

"We're supposed to come for lunch tomorrow, Father Dom and me, if it's all right. Is there any food you can eat that we can bring, anything special you have an urge for?"

"No, nothing," I said. The pain was knocking against the inside of my hipbones now, and I wanted him to leave but I didn't know how to say so. He pulled over a chair and sat down next to the bed, and after a minute he said, "Aunt Lucy. I'm sorry for what happened."

"What happened?" I said. "Is Peter hurt?"

"Peter's okay. I'm sorry for what happened . . . with my mother."

"You didn't do it."

"I know. But she felt sorry about it too, that's what I'm trying to say."

"Sorry is something I never heard from her, Alfonse."

"I know that. That's my fault. She told me only at the very end, the last day. And after she told me, she asked me to go and get you and bring you back to the house on Ambrose Street so she could ask your forgiveness face-to-face before she passed on. . . . I promised her I would. I got in my car and started to drive over here, but halfway up Park Avenue I started to think it would be too much pain for her at the end of her life, when she already had all the pain she could deal with. So I just drove around a little bit and went back and told her I had given you her apology, and you accepted it and were praying for her."

"I was."

"And about three hours after that, she died. . . . I never had the chance to tell you this, I never had the courage."

"Now why tell me?"

"Because I'm having a day when I'm in a mood to tell everybody the truth."

"Did you tell Peter the truth?"

"Not about this. Never."

"Vito?"

"No. But a hundred times I wanted to."

The pain was crawling down my legs now, up into my back, out my arms and fingers. I didn't think I could talk very much longer. Or listen. I was glad, still, to have Peter and Joanie not know who Alfonse was to them. Even now, at the very end of my life, I held on to that like a revenge. Which was a sin, a kind of lie, a kind of hate I had prayed about for years and still couldn't get over.

"Father Dom?" I asked.

"I told him. My mother told him."

"Dommy knows everything about everybody," I said. "God's ear. If he ever tells anybody, they'll know what terrible people we are, all of us. Good Catholics, and under the surface we're lying, we're keeping secrets, we're loving somebody else besides our wife, we're hating."

"There's always a difference between what people see and what really goes on," he said. "There's always the person-for-show and the real person underneath."

"Not with Peter," I said. "Everybody else's problems are buried so deep nobody sees them, Peter's problems are all in the open."

"That's right," he said. "That's why we love him," and I smiled into the pain a little ways and wanted him to leave.

He understood, then. He squeezed my hand, very gentle, and said he would see me tomorrow.

I was having to close my eyes against the pain, but I got all my strength together and I said, "Take the little notebook I keep on the TV, under the saint. The nurse will show you."

"What notebook?" he said.

And I told him—because I was in a mood to tell everybody the truth that day too—"The little notebook where I marked down all the prayers I said for your mother over the years because of all the times I hated her. I'm sorry for the hate part. I'm sorry for the things I said to you those times."

"Don't worry about that, Lucy," he said, leaving off the "aunt" for once. "Anybody would have had those feelings if something like that happened to them. Every time you looked at me you saw the worst thing that could happen to a woman in this world. I know that."

"I should have found something better to do with those feelings," I said. "It caused a lot of pain, what I did with them. I should have taken that pain on myself and just kept it there. I spread it around."

He looked at me a long time, and it was like I was lying in a hot bath of pain then; every piece of my flesh and blood and bones was burning. My penance.

"Nobody holds it against you anymore," he said finally.

"Nobody? Not Peter?"

"Peter least of all."

"Not Vito, not Joanie, not you?"

"Nobody," he said, staring straight into me like I was naked in front of him there on the bed. I could see what kind of a person he really was then. I could see it was a good thing he had been born onto this earth. I could see that he never could have come out of a woman like me.

48

Three times on the way home from Eddie's I had to stop and rest. Near the top of Revere Street I sat down on a concrete wall in front of somebody's house that had just had new paint put on, and the woman who came outside to ask me who did I think I was, sitting on her property, it turned out this woman was Phyllis Mastromarino, who I went to school with when I first came over from the Old Country, 1936, and who had been good friends later on with Alfonse's mother, Carmellina.

"Vittorio," she said. "It's you."

"Sure it's me."

She was smiling like I knew whose wall it was when I sat down on it, like sitting on a person's wall was a new way of saying you were in love, seventy-three years old.

"Come inside for cake," she asked me.

"No, *grazie*, Phyllis. I was just taking a one-minute rest."

"So take your one-minute inside. I have some chairs, even, for you to sit on. Have a nice piece of cake with a widow."

Phyllis was smiling at me with the same nice smile she used to have in high school, and it made me think that whenever you looked at a person, you talked to the whole picture they made in you memory, not to the real person of this minute. A little while ago I had been talking to my idea of who Eddie Creviniello was, and Eddie had been talking to his idea of who Vittorio Imbesalacqua was, and we had both of us been talking about our two different ideas of who Peter was. I could see now that Phyllis had the same problem: She was talking to an idea of me that was nothing like the real me at all.

"Where are you walking from, so far?"

"Church," I said. "Confession."

She moved a little ways towards me where I stood. She was wearing a nice purple dress that showed her figure, and she ran her two hands down over the hipbones in a way as if to smooth the material, but really to make sure I saw that, at her age, she still had a figure. Nothing against you, Phyllis, I wanted to say, nothing against you, but it doesn't mean anything to me now, the figure. Today, this minute especially, it doesn't mean any thing.

"What does a nice man like you have to confess?"

"Plenty," I said.

"Really?"

"You'd be surprised how much."

"Really, Vittorio?"

The big amount of my sins seemed to make Phyllis happy. She asked me in for cake again, for coffee with the anisette, but I told her I had to get home. "Lucy's sick," I said. "And Joanie our girl comes for supper. I'm suppose to cook."

"You cook!"

"There's a nurse who cooks, but she cooks plain. On Saturdays Joanie comes over and I make a real supper."

"I watch her on the TV," Phyllis said.

I explained her that Joanie was taking a vacation now from the TV, and that when she went back she was going to do something special, over and beyond the regular job. But Phyllis did not seem to be listening about Joanie, did not seem to care too much about Lucy bein sick. She was drifting away into her memories and her dreams. She was trading away now for then and then. I would have to try harder myself not to do that.

"Did you hear about Angelo Rotazzi?" she said.

I told her no, I hadn't heard.

"They broke in his house and tied him up in a chair and put tape over his mouth. Then they took everything he had and smashed up everything else. The Cambodians did it. They're like animals when they get together in a group."

And the Italians, I thought, we're like altar boys. But I didn't say it. My mind was pulling me away from Eddie's house and back towards Proctor Avenue. I was tired now, and worried about nine different things, and the last thing I could make myself think about was the Cambodians and the Vietnamese. Let them live their lifes, those people. I had my life I was trying to live. Let them take care of their children and their families like I was trying to do.

"Come visit me again sometimes," Phyllis said, when I made as if to leave.

I promised to her I would.

"Next Saturday after confession, will you, Vittorio?"

I said I would try, and I put back on my hat and said thank you—even though I didn't know for what. For the cake I didn't eat, for the wall I was sitting on one second, for helping me forget a little while about Eddie Creviniello, I didn't know. I just thanked her, and then I made a little bow with my back that was sore from too much walking, and I went away.

After Tapley Avenue it was all downhill and I felt stronger again in a little while. It began to seem to my mind that I done the right thing, going to Eddie's house. No matter what Alfonse said, no matter what Joanie was gonna say now. When thoughts came about the eleven thousand, I said a prayer and pushed them away, because the right thing was to love your own son, and this was my way of loving. I would be different to Peter now, things would be different. Money wasn't the most important thing.

49

When I got home, Lucy was solid asleep in the back bedroom, resting under the covers with her face the color of concrete. I sat next to the bed a little while and watched her, and I wondered what she would say about my talk with Eddie Creviniello, about the money, about Peter. We had a lot of fights over things like that in our time. No more than anybody else husband and wife, but still. . . .

And there were other times that were good times. I tried to bring them back now, to my mind. I remembered we used to have all Peter's whole basketball team over the house after they finished their games, and Lucy would make a big lasagna for them that they would eat in about one minute. . . . And we used to go to Joe and Eleonora's house on Essex Street on Sundays sometimes, the four of us, and Joanie and Peter would run out and play with all the children in the big yard there, and we would sit under the grapevine drinking the wine Joe made, eating Eleonora's antipasto, talking about what there was to talk about in this world in the days before we had a son who borrowed money from the Devil.

Maybe she'd be happy at the way I talked to Eddie, and maybe she wouldn't be. Either way, I wouldn't tell her about it now. I knew just from looking at her face. No sense telling her now.

In a little while I went outside. I picked some salad from the garden and mixed it up in two bowls with my tomatoes and my peppers, fresh, and a little bit of dandelion because Joanie didn't like too much. For the gravy I just took two small jars of the tomatoes I'd put up with salt from last year's garden, stirred them in a pot with spices, handful of sugar, chopped-up garlic, olive oil. There were four bottles left from the wine Rafaelo made right before he died. I opened one and put a spoonful in the gravy, then poured a glass for myself and sat with the baseball on, not really watching, while the gravy cooked. When the commercial came, I went back to check on Lucy sleeping, to pull the blanket up one inch more on her chest, to say in a low voice that I lit a candle at Saint Anthony's for her and was cooking a nice supper for Joanie.

Three times I went in to see her; then I thought maybe all I was doing was bothering her sleep, so I left her alone, praying for her at the commercial instead of getting up. My back was sore, and I was worrying about the eleven thousand, about what Joanie was gonna say. Confession or no, right thing or no, my mind was not giving me that much peace about it.

In a little while the baseball was over. A little while after that I heard a noise in the driveway and I pushed myself out of my chair and went to the door. It was Joanie, the fancy car they made in Germany. Green, like money.

50

She always kept herself nice, Joanie, even when she was a little girl. When she got out of the car I saw she was carrying a handful of flowers, but she was like a flower herself in the yard, with a dress that was blue and green and a little too short. Her hair was looser than it looked on the TV, held back a little bit so her face was full and pretty. I couldn't tell if she was wearing makeup or not, but I thought she was, and if she wasn't, she didn't need to be.

She came walking up the driveway towards the steps, and in her eyes there was something like looking down into water. I wanted to tell her she didn't have to be so sad like that, even now, but I didn't know the right words, and I didn't say that even to myself sometimes, so I kept quiet.

Joanie hugged me and kissed me and right away took over the house: setting up the flowers in a vase and bringing them in to her mother (who was sleeping still, and who already had the big package of flowers from Peter); straightening my books on the living room coffee table so the mark came out of the one I was reading; saying some order to the nurse, who was making up the medicine in the den and who had been quiet all day the way she always was, this one, a spy in the house.

"Why don't you put the butter in the fridge until we're ready to eat, Papa?" Joanie said, when she came back in the kitchen. "They did tests that show it causes cancer if you leave it out in the air too long."

I felt something go through me, something from the way she used to be a long time ago when she would come home from the college, bossing us about the government, knowing everything. Cancer from the butter now, when it was already too late. I thought about Phyllis Mastromarino, about how you needed to concentrate on what was going on now, not then, but I said, "Leave it to be soft," in a way that had all the past in it.

Joanie was opening the frigerator door already—five minutes before we were going to use the butter anyway—and so I said it a little more strong than I meant. She heard the past in me and looked up. "But the oils turn rancid, Papa, and then the bacteria—"

"No. A few minutes now we're eating. You're too fussy, thinking that way."

"I'll just put it in to get firm—"

"Leave," I said, too strong, but it was my house still.

"Don't shout at me like that, Papa."

"Don't take over, then."

She hit the butter down on the table and put her back on me. After a little while she went over to the bottle of wine and made a glass for herself, and I didn't say nothing else to her, or her to me. For a minute I was afraid she was gonna go out the door and drive right back to Boston without even eating. The gravy was spitting red spots on the stove, I had the pasta sitting dry on two dishes, all measured out, and I hadn't even put it with the water yet.

When I put it in, the ziti seemed to be slow cooking. I stirred them once or twice, so they wouldn't stick, stirred the gravy but not too much. In between, I took the two bowls of salad to the table and sat them there on both sides of the butter. But now, instead of being two bowls of love that I made up special for Joanie the way she liked it, they were two bowls of something else, my stubbornness, my having to be the king in this house every minute. Lucy was dying. Peter was in trouble. And when my daughter came by to visit I raised my voices at her. Over what? Butter. Over nothing.

Outside, Jimmy Haydock's lawn mower was going, and a nice breeze was coming up Proctor Avenue from the direction of the beach, and the air blowing in past the curtains was beach air with the smell of grass in it, as sweet a thing as could be. But there was only bad feeling flying around me now, cutting me, cutting me. How much more time did I think God was gonna give me to learn how to talk to the people I loved?

Joanie was standing with her back on me. Walking past her from the table to the stove, I was ready to put my hands on her shoulder and tell her I was sorry. But some devil whispered to my ear that *she* should be the one to say she was sorry. And I told myself if I didn't get it out now, the macaroni would go soft, like macaroni in a restaurant, like a sponge with gravy on it; then neither one of us would want to eat.

I strained the water off in the sink with the steam burning my hands, and when I poured them out onto the two plates, the ziti seemed like they were alive, shining and bumping there like white little cutup eels. Very careful, I ladled the gravy on the way she liked it, thin little strips.

One in each hand I carried the plates over to the table and sat them down, and the sound of them made Joanie turn around. Her face was a broken-up face now, and who was I to tell her to put it back together again? Who was I, a saint, to tell her not to be sad about her mother dying? What was she gonna be left with then, when Lucy was gone, a prize like me for a father? Me and Peter, that other prize?

That one time, because she didn't like me to, I didn't say the grace out loud. I poured myself wine and put a little more in her glass to make the peace.

"Eat a little bit," I said. "Get started. You stomach will take over."

She picked up the fork and pushed the ziti this way and that way.

"You father's a *chidrool*," I said (which means, in the dialect, stupid as a cucumber, only worse), "but eat what he cooks for you anyway."

She looked up at me, a flood situation in the eyes, a face that made everything inside you turn over.

"He's a stupid man, you father," I said. "His girl comes to have supper and see her mother, and he takes the hammer out and smashes all his fingers."

She let her mouth come open and I thought maybe she would say something then, but she could not seem to talk, which used to happen when she was a little girl and something was hurting her inside. Sometimes—even when she was in high school, even when she came home from the college—she would sit out on the patio with me and Lucy and not say one word for a half hour at the time. She was such a beautiful girl when she was young, and seeing her sad like that used to be for me like somebody tearing off my skin. I looked down at the table now in order not to make her think I was watching. Something missing.

The bread. I looked up and saw the empty dish I put out on the counter right before we had the little fight about the butter. I went over to get it. The dish, the bread bag with the little piece of metal in a little piece of plastic wrapped around the neck to keep it tight that you couldn't take a hold of unless you had fingers skinny as a pencil. It was impossible the way they made it. The ziti on the table, getting cold. The nurse in the kitchen now, interrupting us with her quietness because right in the middle of supper she had to get the scissors out of the drawer to cut something. I pushed the bread bag straight at her. She gave me a look that could blind a person, but after a second she took and opened the bag as easy as me knocking a six-penny nail into pine in the old days: bang, once. Open.

Joanie was eating the salad when I sat back at the table, and I was pretty sure telling her about Eddie would not be that good of an idea, now especially. But it was pushing against the insides of my teeth.

"What did you do today?" I said, instead of telling her. She had eaten two mouthfuls of the ziti and one mouthful of the salad, even though I always taught them to eat the salad last, which was the right way for the stomach. A little bit of the sadness was washed out of her face.

"I went sailing."

"You have a sailboat now?"

"A friend of mine has. A lawyer friend. The boat's name is *Getting Me Off*."

I could tell the way she said it that this was suppose to be funny, but I didn't get the joke so I didn't smile. She was going out with lawyers, though, which was something. What I said to Father Dom must be wrong, then, if she was going out with lawyers alone in their boats.

"She's a defense lawyer, Papa. You see?"

I nodded my head. I saw. A lawyer she.

For a little while we ate together without talking. In the back room one of Lucy's machines went on, pumping something into her or out of her. Jimmy Haydock and his mowing was on the far side of his yard now, getting ready to quit, and Antonelli had his TV on loud enough for the whole neighborhood.

Joanie took a piece of bread in her hands that were like hands Michelangelo made. She broke it in half, and put one end of it in the salad so it came up with oil and vinegar soaking it, and small pieces of the dandelion sticking here and there. She held her other hand under the bread when she put it up to her mouth so it wouldn't drip, and she leaned a little bit forward so the front of her dress pushed open and you could see too much.

"I didn't put that much of the dandelion in," I told her, "because that's how you like it."

She nodded her head. A little bit more of the sadness was gone. A nice feeling was starting to fill up in the room.

"You can't find bread like this in town. This is Revere bread. I love this."

"They use to put it in the paper bags," I said. "It was even better that way. You could even open it."

She did not hear my little joke. For a minute my mind got taken away by a memory of Anthony DeMarco coming up the house on

Saturdays with his bread truck, opening up the two back doors with all the loafs stacked very neat inside, and the smell, and the sesame seeds falling out the back, so that when he drove away the birds would come and pick them out of the street. I would stand very still on the edge of the yard and watch those birds, because they reminded me of me: working, working hard, always a little afraid, flying back home to their families with the one piece of treasure.

"Mama looks tired today. Has she been having a lot of pain?"

"Not too much," I said. "She stopped taking the medicine."

"Which medicine?"

"For the pain."

"You're kidding."

"Why should I?"

Right away the flood came back.

"Her cells are eating away at themselves, Papa. Her body is consuming itself. She won't be able to stand it."

"So far she's standing it. When she had the babies she stood it okay."

She looked at me like I'd just slapped her, which never in my life did I do.

"She has the sleep medicine she's takin," I said, but Joanie was going down the saddest road in herself now—you could see her eyes going, the muscles near her mouth going—a long long road of sad thoughts. Nothing you could say could call her back.

"This is so insane. This family is insane. Why?"

"She wants her head to be clear, that's why."

"But that's insane. It's absurd. How could you let her? How could the doctor?"

"You mama, she's stubborn. Like me. Like all of us. Eat."

But Joanie was given up on the eating. Another mistake, telling her this now. Another worse mistake, talking about babies.

"We have to make her take it. I'll mix it up with some ice cream or something, with some applesauce. We have to."

Now I could see that Joanie was afraid of the pain, not that much only in her mother but in herself. I could see that, and I almost said it to her because I was afraid of the pain in myself too, and afraid of watching Lucy with that much pain, and afraid what life would be like without her in this house. But all during the walk to confession I thought about it, and it seemed to me this once I shouldn't argue. The medicine was there if Lucy wanted to take it. She could change a mind when she wanted to, or not, dependin.

"Let you mother decide on her own now."

"But she's out of her mind, Papa."

"Don't say that now."

"But no sane person would bring pain on themselves when they could just as easily avoid it."

"Don't say that, I'm telling you."

"Don't tell me what I can and can't say. This is absurd. I'll have her taken and put in the nursing home if you won't—"

I held up my hand.

"She doesn't want to die in the nurses home," I told her. "She wants to die here. That's what we're doin for her, you and me. Now she wants to die without the medicine, so that when her own children come see her she can talk to them and listen to them like a regular mother."

For a minute then I thought I was gonna have to catch Joanie from falling face down in her food. Something I said was like knocking her out. I tried to think what it was.

"Eat," I said, but there was no chance now of her picking up the fork even. When I tried to get up from my chair, my knees wouldn't work right; I walked too much that day. I pushed down so hard on the table it almost flipped over, and I went to her and put an arm under her arm and lifted her to standing and pulled her to the door. The napkin was in her hand, the makeup running down from one eye like black blood. Gentle, one hand on her arm, I led her out the door, away from the ears of the nurse, and when we were out in the yard I walked her a little ways past the garden towards Rafaelo's house where no one lived now, where no one could hear.

"Joanie," I said. Her arm was like steel in my fingers. "I know you don't believe in God, and I'm not tryin to make you. I'm not so sure about Him either some days."

She was making a frown on her face.

"God isn't the style now. And maybe when you get smart like you, you don't need Him helping you. Maybe that's how it's set up, I don't know. But—listen me, let me hold you arm—when you die, you only die once. For a person like Mama, she didn't want to be in the nurses home, dyin in public. Even, if she had her way, she wouldn't have the nurse in her own house, but we can't do it without the nurse. . . . When a person's dyin, it's important to let them have what they want. It's important not to upset them too much because they're getting ready to see God. Even if you don't believe it, they're getting ready. And you don't want them to be upset, seeing God. You don't want that when they leave they have bad feelings on you. You mother she wants no medicine now, she told me that herself. The medicine is always there. If she changes a mind, she can take it right away. But if you make some kinda big fuss out of it now, you make it hard for her to change a mind when the pain is too bad. Okay?"

She looked over my shoulder at Rafaelo's yard. Her lips were shaking, her beautiful face that so many people saw only happy on the TV. I waited for what she had to say. Nothing came.

"Go in and sit with her now a little while," I told her. "She only wants to be able to talk to you in a regular way, like a mother, that's all. You see?"

Joanie did not say yes or nod the head, but I could tell from the way her eyes were, and from the soft feel of her arm, that she heard what I was saying. In some way, she heard it, even though she had a bad look now, like she was drifting far away inside herself where you couldn't reach. I decided I wasn't gonna tell her about Peter and the money. In the worst way I wanted to, but now I wouldn't. She turned away from me without saying one word, and I watched her walk across the yard to the back door in the exact same body her mother had once, only she didn't know it.

51

I left my father in the yard and walked into the house, through the kitchen, down the hallway toward my parents' bedroom. Through my sad little mist of self-pity, I could see a bouquet of gladioli sitting there on the table at the foot of their bed, absolutely enormous. A gift from one of my parents' friends, it had to be.

I sat beside the bed and took the fingers of Mama's right hand into my own. Her face was drawn, ashen, all but the last embers extinguished. Coarse whiskers, sunken eyes, skin draped over bone and cartilage that had once been the superstructure of real beauty. What kind of a life had this woman had, married to my father? What had she hoped for in her youth and middle age, besides the obvious things women of her generation had been programmed to hope for? Why had she turned vicious on us for three years, ranting and shouting and saying things at the top of her lungs that no mother, no parent, should ever even whisper?

Why, as an adult, had her only daughter never asked about any of this?

I had never asked, really asked, because on the two or three occasions when I'd so much as tiptoed anywhere near that territory, my mother switched into a slightly false and completely upbeat mode and said something like, "Oh, Joanie, we didn't think about those things then. We didn't ask ourselves what we wanted the way you people do now. We had our house, our husband, our children. That was enough for us."

"But what did you want that you *didn't* have, Mama?"

"Oh, please, honey," she would say. "It just never entered our minds to think that way."

And I had never asked about the bad years because it would have been like unearthing radioactive waste that had been buried in the back yard for a quarter century. Some part of me did not want the answer for that, did not believe there was an answer, did not want to touch that sore place again. . . .

A few minutes passed, unasked, unanswered questions resting in a fine film on every surface. My mother stirred, pressed her lips together, and let them fall apart. A trickle of saliva slid down her chin. "Joanie," she said, before even opening her eyes.

I wiped a washcloth very lightly across her forehead and mouth and told her I loved her. "Are you in pain, Mama?"

"Not so much . . . today."

"Papa said you stopped taking your pills."

"It's temporary," she said.

"Did you stop taking them just so you could talk to me?"

"Not just . . . no." She closed her eyes, took three slow, shallow breaths, seemed to be summoning energy from the distant reaches of her shrunken body. She made a sign that she wanted to sit up. I helped her ratchet herself a few inches farther up on the pillow and watched a wave of pain take hold of her, shake her, slowly let her go.

"What about . . . your brother, have you seen him?"

"Peter and I had dinner together on Thursday night."

A flicker of joy played at the corners of her lips.

"Because he's in trouble? Tell me."

"Not really, Mama. Just the usual."

"Joanie." She squeezed my fingers. "Tell me."

"He says he's in a little bit of trouble, but with Peter you never know. He says he owes someone money, but he's said that two or three hundred times over the last ten years."

"I worry about him, don't you?"

"I'm tired of worrying about him, Mama."

"We can help him."

"Okay, Mama. Don't talk now."

"Peter—"

"Mama, please. Shh. . . . Rest now."

"That's the way he is . . . Joanie. We should . . . you're the way you are. Peter the way Peter is. Vito—"

"Fine, Mama. Please."

"Look at me."

Her eyes were blue death beacons in a skin-sheathed skull. The tears rose up through me.

"What are you thinking, Joanie?"

I shook my head.

"Joanie."

"I'm thinking this might be the last time I'm ever going to see you, Mama, and even now all we're talking about is Peter. Peter's gambling, Peter's troubles, Peter's life. I'm just tired of it. I just wish we could have a normal family, some kind of sane balance. We—"

"It's important not to hate a person, Joanie, not to judge them too much for what wrong things they did to you."

"I don't *hate* him. Of course I don't."

"Even if you think what that person does is terrible, disgusting . . . you should look at them with the same eye God does, see? I didn't know this then . . . before . . . with your father . . . understand?" She stopped and took a breath, swallowed, winced. "I should have forgiven your . . . I kept . . . in my heart. . . ."

"Rest, Mama. Please."

"The eye God sees you with . . ."

Another wet wave of sorrow broke over me, sweeping me out to sea and stranding me somewhere in a lonesome land between Leslie's cool logic and this: my mother's Sunday-school love, my father's sweet God-in-the-sky. They should have co-hosted the church hour on SBT, I thought, two devout Neapolitans talking like this in the face of death and addiction. But then something else occurred to me, and I let go of my mother's fingers.

"Hold my hand, Joanie. What are you thinking?"

I shook my head and stared at the window.

"Joanie?"

A plate fell and smashed in the kitchen. I tried to take a deep breath and made a loud sucking sound, childish, humiliating.

"Honey?"

"You're really talking about me, Mama. The disgusting . . . judging. You know. . . . I know what you're thinking, that I'm—that . . ."

"I look at you and I don't even think about that part of you, Joanie."

"But I *want* you to think about it, don't you know that? Peter's ruined his life by what he does. You make what I do out to be the same thing. I *love* women. That's the way my body is, my emotions. I don't burn money. I work hard. I don't borrow. I don't lie. I *love*."

"It's the same."

"It is not the same! It's not an addiction! It's not wrong!"

"It's the same. . . . When Peter walks into the room I see his spirit, not what he wears . . . how much money . . . who his girlfriend is—same with you."

I shook my head and turned my eyes away from her. Mystical mumbo jumbo. Sweetness and Jesus instead of hard psychological fact. My mother and father and Peter had always been this way, and it had always been a sheet of cold metal between me and them, the people I loved.

"What happens in the outside world is not that important," my mother was saying, slowly, in a weak voice, but with some kind of absolute certainty that was new for her.

I squeezed her hand and felt her pain just swallow me up. Suffering everywhere, in every news report, every body, every life. And the people who were supposed to be closest to me clinging to it as if it were bliss and treasure. Not taking their pain medicine. Not paying their debts. Not listening to logic. Plowing the same mind furrows again and again, sowing the seeds of more misery, not changing.

I leaned forward and rested my head in the bedclothes covering my mother's middle, the life place and the place of death. The same cells in which Peter and I had once taken our warm, watery refuge were consuming my mother now, eating up my last hopes for some kind of normal, logical family.

Without putting any weight there I held the side of my face against my mother's body, felt her hand settle in my hair, the smallest of tremors running through it like life's fleeting current. Still there. And the sheet of metal still between us.

"Do something to help Peter, sweetheart" was the last thing she said to me.

52

When Joanie went inside to see her mother, I followed her at first, far as the kitchen, but then I stayed there and didn't go to the back room. In the kitchen, even though it was the nurse's job to do it, I cleaned up the table. I put our salads together in one bowl. I covered the bowl with a plate and put it on a shelf in the frigerator that had never been so empty. I scraped the ziti Joanie didn't eat into the plastic bowl we took out to the compose, even though it seemed wrong to keep a compose for the garden for next summer. My life and Lucy's life had been nailed together now so many years it seemed like almost an unfaithfulness, planning for something she wouldn't never see.

But I did it, throwing away good food, thinking all the time whether to tell Joanie about the eleven thousand or not tell her. I let her know about the pain medicine and look what happened.

We always kept our money papers in an envelope, sticking out between Lucy's yellow ceramic jars, sugar and flour, but I didn't have to look at them. I had the numbers in my head—what was in the bank, what was in the investment Joanie's friend set up for us with the stocks—I knew it almost down to one penny. And when I paid Peter's debt Monday I would have less than one half what I had now. Less than one half. And how was I gonna put that into cash, that much, and carry it over to Mercury Street without telling nobody? And give it to Eddie Creviniello without wanting to kill him? And, after that, how was I going to look my own son in the face?

While I was thinking about this, one of the pasta plates jumped out of my hands and smashed in pieces on the linoleum on the floor, but I didn't get upset over it like I used to when I was young. That was the plus in being old; the temper got smaller. The minus was, when you bent over, the back went all stiff on you.

It took me a few minutes, but I swept up the pieces and put them in the wastebasket in a paper bag and finished cleaning the sink, all the time listening for some signal from the back room, some sound that they were calling me in to sit with them. But they were quiet in there.

When I finished the dishes I swept the floor, and still they were quiet. Lucy was sleeping, maybe, or else they were talking so soft you couldn't hear. The nurse was making herself busy in the living room, separating tomorrow's pills into the plastic holder they had now so you wouldn't mix up the days and lose count, and when I looked at her I thought: Eleven thousand! How could it be?

For a little while more I went back and forth in the kitchen, pressing my fingertip down on top of crumbs and brushing the finger and thumb together over the wastebasket, running the sponge over the stove where the gravy made trouble. Even although I wanted to walk down the hall and sit with Joanie and Lucy in the back room, it seemed the right thing now to let them have a talk by themself. Let the girls talk by themself now a little while, it didn't mean nothing against me. I pushed open the screen door and went out in the yard.

Always this was the time of day I loved. It was so late now in the summer—tomorrow would be September—that the sun was already behind the hill after supper, and the ground was throwing her smells up into the cool air, filling the space the heat left empty.

My father loved this time, too. Eighteen years he worked in the shoe factory in Lynn once I brought him over to this country. And after a day of that work, it was a good enough thing to be able to sit in a back yard with a cigar in your hand, if you had money for cigars, and make yourself small there with the world singing her noises all around you. My father tried to speak English with us sometimes so that he would be like a real American, but it gave him a lot of trouble, the English. "You life she goes by like-a one second," he said to me once. And that was true.

I was thinking about that one second then, about the things I knew from living it. More than anything I wanted to pass those things on to my children. But there was no language for me and Peter to talk, and with Joanie I said one and she heard two. Maybe Lucy was saying it to her, right now, and so it was better for them to have a talk on their own, without me sticking my man's nose in. Another time they'd call me in. Next time they would.

But then, right there in the middle of my yard, a terrible idea come to me. I began to imagine Lucy and Joanie were in there talking about Carmellina, and Alfonse, and the one big mistake I made in my life . . . so many years ago now it seemed like another person had been making it.

No, never, I said to myself. But then the Devil came back and told me when people were dying, all kinds of things happened to their mind. Maybe the pain of it had been so bad in Lucy all these years she had to tell somebody finally, the way I had to. I walked three steps to the fence between my yard and Rafaelo's yard—the garden all a mess now since he passed away—and I held on to the top of the pickets there.

In the years when I was still working, I used to go out sometimes after supper and stand against this fence and talk to my old friend Rafaelo, who was from the same *paese* as our family, near Avellino. In Italian we would talk, in the dialect. And once, when Alfonse came into the yard to get Peter to go someplace with him, Rafaelo said, in a way that didn't mean nothing bad, *"Come due fratelli"*— They're like brothers, the two of them. And that night we stayed out there in the yard until late, and I told him my secret, even though it felt like another unfaithfulness, doing that.

There was a fog coming in that night over Revere—a Saturday night like tonight—and it was a little bit cold on our arms, I remember. But we stood out here and I told the whole story: about Carmellina's no-good husband Louie going with other women and not caring who knew, drinking and yelling in the yard at night, hitting her. Louie went away and never came back, and for a long time there was nothing but crying coming from the back yard there. Carmellina, she took a job in the mornings at a shoe store on Shirley Avenue, for a nice Jewish fella, and the fella let her work as much as she wanted to, and he paid her pretty good.

And so sometimes on the weekend I would go over there and do a little carpenter work for her in the house—because it was all run-down, inside and out, thanks to Louie. I had been trying to do good, at first. Then, later, I started thinking all the time about what a beautiful woman she was, what a beautiful woman's body, how alone she was, how it wouldn't be a sin to spend time with her because it would be taking away some of the pain of her aloneness, making up a little bit for all the bad things Louie done.

Sometimes I would be with Lucy and I would be thinking about Carmellina in secret and telling myself it wasn't a sin. And then I was going over there, and telling myself I was just going to help her fix up the house, and lying straight in Lucy's face when she asked me was there something bad going on in my mind.

All this was like the Devil planting an idea in my body, and the idea growing, steady as a plant, and the roots going into my brain and little by little taking over. But I couldn't see that then.

And then . . . then Lucy was pregnant and it wasn't good for her body to have the lovemakin. And after we been that way two months or three months, my own body was like a wire somebody was sending the electric through. One day it was another Saturday, and Lucy and little Joanie they went into Boston to buy the presents for Christmas, and I went over with all the holy thoughts in the world in my mind to do a little work for a woman whose husband run away from her, and . . . it was my fault, not Carmellina's. All my fault, everything was. My body started it, not hers.

But her body finished it, though.

After that day I stopped going to see her. At first, the sin seemed to be stuck on me no matter where I went, a voice talking all the time in your ears. Then I went and confessed it to Father Dom and I swore I would never touch another woman besides Lucy for the rest of my life, and even though Father Dom said God would forgive me for it, and even though I felt a little bit better, I was never really the same man after that, never really the same. I would see Carmellina in her yard, and I would go to another part of the house. I would drive by Rigione's Market in my truck and pretend not to see her coming outside with her bundles. Some time went by and Lucy was starting to get very big, and one day I came home from work and Carmellina was standing there at the top of Tapley Avenue, a little ways off the sidewalk, in the street. She was wearing a plain dress with a sweater over it, and she was holding her hands together down in front of her, I remember. When I turned the corner in my truck, she stepped out so I had to put on the brakes.

Even now I can see her face when she told me. She was standing by the window of my truck with just the sweater on over her dress. It was the end of March, just going dark so that there was a light like the color of roses between the houses there, and on her skin, and the lights in the street coming on one after the other like little white moons.

"Vito," she said, "I don't want to tell you this but I have to tell you."

And then it was just like somebody took a big crowbar and hit me with it in the middle of my face.

Now my hands were squeezing the pickets on Rafaelo's fence so hard that little splinters were breaking off against the insides of my fingers. I was thinking about Lucy sitting near the window in the soft chair, with her belly out in front of her and her two hands on it, and me trying to make the words come out. Six different nights I tried before finally I told her. At first, for one minute, there was a look on her face like she hoped I was making some kind of a joke. And then something else fell down across her face and everything changed. Everything.

I was thinking about that everything when I heard the screen door of the house knocking closed too hard, the way I always told the kids not to do and they always did anyway. I heard Joanie come out on the steps and stand there. I could not turn around to look.

Lucy stayed living with me then only because she made me promise never to let the children know about it and never to say in public what happened. I promised. She made us move away from Tapley Avenue, where I had lived all my life after coming to this country. And I moved. She made me go to Carmellina and tell her we would help her with the money for the child, always, but that she should never say a word to nobody about who the father was. And even though it was a disgrace for her, Carmellina did what Lucy wanted. And even though it was a terrible stone on our backs for all of us—for Lucy, number one; for Carmellina; for me—we all did it the way Lucy wanted. At first it was like living in the fire in hell— me bringing the envelope with money up the front steps of Carmellina's house on Ambrose Street with the squeaking porch boards, Joanie with me, and Lucy waiting in the car with Peter, who was a little baby then, just barely one. Carmellina answering the door, sometimes with the new baby in her arms, and me giving the envelope, and looking at her in the eyes, and feeling Lucy in the car at the curb behind me. Two sons, one on either side of me. Two women, one on either side. It was like sitting in the fire in hell, and out of all of them I was the only one who deserved it. Ten minutes of a sin, and then years and years and years of suffering for that sin—sometimes it didn't seem fair to me. But who was I to talk fair?

The way God made it turn out then, Alfonse and Peter became best friends in the sports, even though they didn't live too near each other. Alfonse was always over our house, for years and years, which was a hard thing for Lucy. Uncle Vito was what he always called me, Uncle Vito and Aunt Lucy, and he was always over the house—playing the basketball, eating at our table, looking at Joanie like he wanted to be her friend too. That was the way God set it up for us.

And then it was a spring night, I could remember it like yesterday. The kids they were in the high school, and there was some kind of a big dance going on, and Alfonse, after so many times of being around our house all those years, he called up and asked Joanie would she go. We were in the kitchen after supper, and the phone ringing, and Joanie in the hallway talking quiet, like she was embarrassed and happy at the same time. Then saying good-bye and hanging up. Then telling her mother what the phone call was about. Then, instead of just telling Joanie the truth, Lucy went running through the house with the windows wide open, screaming that he was a no-good, this Alfonse, that she would never let her daughter go on a date with a no-good like him. Never! That she would kill herself first.

She took a steak knife from the kitchen drawer and ran in the bathroom with it and locked herself in. I had to smash the door off the hinges with my shoulder and take the knife away from her, and Joanie went in on her bed crying like somebody just died, and Peter ran out of the house and started playing the bocce all by himself, back and forth, back and forth, because he couldn't stand it.

The next day, nobody said one word about none of it, but it was like a new person come to live with us in the house. Lucy went around with a mask on her good heart from the morning until the night, and when she said something to me or to Peter, or even sometimes to Joanie, it was a horrible thing. "I never even loved you," she would say to me. Or, "I never even wanted you as a son," to Peter. Her voice changed, her eyes changed. She told Peter a hundred times he was a no-good, that his face was ugly with the pimples, that he was lazy, that he had the Devil inside his body—like all men did— and it was at the age when you can't say things like that to a boy. I tried hard as I could to stop it, but some things you can't stop.

This wasn't a mood that lasted a few days or a week, neither. This went on and on, my own wife screaming out through the screens on the windows, a coldness in her when she talked to me and to Peter and even sometimes to Joanie. They didn't go to the dance, naturally. And Alfonse stopped coming by then. But even so Lucy went on and on, like a flood can go on even a long time after the rain stops.

Finally, because I didn't know could I stand it anymore, I said something to Father Dom. Dommy came to the house many times after that and tried to talk to Lucy, but there was no talking. "Lucy, how are you?" he would say. And she would say, "Fine," in a voice that meant, *Stay away from me.* "Vito says you've been upset these last few months," Dommy would say to her. And she would say back, "It's Vito who's upset, not me. I'm the same as ever, Father." "But he says you're saying bad things to Peter." "I would never say bad things to my own son, Father. That's my flesh and blood, why would I say that? Why is Vito telling you lies?"

Like that.

So instead of Lucy changing, we all the rest of us changed a little bit. Me, Peter, Joanie, we made up a new type of family in this house, but it was a lie, this new family, and it made inside you a pressure that wanted to burst open you skin.

In those years sometimes I used to go out after supper and stand against this fence, like I was doing now. And I would think how all I had to do was to tell the truth to everybody and things would straighten out. But I didn't do it. For Lucy's sake, I didn't, and for my own. Little by little the time went by and things seemed to fix themselves without me telling everyone the secret. But then, after another few years, you weren't so sure they were fixed.

I heard Joanie's shoes on the patio now, and I stood still like a frozen man, staring into Rafaelo's garden.

Joanie came and stood beside me and rested her hand inside my elbone in a way that made me know right away they hadn't been talking about Carmellina in there.

I squeezed her hand between my arm and my body, but I didn't look at her, and I couldn't think what to say.

"She was awake for a little while, Papa. Now she's sleeping."

I looked at her pretty eyes, then away. "You had a good talk?"

She swallowed; she looked at Rafaelo's house. She said, "Pretty good," in a way I didn't believe. We were quiet a few minutes, thinking our own thoughts, a nice peace between us, the way it had been with me and Lucy watching the moon coming up, the way it had been with me and Peter, playing bocce.

"I didn't make a fuss about the pills."

"That's the girl."

"I have to leave," she said after another minute, very sad. "I'm going out with some friends, but call me anytime, all right, Papa? If anything changes, call me in the middle of the night. If I'm out, I'll check my messages every hour, so don't worry if I'm not there, okay? Just talk into the machine after it beeps."

"I'm not getting used to talking into the phone if nobody's there," I said. I took my hand out of my pocket and put it on her arm, but still I didn't look at her.

We went over near her car. The night was making herself still every minute, the stillness breaking now and then by somebody's talking in one of the other yards, or a car door knocking shut, or a dog. But whenever she was broken, the night would swallow the sound again like a lake eating the stones you threw in it. Whatever happened, the splash, the little round waves, the lake always went back to being still, which was the way the mind could be sometimes in some people.

When we were next to the car, Joanie asked me, "Have you talked with Peter recently, Papa?"

I told her Peter came by to visit just the night before this one, Friday, and that he brought the big flowers in her mother's room. She was surprised.

"Did he talk about the debt?" she asked me then, and it seemed wrong, telling another lie to my family, when it was lies that got us into trouble in the first place. She was looking at me; she cared enough now about her brother to ask. How could you lie to her?

"There's no debt no more."

"What do you mean, Papa?"

"I went to Eddie," I said.

She took her arm away. "When?"

"Today, this afternoon, like I said I was gonna. I walked down his house after confession and we had a little talk."

"And?"

I looked at her, then away.

"And?"

"Don't talk to me with that voice, Joanie," I said. "I'm still you father."

But it was like she could not hear those words.

"And?"

"He took a lot of money off and I told him I'm gonna pay it. Monday."

She walked around so she was standing between me and the door of her car, blocking.

"Papa, tell me you didn't do that."

"I did it. I knew you wouldn't think it was right."

"Please tell me you didn't."

"It's wrong to talk to you father with a voice like that," I said, but she wasn't hearing now.

"How much money?"

"How much? What difference does it make, how much? It's my money." I said it in as strong a voice as I could without talking so loud the neighbors would hear, but it was no good, and not the truth anyway because Joanie been giving us money for the nurses for a long time now.

"How much, Papa?"

"How much? From twenty thousand he made eleven. Eleven thousand."

She looked at me, almost as tall as me now because I was shrinking. Her mouth was shaking and her face had blood in it, and if she was a man I would have been sure she was getting ready to hit me now, the way Lucy had hit me. Once. One time twenty-five years ago—April fourth, a Wednesday, when she was crazy—and I walked out of the house and went and stayed with my brother two nights and almost never come back.

"Say what you gotta say," I told her, but the sound of the words came out wrong. I meant to let her yell at me—because there was a lot of weight on Joanie now, a lot of reasons for her to want to yell at her father, a lot of sadness in her life—and then to make the peace. But the sound of the words come out through something bad in me that I didn't know was there. For one small part of one minute, that sound floated in the air, and I thought I might have a chance to pull it back into myself. I reached out both my hands as if to catch the words, to put my hands on my daughter's shoulders and stop everything for a minute so we would both of us be able to fix everything, so we would be able to love each other again like years ago.

But before I could touch her, Joanie let a noise out of her, a crazy noise, and held her arms straight out, like I was a man attacking and she was holding him away. It wasn't much against me, her weight even now against my weight, but when she put out her hands that way it caught me by a surprise and knocked me one step back. And while I was going back I hit the heel of my shoe on the brick border of Lucy's flower garden that ran alongside the driveway, and before I could know what was happening I fell on my behind, hard, and there was a pain shooting up in my back that almost knocked me out.

I didn't see Joanie getting in her car. What I saw next after the first pain was the car backing out—she wasn't looking, just backing, wild—the headlights running over my face so I had to close my eyes.

I listened to the car speed away. After a minute, I made like I was picking the dead flowers off in Lucy's garden, so somebody driving up the street would think that was what I was doing, sitting there like that, an old man on his bum in the dirt.

53

I took the hospital cross street and drove down Mountain Avenue at fifty miles an hour—as if it were possible to drive away from the person I was, the family to which I belonged, the city I had been born into. Parked American cars along both curbs, fire hydrants, electric wires, trash barrels, weeds in the cracks in the sidewalks, hedges, chain-link fences, neatly painted wooden porches, windows glinting like eyes looking out upon tiny quilt squares of lawn on which children's pools and statues of the Virgin stood; mothers on the stoop smoking and talking, kids shrieking, a close-quartered American kingdom fraying unstoppably at every beautifully tailored hem and cuff. I did not have to really look at any of it. The monuments and commandments of this place were as familiar to me as the letters of my name, and I pushed against them on that night, and the harder I pushed, the more tightly they took hold.

Go back, I thought. Go back now and apologize. Sit with Papa in the yard. Spend the night. Make peace. This is your brother; there is nothing wrong with helping him, with letting an old man help his son. Go back.

And then: eleven thousand dollars! Eleven thousand dollars' worth of stubbornness and stupidity.

At the corner of Broadway, half a mile from my parents' house, I pulled to the curb, leaned back against the headrest, and closed my eyes. I drew and expelled a breath, two breaths. Why should it matter? Why couldn't I just walk away from it, send a check and a note, not care? Cut the cord, Leslie said. Just cut the cord and be done with it.

Someone waiting at the stop sign in the car next to me was playing rap music very loudly out the windows, the violent beat echoing against the fronts of the houses and the short row of stores near the corner. I waited for it to move on, but even when the driver had made the corner, that music seemed to hang in the end of day like the hot street's heartbeat: *anger here, anger here, anger here, all buried.*

I should go back. Sit for a minute to settle myself, call Leslie and tell her not to wait, then go back. An apology for my father, another few minutes with Mama.

But I sat and sat, and when I opened my eyes it was because of a cacophony of blaring horns. Though there were three open parking spaces in plain view just fifty feet farther up the curb, someone had double-parked next to the deli across the street from me, forcing cars making the tight corner to squeeze around him, blocking the street and fouling the air, engine running, oblivious. One more drop of irrationality in an overflowing cup.

In a minute the driver came outside carrying a six-pack of beer in one fist and a paper bag inside the other elbow, swaggering, arrogant, making the reasonable world change to suit him. I had to close my eyes against the sight of it and lean back on the headrest.

One wise decision now, one brave gesture, and I would strike right to the heart of everything I hated about this place. It was obvious what I should do, it had been obvious all along but I had been blinded to it by my own craving for Family. That had been the mistake. I had been dazzled by the idea of some imagined, sugary solidarity, some myth. I would take care of the myth now. I would settle my score with this imaginary Family. With both Families.

"Do something for Peter," Mama had told me. Fine, I would.

The car's digital clock read 7:59. I lifted the telephone out of its cradle, fished in my daybook until I found the business card D.B. had given me, and dialed.

54

I had been instructed to be at the Parkway Grill and Lounge at 8:30 P.M. sharp, to sit at the bar, and not to order dinner. I did more or less as I was told, except that there were only a few drops of gas in the T-bird, and I thought the ocean air might clear my head, so instead of driving, I set out from my condo on foot, and since I wasn't much of a walker, I didn't figure the time just right and ended up strolling into the Parkway Grill and Lounge eleven minutes late by the bar's digital clock. No huge deal.

No huge deal, except that Xavier was there already, twitching his forehead muscles, looking not that happy to see me.

I swallowed, I smiled, I turned my hands palm up, as if to say, You know me, man, nothing personal. "Sa-sorry I'm late, Zave," I told him, when I was close. "Traffic was wi-wi-wi-wild on the b-boulevard tonight. Crazy teenagers, you know?"

Xavier took a last sip from what appeared to be a glass of ginger ale with a dozen maraschino cherries in it and hoisted himself off the bar stool. Without leaving any money, and without so much as hooking a finger in my direction, he moved towards the back door, slow and heavy, like a bull. I followed.

The back door was not used by customers. It let out onto a flagstone patio with a dumpster in one corner and cases of empty beer bottles stacked against the stockade fence. When we'd taken three steps across it, Xavier stopped, turned, and frisked me in what seemed like a casual way . . . immediately felt the lump in the sportcoat pocket, fixed his eyes on me like two light-blue rifle barrels.

"The money for Eddie," I said, and keeping the same innocent expression on my face while my bowels went loose, I reached in as if I was all ready to hand over the contents of that pocket. But Xavier only gave a tiny shake of his head, a nasty look, and ran his huge mitts up and down my legs and across my back. Before he could turn away I put a hand on his arm. What I wanted was to take an iron bar and break his face open with it, as a type of lover's revenge on him for scaring Elsie. But the lover's revenge would have to wait. What I did was cough a little to clear my throat, and say, in as close to my normal voice as I could manage, "Zave, a small fa-favor, buddy. What kind of ma-ma-m-ma-m-mood is he in about me? What should I do? How should I p-play it?"

For ten or fifteen heartbeats, Xavier only stood in the yellow neon twilight, studying me. And it seemed to me then that there was a twinkle of respect beneath the bushy eyebrow, a beast's affection. "What you should do?" he said.

"Yeah, I mean—"

"What you should do was left town."

"What, run out on him? I couldn't do something like that, man, ya-you-you know me. And anyway, I'd be na-nothing outside Revere. I wouldn't survive t-two minutes."

Xavier shrugged, peered at me in a kind of half-admiring disbelief. "What you should do was found a good doctah."

"What?"

"Get a operation. Get the bullshit cut outa ya." He lifted an index finger the size of a small banana and poked it once into the middle of my chest, for emphasis. Half inch this side of real trouble.

We passed through a squeaking gate and came upon the limo there, parked on a little unlit scrap of asphalt between the stockade fence and the street. Dark territory. Dirty. The perfect habitat for a rodent like Chelsea Eddie Crevine.

Xavier pointed towards the right rear door with his chin. As I ducked in and pulled the door shut, the back of Eddie's right hand caught me on the side of the face. It shook me, drew a little blood inside my mouth, but Eddie was no boxer and the pain passed right away.

"For being late," he said, too quiet.

To hell with you, then, I thought. To hell with the both of you. And whatever small little drop of doubt I'd been carrying around with me just evaporated.

Xavier pulled out into the street, slow and smooth as a snake sliding. I turned my face full to Eddie and tried to hold eye contact in
the shifting shadows. "When they come fa you," Uncle Peter told me
once, "they come fast. No nice hellos. Nothing but four-letter language and hands. I hope they never come fa you, Petey, but if they
come, you stall. And if you can't stall no more, then you keep your
eyes straight on them and you don't whine. These are like sharks,
these people. You whine, that's like goin swimmin bleedin in Aus-
tralia. See?"

I saw. I could feel the truth of it in the air around me, in the way
Xavier was ticking his ruby ring against the steering wheel, in the
way Eddie was sitting—knees spread apart, toe tapping the carpeted
floor. They were watching me without watching, waiting for me to
give them any excuse to do what the sick little sadist inside them
wanted to do anyway.

Eddie had his face half turned out the far window and was flipping
the armrest ashtray open and shut with his left little finger. After a
minute I turned forward again, but I watched him out of the corner
of my eye, and I watched where Xavier was taking us, and I kept my
hand near the door handle on the chance I might have to risk a run.
Run where? was the question. Alfonse's house? FBI headquarters?

We went along the boulevard in a hideous silence, past Stevie's,
Kelly's, the front of my own building, full darkness settling slowly
down over the city. I could feel my heartbeat in my face. Out of
some old habit, an old reflex that would do me no good now, a thousand excuses pressed out against my lips. I chewed them all up and
swallowed.

At Point of Pines circle I hoped we'd make a U-turn and head
back down the boulevard, which would mean we'd be staying in Revere tonight, just driving back and forth, working things out. But
Xavier plowed straight on through, over the drawbridge, along the
Lynnway. Teenagers in Corvettes, cops at stoplights, Dunkin
Donuts, McDonald's, car dealers with their triangle flags waving—
the entire rest of the world living their normal little lives while I
sucked blood out of my cheek and peed myself in the back of
Chelsea Eddie's limo.

Still, in some weird way, I almost liked it. The feel of your own fate rubbing against you, the chance of victory here, victory against huge odds. The arrogant big shot Eddie Three Hands thought he was on top here, and he wasn't, and there was a real satisfaction in that for me, I admit it.

So we cruised on: Lynn Beach, the Swampscott line. I kept my lips ironed tight together, my hands palm down on my legs. The essential fact to keep in mind here was that Eddie had always been a little bit smarter than your average Mob type, which was why he'd survived while the rest of the New England Mafia was either rotting in coffins or doing old-age time in Leavenworth. A little smarter, a little sneakier—it was important to be ready for anything now, any possible thing.

After ten minutes of silence you could have taken a bite out of, we crossed into Marblehead, then Marblehead Neck, where the houses weren't houses at all but mansions, castles; where, instead of working for a living, guys my age spent their days on the golf course, or out on their yachts, and their nights reading the stock pages to see how many more thousands they'd made that afternoon off of somebody else's sweat and somebody else's brains. They weren't gamblers, though, those people. No, of course not. They were *investors*.

At last, when we'd made one loop around the Neck, Eddie spoke. "Tell me," he said, very calm-sounding, very vicious. "What am I gonna do with you?"

I felt a little nervous laugh bubble up against my teeth then, because that was exactly the same question my father and mother used to ask me over and over when I was growing up. What were they gonna do with me, what were they gonna do?

Then and now, I hadn't the foggiest idea.

"Take my b-business," I said, in some voice I had never heard. "Take my car, the condo. . . . You could have sa-somebody ki-ki-kill me if you wanted to, I know that, Eddie. There's na-nothing I can do."

"The condo and the car are worth zero," he said, so quiet the words seemed to be instantly absorbed by the carpet and the leather seats. "We checked. Your so-called real estate business is worth minus zero."

I listened to the voice, gauged it, kept my face blank and my mouth closed and the lapels of my sport coat close together.

When he spoke again it was half a decibel higher. "In the old days, the guy you owed, he'd chop off your fucking leg with a butcher knife and let you walk around the city that way for the rest of your fucking life. Understand?"

I nodded.

"Something like that does me good, because people would see it and pay me what they owe. Year after year, no excuses. You'd be an advertisement on crutches, a fucking cripple billboard. I'd give you a drink, I'd lay out a piece of plastic in the cellar and turn the stereo up loud. I'd have Xavier hold you down and I'd chop off your leg at the crotch. Myself. With a fucking butcher knife."

I looked down at my legs, accidentally, then out the side window again. We'd left the Neck now and were crawling through summer-evening traffic in downtown Marblehead, as if God was giving me my opportunity to jump out and make a run if that's what I wanted. I considered it. I stared out at the shadowy streets and wondered if that was the better move. A bookstore, a Chinese restaurant, an old-style ice-cream parlor. Quiet. Rich. People walking along under the streetlights with kids in strollers and ice-cream cones in their hands. Another universe compared to Revere. I pictured myself going into exile in some universe like this, a thousand miles from here. Forged papers. A new face. I thought of my mother and father, of what people would say about me in the city when I was gone. I called to mind some of the things I'd heard about Eddie and his operation, but compared to the sweat and smell of this minute, those stories seemed like only a softer version of underworld life . . . in just the same way Marblehead was a softer version of Revere. We lived real, at least. In Revere, we lived real. I was living real now. . . . It had its drawbacks.

"I mean," Eddie was saying, letting the voice rise a little and turn harder, "instead of coming to me yourself, like a man, what do you do? Instead of answering my phone calls, like a man, you run, you make up stories, you try to bribe my guy here with a lousy hundred bucks."

I flexed my toes inside my shoes.

"Instead of coming to see me yourself, you send your half-senile old man *to my front door* this afternoon. You coward asshole, you. You *strunze.*"

"My fa-father came to you?"

Eddie raised an open hand and held it, knuckles forward, a foot from my face. "You start lying to me now, and I swear to Christ I'll beat you unrecognizable, right here."

"No lie, Eddie. I didn't know. I sw-swear."

Eddie held the hand in place another three seconds, then dropped it back onto his leg and swung his head closer to me, like a cow. It was almost dark in the car, and I could see only part of his jowly face in the passing strobe of the streetlights, the pouch of his neck, the fat button nose. If there was any emotion at all showing there, it was disgust. Eddie seemed about to spit. "Who told him then?" he said.

"N-not me. Did he say I told him?"

Nothing, not a twitch around the eyes, not a word. Xavier turned off the main drag into a dark, quiet road and drove past a little over-look where you could gaze down on the stock-market guys' yachts and sailboats; then he swung back onto the main street again, just cruising now, waiting for the order.

"One of two things," Eddie said. Something new was beginning to crawl into his voice now—some old fear or humiliation, some old hurt—and it made him seem almost human for a few seconds, which scared me worse than anything. "Either you're the world champeen fucking liar when anybody else would be shitting their pants, or you have a family more fucked up than any family that ever lived. . . . You didn't tell your old man to come see me?"

"No w-way, Eddie."

"He wasn't setting it up so your sister could catch Eddie Crevine by the balls on her TV show?"

"Ab-ab-absolutely not."

"And you don't know who called me *at my fucking house* tonight, fifteen minutes before I left?"

I shook my head.

"Take a guess."

"I ca-can't."

"I'll give you a fucking clue. Same last name as you. A she. Not your mother."

At this piece of news, the whole tone of things did an about-face. All of a sudden I wanted a cigarette in the worst way, but there was only an empty pack in my other pocket.

"What'd you, give her a story about me for her TV show? Is that what's going on? I think that's what's going on, you little cocksucker."

"No wa-way."

"No? Did you hear what her little show is about?"

"N-not exactly."

"Who gives her her bullshit information?"

"I don't know."

"Not you, though."

"I'm not that stupid, Eddie. I'm a ga-gambler, a ba-bullshitter, but I'm not stupid that way."

"Alfonse Romano, maybe?"

Eddie was peering at me now, very close, and it required every ounce of acting skill I had in order to hold the surprise in my voice, not to react to Alfonse's name, not to show. I brought my eyebrows down and together as if the name just irritated me, which, actually, at that particular minute, it did.

"Captain Romano, your good buddy. The Romeo of Revere Beach."

"He hates my guts now, that g-guy. He has me picked up if I so much as ba-bur-bur-burp in p-public."

"Your piece-of-shit sister is friends with him, though, isn't she?"

"That was a long ta-time ago, Eddie."

"He's been single ever since that terrible accident with his wife. Maybe he has the hots for your sister, could that be?"

"Anything could be."

Anything. They could have seen me with Alfonse at the beach, they could have seen me with Joanie at the Top of the Hub. Eddie could be having Alicia watched, which meant he would know about her and Alfonse (why else in the world would anyone call him "Romeo"?) and was trying to trick it out of me. Or Billy could be feeding Alfonse and the FBI all the information they'd ever wanted to hear about Eddie and then turning right around and feeding Eddie information about them an hour later. Anything.

I tried to clear my mind and see it straight, but I kept knocking up against this vision of my father driving the old family car to Eddie's house, parking it there, climbing the front steps with a necktie on, rapping on the door with his scarred carpenter's knuckles, and offering to pay my debt. Somehow, it gave me a little courage.

"Maybe that's something you could do for me. You could get your sister to keep her little pussy mouth shut."

A small laugh flew out from between my lips, perfectly unplanned, perfect. "She w-wouldn't even think of ba-buying the Curtis house, never mind hurting her pr-pr-pr-precious career by doing her brother a fa-favor like that."

"Maybe if somebody mailed her her brother's leg in a plastic bag she'd think about it."

"She ca-can't stand me, Eddie," I said. "She'd just as soon see me da-deh-deh-dead, I'm telling you. It would be a load off her mind."

True as I had tried to make them sound, when those words were actually out in the air, they rang against the leather interior in a bad way. I did not know if Joanie being mad at me was a plus or a minus in this situation, I did not know how to play it, whether to make myself out to be the only person who could get her to cancel her report on Chelsea Eddie, or whether to stay with something like the truth and just hope to step into the world beyond these windows one more time alive. One more time. It did not seem like so much to ask.

I decided just to keep talking. "If she di-didn't do her series, somebody else would f-finish it now," I said. "I don't know where she gets her information. There's lots of stoolies around—j-junkies, pa-punks, l-liars. You know that. It could be anybody."

"Cops," Eddie said, all sarcastic. "Priests. Housewifes." He flipped the ashtray shut and showed me his full face again. His hair was thick and very short, white as a businessman's shirt, and his face was round, a fat man's face, a terrifying clown's face. Murder in it now, plain as day. "You know what you owe me," he said.

"Eleven and ch-change."

"And you don't know your old man came and said he was gonna pay it off?"

"I swear to God I don't. It's un-un-un-unbelievable to me. I can't even m-make myself imagine it."

"Mister Italy himself, who's been in this country how long and can't talk right?"

"He gets nervous, that's all. He was probably afraid when he c-came to your house."

"And you don't know your sister calls me and says your father isn't paying?"

"T-to-to ha-hell with her. I didn't know any of this. I've been la-laying around my apartment all day li-listening to the phone ring and sweating blood. I went to Stevie's for breakfast, that's all, because I was starving and he lets me run a t-tab."

"So then, tell me. What am I going to do with the debt?"

"I don't know."

"You don't know. And you say it like you don't give a shit."

"Of course I g-give a shit. But I can't *make* people buy a house. I can't ba-borrow ten cents from anybody in Revere anymore. I went to the track and won n-nine hun-hundred dollars yesterday. Here." Very very carefully, steadying my shakey fingers, I reached into the inside pocket and pulled out the envelope. Xavier turned his head one inch and watched my hand in the mirror. "It's the best I can do ra-right now."

Eddie did not seem to have the smallest interest in the money, which struck me, for about one second, as a piece of good luck. I set the envelope down on the leather seat and made myself not look at it.

"You still didn't give me no answer."

A little creek of sweat rolled down along my ribs, I tried to get my thoughts in line. Xavier was driving in big circles now, just driving, wearing me down. We had crossed back into Swampscott, and Swampscott was where Alfonse made love on Saturday nights with the one woman in America he should have left alone. Another minute and they were going to take me to the motel, strangle me, and leave me dead in one of the rooms there, Channel Eight going on the TV. A double message.

"You think somebody like your sister means anything to me?"

I moved my head back and forth in two slow shakes. Things were spinning out now, just spinning out past my reach. Eddie was pulling a Three Hand on me.

"You know what I do with broads like that?"

"I na-na-know."

"I have Xavier and Michael pick her up one night when she's walking into her new apartment on the waterfront. I have them take her to Billy O's place in the West End and do whatever they want with her for a couple hours. Then I have them drive her up to a friend I have who runs a business about half a mile from here. Tree business. Into the fucking shredder she goes, and she comes out in twenty thousand little wet pieces, and we mix the tiny pieces in with a pile of other shit—stone dust, construction scraps—and we mix it with concrete, and we pour somebody's fucking cellar floor with it someplace in New Hampshire. All of a sudden your bigshot sister is a brown spot in Joe America's playroom, and all the reporters get upset because she just dropped off the face of the earth, but how do they trace it to Eddie Crevine? One way—if this guy here talks." Eddie pointed a finger at the back of Xavier's head. "You're a betting man. Tell me, what do you think the odds are of that happening?"

"N-not good," I said.

Xavier gave me a hard look in the mirror.

"The ah-ah-ah-odds are za-zero," I said very fast.

"Right. So how afraid am I of your sister?"

"Not too afraid."

"Right. But here's the problem. Your sister has the balls to start calling my house all of a sudden. Why is that?"

"I don't know, Eddie."

"How does she get the fucking number of my house? Nobody has that number."

"N-not from me. I don't even—"

"Better not from you. It's a mystery, though, isn't it."

"She's a re-re-reporter. She has her sources, I guess, la-like every-body."

"Not you, though."

"I swear on my ma-ma-ma- my moth- my m-mother, Eddie."

"She calls my wife and says who she is and that your old man won't pay and then she hangs up like a ignoramus. That's fine. Your old man won't pay. You can't pay. But the thing is, you still owe me. And every other fucking piss-drinker in the city knows it and they're watching to see what I do. And sometimes when a person gets in a situation like you, they go desperate, and the desperateness makes them crazy, and they get it in their heads to go talk to somebody. . . . Maybe you already did that."

"I didn't. I wa-went to my sister and asked her to buy the Ca-Ca-Curtis house because you said that was a wa-way I could pay off my debt, and because I know she has the ma-money. She laughed in my face. After I ate at Stevie's today, Al-Al-Alfonse waylaid me and sa-said he'd take me to the station and book me if I didn't go for a ride with him, and he fed me all this bullshit about Ga-Gamblers Anony-mous and c-counseling and religion and so much cr-crap I could have thrown up all over him. Those are the only people I talked to since Billy O on Friday afternoon. . . . I'm not the st-stoolie type, you know that about me. We had ba-business a l-long time ago and I paid you back then and nev-never said a word about it to anybody. And I'm going to p-pay you back now and not say anything this time, either. I swear to G-G-G-God."

Eddie mumbled something that sounded to me like, "Don't bet on it," and after that there was a terrible silence, just a terrible, aw-ful silence, the world floating by in black slow motion, sweat com-ing out of me everywhere. It had been a mistake even to show up, that was perfectly clear now. A mistake, a Hollywood move. Eddie was pissed off the way a bear gets pissed off: jealous about his wife, worried about Joanie's series, furious beyond thinking about it. He was going to play with me for an hour or so like a bear with a squir-rel, try to see what he could find out about Joanie or Alfonse, and then make me disappear like I was a slice of salami in a sandwich.

Just like that: gone. I could feel it now. I could feel the death air against my skin.

But then, in response to some silent signal I did not see, Xavier turned the car back towards Revere, cruising still, five miles an hour under the speed limit.

Which meant we were going back, away from the house of the guy with the tree business, away from the motel. Just when I'd started to lose faith, we were going back.

Eddie was sitting perfectly still and quiet, radiating hate. When we reached the rotary at the end of Lynn Beach again, he said, very calm now, "Curtis wants his house burned."

I whipped my head around and saw that he was serious. This was the Three Hand move, then, Eddie's ace. "If Ca-Curtis g-gives me a little more time," I said, "I'm a ha-hundred percent sure I could sell that ha-house for him, I know I could. That way we could b-both pay you. I almost had it sold to this Cam-Cam-Cambodian couple the other day—"

At the mention of the Cambodian couple, Eddie smiled. He held up a hand. "You ran out of time, I just told you that. Curtis wants the house burned, and I think I found the absolute perfect person to burn it: the Prince of the Revere Beach Boulevard Bullshitters. Whose sister is a TV lady sticking her nose in, whose best friend is a cop. It makes me happy when things fall into place like this. It gives me faith in *G-G-G-God.*"

"There's twelve fa-families in that house, Eddie. There's ki-kids."

"Curtis wants it burned, and so do I. We think tomorrow would be a excellent day for the fire, before you start to go a little mental on me, before your sister gets any more involved in your private life than she already is, before your old man gets frustrated that he can't bail out his son and starts to consider his other options. You burn the house. And then, if your sister tries anything, if Alfonse tries, if your father tries, then we feed you to the proper authorities with the proper evidence. Their excellent little stutter-mouth Saint Peter is an arsonist who made kids die; we can prove it, eyewitnesses, and so on. You get the picture now, right?"

I nodded.

"All those families will be in church tomorrow. All the firemen will be taking their Sunday naps, see?"

"They're all Cam-Cam-Cambodians and Vietnamese living in those apartments now. They don't go to church."

"Then you shouldn't worry about them so much, if they're all *Cam-Cam-Cambodians.* You don't owe the *Cam-Cam-Cambodians,* and you don't owe the Vietnamese. You owe me. You don't seem to appreciate what that means. And I don't know what else I have to say to fucking convince you."

"There's things I ca-can't do, that's all." I tried to roll down my window to let a breath of air into the back seat, but there was some kind of lock mechanism on the electric button, some kind of smirk on Xavier's face. On the one hand, I should have just shut up, just said yes and got out of the fucking limo alive, with the little mojo in my pocket. I knew that. On the other hand, it would have looked too easy. Eddie would have smelled something. On the third hand, my stomach and my chest and my legs were vibrating with a kind of weird manicness, and the only way I knew how to deal with it was to talk.

"You sure?" Eddie said, like he was about to tell Xavier to turn back towards the tree shredder.

"Eddie, I—"

"That's very honorable of you, not wanting to do this. Very honorable. But here's the thing: At some point when the lifeboat's going down, either you push somebody out or you all go down together, get it?"

I nodded.

"And I don't hear you pushing."

You, I wanted to say. I'm pushing you.

"You could still change that, of course, but as of this minute I don't see you being of any use to me except not paying me about half what you owe."

"If I had something to tell you, I'd tell you this minute, this second, be-be-believe me."

"But you don't."

"I don't."

"Not about your sister, not about your good buddy the captain of police."

"Na-Nothing."

"Then you burn the house, that simple. Curtis gave me a key, and we had a pro go into the maintenance closet in the cellar and set it all up with paints and rags and so on, a can of kerosene, everything. That was another debt being paid off; see how it works? Alls you have to do is go in there, tomorrow sometime—whenever you want, you pick the time so long as it's tomorrow—and light your cigarette lighter to a piece of special rag that burns itself all to nothing in about a minute. That's all. The rag runs up inside the wall along the wires so it looks exactly the same as an electric fire. You can get all the little Cambodian kids out, if you want. You can even call the fire department after a few minutes and let them come and chop holes in the walls and flood the rooms with water. I don't give a fancy fuck, so long as there's enough damage."

"Eddie—"

The voice was hard as iron now, Eddie leaning over, Eddie splashing me with little drops of spit. "Or you can act like a moron and still say no. In which case I'll have somebody else light the fucking fire in the fucking maintenance closet and then I'll get one of those stoolies or druggies you were telling me about, or maybe even two of them, and somehow—somehow, I don't know how—I'll convince them to swear on their mothers' pussies that it was Peter Imbesalacqua the real estate guy they saw going in there in the middle of the night when all the fried little Cambodian kids were asleep. And then, instead of walking around a free man in two days, with no debt, you'll have your beautiful face on the TV, where your sister and your old man can both see what happens when people fuck with me, and you'll be in Walpole for twenty or thirty years getting your rear end reamed out by some *animale* I won't even have to pay to do it—"

Eddie ran short of breath, wiped his fingers across his mouth, and tried to get his face back under control. For a moment there, his ugly true self had popped out, and he was trying to push it back down now, to wrap it up in a quieter, more dignified personality that suited him like a silk jacket on a lizard. I watched him for a minute and then turned my eyes out the window, trying to keep one half of one step ahead. The house burning did not make sense. It was some kind of maneuver, another angle. He was working me to get at somebody else, that was clear enough—somebody who could really hurt him, or somebody he was so angry at he couldn't let it go—Alfonse or Joanie or some mysterious other person I could not even imagine. He had somehow found out that his wife was sleeping around—from Billy Ollanno, possibly—but he wasn't a hundred percent sure yet, and he wouldn't go after a policeman just on Billy's word, so he was pressing all the territory around Alfonse, digging for clams, watching for some little squirt of proof to appear when the weight got to be too much. Which was what the house-burning idea must be. They were waiting for me to crack, turn my best friend . . . which would be a very long wait.

We drove past my apartment building without slowing down, and I thought of Elsie sitting at home waiting for my call, Elsie and Austin, who wouldn't be able to sleep until they heard from me. One more little burst of courage.

"You understand now, right?" Eddie said. "Your sister did you a lot of good today. It was all set up nice with your father. Monday, you would have been a free man. You could have gone out and started losing money all over again and borrowing from somebody else. But your sister makes one phone call, and with that call she changes you from a free man into a arsonist, like that. . . . And still you don't have anything to say to me about her."

"Eddie," I said, letting the smallest note of whining creep into my voice, "wha-what if—"

He brought his hand down hard on top of my thigh and moved his face half the distance across the back seat. "Listen. For once in your life, Mister Prince Bullshitter, don't talk, all right? Just listen. You burn it, understand me? There's no choice here, no games, no second and third and fourth and fifth chances. No salesman's talk, okay? Just fucking *burn the fucking house!*"

I shrank back from him and did battle with a crazy urge to smile, to laugh a crazy laugh in Eddie's pudgy face, to thank him for adding conspiracy to commit arson onto his tape-recorded loansharking rap. And in such a nice clear voice.

Xavier was slowing down. They were going to let me go any second now, I could feel it. I had held on, kept myself from saying anything I shouldn't have said, let Big Eddie do all the talking, and I had a little trophy now to carry away with me. A little Swiss-made trophy and brass stones.

At the corner of Shirley Avenue, four blocks from Curtis's house, Xavier pulled the limo to the curb. Eddie squeezed my thigh and took his hand away. "Take a walk up there right now and see what the setup looks like," he said. "I have somebody waiting there to show you the closet." He checked his watch and said, "Right on time," but the voice was changed now. All of a sudden Eddie wasn't making eye contact anymore. He was embarrassed. He seemed in a hurry to get me out of the car. Eddie Crevine had put the squeeze on and gotten nothing, and he couldn't live with himself now, couldn't look another man in the eye. "It's nine forty-five," he said. "Tomorrow night, nine forty-five, it should look different, that house. Different enough so Curtis's insurance company don't argue. You understand now, right?"

I nodded. I kept my eyes on him.

"Nothing else to tell me?"

I did not trust myself to speak.

"You're going by the house now, right?"

I nodded.

"No bullshit this time, right?"

"R-right, Eddie."

"Go."

55

After I made the call to Eddie Crevine's house I started the car again and drove the streets in a kind of trance, passing Peter's darkened office and several Catholic churches—there seemed to be one on every other block—riding very slowly all the length of Revere Street. I did not know how much time passed. I did not call Leslie, or drive back to my parents' house and apologize, or feel any strong urge to find Peter and tell him what I had done.

Driving had always calmed me, but I did not especially want to be calm then. What I wanted was a new understanding of myself, some way of rejoining my two separated halves. Through the shifting fog of feelings it seemed obvious on that night that my relationship with my brother sat at the heart of that disunity, but I could go no further.

After a time I found myself back on Broadway, still trance-driving, and then at the corner of Ambrose Street, so I made the turn there, thinking I might coax a word of wise counsel from Cousin Alfonse. Perhaps he would have an answer, a place to stand between Boston and Revere, too cold and too warm, between just toughness and just love.

It was only a plain two-story wood-frame Cape with a steep roof, a porch, and a small front yard overgrown with lilac bushes, but Alfonse's mother's house held some mysterious and not very pleasant power over me. I did not know what it could be. The squeaking front steps, the old-fashioned doorway trim—it evoked some half-buried childhood moment. I'd been there a few times with Peter—as a gangly eleventh-grader—using his friendship as an excuse to visit, because I'd developed a riotous crush on Alfonse Romano and was ashamed of it. Alfonse was mature and popular and a basketball hero of sorts, but two classes behind me, and it had seemed an admission of all my insecurities then to be even thinking about a younger boy.

There was something else about this porch, though, some echo here of his mother's welcome—glasses of cola and orange soda ("tonic," people in Revere called it) and vanilla ice cream—that made me vaguely uneasy. She had always been too effusive, too nice, presupposing some immediate intimacy that should have taken more time. "Auntie Carmellina," she insisted we call her. It always felt forced.

Climbing the old wooden steps now, I thought of that woman's eager embraces and then of another, more recent memory: coming here to pay my condolences after Alfonse's wife had died, my police detective "cousin" weeping at his out-of-style kitchen table, with Auntie Carmellina in the back room, at prayer. Alfonse and I had been in our early thirties by then. And by then, as far as romantic matters were concerned, the tidal sweeps of youth had long ago left us standing on different sides of an immense and unnavigable sea. Still, there had been some odd sense of connection with him in his grief, not a romantic link, but something else: the sense of being whole—or almost whole—while those closest to us remained confused and miserable; the sense of having passed through some fiery trial and come out on the other side, sane, saner. After that evening I had turned my back on that connection, though—hardly calling, never visiting again—for fear of giving him a false message, perhaps. Or showing him too much of my hidden self.

The window in the house's front door was large and oval-shaped—detail from another era—with a sad, yellowed curtain drooping on the inner side. I rapped four times on the old glass and waited.

Half a minute passed. I rapped again and turned to look for his car. A moist darkness seemed to be sprouting from the shadows of the small yard, almost as if night were giving birth to night, deepening itself, multiplying itself. I saw my father falling, heard the sound he had made. I decided I would sit there on the step for ten minutes and decide what to say when I returned to Proctor Avenue, how to make amends. Peter would have to figure out his own way to pay the debt, to kick his habit, but Eddie would not harm him, not now, not with the vigilant eye of the press focused upon him. A woman had answered my call. "If Eddie hurts him," I told her, sitting at the corner of Broadway with the car phone clutched in white fingers, "if he so much as tears the sleeve of my brother's sport coat, I will personally see to it that his face is on the television screen every night for weeks. I will make it my personal crusade to put his fat Mafia ass behind bars. Is that clear?"

I had, for once, found an almost perfect solution. I had trumped Revere with Boston and retired from the game.

Alfonse's doorbell was coated in a light film of dirt, and stuck crookedly in the pressed position. No one answered my second knock, or my third; probably he'd been called in to work or was out on a date.

I stepped down off the porch and saw that I had left my headlights on again—a habit of mine—and that the passenger-side beam was just catching the left rear reflector of Alfonse's plain dark-blue car, parked halfway back in the driveway. I snapped off my lights, walked around the side of the house and found him there, standing with his back to me, leaning forward with both hands on a lawn chair, staring into a starry city sky.

He hugged me hard against his chest, brought me a glass of red wine with one small golden peach slice floating in it like a crescent moon in blood. There was a cell phone folded into his shirt pocket—totally surreal in this setting—and he tapped it every few minutes, as if for luck. "Your brother might call," he said, after the third or fourth of these taps. He glanced at me, turned his chair a bit closer so we were half facing each other in the darkness. I took a breath and told him what had happened with my father, what I had said to the woman who'd answered the phone at Eddie Crevine's house. "The maid, probably," I added, not quite so sure of myself suddenly. "She probably had no idea what I was talking about, probably didn't even give him the message."

"His wife," Alfonse said, after a minute. "They don't have a maid. . . . She'll tell him." He brought his watch up to where he could read it, then tapped the phone in his pocket. "Peter might call."

"You said that already."

"Sorry."

"What's wrong, Alfonse."

"Nothing."

I let out a little nervous half-laugh, a terrible syllable. "You're going to tell me I made a mistake, calling Eddie."

"No, Joanie. I'm not sure. You might have."

"There's something I don't know. What is it?"

"Nothing, Joanie. I just wasn't aware your father had actually gone to Eddie, that's all. He told me he was going, but for some reason I never thought he would actually get there. I should have called to see. . . . I'm trying to work out how it changes things."

"All there is to work out is my brother. I've fixed it for him now. He'll have to find a way to pay the debt on his own. After that he can get into a program if he wants, but I'm out of it as of this minute. This was my last attempt to save him. I'm finished."

"Peter's meeting with Eddie tonight," Alfonse said, after a moment. He would not quite look at me when he said it. "Right now, probably."

"He'll talk his way out of it."

"I hope so."

What happened to walking him right to the edge of the cliff? I wanted to say. But I turned away a few degrees and kept silent. A car passed by slowly in the street behind us and turned around in the gravel driveway next door. We listened to it slowly drive off.

Alfonse gestured with his glass. "Your family used to live on the other side of that fence, you know."

"I was still in diapers when we moved. I have no memories of it."

He fished into his shirt pocket and drew something out from behind the telephone, a small notebook that looked like one I had seen my mother scribbling in at times, when she was still able to scribble. He started to say something about it but was seized by a sneezing fit. When it ended, he blew his nose in what seemed an apologetic way, half turning, delicately wiping the handkerchief back and forth and folding it into his pocket. He turned to me again, struggling to speak. I listened to the sound of voices from one of the nearby yards, closed my eyes, and offered up a kind of atheist's prayer that what I had done for my brother had been the right thing, and that what Alfonse was struggling to say now would not be a declaration of long-standing love.

"Do you know why your parents moved?" he said, at last.

"My mother wanted a newer house. Something all on one floor so it would be easier with two children. . . . I asked her once."

"And that's what she told you?"

His voice knocked against me like a cold finger tapping skin. A chill rode along the back of my neck, one ripple. "You say that so strangely," I said. "Is there some skeleton here?"

And it seemed like a full minute passed before he could answer.

56

We drops Petah off at the end part of Shirley Ave near where the subway goes undah. Me an Eddie sits in the limo and I watches Petah walk up away, swings his shoulders, Mistah Big Balls, Mistah Walk Away From Eddie No Problem. A little ways up he takes a thing out from his pocket and troes it down on the gutter. Cigarette pack. Don't look right the way he done it, somethin don't fits.

I wait for Eddie to say where, but Eddie's flippin the ashtray: *tink.* I look in the mirra at his face. He's watching Petah go: *tink.* In a minute he says, "Looks too happy."

What I'm thinkin in myself.

"He's just happy you letted him go, Eddie," I says.

"Think so?"

Eddie's bad voice. Makes you sweat on the legs.

Petah goes now over the little hill in the direction to Curtis. No good fa him.

"I didn't, though." The bad voice goes around my eahs. "That's the thing. I never let people go, right?"

"Right Eddie."

"You remember Janice, right?"

"Sure Eddie."

"We didn't let her go, did we?"

I shakes my head.

We dint, neither. Janice is Eddie's first wife, liked to have coffee with a fiyamen on the sly, don't know what else. Eddie finds out, maked him crazy. When Eddie goes crazy he went quiet. The night he finished wit Janice we drives that night way down Milton, and all the whole highway Eddie in the back seat quiet like the piece of wood he has holdin in his hands. Round piece like, long as ya bottom leg.

This guy Angie Bing-Bang has a lumbayahd down Milton. Big fence around, factories around. But the fence has no lock on it that night so I open it. I drived inside, Eddie quiet like a rock in the back. We getted out. In the big buildin wheah they hold the lumba, O'Brien is in theah—guy used to work for Eddie, like me. O'Brien is in, Bing-Bang is, Janice.

Eddie goes on Janice with the round wood piece, easy in the first. The legs, the ahms. He don't say nothin in the first and you don't know if it was no good fa her or what.

Cryin, Janice, in between. "I didn't do anything with him, Eddie. Coffee, that's all."

Eddie goes a little harda, the face once, the knee, little bit a blood.

"Not even a kiss, Eddie. I swear. He'll tell you."

Janice holds the knee, goes backwards in the cohna, cryin.

"It was nothing, Eddie."

Little harda now—the knee, the shouldah, once ovah the top on the head, but still you don't know if it was no good fa her all the way or what.

"I swear . . . Eddie."

Bing-Bang watchin, O'Brien watchin. Me. Janice falls down on the floor and gets the blood from her hand on the stacks a wood theah, tryin to get up. Her feet Eddie hits, hahd now, her hands. The elbow once, and you hears the noise for the bone. Screamin. In the face now once. Now in the face twice. Eddie was sweated, breathes. Janice was now just makin singin little noises. Still you don't know that Eddie could stop, or couldn't.

Janice maked a mistake though then. Eddie might stop, but she maked a mistake. Her mouth is a little with blood, but "I love you, Eddie," she says, quiet, nice. Eddie just went afta the head then—hit, hit, hit. Me watchin. Bing-Bang looks away. O'Brien lets a little laugh out. Hit. No talk now from nobody, just Eddie like he's chopped a tree, hit, hit. The end of the round wood piece is all wet red, all blood on the floor, on Bing-Bang's wood stacks, a spray. Eddie goes and goes till his arm gived out. He stops. He troes the round wood down on Janice. Not much face lef now, Janice. Only eyes. He breathes, breathes, then Eddie says, "Love you too, babe." Voice like you can't listened to.

Same voice goes up the back on my neck now. "You frisked him?"

But I'm memberin Angie Bing-Bang though, not listenin too good. O'Brien and me taked Janice away then, but Bing-Bang he stays and he cleans up the lumba all night, makes a little fiya outside for the blood wood. Next day Eddie sended O'Brien an me to takes him out in the boat like for a thank-you. "We'll cooks you a lobstah out theah, Bing-Bang," Eddie tells him, and Bing-Bang is happy as a clam. We goes way out.

Way way out, O'Brien hitted him once, troed him ovah; Bing-Bang washes up near the airport next night, a accident. I member O'Brien drivin the boat back in, says, "We get the lobstah, I guess, Zave." Then I member what happened wit O'Brien about a month later at the tree guy's house. No good fa him neither.

"You frisked him?"

"Who?" I says.

"Peter. You frisked him, right?"

"Course Eddie."

"Feel anything?"

"Nah."

"Nothing?"

"Lump in the chests pocket. In there was the money in the elevope. On the seat now."

"You saw yourself that it was just money in the pocket?"

"Sure."

Tink.

"You made sure there was nothing else in the pocket? Behind the money?"

I moves ovah to the other side of my reah end. Eddie's eyes in the mirra. "Course, Eddie."

"You looked?"

"Wit my hand I look," I says, but my mind is goin like this heah: Janice, Bing-Bang, O'Brien . . . me.

I wait for him to says where but he's doin ashtray: *tink*. He starts a little whistle, what Eddie does when he's worry, when he's scared. The next worse thing next to goin quiet. You can't listened to it. I watches the light—red, green, red, yellow. I'm thinkin about Janice now, about the way her eyes look at you when she was dead, about how O'Brien and me we putted her away in O'Brien's trunk. She was lookin up at me like: Next you, Zave.

"Give me the phone."

I give.

Eddie punches in a numbah, waits a minute, then he hangs up.

"If he doesn't show now at Curtis's house in fifteen minutes we'll get one ring back in return."

"Right Eddie."

"You know what's gonna happen?"

Too quick for myself I says, "Yeah sure Eddie."

"Who told you?"

"Told me what Eddie?"

I don't look in the mirra, then I look, then I look away. Eddie's eyes. Eddie whistled low a little while. We waits two minutes. Cop car goes by, don't look at us. Train goes undah, street shakes. I'm thinkin about Peter trowin the cigarette pack. I'm thinkin about the fat pocket. I'm thinkin, was Billy tole me, an should I say? "Petey's in deep now, Zave," he says. "He's gone now, if he don't pay. Gone." So who tole Billy? Mistah Big Balls? Eddie's wife? Some otha?

Tink. Finely Eddie tells me, quiet, "Go to the club. When we get there, bring Billy out."

Janice, Bing-Bang, O'Brien . . . Billy.

I turns the car around in the direction towards the club, and we goes.

57

I had been in this neighborhood a thousand times, but not very often after dark, and never after a conversation like the conversation I'd just had, and I was not in the mood for the horns and headlights, the sulking Southeast Asian tough guys on the corners, shadows in the doorways, cruising cars with out-of-town white guys driving— all of it grinding up against the twisted cheering of my own mind. I was just breathing cigar smoke now, not inhaling, just walking toward Curtis's house. For show.

A kid who could not have been more than ten angled out from in front of a building and seemed to put his finger up next to his nose. An itch, maybe. I ignored him, kept moving, swinging my shoulders a little bit, making my face hard.

Curtis's property was not actually on Shirley Avenue but off on a quieter side street. I walked for ten minutes or so, turned two corners, and at the front of a newly repainted house with my competitor's sign on the lawn I saw an old Asian woman sitting on the step, staring at me like I was her son from another world. She wasn't sitting, exactly, but squatting on her heels the way they like to do, a shrunken old bird of a lady standing guard over what had once been a wonderful neighborhood—as if to say it might be wonderful again someday, in some future incarnation. As if to say, Give us a little chance here, a little time to figure things out, a little breathing space to do things the way we're used to for a while, then blend in. I had no problem with that, given the history of my own people, given the kind of night I'd had. At that moment, I had no problem with anybody anymore . . . only I was a little sad at the idea of leaving Revere, that's all.

I lifted the collar of my sport coat, kept walking. In another minute I could see Curtis's house up ahead. The property disgusted me so much, and I felt so sure I was in the clear now, in possession of the goods, that I almost kept going straight on past it. But Eddie Three Hands was a sly bastard. Odds were, he'd have somebody watching from a parked car to make sure I showed up, or somebody following me, or the guy waiting in the basement would have a phone. . . .

Everything was settled now, everything was going to be fine. The smart move here was to just stop in for a minute, pretend to take a peek at the famous closet, have a chat with the famous scumbag who was going to show me how to burn down houses with little kids in them. And then, cool as could be, walk the three blocks back up Shirley Avenue to the Dunkin Donuts, call Elsie to let her know everything was all right, call Alfonse to come and get me, call my folks. Begin the process of saying good-bye to Revere.

As I got closer I noticed there was somebody on Curtis's front porch, a guy sitting on the sagging top step with a little boy on his knee. The guy seemed to nod at me; I could see his head move just slightly in the yellowish light from the windows. When I went through the front gate I was absolutely sure, for one instant, that it was the same guy whose life I'd saved down the beach last year. I stared back at him for a couple seconds, almost went up the walk and started a conversation, hoping for the big favor that was due me, the million-dollar Vietnamese thank-you.

He moved his head again, seemed to shake it one inch either way. Friendly face, kid on his knee, he made a little move with his right hand too, down low, and for a split second I thought he might be sending me a signal, telling me stay away. But it was just the mosquitoes he was waving at. They could be nasty down here on a summer night.

That was it, then—one more chased-away mosquito—that was my huge favor.

I walked around the side of the house, where the exterior light was broken and the concrete path was a minefield of cracks and potholes. All the lies I'd told about this place, all the fibs and exaggerations, all the begging seemed to follow me into the dark side yard like a parade of sins. So much aggravation, so much wasted effort when the an-

swer had been right there in front of me the whole time: Take the
risk, carve out your own territory in this world. After all the sweat
and bullshit I'd been through, I could not help but smile a little bit
at the way it had all worked out. Elsie and I would get married,
finally. We'd have our house and our ordinary family situation,
though it would not be on Reservoir Avenue and not in Revere. Alfonse's FBI friend would find us a place where we had no history,
where there was not much temptation to gamble, and it would be up
to us to make a life there: pool in the back yard for Austin and his
new pals, museums, ball games, barbecues on Sunday afternoons.

The Imbesalacqua Method.

The cellar door, at least, was in working order. I pushed it open
very very quietly—the last thing I needed now was to have one of
the tenants hear me, think I was part of Curtis's operation, and start
bugging me about something, broken this or broken that, bad
plumbing. Just a quick in-and-out here and I was free.

Inside, there was no light and no sign of Eddie's guy, which struck
me as a little bit not kosher. Twenty feet or so in front of me the corridor made a ninety-degree bend—I knew that. And I knew there
was a string hanging down from a bulb close by. I was just about to
shuffle forward, find it, and yank, when I thought, What kind of
scumbag arsonist waits to meet somebody at the end of a cellar corridor with no light on? What kind of a slimeball stands around for
half an hour in the dark?

I stood perfectly still a minute, the way we'd been taught in the
army, perfectly quiet, all ears.

Nothing.

I was all set to go for the light string—I had already started to
move my arm—when I heard a weird little noise around the pitch-
black corner. A cough, sort of, a little choked-off cough caught and
swallowed in somebody's throat.

Without making a sound I reached down and slipped my loafers
off, held them in two fingers of my left hand. Made an about-face.
Made the tiniest little squeak with the door handle. Waited. Pushed.

The back yard was almost black. A little dim light from the street,
a drift of radio noise from the top-floor apartment. Four steps and I

felt grass under my feet. I stopped to put on my shoes. Eleven more steps, and there was a chain-link fence. Hupped, we used to say when we were kids. Petey hupped the fence into Losco's yard. I hupped it and slipped towards the next block like a Revere kid—streetwise, scared but not showing it, expecting nothing from God's bag of tricks but a mix of the possible best and the possible worst.

I started going in the direction of my parents' house at first, and then changed my mind and went in another direction.

58

Everything was like always, working the club that night. The lights blinking, like a circus. The music from the speakers in a sledgehammer against my head. People going in and out the front door, Santa walking back and forth on the other side of the bar making sure nobody tried to reach out and touch someone. . . . But, man, what a bad feeling I had that night, a pinched feeling. Pinched between my pal Petey, who I tried to go warn at his office yesterday about how peed off Eddie was but hadn't really told everything to, on the one side; and, on the other side, natchrally, Eddie.

Pinched between Alfonse the bastard, who I owed one phone call to or he'd send me away, on the one side; and, on the other side, Eddie.

Pinched, thinkin somebody seen me comin out from the church.

LaBelle was up on stage, behind me. We had a very small thing once, LaBelle and me, a relationship. Two dates in Boston that cost me two hundred eleven dollars altogether, and one night at the Town Line Motel. She was nothing like people would ever think. Sweet like a nun, LaBelle, not even the littlest bit dirty about bed. A girl I could marry if she wanted me to. But the way it worked with me was it never seemed to go nowhere past that first or second time. I was thinking about that. I was thinking that was the way it was always gonna be. I was like a entertainment, Billy was. I was the new restaurant you go to once, for fun, and then go back to your regular. I was the guy who went home to his apartment at three o'clock in the morning and laid in bed with his hand in his undapants for two hours thinking about different girls I been with one night or two nights and how they said I was sweet, Billy, not like the other guys . . . and how maybe being like the other guys wouldn'ta been so bad.

I could feel her behind me, LaBelle, behind me and a little up above on the stage. Every once in a while I turned my eyes away from the guys at the bar—the Dead Came Back to Life, me and Richie calls them, because of the way their faces never move—and looked a peek at LaBelle to see if there might be a little chance for me at the end of the night. And there was. She looked at me, turned away, unzipped the side of her skirt. . . . A little chance like the lottery.

So I was pinched there too, little bit shook. Bringing guys Buds Lites when they axed for Miller Lites, spillin ice cubes on the rubber mat around Richie's feet. Drifting inside my mind, sweating for no reason. Pinched, big-time.

And then the no reason I was sweating for come through the back door. My friend, like Alfonse says.

I felt him, man. I looked to the side, and I seen his shoes and his big legs in the hall where the girls go, behind the curtain. LaBelle finishes, picks up her dollahs and her skirts and whatnot, gahtahs, goes through the curtain, and walks by naked next to him so close he could burp and knock her down.

Richie looks over. "Xavier come for you," he says, just with his mouth, under the noise from the speakers. Like I don't already know who he come for.

I wipe my hands. I go through the curtain into the hall where the music ain't so loud, and I hold out one hand on the chance he might shake. He don't move. The hand floats there a second; I put it in my pocket. "Eddie was outside," he says, and everything between where my shirt collar is and the bottom of my zipper drops down like when you put a quarter in the motel machine for ice, boom.

We stand there a minute. He don't make any move to the door.

"He want me?"

The next act walks past, Lady Lee. Xavier rubs two fingers hard on her neck when she goes by—a real class act, this guy. Real tenda. He waits till she goes through the curtain; then he says, "Gonna zinged Mistah Big Balls tanite."

"What?"

"Gonna zinged ya pal."

"What pal, who? Petey?"

"How more otha pals you gut?"

I follow him out the back door. Alls I can see is Eddie's limo in the shadows in the parking lot, tiny little pieces of busted glass in the light at the bottom of the steps. Me, I'm thinking. Billy O is who they're gonna zing, my real pal, the person who sleeps with me one night and is always there the next day afterwards. Me myself and you, is who they're gonna zing is what.

Inside the car it's as close to dark as dark gets, and Eddie . . . it's like Eddie is big as a house. I'm the ant walking up that house's front walk, people coming out, shoes the size of countries. I sit. I close the door. He looks at me. My arms and my legs are going. Before he can start on me, I says, "Bad news, Eddie."

He just looks.

"The TV people were here."

"What TV people?" he says.

"The people from the TV." I feel the first little bit of pee inside me where the ice cubes dropped down, melted now, ready to come out. "They come in the club right after I went on, six, six-fifteen. I seen them up the back, black guy and a broad. Another guy with a camera on his shoulder comes in the door, goes up to the stage. Sheila was halfway through her act. We threw him out, me an Richie."

"How did he get in the door? Where was Santa?"

"In the—you know. In the terlet. Me an Richie threw them out no problem though, Eddie."

Eddie's face is maraschino cherries. His hand is goin on his leg. Next minute that hand is gonna find my face, I can see that. I turn a little so's he won't get the teeth, because last time it cost me what I make on the side in three months for the dentist.

The hand goes a little. Goes a little more. He's slappin himself on the leg to get ready for slappin me. Little bit more with the hand now, little bit faster—but then the phone on the seat between Eddie and me rings once, one time, and dies. I let out a little yell, can't help it.

But Eddie don't pick up.

59

I never seen Xavier drive like that, man. In about a minute and a half we was at Curtz's house, Shirley Ave, and in that minute and a half I'm holdin on to the door fa life, trine to listen to Eddie tellin me what I'm suppose to do. Go in the house, in the sella. Find a guy who's waitin there and find out what happened, where Petey is.

We park up the street from Curtz. I get out. I walk down and go in the gate. Nobody. Eddie said go around the side on the walk there, so Billy goes around the side. Eddie said go in the sella door, so I go in the sella door. Eddie says there's a light in the hall there, so I pull the string and you can see the hall where it turns the corner—spidawebs, rusty shovels layin around, broken windows and a smell like junkies come here to piss. This is where they zing Billy, I say to myself. This is where Billy O gets zinged for talkin to cops in churches. This is where.

But what can I do, man, run? Run wheah, Lynn?

This is the end of the movie, I think, an a drop of pee goes out. Who was I? Who liked me in this heah life? Rafaelo, my godfather, one. LaBelle, two, I think, goin down the cement hall now. Rafaelo, LaBelle. My good buddy Leo Markin, who I helped out once an who moved to a desert island afterwards. I had some friends, you could say. Petey was a friend. I did alrigh. Different from all the otha guys, I was. Billy O.

So I'm down the hall, one foot afta the next foot. I'm around the corner, I pull another string for another light there. Bing, nothing. Nobody. I check to make sure there's no doors, no windows to crawl outa, no places the hall turns that you don't see right away. For a few seconds I stand there and I think: Alive still. Still alive.

I go back out. In the yard there's a Cambodian guy with his little kid. I go up to them, cold now, where I sweated, where I peed a little. "I was suppose to meet a friend of mine here, a buddy," I say. "Petey Imbesalacqua. You seen him?"

Guy slugs his shoulders, like he don't speak American.

"Nice-lookin guy," I say. "About so tall, nose on him like Durante."

But it's the no American zone tonight, the shoulders again, the eye contact looking away. Little kid is staring at my face like the next second it's gonna make him cry. I squash down a little so I won't scare him. I slap myself in the front a few times. "Me," I say, desperate now. "Billy O." I point to my eyes. "Looking for a guy." I stand back up and hold my hand over my head about where Peter would be. "Like about so tall," I say. I hook a finger in front of my nose. "Shnozzola like this heah."

For about three seconds they stare at me, the guy and his kid. Then the guy says, "We haven't seen anyone here tonight." Just like that.

You could feel Eddie from a hundred feet in front of the limo, giving off heat like the engine. Even Xavier was afraid, even Eddie himself, it felt like to me when I opened the door, even though for what he could be afraid of Petey for I couldn't really figure.

"No luck, Eddie," I says, when I get in. "No Petey theah. No otha guy."

Boom, he whacks me, right off. Anotha effin dentist bill. I take the hankachif out, spit a little blood in it. I wiggle the tooth with my tongue. Used of it now, just used of it.

"Where'd he go?"

"How would I *know*, Eddie? I—"

"You tipped him off, you fuck." Boom. Whacks me again.

"Tipped him off, what? I neva even seen Petey all day, Eddie. The hall in the sella, nobody was in theah. One Cambodian guy with his little kid out in the back yahd. Says nobody been around all—"

Boom, again.

Boom, anotha time. I'm press back against the door now. I gut my hands up to covah. Boom. Alfonse turned me, I'm thinking. Boom. The priest in the church turned me. Boom, boom, boom. I'm down now, almost on the floor, droolin blood. Eddie's not even talkin no more, not even askin, just all hands.

One last shot I give it: "Maybe up his parents' house," I say, from out from under theah. "Procta Ave."

So that's where we go.

60

After the terrible thing that happened with Joanie I sat out in the yard a little while in the dark in a chair near Rafaelo's fence, the back sore as she could be. The night came down over me. The air went cool on my arms and on my neck, but I stayed out there, trying to let the feelins go, and trying to let them go. But they stuck to me, those feelins.

Over and over again my mind kept bringin me pictures of all the times somebody hurt me and I didn't hurt them back—customers, family, a fella who embarrassed me once at the Holy Name. I could feel every one of those times like pieces of charcoal in my chest. And the worst one of them was this what just now happened, tonight, with Joanie.

This was what it felt like for Lucy all those years, then, this burnin.

This was what could make you into a different person if you let your mind keep goin back to it.

So I tried to hold my mind in just that minute. I used a little trick Dommy taught me. What are you hearing now, Vito? I said to myself—now, not then. . . . I'm hearing a bird on the telephone wires, a little wind in the trees. What are you smelling now? . . . I'm smelling the way the tomato plants smell when they're only a little time away from being dead. What are you seeing now? . . . I'm seeing Rafaelo's garden, his house. I'm seeing . . . somebody—a kid, a robber—comin through Rafaelo's yard in the dark, comin up to the fence, lookin, jumpin over.

It was a surprise to me so much for a minute I didn't move. He come right over the fence, this robber, a kid I thought at the first, and then maybe not. He jumped down on my property. He made one step towards the direction of the house, two steps, not seeing me, I was sitting so quiet. At the first I thought he must be the Cambodians who broke in Angelo Rotazzi's house and put tape on his mouth and took everything else, but in another step he wasn't a Cambodian unless I was.

One more step after that I started to move, to protect Lucy and the house, to break him in a half like a stick, this robber. But the pain in the back came on strong again, I couldn't get up the first time but only made a little squeakin noise in the chair.

The robber heard it. He stopped. He saw me. And he was so surprise he yelled the way you yell when you bring the hammer down full pressure on the side of your second finger. He jumped back one step; then he stood there not too far away from me, like a statue. After the yell, I thought then maybe the nurse would come out to see, but she must be sleepin. I thought maybe the neighbors would come—but who were the neighbors now? Rafaelo Losco, who was seeing from heaven. And Patsy Antonelli, who wouldn't hear if you had the navy ship in your yard shooting the guns over his fence.

Back or no, I was gonna get up then. Help from the neighbors or no, I was gonna take this person and break him in a half. . . . And then I heard him say, "Mistah Imbesalacqua," like I knew him. And a minute later I did.

He walked over to me, this person, and stood in front of me, and it seemed like he was shaking, breathing too hard, a runner. He put his hand out, sweaty, and we shook—you have to. "Member me?" he said.

The face, not the name, I remembered. "Rafaelo's godson."

He smiled now, a shaky smile, a smile with lie written on both the lips.

"I came for Petey," he said, and I remembered this same boy saying this same thing many years ago, only from on the other side of the fence. In Rafaelo's yard he was standing then, with the back of his feet on the garden, small for his age even in those days like the carrots at the end of the row who don't get enough sun. Small, and smiling like you were gonna hit him with the back of your hand if he let his mouth relax one second. Ears stickin way out. Something bad laying there behind the face. In a million years you couldn't never forget this person.

"There's a walk in the front," I said. "Flagstones. Most people who come here lookin for Peter, that's the way they do it."

He laughed a little, like he thought I was making the joke. But I wasn't.

"Is he home?"

I just looked on him. A man now, even though he never really grew. A man carrying this little bad part of him over your back fence on a Saturday night the time people are in bed already. You didn't know whether to feel sorry for him or afraid.

"You member me, right? I'm his good pal. Billy O, people call me."

I didn't care that much then what the people call him. I knew him, I knew his face. I knew Rafaelo told me he used to work in the barroom in Boston where the girls take off they clothes for you, and then he went in jail the first time. Then he got out. Then he went back in again. "Vito," Rafaelo said to me, "this one is the snake you pick up because he's so little, but he's the one that bites."

"Mistah Imbesalacqua, I'm tryin to find Petey, desperate. He heah?"

"Sit," I said.

"I would but I can't. I hafta find him. You seen him? He inside or anythin?"

"Sit," I said again. He sat on the edge of the chair the way a bird sits, ready to take off any second, lookin around, listenin, shakin the wings.

"Whatta you doin?" I said to him, straight.

The smiling still, the lie. "I tole you, Mistah Imbesalacqua. I'm lookin for my good pal Petey. It's important."

The way he was talking reminded you a little bit of the way Peter was always talking to me and Lucy over the years. You were the guitar and they were the finger. I was tired now of making the noises I was supposed to make underneath that finger.

"It's life or death. I wouldn't say it if it wasn't."

"Why you didn't call on the phone if it's life and death?"

His eyes went around the yard, over the driveway, over the windows in the house.

"It's a emergency. I didn't have time to call."

"Why you didn't come up to the front of the house in you car, like everybody, if it's the emergency?"

"He's in trouble, Petey. I came to help him."

I just looked on him then. And then all the feeling that was inside me from Peter all those years, from Lucy, from Joanie, she all came up; I could feel her coming, I could feel her goin into my hands. I squeezed them tight together.

"He's really in trouble. I wouldn't lie to you about it."

"Not no more," I said. "I fixed it."

"No you didn't. Really. Can I go check in the house?"

"Only the nurse is in the house now," I said. "And my wife, dyin . . . With Peter I fixed it already."

But he closed his ears off and was using his eyes instead, running them everywhere, and you could see now he had cuts on his lip where there was blood a little while ago, and that his arms and his legs they were goin a mile a minute. He was a bird there, he was gonna take off.

"Whatta you doin in you life, except bein a liemaker?" I said then.

That made him look at me, and all of a sudden I understood this was nobody you didn't feel sorry for. "What am I doin in my life?" he said, loud now, mean. He leaned his little face in. "What am I doin in my life? I'm trine ta just keep *havin* a life, that's what I'm doin. I come heah and I ax you nice about Petah, and it's the song-and-dance. You—"

"You gonna hit now?" I said, in the middle of what he was saying, because I could see all the bad rising up in him, the rotted beam under the paint and the shingles. I could see he was next on the line to hit.

"I *know* you," he said then, crazy, because he wanted to hit but now he wouldn't, and he was small anyway, and afraid, and I could still break him in two pieces, even tonight, even now. "I know everything about you. My godfather was drinkin with me once, New Yeahs, an he let it slip, man, an I figured it out. Me, *me*! Everything!"

"You godfather wasn't no drinker. I knew him my whole life."

"One time he was. You're Mistah Good Guy, do everything right, go to church. But you're Alfonse's old man, is who you are, Mistah Good, and you're walkin around lying like I breathe, man. Like I *breathe*!"

I knew who this was, then, in my yard. He was gone red in the face, ears big as apples. You knew. Now he reached over with his hand and grabbed me on the arm, and I let him grab me, even though his arm was like a toothpick arm next to my arm, even now.

"Listen to me, old man. Listen! You know whose car is ovah theah on Mountain Avenue? Chelsea Eddie's car. Know who he is? I just got outa that car, and I hafta go back and get in it, and tell him where Peter is, and if I don't tell him then I'm dead, man. Dead. Dead!"

"Then it means if you do tell him then Peter's dead."

"Peter, Joanie, Alfonse. Your whole family will be dead by the end of today if you don't tell me. If you tell me I can maybe try to save him then, but about five more seconds and the next guy who comes ovah that fence ain't gonna come ovah it, he's coming through it, man. With . . . with a gun."

I knew who he was, clear as I knew my name. Dommy told me this, the Bible tells you. He was the One who tries to make you hate yourself. The One tries to make it so you can't forgive yourself for the bad things you did to other people—so then you can't forgive when people do bad things to you.

Clear it was to me, like my name, and clear what I was suppose to do.

"Peter's at my son's house," I tole him. "My son Alfonse is where Peter is now."

One second he looked on me. Two seconds. The third second he was on his way over the fence again, and the fourth or the fifth second, the back hurting me now like a fire burning the muscles there, I was walking in my house and going over to the little table in the hallway. And making sure, when I dialed Alfonse's number on my old-fashion phone, that I did it slow, so they wouldn't be no more mistakes now from my side of life.

61

Tink. I sits in the limo in the dark on Mountain Ave with the lights not on, waitin for Billy, and I thinks: Run, you little mook. If you're any smaht in theah, run.

For a little while seems like he did. Quiet in the limo. Long time we waited theah. Eddie don't say nothin, don't hand me back the phone, don't look out the window, don't whistle no more. Two kids go by holdin hands, looks in, keeps walkin.

Little by little I'm figured it out. For a cup a coffee wit a fiyaman whadduz Eddie do wit Janice? For watchin what he done wit Janice, whadduz Eddie do with Bing-Bang? For doin what he done wit Bing-Bang, whadduz Eddie do wit O'Brien?

Heah he comes now, out the yard acrost the street, lookin every way around.

Run, little mook.

Tink.

But Billy don't run. He getted in, no breath. "Petah's at Alfonse's. His old man tole me."

Any minute I'm lookin in the mirra for the cops to stop us, Eddie's makin me goin so fast. Mountain Ave. Broadway corner. Broadway. The light just goin red but Eddie says go tru it, quiet voice now he says it, quiet like dead. Ambrose Street.

"Slow now," Eddie says, a spidah on ya neck. "All the way down on the left."

Slow now. Pretty dark.

Out from the quiet, Eddie says, "He had a wire on, that little bull-shitter."

I don't say nothin fa that.

Captain Alfonse lives down on the end part. Bushes in front. *Tink.*

"Who's this?" Eddie says, because a car's park there, not the cop's. Green GMW. SBT-ANCH the license says. I knows who dis is. I knows the tires. Eddie knowed.

Billy maked a squeak. "Joanie."

"Pull up," Eddie says. "No noise." I cut the engine and rolls up; I kilt the lights. For a minute we sitted there. No cop's car, no lights in the house.

"The pistol," Eddie says.

I takes it out and gives.

"If he gets heah with the wire . . ." Eddie says on himself.

Same what I'm thinkin.

"You go in the side yard and take a look," Eddie says now, to Billy. But Billy don't move. He knowed what it meant now, Billy. "I'll give you three minutes in there. You come out in three minutes or I'm gone, understand?"

I watches the house. Billy don't say nothin, like he don't under-stand. He understands, though. Send him into the cop's yahd now, the TV lady, Eddie behine him with the gun. Sure he understands. Anotha minute I'm gonna turned around and push Billy out the door, but then Eddie's hand touches me soft on the shouldah. "Walk quiet," he says.

"Me?"

"Billy and me need to stay here and talk. If his good friend comes running down the street, we need to be here."

Me bein sended into the cop's yahd then. Eddie behine *me* with the piece.

I gets out. Slow I goes, quiet, on the grass, not on the hottop, po-lice yahd, air behind ya neck, past the bushes, past the side of the house, no car in the driveway theah, no lights in the house, no noises.

No nothin but in the yahd Petah's sister sittin wit her back on me, waitin fa her cop friend to get home from the office, fa her brother to get there wit the wire, Mistah Walk Away. Instead she's gonna gets somebody else.

I go up quiet. I starts to put one hand on the back of her troat to takes her out to Eddie, just starts to, didn't even touched her and she maked one little tiny noise, smallest noise you ever heard of. But just at that minute near the back of my eah I feel this cold spot. No good. I hears Alfonse's voice, the cop. Alfonse's voice says, "It doesn't matter that you're under arrest, Zave. It doesn't matter that you have the right to remain silent. What matters is, if you so much as twitch, I swear on Jesus Christ I'm gonna blow your brains to fucking Beachmont."

No good fa me then.

62

I made Xavier lie face down on the grass when I put the cuffs on him. I knew it would do no good to ask him whether Peter was alive or not. In a quiet voice, with Joanie standing next to me, I read him the rest of his Miranda, then made him stand up with his back to us.

Xavier was my height, wide as two men, silent as a block of stone. Joanie, who'd been through three kinds of hell that night already, who'd had the courage to sit there very still the way I told her to even when she knew somebody was coming into the yard—Joanie all of a sudden seemed to be losing it, all at once. She was breathing wrong; she was wobbly. She kept shifting her eyes to Xavier's body, as if the cuffs could not possibly hold something that size. In a few seconds, in a wobbly voice, she asked to use my phone, but we had to keep the line free. Then in another few seconds she said she wanted to go out front to her car to use the phone in her handbag there. "I have to call my father, Alfonse. I have to call the station."

I stalled for a minute or so. Then, instead of waiting in the yard for a little while longer to see who else might wander in, which is what I should have done, I marched us slowly out along the other, darker side of the house—Xavier in front, me with the barrel of my pistol between his shoulder blades, Joanie just behind and to the side, breathing harder now, crying, but quietly, like she was angry at herself for it, which she shouldn't have been.

My mother had planted lilac bushes in the front of the house, years ago, when my father was still with us. They were past their bloom now, no scent, very tall, and they hid us from the shadowy street and the shadowy street from us. We went past the corner of the house, paused there a few seconds, listening, brushed between two of the lilacs. There was Joanie's car at the curbstone, a neighbor's car a little farther up the way, my car in that neighbor's driveway. We saw nothing else at first. Then, slowly, we went across the little unfenced lawn and onto the sidewalk, and there was the body lying in the rough circle from the streetlight, in a way no living thing could possibly lie. Posture of death, as they say around the station. You knew it instantly.

Xavier saw it first. I saw it. Joanie, for the count of five did not see it.

"Is it Peter?" I said to the handcuffed block of stone, thinking to take hold of Joanie's arm and keep her away if it was.

But she let out a scream then that was like the song my mother's property had been holding on to for forty years, a scream to turn your skin inside out. At the same instant the phone in my pocket rang. Joanie sprinted into the street. I made Xavier lie down again on the grass and watched her sobbing and weeping and taking hold of the shoulder of the body on the street and rolling it onto its back. A second ring. Pistol in one hand, the other hand working to get the phone out of my shirt pocket, I took two careful steps towards where she squatted and saw enough of the body to know what I had to know. Third ring. There was a pool of blood beneath him, and she was kneeling in it, thinking it was her brother's. It wasn't. There would be a small hole in the back of the head, I knew, because where the cocaine puppet face had been there was nothing now but misshapen bloody flesh touched with lamplight, bits of bone. Joanie was screaming in a kind of rhythmic way, like she was letting out small breaths and they were catching fire as they left her lips. But when she finally understood who it was—who it wasn't—the screams changed so that they sounded almost like laughter, a terrible thing to hear. Neighbors on their porches, coming down their walks, quickly at first and then slowly.

The phone rang a fourth time, in my hand now. Xavier at my feet, Joanie hysterical in the road in the puddle of blood in the lamplight, the neighbors moving closer, Vito waiting for some word from me, Eddie gone. . . . I was finally able to flip open the phone and answer it, and I heard a voice I knew then, and the voice said, "Alfonse, it's me. Your br-br-br-brother."

63

Father Bucci, I never saw my mother like I saw her that night, not even when she and my father were getting divorced and having a lot of trouble about it. She was watching the Red Sox game with the sound off, but every few minutes she'd get up and peek out the front door and then the back door from behind the shades, then go and touch the kitchen phone to make sure it wasn't off the hook. She'd stand next to the couch with her hand on my girlfriend Darcy's shoulder. She'd turn the back outside light on, turn it off again, pour another few ounces of root beer on top of her six ice cubes in a glass, take two sips. Darcy thought she'd been doing drugs and couldn't look at her. For almost two hours we went on that way.

In the top of the eighth inning there were three taps of a fingernail on the glass of the back door. My mom let out a small scream and whipped around so that the root beer and ice cubes came flying out of her glass and made a half-circle mess on the carpet.

I beat her to the door and peeked out. Peter was standing there on the step with his coat collar up and his back half turned, practically vibrating. The first thing he did when I let him in was to go for my mother and hug her hard enough to break her in half; then he made us turn off all the lights and the TV. Darcy was holding on to my neck in the dark. I heard the phone come off the hook. I saw the refrigerator door come open two inches, and my mother's forty-year-old boyfriend squatting down there, dialing by that light. I couldn't hear any ringing or anything, but it seemed to take a minute or so, Peter breathing, tapping his knuckles on the floor. "Come on," he said. "C-c-c'mon, Capitano." He closed the door again when the person answered. He said this—I'll always remember this—he said, "Alfonse, it's me. Your br-br-br-brother . . . I'm at Elsie's house. Send ev-ev-ev-every sireen in the city." And his voice sounded like someone had attached an electric wire to it and was running current.

We all four of us were squatting in a circle near the kitchen sink. I could hear my mother breathing. She reached out her hand to touch me and just about poked my eye out. After a few seconds, somebody, Peter, knocked my knee with his arm and said, in a quiet voice that was running with something else now, not fear: "Ey, Bellini. Count backwards slow from fifteen, not too loud."

I didn't get it at first. Darcy did, though. "Fifteen," she goes. "Fourteen." We all join in, quiet as a prayer, four shaking voices. At "eight," I heard something way up the beach like a cat crying. At "five," I heard something else, electric guitar. By zero it was like every cruiser in the state of Massachusetts was bearing down on us.

Peter stood up and flicked on the small light over the stove. He kissed my mother once on the mouth and straightened the lapels of his sport coat like he was getting ready to have his picture taken. "He-hear that?" he said to me, as if there was any way not to hear it, with sirens screaming out front and blue lights strobing the window shades. "That's what the a-a-a-angels sound like when they sa-sing."

And I'll never forget that either.

EPILOGUE

In Revere, among our people, the wake is a kind of festival of farewell. Everyone comes: relatives, family friends, people who did not know the deceased at all but happen to work with a member of the family, enemies hoping to fashion some kind of posthumous peace, even a few professional wake-goers who regularly make the funeral-home rounds, because no one is denied admittance to these affairs, and because it gives them a sense of belonging to the community of humanity.

Lucy Imbesalacqua's wake was no exception. Executives in suits from WSBT, old stooped housewives from Proctor Avenue, Cambodian grocers, retired Italian stoneworkers, Jewish policemen, rectory housekeepers, bank clerks, Holy Name carpenters, and a collection of very somber fellows—uncomfortable in their shirts and dark sport coats—who seemed to have driven over from Wonderland Dog Track with racing forms hidden in their inside breast pockets.

According to custom, the wake continues for two afternoons and two evenings, and the family stands in a row near the casket and receives condolences. From this short file of mourners—Joanie, Vito, a few stray cousins—Peter was conspicuously absent. Many people asked about him. There were whispered speculations. Within range of my hearing, at least one person seemed to make a connection between Peter not being there and the events of that week, front-page news in all the newspapers: the murder on Ambrose Avenue, the arrest of Eddie Crevine's henchman, and the indictment and disappearance of Crevine himself. The city was full of idle chatter on the subject.

At the close of the second evening, just as Larry Bruno and his crew of undertaker's associates were gently ushering the last visitors toward the door, Vito approached me where I sat in the front row and asked if I would stay a little while longer. I agreed, of course. Half an hour passed; the room gradually emptied. Vito and Joanie and I sat on the folding chairs in silence, or wandered about the room, reading names on the banks of floral arrangements, glancing occasionally toward the open coffin.

At last, I heard several cars pull up outside the building. The front doors opened. Peter walked in, somberly, with Elsie on his arm, Alfonse and Austin trailing, and a posse of state policemen—some in uniform, some not— fanning out to cover the various entrances, as if this were the President of the United States come to pay his last respects to his mother, and not a newly unemployed real estate salesman.

Peter went straight to the coffin and knelt before Lucy's body; she seemed so stiff and small amidst the satin pleats and flowers, so much diminished. A long while he knelt there, wiping his eyes with an oversized handkerchief, dripping a tear down onto his shirt. At last he stood, leaned over and kissed her waxy forehead, toweled off his face again, blew his nose. He embraced his sister, stepped back to let Elsie embrace her, then took Joanie's arm, walked her toward a corner of the room, and stayed there for several minutes, talking and talking while policemen went in and out the front doors and Austin and Vito and Alfonse and I stood in a little knot of awkward masculinity on the soft maroon carpet.

When Peter approached his father, we all moved away a few paces and averted our eyes, but I could not restrain myself from peeking over at them. The usual vibrant personality was dampened, of course, appropriately dampened, but Peter seemed to be selling something still. Himself, perhaps. And Vito seemed ready to buy. Observing Peter for those few seconds—he was leaning in and down toward his father, speaking earnestly, somberly, gripping the top of Vito's arm with his fingers—it occurred to me that, even in this quieter version, he was not so unlike a candidate working a room . . . though what he was after was not votes or money but some sense of himself as being loved without qualification—a sense that can never really come from the external world, not after a certain age, no matter how lucky or courageous or obedient a person is, or how many friends he has, or what those friends are willing to do for him. That endless outward search, I saw then, was what had always driven him, and what would continue to drive him. And, even with Elsie there, I worried about how he would manage in his enforced exile, and by which lights Austin would sail into the rough waters of adulthood.

In a certain sense, the scene in that room on that night was very much the culminating role Peter would have given to his own local legend, a sad but nevertheless triumphant final exit from the stage that was the city of Revere.

But Revere is not the world, as I could have told him on that night, as I wanted to tell him. There would be another life for him now, true enough, but into it he would carry all the same habits and tendencies that had haunted and delighted him in this one. How, though, does one say such a thing to an optimist?

At last he kissed his father, came up to me and shook my

hand, then squeezed me in a long embrace. Somber as he was, a tiny spark of hope played at the edges of his lips. Sad as he was at his mother's death, shaken as he was, still, by the events of recent days, he'd won a sort of victory over the forces of the external world, I could see that, and I was grateful for it, even though all these years it had been an internal victory I'd been praying for.

I told him how very sorry I was to lose the friendship of his mother. He paused, nodded, met my eyes. "D-Dommy," he said, after another moment, "tell me. Does G-God have anything like a Wa-Witness Protection Program? Any sh-sh-shortcuts to salvation for a wa-wise guy like me?"

I laughed—he had always made me laugh. I squeezed his arms with my hands and pulled him against me again. But I could see, when we separated, that he was, in fact, waiting for some last word, some ecclesiastical cure for the doubt that lay like a soft underbelly beneath his armor of doubtlessness. No clever priestly answer came to me, for once. I could sense a stir of impatience around us in the room, and so I simply blurted out the first thing that leapt to my mind. "Your mother loved you," I said. "Love yourself."

Something between a smile and a smirk touched his lips, but behind it I thought I detected one droplet of ... I'm not sure what it was, wisdom, perhaps—that had not been visible in Peter prior to those four days. Perhaps I only wished it to be wisdom; perhaps it was something else. But I choose now to believe it marked a very small change in him, the first step toward his ultimate internal victory— paid for by the efforts of the people who loved him.

"Write," he commanded me, before turning away.

And I promised that I would.